DO THEM NO HARM!

DO THEM NO HARM!

Lewis and Clark among the Nez Perce

ZOA L. SWAYNE,
Author and Illustrator

Edited by Carol Ann Goodrich Bates

CAXTON PRESS
Caldwell, Idaho
2003

Originally privately published as *Do Them No Harm: An Interpretation of the Lewis and Clark Expedition among the Nez Perce Indians*, by Zoa L. Swayne, 1990.

Library of Congress Cataloging-in-Publication Data

Swayne, Zoa.
Do them no harm! : Lewis and Clark among the Nez Perce / Zoa L. Swayne, author and illustrator ; edited by Carol Ann Goodrich Bates.
p. cm.
Includes bibliographical references and index.
ISBN 0-87004-427-3
1. Lewis and Clark Expedition (1804-1806)--Fiction. 2. West (U.S.)--History--To 1848--Fiction. 3. Lewis, Meriwether, 1774-1809--Fiction. 4. Clark, William, 1770-1838--Fiction. 5. Nez Percâe Indians--Fiction. 6. Explorers--Fiction. I. Bates, Carol Ann Goodrich. II. Title.
PS3569.W345 D6 2003
813'.54--dc21

2002152235

Printed and bound in the United States of America by
CAXTON PRESS
Caldwell, Idaho 83605
169243

Dedicated to
the Nez Perces
whose ancestors befriended
the Lewis and Clark Party
in the Clearwater Valley of Idaho
September 20 to Octobcr 11, 1805
and May 4 to July 4, 1806.

TABLE OF CONTENTS

PAGE

PREFACE xiii
ACKNOWLEDGMENTS xvii
EDITOR'S NOTE xxi
THE CHARACTERS xxiii

The Nee-mee-poo—The People • The So-yap-pos—Lewis & Clark Expedition Members

NEE-MEE-POO CALENDAR AND GLOSSARY xxvii

* * * *

CHAPTER 1—THE PEOPLE 1

The annual root-gathering on Oyaip Prairie • The return of four hunters with Wat-ku-ese • Wat-ku-ese's story • The killing of three warriors on a peace-making trip • Chiefs Broken Arm, Red Grizzly Bear, Fierce-Five-Hearts, Cut Nose and warriors go on the warpath to avenge death of three peace-seeking warriors

CHAPTER 2—WE-YA-OO-YIT 12

The coming of the first white men to the Koos-koos-kee Valley

CHAPTER 3—CLARK TO THE RIVER 20

The advance party of Clark and six men from the Lewis and Clark Expedition trade beads for food • Clark inquires way to river that will lead to Big Water • Told Twisted Hair knows the way • Clark and his men go to Twisted Hair's fishing camp guided by Joyous Heart

CHAPTER 4—SO-YAP-POS! DO THEM NO HARM! 28

Wat-ku-ese rides back to Oyaip from Twisted Hair's fishing camp to protect the remaining Lewis and Clark party from harm

CHAPTER 5—THE OYAIP COUNCIL 43

Captain Lewis calls for a council • Clark starts the council fire in a mysterious way • Lewis explains that the Great White Father wants peace for all men—white and red • Twisted Hair agrees peace would be good • Tamootsin and friends play harmless prank on Sa-ka-ka-wea's baby boy • Hawk and Mets-et-pus lead gang to find out what makes York black

CHAPTER 6—IN SEARCH OF CANOE TIMBER 53

The So-yap-pos and many Nee-mee-poo leave the Oyaip Prairie and go downriver • Twisted Hair and his sons guide Clark to find suitable wood to build canoes

CHAPTER 7—CANOE CAMP 62

The So-yap-pos are miserable with hunger and adverse reactions to the unusual Nee-mee-poo food and the heat • Working sluggishly they chop down enough trees to make five canoes • The Nee-mee-poo show the So-yap-pos how to hollow out the canoes with fire • Twisted Hair and Te-toh-kan Ahs-kahp agree to guide So-yap-pos downriver to Celilo Falls but leave before the white men depart • So-yap-po horses turned over to Twisted Hair's men • Clark's pipe tomahawk missing • So-yap-pos leave

CHAPTER 8—DOWNRIVER 78

The route and mishaps of the So-yap-pos' trip down the Koos-koos-kee until they come to Tsce-min-i-cum • Big Heart and the lead canisters • Little Lee-tsu and her dog Mox-Mox • The myths about the rock formations

CHAPTER 9—THE COLD MOONS 94

The COLD moons—Ho'plal • Seekh-le-wahl • Ha-oo-khoy • Wai-lu-poop • These winter months have forced the Nee-mee-poo to seek shelter, venturing out only when the food supply is exhausted • The Nee-mee-poo occupy their days and nights making clothes, baskets, dance regalia • They hand down their history to the children by means of story telling—Deer Hunt • The Path for the Water • The Kamiah Monster and the Coming of People • The Coming of Fish • Finding the Trail Through the Mountains • Coyote • The Chipmunk and Grizzly Bear

CHAPTER 10—RETURN OF THE SO-YAP-POS 121

The Moon of La-te-tahl is a liar • COLD still prevails, forcing the Nee-mee-poo to stay in their houses • The Moon of Ka-khee-tahl finally allows the women to dig for ka-keet roots • The Moon of Ah-pah-ahl brings warmth and The People may now move to their first camas root-digging on Camas Prairie • Twisted Hair and Te-toh-kan Ahs-kahp prepare for the return of the So-yap-pos • The So-yap-pos return to the Nee-mee-poo country led by Te-toh-kan Ahs-kahp • The So-yap-pos visit a village where Prankster throws a puppy at Captain Lewis • Captain Clark treats the sick • The So-yap-pos move to Nez Perce Prairie • They recover horses, saddles and black powder

CHAPTER 11—THE KAMIAH COUNCIL 145

So-yap-pos visit Broken Arm's village • Lewis tells Nee-mee-poo chiefs about their mission to bring peace to all red and white men • Gifts are exchanged • Clark administers to the sick • Red Bear, Red Grizzly Bear's father, tells council the Nee-mee-poo will accept the Great White Father's pleas for peace • Broken Arm gives ultimatum • Twisted Hair is given first gun for caring for horses

CHAPTER 12—WAITING FOR THE CANOE 168

So-yap-pos leave Broken Arm's village • Waiting for a canoe to transport men and baggage across the Koos-koos-kee, the Nee-mee-poo play the Badger Game with unsuspecting So-yap-pos • So-yap-pos race their horses

CHAPTER 13—BEARS! 174

So-yap-po hunters kill several bears • Ya'amus Wakus, Twisted Hair's oldest son, borrows his father's gun to go hunting • Not in the usual manner, Ya'amas Wakus brings down his own Hah-hahts (grizzly bear)

CHAPTER 14—HORSES 181

The caring for the sixty-five horses the Expedition needs to survive and get across the mountains to home • What horses mean to So-yap-pos and Nee-mee-poo

CHAPTER 15—GOOD MEDICINE! 195

During Lewis and Clark's homeward-bound trip they treat many Nee-mee-poo for various ailments • Eye drops are in high demand for sore eyes • The strange affliction of Moves-No-More

CHAPTER 16—MOON OF AH-PAH-AHL 211

The So-yap-pos wait for the snow to melt enough to make their homeward route passable • They prepare for the trip and procure food from the Nee-mee-poo • The Nee-mee-poo gather kouse

CHAPTER 17—BREAKING CAMP 237

Despite warnings that it is too soon to cross the Bitterroots, Lewis and Clark decide to leave

CHAPTER 18—THE FIRST ATTEMPT 254

Impatience overcame discretion! The route was too hazardous with slippery, deep snow and no exposed grass for horse feed • The Corps of Discovery is forced to make its first and only retrograde march • The So-yap-pos are sent back to obtain guides over the Bitterroots • The larger party returns to the Oyaip Prairie to wait for help

CHAPTER 19—KA-OO-YIT 273

Life carries on for the Nee-mee-poo • They celebrate the ending of the winter season and the beginning of the warm food-gathering season • Two of the best So-yap-po communicators return to the Nee-mee-poo, pleading for guides • With the promise of two guns and ten horses, the Nee-mee-poo are persuaded to let three of their young men go as guides for the So-yap-pos

CHAPTER 20—CROSSING THE MOUNTAINS 282

With the help of three appointed guides and three other Nee-mee-poo travelers, the So-yap-pos finally make their difficult way over the Bitterroots • Lewis and Clark prepare to separate, with Lewis detouring to inspect the Marias River • The two captains plan to reunite at a distance • The Nee-mee-poo are given rewards • They agree to show Lewis the route to Marias River before they join their friends and relatives, the Shalees

CHAPTER 21—THE PARTING 305

Captain Clark and his party take leave of Captain Lewis • Captain Lewis and his men, along with the party of Nee-mee-poo, cross the Missoula River • The guides show Captain Lewis the correct path to take, but decide not to accompany Lewis to the Great Falls • Rewards and exchanges of gifts take place • The So-yap-pos and Nee-mee-poo part with emotion • The Nee-mee-poo guides and friends visit the Shalees • A young maiden, Tom-sis, from Kamiah Valley, crosses the Bitterroots to find her So-yap-po man • Tom-sis decides to stay at the Shalees' village • The young guides and friends return to their homeland • The Nee-mee-poo share their memories of their friends, the So-yap-pos

* * * *

CHAPTER NOTES 319

APPENDIX 332

Nez Perce Chiefs Named by Lewis and Clark • Definition of Chopunnish • Nez Perce Names • Sa-ka-ka-wea, the Bird Woman • Twisted Hair

BIBLIOGRAPHY 337

INDEX 342

PREFACE

FIRE DUST

LIKE COALS, SMOLDERING UNDER THE DUST OF BURNED-out fires, unwritten stories from the past that survive into the present cast a warm glow of insight on recorded history. Such stories, like those kept alive orally by the Nez Perce Indians, sparkle with human interest and add to our understanding of what the coming of the Lewis and Clark Party meant to them.

Long before our great-grandparents' days, the Nez Perces living along the Kooskooskee (the Clearwater River of Idaho) saw white men and a black man for the first time. As long as these people lived, they recited memories of what happened after the Lewis and Clark Party struggled out of the Bitterroot Mountains into the Nez Perce encampment on the Weippe Prairie.

What spellbinding tales these people must have told after Lewis and Clark left the Clearwater Valley! Those strange men, the "So-yap-pos," had been among the Nez Perces, the "Nee-mee-poo"—"The People," altogether some seventy days. From September 20, 1805, to October 10, 1805, they camped among the Nez Perces while they built five canoes to carry them to the Pacific Ocean. Returning to the Clearwater Valley May 5, 1806, they stayed until June 23, 1806, when they started their final push across the Bitterroots towards the United States. Everyone—those who had bargained with the white men; those who had guided, hunted, and fished with them; those who had traded horses with them, gambled with them, made love with them, had been healed by them; or those who had only caught a glimpse of them—had memories to keep alive.

They told their stories to their grandchildren, and that generation retold them to their children and grandchildren. If no one remembered well enough to pass them on, some tales died out with their narrators. No one knew how to write them down.

It has been my privilege to have heard some of these stories from the lips of Nez Perces. A few came from the pioneer, Walter Sewell, who had heard them from Charlie Adams, grandson of Chief Twisted Hair. Some came from newspaper articles that recorded stories written years ago by pioneers who had heard them directly from the Nez Perces. Some came from the manuscripts of Pauline Evans, co-owner of the Sacajawea Museum at Spalding, Idaho (about 1940-1948). When buying artifacts from the Nez Perces, she wrote down the accounts they told her concerning the heirlooms they were selling.

Was there any definite historical foundation for these stories? Did some of them refer to incidents dealing with white settlers instead of with Lewis and Clark? Who was the Tetoharsky mentioned in the Lewis and Clark Journals? Did the name "Tinnachemooltoolt" really mean "Broken Arm" as Lewis and Clark called the chief at Kamiah? Who were the three little boys who first saw Captain Clark on the Weippe Prairie?

Over the years some of these questions have been answered and some have not. The story of Wat-ku-ese has historical foundation, for such a woman was mentioned in Clark's records. No living Nez Perce can make the name "Tinnachemooltoolt" (as it is spelled in the Journals) translate to "Broken Arm." The name of Tetoharsky, as Lewis and Clark wrote it, meant nothing to the Nez Perces. (There is no "r" in the Nez Perce tongue.) But the real name came out in casual conversation with a Nez Perce as did the names of the three little boys who first saw Clark.

Such disclosures reassured me that this account would be a valuable contribution to Lewis and Clark lore. After more than fifty years of listening, learning, reading, accumulating, culling, verifying, starting, stopping, and starting over, the time has come to complete the writing.

In this book pertinent excerpts from the Lewis and Clark Journals are printed in smaller type. Following, in regular type, comes the interpretation of Nez Perce activities that relate to the daily entries in the Journals.

Where Nez Perce names have been supplied by written record or by oral history, they have been used; but when no name was preserved, it was necessary to improvise. All the characters were real people mentioned in the Journals, though some have unauthentic names.

Chapter Nine ("The Cold Moons") and Chapter Nineteen ("Ka-oo-yit") are distinctive chapters. They do not follow Journal entries. To give a better picture of some activities of the Nez Perces during the periods Lewis and Clark were not in the Nez Perce territory, incidents were taken from later periods of Nez Perce life as told to me. All of these activities could have happened during the winter months and at the encampment mentioned in the Ka-oo-yit Chapter where Drewyer and Shannon went to get guides.

Those superb Nez Perce guides rendered a vital service to the Lewis and Clark Expedition. Without the knowledge and skill of their guides, it is doubtful that the explorers could have crossed the Bitterroot Mountains safely in 1806.

ACKNOWLEDGMENTS

IN THE FIFTY-FIVE YEARS (1934 to 1989) THIS BOOK HAS BEEN taking form, many persons (both Indian and non-Indian) have helped, some knowingly and some without realizing it. Though many are now deceased, I am grateful for every kindness, for every question patiently answered, for all the meetings and visits where knowledge of customs was shared.

I first heard the story of Wat-ku-ese from Walter Sewell, a 1904 pioneer. His friend Charlie Adams, grandson of Chief Twisted Hair, had told that story to him along with much Nez Perce lore. Sewell also introduced Camille Williams, an elderly Nez Perce man who willingly retold the Lewis and Clark stories he remembered. In 1944 Sewell guided the author and her family along the Lolo Trail in the Bitterroots as far as Indian Post Office, pointing out Lewis and Clark campsites as marked by the U.S. Forest Service. I gratefully acknowledge Walter Sewell's help.

The daughters of Charlie Adams—Mary Kipp, Sophie Payne, and Louise Powaukee—were helpful in sharing their knowledge of Nez Perce customs and culture.

Other Nez Perces have helped in many ways. I thank Angus Wilson, Allen Slickpoo, Phil Types, Earl Gould, Frank Penney and Mose Thomas of the Nez Perce Development Advisory Committee. To Irving Allen, Joe Blackeagle, Ida Blackeagle, Lydia Corbett, Austin Corbett, Rose Corbett, Joe and Pauline Evans, Alta Guzman, Joe and Sally Joye and their children—Melvin, Marvin, Darlene, Marlene, and Calvin—Corbett

Lawyer, Mylie Lawyer, Lillian Major, J.J. Miles, Rev. David Miles, Beatrice Miles, Richard Moffett, John Moffett, Albert Moore, Alec Pinkham, Josiah Redwolf, Patricia Slickpoo, Leroy Seth, Edith Types, Edna Thomas, Mari Watters, Elizabeth Wilson, Harry Wheeler, and Ida Wheeler go my thanks for sharing their knowledge of Nez Perce history, customs, and language. I also thank David Miles and Horace Axtell for Nez Perce language tapes.

The intense interest of Jack Harlan and Marc Ware and the dedication of Ralph Space in locating Lewis and Clark campsites and trail have kept me on the track more than once.

I am indebted to Ralph Williams and Ernest Robinson for sharing their wealth of information about the early Nez Perces. Also I thank Wilma Ogston and Doug Marsh for introducing elderly Nez Perce friends who answered many questions.

For their professional advice and information I acknowledge the help of Dr. Jerry Swinney, former Director of the Idaho State Historical Society; of Dr. Merle Wells, former Curator of the Idaho State Historical Museum; of Dr. Haruo Aoki, Department of Linguistics, University of California, Berkeley; of Darby and Julie Stapp, Department of Anthropology, University of Idaho; and of Steve Evans, Assistant Professor of History, Lewis Clark State College, Lewiston, Idaho.

The librarians and staff from the Spokane Public Library, the Library of Washington State University, the Library of the University of Idaho, the Idaho State Library, and the Clearwater Memorial Library have been most helpful through the years.

Words are inadequate to express my appreciation for all the services rendered by Carol Ann Goodrich Bates. She has been editor, secretary, chauffeur, and friend throughout the final years of preparing the manuscript for printing. Without her dedication and enthusiasm, and her skill with the word processor, this book would not have become a reality.

Also I thank my friend Marcia Smith, a Spokane, Washington artist, who designed the handsome dust-jacket for the book.

Finally, I gratefully acknowledge the unfailing interest and encouragement given by my husband Samuel and our four sons. David, James, John, and Mark have grown to manhood, never knowing a time when their mother was not trying to learn more about Lewis and Clark among the Nez Perces.

ZOA L. SWAYNE

November, 1989
Orofino, Idaho

EDITOR'S COMMENTS

MY FIRST INTRODUCTION TO THIS MONUMENTAL UNDERtaking was on a spring morning in 1984 when Mrs. Swayne asked me to type the story of Wat-ku-ese, ending it with the words, "Do them no harm." Four years later I was still typing "Do them no harm," but with the realization the book would soon be completed.

During these years I was to learn that Zoa had been working on this manuscript for over fifty years. Throughout her home were to be found her records of research and conversations regarding the Nez Perce. They were on small note cards, large note cards, standard sized sheets, note pads, legal note pads, sketch books. She also had innumerable files of illustrations and clippings. Zoa knew the material for her book so well she had basically written the text three times, each from a different viewpoint as her life progressed.

As I gained access to all these bits and pieces of information, I became excited, not only because they were interesting and entertaining, but they had historic value. What a challenge it was to help fit all this information into one organized whole!

It is my joy to have been introduced to Nez Perce culture, to have been reintroduced to the historic importance of the Lewis and Clark Expedition, and to have had a part in the compilation and completion of *DO THEM NO HARM!*

CAROL ANN GOODRICH BATES,
Secretary-Editor

THE CHARACTERS—THE NEE-MEE-POO AND THE SO-YAP-POS

THE NEE-MEE-POO—THE PEOPLE

Following are two lists of Indian names found in the text. *LIST I* gives authentic names of the people living at the time of the Lewis and Clark Expedition. Many of these names can be found in the Journals. With the help of many people, an attempt has been made to give the English interpretation of the names.

LIST II contains fictitious names assigned to real Nee-mee-poo mentioned in the Journals but not named.

For additional information on real people of the Nez Perce tribe and other characters mentioned in the text, please see the Appendix.

LIST I (AUTHENTIC NAMES)

A-hot-mo-tim-nim—Joyous Heart
Alle-oo-ya
Al-pa-to-kate—Father was Daytime Smoker
Hahahts-il-pilp—Red Grizzly Bear; also Many Wounds
Hat-itt
Heume-ya-kah-likt—White Grizzly Bearskin Folded
He-yoom-pahkah-tim—Fierce-Five-Hearts
Iscootim
Nusnu-ee-pah-kee-oo-keen (upriver people)—Cut Nose
Neesh-ne-ee-pah-kee-oo-keen (downriver people)—Cut Nose
Red Bear
Sa-ka-ka-wea—Bird Woman
Ta-moot-sin
Te-toh-kan Ahs-kahp—People Coming—Look Like Brothers
Timuca
Tin-nach-e-moo-toolt—Broken Arm
Toba
Tsap-tsu-kelp-skin—Twisted Hair
Wat-ku-ese—Gone-from-Home-then-Come-Back
We-ah-koomt
We-ya-loo-hom
Ya'amas Wakus—Looks-Like-Mule-Deer-Doe

LIST II (FICTITIOUS NAMES)

Ahs-kahp—brother
Akh-akh—Magpie
Al-la—grandmother (father's mother)
As-ah-ek-sach-t-nim-e-wai-oo-ko-i-in-sam-ne-pah-hak-e-nee—Crows-Flying-out-of-Rock-Creek-Canyon-with-Mouths-Wide-Open
Ahtway
Ayat
Bad Horse
Big Eagle
Big Heart
Black Cricket
Black Tail
Crane's Legs
E-wap-na—wife
Fish Hawk
Follows-the-Trail
Gray Cloud
Hahahts-tah-mal-we-yaht—Grizzly Bear Commander
Hawk
Horse-Breaker
Ka-hap—Wildcat
Kah-hah-toh—Short One
Kah-lah-tsah—Grandfather
Khai-yoon—Old Man
Koolkooltom—Red Arrow Point
Koots-koots—Little One
Ko-yas-ko-yas—Bluejay
Lah-kahts-koots-koots—Little Mouse
Lee-tsu—Daughter child
Looks-Ahead
Lost-His-Horse
Mets-et-pus—the Naughty One
Me-yap-khah-wet—Baby
Morning Star
Moves-No-More—Also, Moves-Again
No-Horns
Old Dog
Old Man Bobcat

Pee-kah—Mother
Peem—Uncle
Pe-pah
Pika
Prankster
Rainbow
Raven-Flying-Over
Raven Spy
Running Horse
Shalee Woman
Sits-By-Fire
Sleeping Wolf
Speaks-With-Straight-Tongue
Sun-Going-Down
Swift-Moving-Hands
Three Feathers
Tip-yah-la-nah-jeh-nin—Speaking Eagle
Tip-yah-la-nah She-mook She-mook—Black Eagle
Tom-sis—Rose
Tota
Two Crows
Two-Times-Shot
Weasel Tail
White Antelope
White Hawk
White Wolf
Yah-tsah
Yellow Dog

THE SO-YAP-POS— LEWIS AND CLARK EXPEDITION MEMBERS

(From *Lewis and Clark Journals*, Thwaites, Volume 1, Page 12.) Members of the Lewis and Clark Expedition as verified by the official payroll at the close of the venture:

Meriwether Lewis, Captain in lst Reg. U. S. Infantry, commanding William Clark, 2nd Lieutenant in U. S. Artillery.

Sergeants:

Charles Floyd
Patrick Gass
John Ordway
Nathaniel Pryor

Privates:

William Bratton	Francis Labiche
John Colter	Hugh McNeal
John Collins	John Potts
Peter Cruzatte	George Shannon
Reuben Fields	John Shields
Joseph Fields	John B. Thompson
Robert Frazier	William Werner
George Gibson	Joseph Whitehouse
Silas Goodrich	Alexander Willard
Hugh Hall	Richard Windsor
Thomas P. Howard	Peter Wiser

Besides these men, the party included two interpreters, George Drewyer (or Drouillard) and Toussaint Charbonneau; an Indian woman, Sa-ka-ka-wea ("Bird Woman"), Charbonneau's wife; and a Negro slave of Captain Clark's, named York.

Two soldiers, John Newman and M. B. Reed, who had set out with the expedition, were punished for misconduct, and sent back to St. Louis on April 7, 1805. Baptiste Lepage was enlisted in Newman's place, at Fort Mandan, November 2, 1804, and remained with the expedition until the discharge of the men at St. Louis, November 10, 1806.

CALENDAR

Wai-lu-poop—January—Moon of Cold Weather—Eat Moss
Ah-la-tah-mahl—February—Moon of Swelling Buds
La-te-tahl—March—Moon of First Flowers
Ka-khee-tahl—April—Moon for Digging Kaeh-kheet Roots (Wild Potato)—Steelhead Spawn
Ah-pah-ahl—May—Moon of Kouse Bread
Hil-lal—June—Moon of First Run of Salmon
Khoy-tsahl—July—Moon of the Run of Blueback Salmon in Wallowa Lake
Also—Hasoal—Moon of Eels
Wa-wai-mai-khal—August—Moon When Salmon Spawn Up High in Mountains
Also—Ta-yum—Moon of Hot Weather
Pe-khum-mai-kahl—September—Moon When Salmon Spawn in Main River—Elk Bugle
Ho'plal—October—Moon When Leaves Turn Golden
Seekh-le-wahl—November—Moon of Fall Deer Hunt
Ha-oo-khoy—December—Moon When New Life Begins in Cow Elk—Beginning of Winter

GLOSSARY

A-a-a-a—Yes; an affirmative expression.
ah-pah—kouse bread
al-la—grandmother
Al-pa-to-kate—Father was Daytime Smoker
alwi'tas—women's lodge
As-ah-ek-sach-t-nim-e-wai-oo-ko-i-in-sam-ne-pah-hak-e-nee—Crows-Flying-out-of-Rock-Creek-Canyon-with-Mouths-Wide-Open
ayat—old woman

Chopunnish—North Fork River
E-nasa-pahl-we-sah.—Have to keep going.
Enim hah-ma—My man
e-wap-na—wife
Ha-ha-tswal kap-sees.—Those dirty, stinking boys.
Hah-hahts—grizzly bear
Heume-ya-koh-likt—White Grizzly Bearskin Folded
hi-sop-ti-kai—rawhide storage case
ho'-pope—roasted moss from trees
Ipna-ko-tahk-o-tsaya.—You have eaten it all yourself, and your clothes are falling to pieces.
Ipna'naksa.—She thinks herself.
ip-paht-tah-khahts—game of endurance
Iship—frenzied trance
ish-nash—brush shelters
Itsi-yai-yai—The Coyote
Itswa-wlts-itsqiy—Hurry, evening shadows be
Kah-hah-toh—the Short One
Kah-itsi-yow-yow—Thanks
kah-lah-tsah—grandfather
Ka-oo-yit—End of a period; beginning of new period. Spring festival.
khalp-khalp—gusty wind
Ki-moo-e-nim—The Snake River
Kiyu'—I will go
komsit—thick soup
Koos-koos-kee—The Clearwater River
ko-pluts—skull cracker
kullo—that is all
Kum-noo-kun—Come here
lah-mah-ta—wearisome
Lawtiwa-mah-ton—a time of being friends together before Cold Moons; joy of renewed friendship
loo-kits-kin-ne-kai—south
mox-mox—yellow
Ninna-nin-nin—Dear little thing
pa'siwya—war paint
pee-kah—mother
See-kim kap-seese'—Bad horse
Si-kip-te-wat—white man's doctor
Skitsuish—Spokanes
Taats—Good
Ta-ma-nam-mah—The Salmon River

te-cas—a baby board
Tee-e-lap-a-lo—Where many crawfish live in creek
Te-wats—witch doctor
te-wel-kas—enemies
Tom-sis—Rose
Tota—father (equivalent to the word "dad"; the form of direct address)
Tsce-men-i-cum—the meeting of the waters
Tu-ka-wi-ut—Snake Dance
wahk-kee-ma—a time far back from memory of man
Wai-i-let-pos—Cayuses
Wa-tu e-mas pahl-we'.—Don't force yourself.
Wayat ha-mtits—Beat it
We-ya-oo-yit—The Coming; the coming of first white man
Wyakin—Spirit Helper
Yah-ka—black bear
Ya-ho-toin—Potlatch Creek
yah-tsah—elder brother
Yal-lept—contest of gift giving
ya-wits-kin-ne-kai—north

DO THEM NO HARM!

CHAPTER 1

THE PEOPLE

IN THE MOON OF TA-YUM, THE HOTTEST DAYS OF SUMMER, when salmon spawn in the little streams and huckleberries ripen in the high mountains, people from many villages of the Chopunnish Nation gathered on the Oyaip Prairie[1] for the work and festivities of their annual camas harvest.

From far and near The People came. They came from far downriver—Alpowa and Wa-wa-wai; from Lah-mah-ta [the Wearisome Place]; from Ha-so-tin [the Place of the Eels]; from Tsce-men-i-cum [the Meeting of the Waters]; from Hatwai [the Place of the Old Woman]; from Lapwai [the Place of Butterflies]; and Te-wah [the Place of the Deer Yards]; from the Kamiah Valley [the Place of Hemp Fluff] and Tee-e-lap-a-lo [the Place of Crawfish], and Tis-ai-ach-pa [the Place of Granite Rock].[2]

Should a stranger enter their homeland and ask, "Where are you from?" the reply was always, "We are Nee-mee-poo, The People who live here in this place."[3]

It was a time of Lawtiwa-mah-ton—a time of being friends together—when The People came for this last chance to enjoy being together before the Cold Moons kept them close to their fires. The visiting and trading, the foot racing and horse racing, and the gambling and stick games would be remembered and talked about long after they had forgotten the drudgery of digging and roasting camas, picking berries, or drying meat and fish.

Lawtiwa-mah-ton! It was good to be friends together.

As was their custom since wahk-kee-ma, a time far back beyond the memory of man, they set up their camps in the same locations their parents and grandparents had occupied before them. Red Bear's people, from Kamiah, made their camp near the trail that came out of the mountains. Their neighbors in Kamiah Valley, The People from Tee-e-lap-a-lo, had their camp close by. Across the wide meadow, by the great roasting pits, the camps of the Te-wap-poo and Ask-kah-poo were located. The tepees and ish-nash, brush shelters, of other groups nestled in their accustomed areas in and out among the pines in such numbers that they encircled the entire meadow land.

Red Bear's people had traveled all summer with neighboring bands, gathering and preparing roots, picking and drying berries, drying and smoking meat and fish for their winter food supply. Now they were at the Oyaip camp. The women worked hard to dig and cure as many bags of roots as they could during the warm, sunny days, for the sharp night air brought warnings that WARM was going and COLD was coming.

Everyone helped in some way. Most of the men fished or hunted for meat. While many of the women dug and roasted camas, other women and older children picked and dried berries.

And the younger children played. They played at hunting. They played with the babies. They played with their horses and puppies. They learned how to live through their play.

This sun, happiness, peace, and quiet blessed the Red Bear camp. All were busy with their daily tasks, until sudden cries came from the children playing by the trail.

"People coming! People coming! People coming on the trail from the high mountains!" they called as they ran to their elders, who looked sharply at the figures of approaching horsemen.

Were they friends or enemies? Did they bring good news or bad?

"Who can it be? What brings them here?" were the questions in every mind.

"Could they be the four hunters who had gone to Buffalo Country two summers past? Would they have news of the families who had gone long ago to Buffalo Country and never returned?"

It was customary for a hunting party to be gone for more than one season.

"Looks like hunters," the older men agreed. "Looks like they had good hunting. Maybe our four hunters. Been gone many moons."

"Looks like five people—not four," others observed.

Excitement grew as the riders came close enough to be recognized.

"A-a-a-a-a, they are our four hunters! But who is the fifth person?" they asked.

"Looks like a woman. Who is she?"

The hunters rode up to the welcoming crowd, proud to show off the loads of meat, hides, and other trophies of their hunt. They paraded around the encampment for all to see how strong their Hunting Power had been—what great hunters they, themselves, were.

Red Bear's people rejoiced at their hunters' success. Good hunters brought good to everybody. The meat meant plenty of food and the hides meant soft-tanned robes to give comfort through the Cold Moons. But it was the sight of the frail figure of the woman that aroused their curiosity. Who was she? Where had she come from? If the hunters had stolen her, why had they taken one so sick-looking?

"Belongs to Red Bear people. Gone then come back," the hunters said, as they dismounted and unloaded their packs. "Found on trail, almost dead."

Now they could see! She was the daughter of the family gone so long ago! The girl-child who had left came back now—a grown woman.

"Wat-ku-ese!" the women cried. "Gone-from-Home-then-Come-Back. Wat-ku-ese!" And Wat-ku-ese was her name from that time on.

Gentle arms lifted Wat-ku-ese from her horse. The women brought her food and made a place for her to rest. For many suns they cared for her until she became stronger.

One evening Wat-ku-ese told her story for all to hear:[4]

"I was a maiden of twelve summers when my family crossed the mountains to Buffalo Country. We lived among friendly Shalees.[5] Life was pleasant. Hunting good. We had much smoke-dried meat and tanned hides all packed. We were ready to start for home when the Blackfeet swooped down upon us, killing our people and taking all our meat.

"One of the Blackfeet dragged me up on his horse and rode off. I never knew if any of my family escaped. I never heard of them after that.

"The Blackfeet women made me do hard work—scraping hides, gathering fuel—anything they didn't want to do. Men abused me, too.

"Finally, they carried me far off to the Land-Toward-the-Rising-Sun. They came to a big water where men with white skins lived—men who wore strange head-dresses, crowns on their heads. So-yap-pos![6] Good men!

"One of these men bought me. I became his wife. He was good to me. We had a baby boy.

"A So-yap-po woman was friend to me.

"One day she told me, 'Your husband plans to take you across the Big Water in a boat. You will never return.' I thought about that. My man had been good to me. I would not mind staying with him, but I did not want to cross the Big Water, never to return. I wanted to go back to my own people, the Nee-mee-poo, The People-Who-Live-Here.

"One night my friend, the So-yap-po woman, gave me a hatchet and some provisions and helped me escape. I had no horse. With my baby on my back, I turned toward the setting sun and started walking over treeless plains.

"Sun and storms beat down. Wild animals plagued me. Streams barred my way. Always I feared capture by Sioux, Blackfeet, or Big Bellies. I just kept plodding ahead.

"Whenever I felt I could not take another step, my Wyakin, my Spirit-Helper, a Great Wolf, seemed always ahead of me, calling, telling me which way to go. He made me feel safe. Without fear, I went on.

"My food gave out. With nothing to eat, I became weak and ill. I had no milk for my baby. He grew weaker and weaker. I could do nothing but keep going on.

"When I came to a big pond, I knew I had to get across. Using my hatchet, I cut branches from trees and bound them together with limber willow withes to make a raft. I pushed the raft along with a pole.

"Just before I reached the other side, a big bear came out to attack me. I killed him with one blow of my hatchet, and as he sank out of sight, I pushed my raft to shore. I grabbed my child and hurried away. I had left my hatchet on the raft, but I would not go back to get it. None of my people ever went back for something forgotten and left behind.

"Just when I had given up hope of finding food for my baby, I came upon an abandoned camp and found a bone with some dried meat on it. Right there I rubbed sticks into a little blaze and cooked that meat for the baby. But there was something not good about it. Maybe the meat was spoiled. Maybe it was just too late. My little boy died.

"There, beside the trail, I scooped out a shallow grave for his tiny body and covered it with dirt and rocks. Then I went stumbling along the trail, weeping.

"When I reached the mountains, I was too weak to climb the steep trail. I lay down, thinking I would soon join my child in the Spirit World. That is when these hunters, returning from a buffalo hunt, found me. Now I am again among my own people, the Nee-mee-poo."

The Nee-mee-poo listened, absorbed in that story of danger, privation, and sorrow. As often as she repeated it, they listened until they, too, could recite it. The thought of her courage through those hardships kindled their never-ending respect. From then on, Wat-ku-ese held an honored place in the hearts of her people.

So-yap-pos! White-skinned men with crowns on heads! Hard to believe, but Wat-ku-ese had spoken. Who was to doubt her word?

The snows of many winters passed.

Again the Moon of Ta-yum welcomed the wandering food-gatherers to the Oyaip with promise of plenty of camas for all who would come and harvest it.

Hahahts-il-pilp, Red Grizzly Bear, was now the war chief of the band which his father, Red Bear, had led. His people from Kamiah were there to get their share. Next to them, as always, the grand chief Broken Arm and his People from Tee-e-lap-a-lo had set up their shelters. As in the past, they camped near the trail that came from the mountains. Their lodges stood where tradition dictated, and tradition determined the routine of their work.

Some able-bodied women set about digging camas. Some scraped debris from the roasting pits and relined them with flat rocks left from seasons past. Others gathered sticks for fuel and damp marsh grass to make the roots steam.

Wat-ku-ese, now old and frail, still lived among her people and helped where she could, but her tasks were more of her own choosing. Often she rode over to other camps to visit.

While visiting the camp of Twisted Hair, she had learned that the salmon were beginning the fall run in the Koos-koos-kee and that the Twisted Hair family was going down to fish and smoke salmon for winter.

"I am going to the fishing camp with the Twisted Hair people," she announced to her own family one morning. "I can help there. Tend smoke fires." And she rode across the meadow land toward Twisted Hair's camp on the Oyaip.

Now, as soon as Chief Red Grizzly Bear saw his camp settled and the women's work going well, he rode off to a lonely place, where he could think and find guidance through his Wyakin, his Spirit-Helper, Hahahts-il-pilp—the fierce red grizzly bear.

In this moon, three of his young men had gone to carry the peace pipe to the te-wel-kas, the enemies—the Snakes, who infested the territory between the Ta-ma-nam-mah [the Salmon] and the Ki-moo-e-nim [the Snake] Rivers. He had hoped the te-wel-kas would smoke in token of friendship and peace. Instead, word came to Red Grizzly Bear that the te-wel-kas had refused the pipe and had killed the three brave men.

Red Grizzly Bear's heart was heavy with anger and grief. He could not let those deaths go unavenged. The Snakes would harass his people more than ever unless they were driven out of the country before snow came to the valleys of the Ta-ma-nam-mah and the Ki-moo-e-nim.

Red Grizzly Bear settled his mind. He would consult his friend, Broken Arm, the grand chief from Tee-e-lap-a-lo, concerning a war party against the marauding Snakes. His own men and Broken Arm's force of a hundred warriors, as well as those from other camps on the Oyaip, could shed much blood in vengeance. They could drive the Snakes from the region and return to perform the Victory Dance. Then peace and security would brighten the long, dark Cold Moons ahead.

Broken Arm seethed with rage when he learned the Snakes had refused the pipe and killed the three messengers of peace. He knew that other chiefs on the Prairie would also burn with anger against the te-wel-kas. Now was the time to seek vengeance.

"A-a-a-a!" Broken Arm spoke to his friend. "The deaths of those three men must be avenged. I will take the warpath against the enemy."

Broken Arm had only to say, "I am going to take the warpath against the Snakes," and man after man from his village would say, "Kiyu'! Kiyu'!" ["I will go! I will go!"]

"Taats!" ["Good!"] Red Grizzly Bear said. "Criers will call all warriors to war council!" The Crier then made his rounds shouting Red Grizzly Bear's invitation to join the war party.

Men from all over the Prairie assembled that night to hear the chiefs' decision to avenge the deaths of their three friends. They gave the matter grave thought, and the call for vengeance grew stronger in each heart. The chief from the mouth of Ya-ho-toin [Potlatch Creek][7] [later known as Cut Nose, Neesh-ne-ee-pah-kee-oo-keen] called out "Kiyu'!" and "Kiyu'!" came from the lips of his young men. Red Grizzly Bear's warriors responded with "Kiyu'!" and nearly a hundred young men joined in. The chief, Fierce-Five-Hearts, He-yoom-pahkah-tim, from Lah-mah-ta[8] and his men felt relief when they said, "Kiyu'!" for their area was closest to enemy territory; they were glad to have help in driving off the te-wel-kas.

Next sun began the period of preparation before going on the warpath. It was a time for purification[9] of their bodies through fasting and partaking of the sweat house ritual. It was a time for meditation and communion with one's Wyakin. A man had to feel the presence of his Spirit Helper going with him when he went to war. Each man had to see that he had proper equipment and food to sustain him and that his horses were fast and strong before he was ready to go.

Finally the night came for the war dance.

Red Grizzly Bear went to his tepee and opened his hi-sop-ti-kai, the rawhide case which held all the trappings he needed for war. He proceeded with the ritual, pa'siwya[10], daubing his face in horrifying patterns with green, white, and red colors made from earth mixed with bear grease. His shaggy red buffalo suit made him seem the personification of his Wyakin, Hahahts-il-pilp, the Red Grizzly Bear.

That suit was the strongest Power he had, for whenever Red Grizzly Bear wore it, the cunning and courage and strength of the red bear seemed to enter into him. He, himself, had no fear. He was sure of his Power in war. His Wyakin, the fierce, red grizzly bear, always protected him in battle. Already his body carried eighty scars from past battles. "Many Wounds" had become his second name.[11] He was not afraid.

In a level grassy spot near the camps of Red Grizzly Bear and Broken Arm, the pounding war drums called the warriors to the dance. For this climax they came showing off the powerful disguises their preparations had produced. The colored designs on their bodies threatened death to the enemy and warded off death to themselves. As their hideous forms leaped about in the firelight, they howled and shrieked and yelped until all were in a frenzy. All through the night the harsh cries continued with the furious dancing.

When the sky began to show pale light, the dance ended. The warriors then gathered around with their various bowls made of tightly woven bear grass and willows or hollowed out wood. Red Grizzly Bear ceremoniously served komsit, a porridge made from cooked dried kause.[12] While every man ate his fill with his spoon of carved Mountain Sheep horn or of clam shells,[13] Red Grizzly Bear commanded, "Eat! This will make you strong in battle. Eat! This will give you strength and courage!"[14]

As the birds began to twitter in the first light of dawn, the four chiefs, Broken Arm, Red Grizzly Bear, Fierce-

Five-Hearts, and the chief from Ya-ho-toin, led a long file of men away on this mission of vengeance. With many a whoop, but never a backward glance, they left—each one filled with a fierce desire to test the strength of his own Power in battle.

CHAPTER 2

WE-YA-OO-YIT

THE WAR CHIEFS HAD GONE, BUT LIFE WENT ON AS ALWAYS. Every man who did not go to war had his own duties to perform. The headman, who was wise and just, oversaw the well-being of the whole camp. He settled disputes and distributed meat and food fairly.[1] He saw to it that every family received a different part of the deer each time. This would allow every family a chance to get the neck with the hide still attached. This skin made the best moccasins, dresses, and rawhide storage cases, the hi-sop-ti-kai.

The Hunting Chief was the most active. He had full responsibility for the hunt, calling the hunters together, planning the day, assigning some hunters to stalk game, some to herd, some to work from ambush. Whether The People had meat to eat depended on the Hunting Chief's Power.

Another man was Chief of Weather. He watched for signs in nature that signaled change. He could tell by listening to coyotes and other animals what the weather was going to be. When the birds traveled south, going fast, the Weather Chief knew a bad storm was coming and would announce it was time to get in a supply of wood. If the ravens flew high up, going west, he knew Cold Weather was coming and he would tell the Camp Chief. The Camp Chief would then have the Crier announce it was time to move.

In Red Grizzly Bear's camp Big Eagle was the headman. Big Eagle made good decisions. Everyone looked up to him, and the life of his people continued uninterrupted for three suns after the war party left.

Then something happened that no one expected—and, no one ever forgot.

September 20, 1805

". . . proceeded on through a butifull Countrey for three miles to a Small Plain in which I found maney Indian lodges, at the distance of 1 mile from the lodges, I met 3 (Indian) boys, when they saw me [they] ran and hid themselves, (in the grass) (I desmounted gave my gun and horse to one of the men,) searched (in the grass and) found (2 of the boys) gave them Small pieces of ribin & Sent them forward to the village . . ." Clark [Thwaites, Volume 3, Page 77.]

That sun began at Oyaip as many another had begun in Ta-yum, the Moon of Heat. Some women had gone to the camas meadows beyond camp to dig roots and some to the great pits to tend the roasting of the heaps of camas already dug. Red Grizzly Bear had ridden away three sleeps before with the avenging party against the Snakes. Though plenty of men with cunning and wise heads remained behind, the stronger bodied and more active men in camp had gone off early to hunt and fish. Only a few stayed to protect the women and children from danger.

Danger, at least the fear of danger, was always present. With the absence of the chiefs and strong warriors, every sun brought renewed vigilance lest some beast like Hah-hahts, the grizzly, steal from the shadows of the forest to drag off a helpless one. Though scouts guarded the high passes, there was always the fear that te-wel-kas would cross the mountains to murder and to carry away women and the whole summer's catch of fish.

But on this day, the fear of the te-wel-kas was lessened. The scouts had been driven from their lookouts by the first snow. The first snow meant more snow to come—deep snow, four or five men high, piled higher by the wind. It would cover the trail and all the markers that told which ridge to follow. There were too many ridges to count, too many that looked alike, too many going the same way. A man had only to make one wrong choice to be lost. Only a few who had traveled the way many times would dare to chance a crossing after snow fell. The te-wel-kas would not be a menace now, not until the snow had melted many moons to come in the Moon of Hil-lal.

So it was that the burden of fear lay lighter on the hearts of The People than it often did. The three boys who went hunting were not aware of danger at all.

Boys of six or seven summers could find no excitement in watching women dig camas or grandfathers doze in the shade. Neither Alle-oo-ya, Koots-koots, nor Iscootim[2] wanted to sit around and listen to Big Eagle talk with their fathers and their uncles about hunting. And the boys were tired of the endless chipping away at the stones the Arrow Chief always had them work on whenever he found them just sitting around.[3]

Each boy had his own little bow and quiver. Why should they sit and just talk about hunting?

Alle-oo-ya settled his mind. He took up his bow of syringa wood and his quiver filled with blunt syringa arrows and said, just like he had heard his father say, "I am going hunting."

"I am going with you," Koots-koots and Iscootim both said, and they armed themselves for hunting.

They set out with no particular destination in mind, just going along looking for something to shoot—birds or ground squirrels or rabbits.

They had no luck with birds. Rabbits were not to be seen, but ground squirrels were all around.

Near where the trail comes out of the mountains, they came upon a large ground squirrel village dotted with holes and mounds. Everywhere squirrels popped up out of their holes to stand straight as little bears, looking about, cheeping. Good targets!

One of Alle-oo-ya's arrows hit a squirrel, who gave a shrill squeak and dived into a hole. He hadn't killed it, just grazed it. But, Alle-oo-ya was as proud as if he had killed a bear.

So intent were the boys on hunting, they thought of nothing else until the sound of a horse's snorting dust from his nostrils startled them. They looked up, and, for just the blink of an eyelid, froze in place. Quickly, they ducked behind tall grass to see, without being seen by, the strangers approaching.

Seven men were riding up. They were not the hunters that had gone out early that sun, nor the warriors on the war party. They were not Snakes, but they were scary men with hair of different colors on their faces like pieces of buffalo robe stuck on! They had no bows nor lances, just strange-looking sticks. Each one carried one of these sticks. Their horses were poor and skinny. Who were these strange men?

The boys flattened themselves on the ground and moved not a muscle, except their eyes. Those eyes missed nothing.

The riders stopped, quite near. Their leader had thick red hair that covered his face—hair, red as a bright sorrel horse. A high-crowned head-dress sat on top of his head—much different from a chief's eagle-feather war bonnet. A single braid of that sorrel-red hair hung down the back of his neck.

The boys had never seen men like these before. Who were they? Why had they come to Oyaip Prairie?

The man in front dismounted and handed his queer stick to the man behind him. Then he opened a pack on his horse and, with a shiny knife, cut off three strips of red material about as long as a water snake. With these fluttering in his hands, he headed straight for the grass where the boys thought they were hidden.

Alle-oo-ya's heart pounded so hard he thought the man had heard it, for there he was, hands dangling the red strips right over Alle-oo-ya's head. They were huge hands, covered with bristly red hairs!

This man's voice was gentle, but his words meant nothing. Alle-oo-ya could understand the man's sign-talk, though.

"Little friend! Take these gifts! Go to your village. Tell people friends come."

He held out a fluttery red strip to Alle-oo-ya and one to Iscootim; but Koots-koots, the Little One, was not to be found. He had wriggled fast on his belly like a snake, safe out of sight in the tall grass.

The two boys reached out cautiously and snatched their gifts.

"Wayat ha-mtits!" ["Beat it!"] Alle-oo-ya gasped to Iscootim, and they ran. With the thin red streamers fluttering in their hands, their feet skimmed over the trail, scarcely touching the ground, until they reached the safety of their own camp.

One of the grandfathers, looking up, noticed their unusual speed.

"Wonder what makes those boys run so fast," he said. "Looks like they run scared."

"A-a-a-a," another agreed. "Looks like they run out from under their hair. They run scared. Three went out. Two come back. Something happened."

Then the men felt their own hair rise, like the hackles on a frightened dog's back. The boys rushed up to them, gasping, "People coming! Strangers with hair on faces—like pieces of buffalo robes stuck on! Their hands say, 'Friend.' They give these."

They waved the red strips in front of the grandfathers. The grandfathers called to Big Eagle the headman and to the other men in camp, "Come! See what these boys have brought. Hear what they say about strangers. Strangers with hair on faces!"

Strangers with hair on their faces?

The men counseled together. Strangers could mean trouble and danger. Such men as the boys described sounded stranger than any man ever heard of before. Someone had to go out to meet them before they got into camp. If they seemed to have evil intentions, every camp on the prairie must be warned.

Raven Spy the scout went. He rode with courage and caution towards the possible danger. The boys watched him grow smaller in the distance until he disappeared. They watched and waited. Finally, figures appeared and began to grow larger as Raven Spy led seven strangers into camp.

The women who were still digging for roots in the meadow were told about the approaching strange men. They rushed the children to the bushes back of camp where they could watch, yet not be seen. Koots-koots, the Little One, had slipped in earlier, wide-eyed with fear and breathless from running.

Together, the women and children peeked out through the leaves at the meeting of the visitors with the men of their camp. None of their men seemed to be afraid. They stood by Red Grizzly Bear's lodge and greeted the hairy-faced riders with hand-talk.

The men dismounted stiffly. They appeared as weak and thin as their gaunt horses.

Big Eagle passed his right forefinger swiftly under his nose, giving the sign that his people were of the Chopunnish nation, Pierced-Nose people. Pointing to the southwest, he said that the big chiefs had left three sleeps ago on the warpath against the enemy.

Then he asked, "Why you come?"

The red-haired leader explained in signs, "We come in peace. We want to find the river that will take us to the Big Water." He continued, "We are hungry. We have no food."

Some of the fear had gone out of the people hiding in the bushes when they understood the sign-talk. Curiosity drew them forward and they slipped around for a better look at the odd-appearing visitors. Some of them offered roots, dried salmon, and berries, and the men ate as if they had never tasted food before.

The hair on the men's faces puzzled the children. Why did they have such hair? Was it really growing there like that,or, if it was buffalo hair, how was it fastened on and why? There was one way to find out. Mets-et-pus, the Naughty One, could not resist. He reached out and jerked the hair on one man's face, hard! The man did not look pleased. The hair did not come off. It grew on the stranger's face just like it grew on the top of his head. He had not plucked it out as the Nee-mee-poo thought a man should do.[4]

All these things happened in the time called "We-ya-oo-yit" ["The Coming"][5], when the Lewis and Clark Expedition were the first white men to come to the land of the Nee-mee-poo, The People who lived in the Koos-koos-kee Valley.

CHAPTER 3

CLARK TO THE RIVER

AFTER THEY ATE, THE STRANGERS GAVE OUT PRESENTS OF beads—blue, white, and red—and pieces of copper, rolled into little tubes. Then each man in turn took the right hand of Big Eagle and moved it up and down, up and down, in a way never seen before.[1] They shook the hands of the uncles and the grandfathers in the same way. Why they did this, no one knew, but it seemed all right. Some women, watching from a distance, put their hands over their mouths and tittered nervously among themselves.

"Where is the path to the river?" the red furry-faced chief asked with sign-talk. "We want to go there. It will take us to the Big Water."

That path was in Twisted Hair's territory. Twisted Hair would know all about the river down to Celilo Falls.[2]

Big Eagle's hands said he would guide them to Twisted Hair, headman over the valley below.

September 20, 1805

". . . I concluded to go to his village and set out accompd. by about 100 men womin & boys 2 mile across the Plains, & halted turned out 4 men to hunt . . ." Clark [Thwaites, Volume 3, Page 79.]

It was not far to Twisted Hair's camp which lay just across the meadow in the direction of Sun-Going-Down. But, before Big Eagle did anything else, he instructed his camp Crier to carry forth important news.

"Ride to every camp," he told the Crier. "Tell the people: 'Come to Twisted Hair's camp. See strange men from the Land-Toward-the-Rising-Sun. They have strange things in their packs. They say they are friends. We do not know. Maybe they have two faces. Tell the people to keep eyes and ears open. Look for signs these men might harm us.' "

"A-a-a-a-a-a," agreed the men when hearing this news.

Before the Crier had reached the last camp, those people first notified were on their way to Twisted Hair's camp. The prairie was soon full of people.

The Red Grizzly Bear people now felt more curiosity than fear. When they learned that the strangers were going to Twisted Hair's camp, they settled their minds. They did not want to miss anything. They, too, would go along.

A noisy commotion of catching and mounting horses began. Women yelled at children and at each other. Men yelled at horses, and the horses, sensing excitement, grew skittery. In the outcome, many a quiet horse carried a double load and received a double drubbing of heels in the ribs to speed it onward.

Alle-oo-ya jumped on his little cayuse mare, and Iscootim boosted Koots-koots up before he, himself, scrambled on behind both. The little mare had to trot to keep up with the long stride of taller horses, but, then, the boys seldom rode her at a slower pace.

They trotted along, beside one strange man after another. They looked hard at each man's face, clothing, saddle, bridle, horse, and baggage, until the young boys could see them in their own minds. Each man's hair was a different color. The chief's was red. Hair on some was the color of dry grass, on some brown and curly, and on others black, flecked with white. Their clothes were partly of cloth and partly of skins. Their saddles[3] were thin slabs of wood covered with rawhide, like those of the te-wel-kas, the Snakes. Their packs were made of skins and cloth. All their horses were skinny and gaunt. And besides all this, across their saddles the men carried those sticks that shot-black-sand-with-thunder.

The boys had seen strange sticks like these when men from Red Grizzly Bear's camp and Broken Arm's camp in Kamiah Valley had returned from the Minnetares with some.[4] For a while these sticks had killed with a loud noise like thunder. But now they did not kill nor make a loud noise. They could kill only when they used a special kind of black sand. When that was gone, no other sand could replace it. The boys wondered why they should trust weapons that would not work.

The young boys' eyes saw much. Their thoughts went deeper.

It did not take long to ride from Red Grizzly Bear's village to Twisted Hair's camp on the Oyaip, but by the time the boys reached the encampment, they could give a long account of how they were the first ones to see these strangers and what they had observed about them. The proprietary air which went with the story impressed their small friends. It was as if Alle-oo-ya, Koots-koots, and Iscootim thought the strangers belonged to them.

Twisted Hair's camp was simple. His people had built only ish-nash, summer shelters of pine boughs and bark, which gave sufficient protection from sun and rain and did not have to be moved. It was just a work camp. Large heaps of brown-skinned camas bulbs, which lay close by, bespoke the sweaty, back-aching work of the women.

The few men who remained in camp to guard supplies and protect the women while they dug and roasted camas received the sudden appearance of the many visitors with questions in their eyes. No one was prepared for this sudden influx.

Why did all these people descend on them at once?

Why did all the Red Grizzly Bear people come over? They lived almost within yelling distance. Nor did Broken Arm's people have to come over for a long stay. They, too, were nearby neighbors.

Big Eagle was able to make some explanation when he rode into Twisted Hair's camp with the seven strangers.

"Men come from Land-Toward-the-Rising-Sun. Want to go to rivers and on to Big Water. Want to see Twisted Hair," he said.

"Twisted Hair not here," the camp guards said. "Down at river, fishing."

"We need a place to camp," the white chief said with his hands. "We have no food. We need to hunt."

When they learned the needs of the strangers, the guards talked the matter over. There was always possible danger when strangers came among them.

"Strangers sometimes have two faces. Say one thing. Do another. Not to be trusted at first sight. Still, these men have interesting packs. What did they bring?"

Everyone was curious to know.

"If we watch them, what harm could these men do?" they reasoned, and they pointed to a place where they wanted the white men to camp.

As soon as the strangers had settled in, four of them rode off to hunt. They carried no bows and arrows or spears, nothing for weapons except their long, queer sticks.

The hunters came back with nothing. They had not seen any deer. They were weak from hunger and ate heartily of the food their leader had obtained from the Twisted Hair people: dried salmon, roots, and dried berries. They ate until they could eat no more.

When darkness fell, the strangers lay down under their blankets to a troubled sleep. They writhed and groaned with pains caused by the unaccustomed food. Some of them just got up to lie down again, and others grabbed at their bellies, retching.

Sleep did not come to Big Eagle and the principal men of the other camps on the Oyaip, for they stayed near the strangers, watching, listening, and speculating on the meaning of this visitation. Who were these men? Where did they come from? Where were they going? What did they want? Were they friends or enemies? What was to be done?

Each man smoked and spoke in turn: "My son found one of his horses killed, butchered, and hung in a tree along the trail from the mountains. These men must have killed that horse. They mean no good."[5]

"A-a-a-a," agreed his friends. "That was not an act of friendship."

"But what is in those packs?" another asked. "They show us things we have never seen before. There might be more."

"A-a-a-a," the men agreed. "Maybe we can have good trade with them. Maybe we better wait and watch."

And they waited there until dawn.

September 21, 1805

". . . 2 Chiefs of Bands visited me to day. the hunters all returned without any thing, I collected a horse load of roots & 3 Sammon & sent R Fields with one Indian to meet Capt Lewis at 4 oClock set out with the other men to the river . . ." Clark [Thwaites, Volume 3, Page 81.]

With the coming of light, six of the white men rode off to hunt, leaving their leader behind. He acted sick, not moving much, but he made sign-talk with Bad Horse and Yellow Dog who appeared from the Te-wap-poo camp to learn what this leader's mission was.

It seemed that this man wanted knowledge about the rivers. That is what his hands said.

Bad Horse and Yellow Dog squatted down beside the strange chief and scratched in the dust to show the path of the water.

"Here Koos-koos-kee in valley below runs into Kimoo-e-nim, then joins great river from cold country.

That river goes over big Celilo Falls where many fish are caught. At Falls white men sometimes come, trade, sell white beads and cloth."

In that manner they talked until the hunters came back, again with no game. Their chief then rose up and stirred himself into action. His hands began to say he wanted food, much food. "Many men one sleep back in mountains. Have no food, hungry. Send food back to them."

As soon as he drew the colored beads and ribbons, knives, and handkerchiefs from his pack, food began to be brought to the red-headed chief.

"Reuben," he called to one of his men, "load a horse with these three dried salmon and all these roots. Take them to Captain Lewis and the party back in the mountains. Maybe one of these people will go along as a guide."

Then he held out a piece of cloth and asked for a guide.

Old Dog, a hunter who knew the trail well, took the cloth and headed into the mountains with the white man and loaded horse following.

The sun was low in the sky when the red-headed chief and his five remaining men decided to go down to the river to find Twisted Hair. Yellow Dog showed them which path to take, but no one went with them. They would find the trail long and steep.

September 21, 1805

" . . . met a man at dark on his way from the river to the Village, whome I hired and gave the neck handkerchief of one of the men, to polit [pilot] me to the Camp of the twisted hare, . . ." Clark [Thwaites, Volume 3, Page 82.]

Shadows were beginning to lengthen when one of Twisted Hair's sons, A-hot-mo-tim-nim [Joyous Heart],[6] decided to leave the fishing camp and ride up to Oyaip. It would be dark before he arrived, but it made no difference to him. All his life, Joyous Heart had been going up and down that trail; he knew every fork, every landmark along the way. He gave his horse free rein and let his thoughts travel ahead to the fun he expected at the horse racing and stick games at Oyaip.

The rhythmic thump of his horse's feet had all but lulled him into a trance when he felt a tenseness in the animal under him. At once he was alert. His horse's ears pointed forward. Something was coming toward him on the trail.

The dim figures of six riders came around a bend, and in the dusk it appeared to Joyous Heart that each man had his head wrapped in fur. The unexpected sight sent prickles of fear through him. He became guarded.

The leader halted. Talking with his hands, he asked Joyous Heart to guide them to Twisted Hair's camp at the river.

Why did these men want to go to the fishing camp? Joyous Heart was suspicious. Would they kill his family and take all their fish as the Blackfeet did? His hands made no reply.

"We are friends. We come in peace," the leader assured him. "Lead us down to the river. We give this to you." One of the men unwrapped a piece of cloth from around his neck and handed it to him. This was something Joyous Heart had never seen before. Curiosity moved him to reach out for it.

Then, without a word, he gave a tug on the rein and his unquestioning horse turned to shuffle back down the wearisome trail he had just plodded up. Though it grew so dark his rider could no longer see the way, the horse led the strange group on the zig-zag path down the face of the steep ridge to the bottom of the canyon, across a creek, and along the bank of the Koos-koos-kee River to Twisted Hair's fishing camp.

CHAPTER 4

SO-YAP-POS! DO THEM NO HARM!

SEPTEMBER 21, 1805

". . . arrived at a camp of 5 squars a boy & 2 children those people were glad to see us & and gave us dried sammon one had formerly been taken by the Minitarries of the north & seen white men, . . ." Clark [Thwaites, Volume 3, Page 81.]

In the dim light of smoky fires, Wat-ku-ese squatted, keeping watch on the smoke that drifted up through the racks of drying fish. Whenever the fire died low, her thin brown hands poked in willow twigs and punk wood to make more smoke. It was good to have smoke rolling up, good for drying salmon, and a comfort for herself as well. Thick smoke drove off the plague of gnats and mosquitos that tormented everybody in camp.

Wat-ku-ese liked this work. All she had to do was tend the fires and think her own thoughts. Those thoughts sometimes took her far away. They wandered now back to the past, to that time when she had lived among white-skinned people, people who had shown her great kindness. She thought of the one she had called husband. She wondered where he was. Had he ever come back from sailing across the Big Water?

A chorus of yapping dogs jarred her into the present, and she looked up to see the cause.

What was Joyous Heart doing back here at the fishing camp? He had started to Oyaip just before sunset. How could he be back so soon? Who were these men following him?

Strangers!

Wat-ku-ese stared in disbelief as six men rode into the little circle of firelight. Did her eyes speak truth? These men had hair on their faces and hats on their heads, just like those she had seen on men before. So-yap-pos! They were So-yap-pos, the crowned ones, like those white men she had known in the Land-Toward-the-Rising-Sun!

Wat-ku-ese felt her heart stop and then commence to beat wildly. She began to laugh and talk and wave her hands up and down with joy, letting them send out the message, along with her voice, that she knew these men were So-yap-pos. Good men! Her delight touched the other women, and seeing the men make the hunger sign, the women picked out a fat smoked salmon and offered it to the strange men, standing there in the firelight.

Joyous Heart turned aside, cupped his hands around his mouth, and sent an owl's hoot across the river. An owl answered.

"Tota!" ["Dad!"] he shouted back. "Come over! Strangers here!"

The soft splash of a paddle announced the approach of a canoe before it could be seen. The chief was crossing the river.

Before Twisted Hair could beach his canoe, Wat-ku-ese was on the bank calling out to him, "So-yap-pos have come! So-yap-pos, like the men in the Land-Toward-the-Rising-Sun. Good to me long ago!"

And the children, running to meet Twisted Hair, called out, "Buffalo hair on faces!"

Twisted Hair's face beamed with pleasure[1] when he came into the firelight. Now he saw with his own eyes the hairy faces of men Wat-ku-ese had been talking about for so long. And the children were right. It did look like buffalo hair covered their faces.

The So-yap-pos' head man came forward, took Twisted Hair's right hand and moved it up and down, up and down. His words meant nothing, but when they sat down near the fire for a smoke, his hands talked. The So-yap-po said that the rest of his party was one sleep back in the mountains with nothing to eat. Next sun they would arrive on Oyaip, needing much food. The So-yap-po told of his mission and that a Great White Chief had sent them to find a way to the Big Water and to urge all people they met as they went along to live at peace with one another.

Then the So-yap-po presented Twisted Hair with something that was small, round, flat, and hard. Twisted Hair bent close to the bed of coals to examine it. On one side he could distinguish the image of a man's head. On the other side he saw two hands clasped as this stranger had clasped his. The Great White Father had sent this as a token of friendship between the So-yap-pos and the people they met. It meant everybody should live in peace.

"No more killing? Taats! [Good!]" thought Twisted Hair. "If our te-wel-kas, the Snakes and Big Bellies, agree to peace, no more fear when going to Buffalo Country."

When the sign-talk ended, the tired men stretched their blankets out on the warm sandy beach and slept.

Wat-ku-ese could not sleep. Too many thoughts raced through her mind. She had learned through the sign-talk that many more So-yap-pos would come on to the Oyaip before the next sleep. These men faced great danger. With all the warriors gone on the warpath her people would feel threatened by the numbers. The seven men who had first appeared were objects of curiosity; but great numbers of men were a threat.

Wat-ku-ese knew that swift death could come to every stranger in the silence of the night. A man, armed only with a ko-pluts [skull cracker], could slip among sleeping people and deal a death blow without a struggle. Just a few skilled men could quietly wipe out a whole expedition. Knives and spears, as well, could kill people in their sleep.

Wat-ku-ese knew these So-yap-pos were friends, not enemies. She knew that her people did not understand this. A thought came into her mind and would not go away. She had to get to the Prairie before the new, larger party of white men arrived. She did not know if she could get there before they did, but she settled her mind to try at the first light of dawn.

When that time came, Wat-ku-ese was trembling with excitement and fatigue, but she made herself go. That was the only way she would ever get to Oyaip. Long ago she had learned how to keep on going even when she was exhausted.

Before the others were awake, she saddled her tethered horse and was on the trail to the Prairie. The valley was still in shadow; the air pleasant and cool. Only the sound of the horse's hurrying hooves broke the silence as she rode the trail along the river bank.

Horse and rider traveled at a trot on this fairly level stretch until they came to the creek that emptied into the river. As soon as they had forded the creek, they faced a zig-zag trail up a steep ridge which ran from the river level to the prairie above.

The horse could not continue trotting up such a trail, but Wat-ku-ese's urge to get to Oyaip drove her into showing no mercy for the beast. All the way up the long hill, she drubbed his sides with her heels and whacked him rhythmically with a stout stick, giving him little time to stop and get his wind.

The horse began to sweat. Heat from the sun, added to the increased heat from his own exertion, caused sweat to run down through the dust on his hair in muddy trickles. The trickles turned to lather, and muddy lather dripped from him in foam. Still, those prodding heels and whacking stick urged him on.

As relentless on herself as she was on her horse, Wat-ku-ese hung on. At times she felt faint and sick, but she disregarded her own feelings, thinking that as long as the horse kept going, she could as well.

After crossing the prairie, the sun was at its highest when the horse, steaming and caked with mud, staggered into Red Grizzly Bear's camp. In relief he shook himself, all but dislodging Wat-ku-ese from his back.

Wat-ku-ese's cousin, with questions in her eyes, came to help her from the horse. Something important must have happened. What had made Wat-ku-ese ride so hard?

"Wonder how an old woman could ride hard enough to get a horse in such bad shape?" Alle-oo-ya asked Iscootim and Koots-koots when he unsaddled her horse and let him roll.

Wat-ku-ese gave her horse no more thought. She had arrived before the So-yap-pos, just as she wanted, but, at last, she had to face her own condition. Her legs trembled. Her knees buckled under her. She felt faint. Only with help was she able to totter into the tepee and collapse on her pallet where her family left her in a sleep of exhaustion.

September 22, 1805

"... I set out on my return to meet Capt. Lewis with the Chief & his son at 2 miles met Shields with 3 Deer, I ... changed for his horse which was fresh & proced on this horse threw me 3 times which hurt me some. . . ." Clark [Thwaites, Volume 3, Page 84.]

Long after Wat-ku-ese had left the fishing camp in the first light of dawn, the sun's warm rays woke the So-yap-pos. Their leader sent all but one of his men out to hunt, leaving the one to guard their baggage. He, himself, crossed the river with Twisted Hair and son, Joyous Heart, to an island near some rapids. Here on the island Twisted Hair introduced Clark to his younger brother, Te-toh-kan Ahs-kahp, [People-Coming-Looks-Like-Brothers],[2] and another of his sons, Ya'amas Wakus, [Looks-Like-Mule-Deer-Doe]. The group talked about fishing and hunting as best they could with their hands.

Twisted Hair showed the So-yap-po how he fished with spears and how the spears were made.

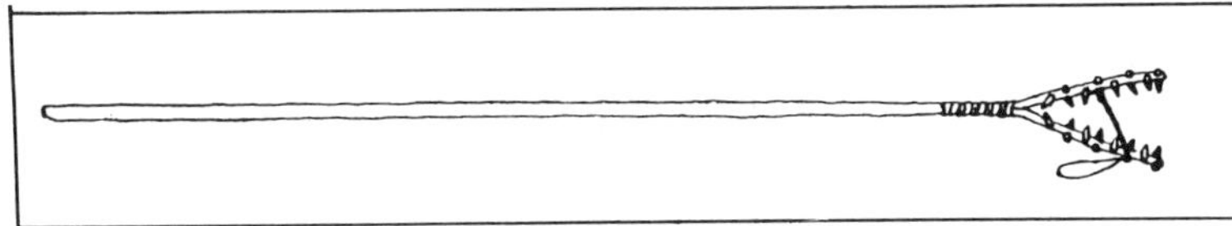

Twisted Hair explained how he, Te-toh-kan Ahs-kahp, and his son, Ya'amas Wakus, had been spearing salmon by pitch-wood torchlight the night before. He showed the green alder torch with its branches forming crotches to hold the pitch that burned with a bright light. He showed the salmon spears he used, one twice as long as a man, with its sharp point, water-proofed with bear grease and bound between the prongs, formed by splitting the big end of the pole the length of a man's forearm. He showed how each of these prongs was fitted with rows of small bone spears, pegged in, then held with glue made from fish skin.

Twisted Hair picked up the long leather thong that was attached to the tail end of a single-pronged spear and looped it around his right wrist. With his left hand he picked up a pole three times his height and thrust it down into the sand and pebbles of the river bottom. From time to time he wiggled the pole. Through the clear water they could see salmon swim up to investigate the disturbance. Then—JAB! He thrust his spear into the water lightning fast, and when he drew it out, a salmon was flipping around on the sharp point, held fast by the bone teeth in the prong.

Twisted Hair, his sons, and brother, Te-toh-kan Ahs-kahp, then asked about the Red-Head's[3] stick. How could it kill a deer? The Red-Head showed them how black sand was poured into the stick and how the thunder came out of the end of it and could hit whatever he aimed at. "Gun," he called it.

Twisted Hair thought, "This stick-that-shoots-black-sand-with-thunder would make me better hunter than young men who now ride faster and hunt better than I can. I could still be a great hunter even when I am too old to race a horse on the hillsides after deer. This could mean much good for my people. I could be important in the eyes of my people long after other men my age give up hunting. I need one of those sticks-that-shoot-black-sand-with-thunder. I want a GUN!"

After a breakfast of salmon, Twisted Hair, Joyous Heart, and the red-haired So-yap-po recrossed the river to the island where their horses were grazing in the lush grass. They caught their horses and started on their long climb back to Oyaip. Te-toh-kan Ahs-kahp and Ya'amas Wakus stayed behind to fish.

The party going to Oyaip had reached a steep and narrow stretch of the trail when they met Shields, one of the hunters the So-yap-po chief had sent out. Shields was trying to bring down three deer he had killed. He had laid two of the deer across his horse's back—one in the saddle and one behind it, with their heads fastened together and their legs bound securely to the horse. The third deer was bound on top of these.

These three small deer did not overburden the horse, but the horse was so crazed by the smell of their blood that Shields had all he could do to walk and control him. The horse had danced himself into a lather. He tossed his head and slobbered froth. The whites of his eyes showed, and he snorted with every breath he took. Shields had to dodge his feet when he lunged forward and jerk him down when he reared.

The So-yap-po chief rode a gentle horse, already tired from the steady climb. This horse could take the meat down to camp with no more trouble. Without those carcasses on his back, the frantic horse might calm down and take the red-haired chief on to Oyaip. Thus, the men reasoned and made the exchange. Shields trudged on down the trail, leading the quiet horse with his load of deer.

It was a different matter with the frenzied horse. Changing loads did nothing to quiet him. He still danced and snorted, though the So-yap-po chief managed to mount and get him headed up the trail.

Twisted Hair's horse stopped and stood quietly to get his wind. The So-yap-po's horse danced and fretted all the while. Suddenly he lunged and reared. He pawed the air with his front feet. For an instant he balanced on the edge of the trail before he toppled backwards down the steep hillside. The rider fell clear, but the horse rolled over several times before he could regain his footing.

The man remounted, but now the horse grew even more excited. They did not go far before he threw himself over backwards the second time.

Again the patient man mounted and rode on a little farther until they came to a sudden steep pitch in the trail. For the third time the horse reared over backwards. Sprawled flat on the ground, his hapless rider caught the hard blows of the hooves that struggled for sound footing.

This fall injured the So-yap-po's hip. In great pain he managed to crawl back to the trail. But he refused to ride that horse again. "Enough is enough!" he said. And his hands said, "No! No more!"

A yearling colt that followed Joyous Heart's mare was safer. This young horse carried the lamed man a short distance until they found one of Twisted Hair's loose horses, grazing on the hillside. Twisted Hair caught the gentle animal and helped the So-yap-po mount.

Slowly, they worked their way up to the Prairie. The sun was low in the sky when they arrived at Twisted Hair's camp. This climb from the river had taken almost one whole sun. Twisted Hair often made it in half a sun.

Red Grizzly Bear's camp was still farther on, and it was there that the So-yap-po believed the rest of his party would be found. He wanted to go over to meet them, but he no longer wanted to ride. Walking would be a relief, even if it hurt. He limped all the way to Red Grizzly Bear's camp with Twisted Hair walking beside him.

They arrived at dark to find that the larger party of men had come as expected, looking starved and exhausted.

"Captain Lewis!" the red-haired chief exclaimed as he shook the hand of the leader of this group.

"Brother-Chief," his hands explained to Twisted Hair.

The So-yap-po leaders located a campsite and bargained for roots for their evening meal. Then the limping chief sat down to rest his injured hip.

September 22, 1805

". . . I got the Twisted hare to draw the river from his Camp down which he did with great Cherfullness . . ." Clark [Thwaites, Volume 3, Page 85.]

After the red-haired chief and the other chief, named Lewis, had talked at length, they signed to Twisted Hair about the rivers. With Twisted Hair seated on the ground beside them, the two So-yap-pos chiefs asked questions about the way the rivers ran. Twisted Hair answered by requesting a white elkskin. When it was brought, he took a stick of charcoal from the campfire and drew lines on it to show the location of his fishing camp and his winter village on the Koos-koos-kee. He drew lines to show how the Chopunnish [North Fork] runs into the Koos-koos-kee, and, two sleeps from there, where the Ki-moo-e-nim comes from the south to join the Koos-koos-kee; five sleeps more, this river joins the big river from the north, and, five sleeps more, all water goes over Celilo Falls.

"White people at Celilo Falls," Twisted Hair said. "Many people fish at falls."

All he knew about the river routes, he drew out on the white elkskin and it seemed what the white men wanted. They acted pleased.

"Twisted Hair does not have it right," said Timuca,[4] chief from Alpowa. In the dust he drew his idea of the way the rivers ran and where the people lived along them.

"Chief Timuca does not have it right," said a headman from Ha-so-tin, and he drew his idea of the way the rivers ran.

The white chiefs welcomed all the accounts. Each man had given information in his own way—none much different from the map Twisted Hair had made first.

What they learned from all the sketches seemed to satisfy the white leaders' questions. Now they knew it was possible to complete their journey on the rivers once they had canoes. Their next step was to get their entire party to the river and build those canoes.

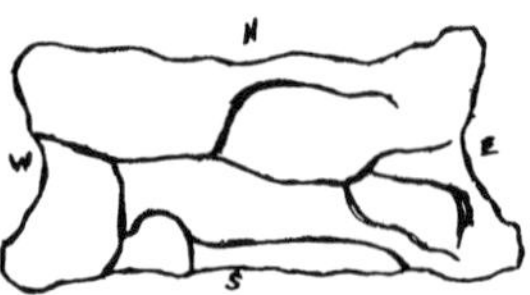

While the white men talked their plans over in their own strange tongue, they had no idea what turmoil this last party of men was causing in Red Grizzly Bear's camp.

Though the Red Grizzly Bear people had known that more strangers were coming out of the mountains and had expected them all that sun, they were not prepared for what they saw when the long line of gaunt, furry-faced men on their bony horses arrived. Other startling humans and beasts were among them, beings they had never heard of, creatures they could not understand at first sight. The fear of the unknown had sent the women and children into the woods.

Even a few of the men, surprised by the unexpected, were not ready to face the unusual creatures which confronted them. They could recognize ordinary te-wel-kas, enemies, like the Blackfeet or the Big Bellies or the Snakes, and they knew how to handle them. They were apprehensive of this new, larger party of the hairy-faced men. Why was that one man painted black as if for night work? What business did those two te-wel-kas, those Snakes, have here? All those things meant trouble, bad trouble. And why was a woman and her baby with these men? They did not belong with a war party.

Good answers did not come to these mixed-up questions. Some suspicious men joined the women and children in the woods where they could all peer curiously, but cautiously, from a distance and ponder.

"I'm scared," one woman whispered to another, but nothing could keep them from peeking out through the bushes at the sight before them.

"Why do they come? Why do they bring those two Snakes, our enemies, among us? Must mean treachery ahead for us," came whispers of fear.

"Not a war party! They bring a woman and baby! But she wears dress of a Snake. She, too, is te-wel-ka. What does it all mean?" some asked.

"Must mean something evil. Look at that big man, black all over! Covered from head to foot with charcoal. May be painted that way for night work. He could bring much harm to us. Look at his hair, not long and straight like ours. Look at his eyes! How he rolls them around! Much white shows like in eyes of mean horse." The observations came from everybody.

"A-a-a-a-a," they agreed. "Have to watch out for him. May be dangerous."

In this way the men and women talked together until Hat-itt looked at his wife, Pe-pah, in horror.

"Where is our baby?" he asked.

"In his te-cas!" she wailed. "Still hanging in the tree! We forgot him when we ran!" And Pe-pah began to weep and wring her hands.

Hat-itt loved that baby. He could not leave his son exposed to unknown danger from these strangers. Fear and love gave wings to his feet as he raced back to snatch the te-cas with his baby from the limb of the tree.

Around the winter fires laughter would always follow this story of Hat-itt rescuing his baby, but just now there was nothing to laugh about.[5]

Not every man and woman had fled when the new arrivals approached. Alle-oo-ya, Iscootim, and Koots-koots did not run. Their fathers and mothers had not run. They had developed a trust in these strange men. They stayed to welcome the newcomers.

Now the young boys could get a better look at things they had never seen before. Their eyes widened with wonder, and a little fear, when the big black man walked past them. They could look at nothing else and for a while they dared not speak.

"Is that black real?" Alle-oo-ya finally whispered. "Maybe just painted black with charcoal. And look! No fur on his face, but fur all over his head! Wonder what makes it frizzy?"

The boys saw another man, younger than the others, who had no thick fur on his face, just fuzz like the down on a baby duck. He grinned at the staring boys. They did not grin back. Nothing to grin about. But they thought to themselves that this one might have some fun inside him.

The dogs in the encampment began to growl and bristle up and walk stiff-legged around the dog that had come with the strangers—a black dog almost as big as Yah-ka, the black bear[6]—so big he could have killed their dogs had he wanted to fight. He paid no attention to them. Instead, he just walked on past at the heels of the chief of these new strangers.

"AH-HEE-AH-HEE-AH-AH-Ah-ah-ah-ah!" came a

deafening blare from one of the pack animals. The sound was so unexpected and terrifying it startled everyone, and all eyes turned toward the beast with the hideous laugh. He looked like a horse with rabbit's ears! That ridiculous idea—a horse with rabbit's ears—brought laughter even to those who had not seen the beast.

Maybe it was that frightful noise or maybe it was just the voices on the outer side of her tepee wall that woke Wat-ku-ese. Still tired and sick, she was at first only dimly aware of the commotion around her; then she remembered. She had come to Oyaip to see the rest of the So-yap-pos arrive. She remembered they were expected that sun. They must have come while she slept.

Men had gathered just outside the tepee where Wat-ku-ese lay. Their low voices reached her ears.

"What should we do?" one man said. "They bring te-wel-kas with them. That does not mean good for us. Te-wel-kas are not our friends."

"What of that black man?" another asked. "No one goes around painted black unless he means to steal upon an enemy in the dark and kill him."

"White men makes big talk, acts like friends. Black man makes them liars."

"Maybe we better kill them."

"A-a-a-a-a!" others agreed. "In the darkness, while they sleep, we kill them. Kill them, before they kill us!"

Wat-ku-ese was now wide awake and alarmed by what she had heard.

She thumped on the tepee wall and called out, "Roll up the wall so I can see out! Let me see!"

The men heard her and rolled up the wall. Wat-ku-ese looked out at what she had wanted most to see: hairy-faced men with queer headgear, asking for food while their bony horses cropped grass around them. So-yap-pos! White men with crowns on heads like those who had been good to her long ago.

Wat-ku-ese called to the men she had heard plotting to kill the strangers. Though the effort took all her strength, she spoke in a quavering voice words they would never forget: "These men are So-yap-pos! Good men! Men like these were good to me. Do not kill them! DO THEM NO HARM! DO THEM NO HARM!"[7]

With that, she sank back on her bed into a darkness from which she did not waken, for her spirit left her soon to dwell in the Spirit World.

No So-yap-po knew of this, but her words lived on in the hearts of her people. The chiefs kept them in mind when they deliberated around the council fires, and the storytellers repeated the words around the fires in the winter lodges.

"So-yap-pos! DO THEM NO HARM!" The words seemed to echo.

"DO THEM NO HARM!"
"DO THEM NO HARM!"
"DO THEM NO HARM!"

CHAPTER 5

THE OYAIP COUNCIL

SEPTEMBER 23, 1805

"We assembled the principal Men as well as the Chiefs and by Signs informed them where we came from where bound our wish to inculcate peace and good understanding between all the red people &c. which appeared to Satisfy them much, . . ." Clark [Thwaites Volume 3, Page 86.]

When the next sun came up, the So-yap-pos let Twisted Hair know that they desired to hold a council. The chief sent out Criers who rode out to every camp on the prairie to inform the remaining chiefs and principal men.

"Now let my words go through your ears," the Criers shouted. "A council with the So-yap-pos is about to take place over by Red Grizzly Bear's camp. All are urged to attend. Use your eyes. Open your ears. Learn all you can."

Their messages did not float away on the breeze, unheeded. The words passed from one person to another until getting to the council seemed the most important thing to do.

Each man gave thought to his appearance. He smoothed his hair and put touches of bear grease on the braids that hung down on each side of his face; the rest of his hair hung loose over his shoulders.

Twisted Hair was different. Instead of braids, he twisted thin strands of hair. No mark of honor, it was just the way he chose to wear his hair.

The head men came in their fine regalia to the So-yap-pos' camp where the white men welcomed them. The council circle was not large, for many, who otherwise would have attended, were away at war with neighboring tribes. Around the circle of leading men stood The People—the Ask-kah-poo, the Kamiah-poo, the Te-wap-poo and those from more distant regions of Chopunnish bands. All The People pressed close to see and hear everything that took place.[1]

"Wonder why nobody lit the council fire?" some asked, seeing the pile of dry wood in the center of the circle. "Must have got busy and forgot."

They wondered more when the red-headed chief walked to the pile of sticks. Over them he held something that looked like a thin piece of ice—round, flat, clear, and shiny.[2] Where would he find ice in this hot weather? What was it? He held it so the sun shone through it on to the dry twigs of the woodpile, but no water dripped from his hand. It did not melt! A spot of white light appeared on the sticks and smoke began to curl up as the wood burst into flame.

It was something to think about. Nobody made a sound. The flame blazed up and encompassed the larger branches, and the little twigs died down to embers. The council fire was blazing—set afire by this ice that did not melt!

"Bring a coal," Twisted Hair asked of Ta-moot-sin,[3] the small son of his sister, wife of Timuca, Chief of Alpowa. Ta-moot-sin, with great care, picked up a coal between two long sticks and carried it to his uncle.[4]

Twisted Hair took the coal and dropped it into the bowl of his pipe. He smoked three times and passed it to one white chief who passed it on to his brother-chief. After they had smoked, the pipe was passed to the others in the council circle. Smoking took a long time. It gave a chance to think before talking.

The leader of the last arrival of So-yap-pos, Captain

Lewis, stood up, and, speaking with his hands, said to the men around the council fire, "We are friends. We bring a message from our Great White Father. We have come far, up long rivers, over plains, across high mountains, to carry this message to all people on the way to the Big Water. Our Great White Father wants all people to live in peace. He wants red men and white men to be friends. He wants red men to be friends with red men. All people should live in peace together."

When Lewis had finished, Twisted Hair spoke with signs: "The Great White Father speaks good words," he said. "My people want to be friends with all people. No more fighting. No more killing. But we have bad neighbors. We work hard. We catch much fish. Smoke it. Dry it. Store it for winter food. The women dig roots. Prepare them for winter. Then from Buffalo Country the Blackfeet come across the mountains, attack us, kill our men, take our women, and steal our winter supply of fish and roots.

"We go to Buffalo Country. We watch. When we see Blackfeet with much dried buffalo meat and fine buffalo robes, we attack and wipe them out. We bring back meat and good robes.

"Our enemies, the Snakes, always near, watch for every chance to steal our fish and root supplies, our horses and our women. We have bad neighbors.

"My people want peace. If our neighbors will also agree to peace, we will live in peace."

Everyone else in the council had his chance to say a few words. After that, the white men distributed gifts.

Two small, flat pieces of metal with the image of a man's head on one side and of two clasped hands on the other, like the one Twisted Hair had received at the fishing camp, went to two of the principal men.

"To show white men and red men are friends," the So-yap-po man said with his hands.

Twisted Hair received a shirt of woven material and

a large piece of cloth, all red and white stripes except for a patch of blue in one corner that was filled with white stars.

"Flag," the So-yap-pos called it, and the red-haired chief showed him how to fasten it to a sapling stuck into the ground. There it stood like a warrior's lance, waving in the breeze, silently proclaiming the honor and prestige of its owner.

The men left a larger flag for the grand chief Broken Arm, who, with Red Grizzly Bear, Fierce-Five-Hearts, and the chief from Ya-ho-toin, was away with the war party against the te-wel-kas, the Snakes. They also left him some white material which they showed others was for wiping the nose.

Each of the other men in the council circle received one of those nose wipers, a knife, and a piece of tobacco to smoke instead of their kinnikinnick.[5] These gifts delighted those who received them.

But the bystanders wished they might also get the white men's things. They were thinking about this, when the Red-Head announced that he would like to get more food for his hungry men, as his hunters had killed no game. The women understood perfectly what he wanted, but they just stood there. They were not going to give food for just the asking. However, when the white men began to delve into their packs again, the women began to move fast. It did not take long to bring out roots, bread of roots, and smoked salmon to exchange for the coveted presents.

There were awls for making holes in buckskin and needles sharper than thorns. Tiny hard caps shaped just like women's beargrass hats were to wear on finger-tips and push needles through tough leather. Another tool, like two sharp knives fastened together, could cut leather faster than any flint knife. Combs with long, strong teeth did not break like syringa twig combs.[6] How could there be so many wonderful things? Women who were fortunate enough to receive these tools felt richly rewarded for sharing their food.

Twisted Hair, thinking to learn more from the strangers and hoping to profit through more trading, invited the entire group of strangers to his camp by the camas roasting pits.

When the council ended and the white men prepared to leave for Twisted Hair's camas digging camp, the bystanders wondered what more the So-yap-pos had in their packs. They decided to follow these men to see what they had that might be new and useful to them.

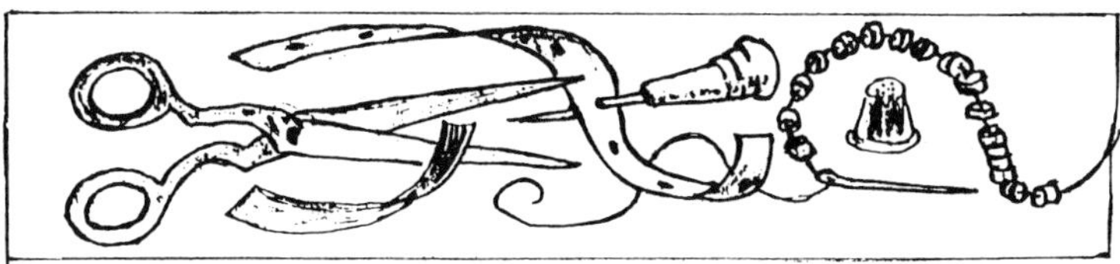

After the group of So-yap-pos had arrived at Twisted Hair's Oyaip camp, the So-yap-po chiefs asked many questions in signs about the harvest and roasting of the camas.[7] Twisted Hair showed them how the women were kept busy sun after sun. Some brought the bulbs from the meadow. Some carried marsh grass to lay over the bed of hot stones in the bottom of a knee-deep pit. Others dumped fresh camas on the marsh grass and then laid more grass over the top of the camas. Then they covered the grass with a thick layer of dirt. When the sun went down, they would build a fire on top of it. Every sundown they would build a fire there—five times. Then they would scrape off the dirt and take out the layers of grass down to the camas. Fresh camas meat was white and the juice milky. Roasted, the meat was brown and the juice sweet and syrupy.

The women pounded some of these roots and made loaves and flat, round "patty-cakes" which they dried and strung on strings of hemp. These would keep for a long time and made handy food to take on journeys.

After the camas was sacked up in hempen bags for winter, another fire was built on the rocks until they were hot and more camas was roasted in the same way. Much work for many women, but people did not die of hunger in winter when they had plenty of roasted camas.

Whatever ideas Twisted Hair had for monopolizing trade and profits were soon dispelled. Such throngs of people came trooping along as to throw everything into great confusion.

But in spite of the congestion around them, the Twisted Hair people exerted themselves to bring out food for trading. All the while they scuttled around through the crowd of greedy spectators, they strained their throats with much loud talk. "Get out of the way! Go back to your own camp!" the Twisted Hair women shouted at their neighbors. "Do you think you will get anything hanging around, getting in our way? We have work to do. Wayat ha-mtits! Beat it!"

But the spectators were not frightened away by words. They stayed where they were and defended themselves with louder words. “And who do they think they are? Ipna’naksa!” [“She thinks herself so high and mighty!”][8] they yelled back. “Do they think they will get all those fine things and leave us nothing? They may end up with nothing themselves.”

Undaunted, the women continued to bring out food and trade goods. Some brought roots and root-bread; others brought tanned elkskin. In return, the women received from the So-yap-pos items like the metal containers that were good for storing food safely away from mice and weevils. Trading kept on until the white men had all the food their scrawny horses could pack for their trip down to the river.

Even after the So-yap-pos had put away their bags of trade-goods, nobody wanted to leave. Some still stood around watching, hoping to get their hands on a new treasure. Others gathered in small groups to talk about the wonderful gifts.

Ta-moot-sin, he who had carried the coal for lighting the pipe, joined his friends, Alle-oo-ya, Iscootim, and Koots-koots. Wandering through the throng, they came upon a group where Ta-moot-sin’s mother and sister, We-ya-loo-hom, sat visiting in sign-talk with the Snake woman who had come with the white men. The boys were interested, but not wanting to be seen by those women, they slipped around into the bushes behind them.

From the sign-talk, they learned that the Snake woman’s name was Sa-ka-ka-wea, meaning Bird Woman. Her man was the one who looked like a badger. She called her baby son “Ba-teese.” She had carried him on her back all the way from the land of the Minnetares. He had been very small when they started. Now he could sit up alone.

That baby, Ba-teese, was sitting up now, and all the girls and women were laughing as he tried to grab a feather We-ya-loo-hom waved before his eyes. The sight of his sister We-ya-loo-hom, sitting there all dressed up with her beargrass hat on her head, gave Ta-moot-sin an idea.

Making no sound, he crept behind her, snatched off her hat, and dropped it over the baby's head. Ta-moot-sin had one good look at that hat with little arms waving wildly under it before he slipped out of sight.

We-ya-loo-hom shrieked, "Ta-moot-sin!" for she knew, without seeing, who had done this thing. "The Whipping Man[9] will get you for this!" Her words went out into empty air, for by that time, the laughing boys had vanished into the crowd, far from scolding and threats.[10]

At the same time the young boys were making mischief, the boys' elder brothers and cousins, led by Hawk and Mets-et-pus, the Naughty One, were clearing up a matter that had puzzled them since their first sight of the black man, York. These fellows of fifteen and sixteen summers, all strong and agile, yet too young to be warriors, thought up a way to satisfy their curiosity.

When the sun was going down and the So-yap-pos began to prepare their evening meal, the boys saw their chance. The black man, York, pushed through the crowd that pressed around the white men's activities and jauntily set off for the creek with a bucket in his hand. The boys joined the group that tagged after him. Now they would learn his secret!

The boys watched York's every move and when he bent over to fill his bucket from the creek, they pounced upon him and their strong young hands pulled him back, back and down, until he was sprawled out on the damp sand of the creek bank—powerless to rise. Two husky youths were on each arm and each leg, one at his head and one astride his body. Although he writhed and squirmed violently under them, yelling at the top of his voice, he could not shake off his attackers, and the boys proceeded with their plan.

"Now we'll see what makes him black!" Mets-et-pus, the Naughty One, said as he grabbed a handful of wet sand and began scrubbing on the black skin.

They paid no heed to the black man's howls and yelling. They scrubbed hard, then looked. The skin was still black! Wet sand should take off any paint!

They scooped up more sand and scrubbed faster. This time when they looked there was no black skin—just red blood oozing through raw flesh! Bright, red blood—like that which flowed from their own wounds!

They understood now. He was in truth made black, not painted!

Hawk thought fast, and he talked fast. They had made this York bleed. He was too big to be so angry. They would all have to get away from him in a hurry.

"Wayat ha-mtits! Beat it!" Hawk yelped, and, at once, all who had participated in the scrubbing, leaped free of the kicking black man and scurried to the anonymity of the crowd.

No one laughed this time when York rolled his eyes at them. Much white showed, but it looked fierce, not funny. When he went back to camp, they did not follow close upon his heels as they had come.[11]

Now the wind began to blow hard and the dark clouds that had covered the sun emptied their waters over the prairie. The So-yap-pos moved fast to protect their packs from rain, and the spectators welcomed the cooling drops.

Darkness fell. People still lingered. They had nothing more important to do. They might as well see all they could. Wait and watch. When the sun came up again, The People would be ready for more trading.

CHAPTER 6

IN SEARCH OF CANOE TIMBER

SEPTEMBER 24, 1805

"Set out early for the river and proceeded on the same road I had previously gone to the Island . . . several 8 or 9 men sick, Capt. Lewis sick all Complain of a Lax & heaviness at the stomack, I gave rushes Pills to several . . . maney Indians & thier gangues of horses follow us hot day Hunters had 5 Deer . . ." Clark [Thwaites, Volume 3, Pages 86, 87.]

When the new sun rose the So-yap-pos prepared to move down to the banks of the Koos-koos-kee River below. There they hoped to find wood for the canoes they would build to take them to the Big Water. Whoever wanted to see more of the white men would have to follow them down to the river. The women in Twisted Hair's band made up their minds it was time to leave the Oyaip Prairie.

"Might as well follow," they said. "We want to see what these men do. Will have to go down to the valley anyway to our winter homes."

The noisy bustle and confusion of catching horses was followed by the loud talk that went along with getting their loads on the horses' backs: bundles of mats and hides, cooking baskets, rawhide cases of clothing and finery, and hemp bags full of precious roasted camas, dried berries, and smoked salmon. The women worked hard to make sure they left nothing behind they would need; but they left the heavy stone pestles[1] which had been brought up from the river by their mothers or grandmothers, or maybe their grandmothers' grandmothers long ago. The stones would wait there until the next camas harvest.

When the loading was finished and the boys had rounded up the loose horses, the different family groups set out. After the heavy shower of the night before, the sun seemed hotter than usual. The air was humid and sticky. The earth dried. Dust rose from the hundreds of hooves that traveled the trail to the Koos-kooskee as one rider after another filed down the steep, zig-zag path to the valley.

Travel was slow-paced at any time, but more so on this day, for the So-yap-pos, who were in the lead, had to stop often. Many of them were too sick to ride and slipped off their horses to lie beside the trail until they felt better. Even then, some were too weak to remount and had to be lifted back into their saddles.

Through it all the women broke the monotony of the ride. They sang a wordless song and drummed out the rhythm with their fingers or sticks against the packs, or by gently kicking their horses' sides. The songs carried all along the line of riders. The children who rode behind their mothers or grandmothers remembered the beauty of the singing long after their bellies recovered from being poked by those antler-pronged saddles.

From the brink of the canyon the silver river appeared below, winding in and out and around those claw-marks which Itsi-yai-yai, the Coyote, had dug long ago for the path of the waters.[2] On the ridges exposed to the south the ripened cheat grass glowed with a faint amethyst tint, while, in contrast, the northern slopes carried blue-green pines to the river's edge. A blast of searing heat rose up from the valley to meet the heat of the sun.

Once in the valley the trail followed the river downstream to a rocky ridge which turned the water abruptly to the left and forced the trail to climb suddenly up and over its steep flank. On the far side, a trail led down to the water which separated the cliff-like foot of the ridge from an island in the river. This was the trail over which Twisted Hair guided the So-yap-pos to their camp on the island. Though it was formed by river-washed rocks and pebbles and sand, the island supported cottonwood trees for shade and ripe grass for horse feed. It was a safe place for the So-yap-pos. Here they could neither harm nor be harmed.[3]

Before the river made its bend to the left, all The People who had followed the white men down from Oyaip crossed over to a broad, tree-shaded flat.[4] Many people could camp here. Many horses could pasture on the tall dry grass. Many fish swam in the eddy and riffles at the foot of the cliff. Polliwogs and baby frogs darted around in the shallow backwaters of the river to delight the children who splashed off the sweat and dust in the cool water.

Twisted Hair's foresight had settled the So-yap-pos on the big island across from his camp. He could see everything they did, but they did nothing suspicious. Eating too much dried salmon and camas had given them cramps and dysentery. Five deer which the hunters had brought in gave little relief to some who were too sick to eat. Most of the men sprawled on the ground and moaned.

When the evening breeze sprang up, the heat moderated and the flies stopped tormenting man and beast. All activity in the So-yap-po camp ceased. They could do no harm this sleep.

September 25, 1805

"... I Set out early with the Chief and 2 young men to hunt Some trees Calculated to build Canoes, as we had previously deturmined to proceed on by water, I was furnished with a horse and we proceeded on down the river . . . on N side . . . to a fork from the North which is about the Same size . . . I crossed the South fork and proceeded up . . . thro' a narrow Pine Bottom in which I Saw fine timber for Canoes . . ." Clark [Thwaites, Volume 3, Pages 88, 89.]

Twisted Hair sat through the long twilight discussing the recent events with his brother, Te-toh-kan Ahs-kahp, and with his sons, Joyous Heart and Ya'amas Wakus. So much had happened that the routine of the family was upset. The new experiences had jolted the men into thinking about things they had never thought about before.

"These So-yap-pos bring change to our people," Twisted Hair said. "They speak of peace. No more killing. No more raids from te-wel-kas. Nothing to fear. Taaats, good, if te-wel-kas agree and live up to their promise!"

Te-toh-kan Ahs-kahp spoke up, "If we had sticks-that-shoot-black-sand-with-thunder, te-wel-kas would be afraid to bother us. We would have advantage. We would have peace."

"I, too, was thinking we could have better luck hunting in winter if we had one of those weapons," said Ya'amas Wakus.

"A-a-a-a-a," his father agreed. "Even old man like me could hunt as good as young man."

"So-yap-pos say 'gun.' We need guns. Maybe we can bargain for guns," Joyous Heart ventured.

"A-a-a-a," the men agreed. They knew what they wanted from those white men. Guns!

When daylight came Twisted Hair looked out over the river toward the So-yap-pos' camp. Nobody was stirring. Finally, there was the first sign of movement and Twisted Hair crossed over to the island in his canoe.

Only the red-headed chief, Clark, seemed to have any life in him. Even though he still limped from his fall with the frenzied horse, he was up now, giving medicine to sick men.

After greeting Twisted Hair, he stopped to ask with his hands, "Where are good trees for making canoes?"

"Downriver," Twisted Hair motioned. "Will guide you. Find big trees."

Together they crossed back to Twisted Hair's camp where Joyous Heart and Ya'amas Wakus brought up four horses.

"Kiyu'!" said Joyous Heart.

"Kiyu'!" joined Ya'amas Wakus.

Te-toh-kan Ahs-kahp remained behind to do more fishing.

The four crossed to the north bank of the river and followed the trail downriver to the stream which came in on their right. Here, they picked their way through large boulders that had been deposited at the mouth of the creek[5] by countless spring run-offs. The deer yards lay on the other side of the creek—a large flat where deer often wintered and where the Te-wap-poo lived. At its edge the men came to a gravel bar which angled across the river, the place where everybody forded the Koos-koos-kee.[6] But, instead of crossing here, they continued downstream to some pines which they thought might make canoes.

The trees were big, plenty big, but did the grain run straight enough to work up easily? The red-haired So-yap-po could not be sure until he had cut one down.

"Axe!" Clark said, showing Twisted Hair and his sons a sharp-edged tool before he began to chop.

Blow after blow he struck the tree, and chips flew fast.

Joyous Heart stood motionless, absorbed in watching those chips fall with every thrust of the axe. Big chips flew out as each cut sank deeper into the heart of the tree.

"Faster than beaver," Joyous Heart said in amazement when the tree finally toppled over. And, at that moment, a great desire possessed him.

"Like magic that axe cuts! With axe I, too, could cut faster than beaver. I want AXE."

But the tree just cut down was no good for making a canoe. The grain of the wood was crazy and twisted. It would take too much hard work to make a canoe from such wood. They left the log by its stump and rode on.[7]

They rode all the way to the point where the Chopunnish and the Koos-koos-kee meet without finding suitable timber for canoes. The So-yap-po then stood on the point and looked at the trees growing on the opposite bank of each river. Across the Chopunnish he saw nothing worthy, but on the south bank of the Koos-koos-kee grew pines larger than any he had seen in this valley.[8] A man standing on his horse could not reach the lowest branch.

Turning to Twisted Hair, Clark pointed to the south side of the river and signed, "Good!"

Twisted Hair beamed and answered, "A-a-a-a!"

Meanwhile, the sons of Twisted Hair had speared six fat salmon and had roasted two of them. The four men squatted down around the little fire and were enjoying the good food when two canoes approached, coming upstream.

"Good canoes," Twisted Hair said. "Hold plenty. Two families, heavy loads. Canoes ride on top of water. Not deep in water."

The So-yap-po chief stood up to watch as the canoes beached. He walked down and rubbed his hands over the shell. Then, with sign-talk, his hands said, "Good! They do not sink deep in the water. How do you make them?"

The newcomers sensed that the strange man liked their canoes, but they could not explain to him how they were made or why they rode high in the water.

"We push canoe upstream fast as a horse can walk," they bragged. "We show you fast canoe."

But the horsemen were not ready for such a demonstration. They left the men with the canoes at the point and forded the low water of the Koos-koos-kee to a wide flat covered with huge yellow pines. There could be no doubt about these trees. One man could not reach around their trunks. The bark of the trees ran in straight, smooth patterns to indicate straight grain. The So-yap-po was satisfied.

Twisted Hair and his sons rode around the flat with the So-yap-po, pointing out the slough[9] which ran back from the river and curved around the foot of a cliff—a good place for launching and loading the canoes. Big pines growing along the edge of the slough could be cut for canoes.

"We make canoes here," the So-yap-po said. "We go on in canoes. Leave horses here. Will your people care for our horses over winter? We come back in spring. Get horses. Go back over the mountains to the Land-Toward-the-Rising-Sun. In return for the care and feeding of our horses, would Twisted Hair accept one of the sticks-that-shoot-black-sand?"

Here was the chance to bargain for guns! Excitement welled up in Twisted Hair's heart. He glanced sidelong at his sons and saw in their eyes that they felt as he did, but no muscle in the three faces betrayed their eagerness.

Thinking, "If he gives one gun, maybe will give two," Twisted Hair looked straight into the eyes of the So-yap-po and gave the message with his hands, "Two guns and black sand."

The So-yap-po looked hard into the eyes of Twisted Hair, while his hands said, "You bring us all our horses when we come back in the spring. We give you TWO guns and black sand." Twisted Hair was satisfied, but he did not gloat. He did not have the guns yet.

The So-yap-po rode slowly along the bank of the slough, looking at one, then another, of the big pines that grew there, looking at how close they were to the water. He looked over the ground for a good place to camp and pasture the horses. Then he pointed upriver and started back to the camp on the island.

They did not cross back over the river as they had come. Instead, Twisted Hair, his sons, and Clark followed a good trail that led along the southern bank of the river up to the shallow ford. This was the trail the So-yap-pos would take next sun when they moved down to make their canoes.

IMAGES OF BEARS TAKEN FROM PICTOGRAPH

On the point between rivers where they had beached their canoe earlier, the men in the dugout watched for sight of the red-head. They planned to show him how fast a good dugout could travel.

"We watch," two men decided. "When we see Twisted Hair and his sons start upriver with that stranger, we will pole a canoe along side. Maybe we can go faster than their horses."

With long poles ready, they sat in one of the dugouts until Twisted Hair's party appeared heading upstream. At once they pushed their canoe into the current and were soon abreast of the riders.

Where the water ran smooth and deep they were able to keep even with the horses. But the river was at its lowest level. Here and there they came upon riffles too shallow for their high-riding dugout. Whenever they had to get out to drag the canoe over the shoals, the riders forged ahead. In deeper water once more the canoe gained. Although they could never again draw even with the horses, the dugout was close behind when the riders reached camp.

CHAPTER 7

CANOE CAMP

SEPTEMBER 26, 1805

"Set out early and proceeded down the river to the bottom on the S Side opposit the forks & formed a camp had ax handled ground &c. our axes all too small. Indians caught sammon & sold us, 2 Chiefs & their families came & camped near us several men bad, Capt Lewis sick I gave Pukes Salts &c. to several, I am a little unwell. hot day" Clark [Thwaites, Volume 3, Page 88.]

When daylight came again, most of the So-yap-pos sluggishly made preparations to move downriver to the big pines. Some made little effort to move at all. The few able men put the packs on the horses and boosted their comrades up into their saddles. The sick men rode doubled up with cramps, gripping the horses' manes to keep from falling off.

The red-headed chief led the way when they left the island single file. Without being guided, each horse followed the one ahead, across the ford, and down to the pine grove opposite the point where the Chopunnish and the Koos-koos-kee rivers meet.

Twisted Hair, his brother, Te-toh-kan Ahs-kahp, and their two families followed. When they came to the place where the So-yap-po chief had cut the tree with his sharp axe, Twisted Hair stopped to show his people the stump with the big pile of chips beside it and the log lying near.

"Like a beaver," they said. Each one had to feel the axe marks on the stump. Even small children remembered that stump, and, in time, would show it to their children and tell them how they had seen it freshly cut.

Twisted Hair's family forded the river and followed the trail downstream until they came in sight of the So-yap-pos' camp. Here, the men left the women to set up camp while they, themselves, went over to see what the white men were doing.

The jolting ride through the heat of the day had made the So-yap-pos worse. Most of them were bloated with gas, vomiting, and doubled up with pain. Even their two leaders were sick. No one entirely escaped the dysentery brought on by too much unaccustomed roots and fish and the sudden change to extreme heat in the valley.

The red-headed chief, though he did not feel well, managed to give medicine to the others and to oversee the ones who were able to work. These few men sharpened their metal axes and fitted them with handles. No man worked fast. It was too hot to work hard.

Some fishermen came down the Chopunnish on a raft loaded with salmon. Seeing the unusual number of people and horses on the flat opposite the point, they started across to find the reason for the gathering. Midway, their raft stuck fast in shoals. After much tugging, they freed it and finally reached shore to find strange white men in the midst of the throng.

The So-yap-pos, upon seeing the fine catch of salmon, brought forth their sharp-pointed fishhooks and thin fishing line in hopes of exchanging them for the fresh fat salmon.

A curious crowd had gathered to marvel at the sharp points of the hooks and the strong thin line to be fastened to them.

One woman, always curious and wanting to learn how things worked, picked up a fishhook. She ran her finger along the hook to the barb at the end. She did not understand about the barb and felt of it again to test how sharp it was.

"Ow-ye-e-e-e-e-!" she yelled, as the barb pierced her finger and stayed there.

With blood dripping, she hopped around, first on one foot, then the other, moaning and yelling, while she tried to free the hook from her finger. The harder she pulled, the deeper it went into her flesh.

Finally, the woman pulled hard enough to tear the hook out, but her finger was an aching, bloody mass. Sucking her bleeding finger, she hobbled off, moaning. For once, she had seen enough.[1]

The onlookers were astounded. "That hook has magic in it! If it can hold so tight to a big woman, then it can hold tight to a big fish!"

That convinced everybody that these new fishhooks held fast. Desire to possess a fishhook and line began to grow as the people watched the exchange of hooks and line for salmon.

Visitors from downriver who had stopped to watch the So-yap-pos measuring out fish line in exchange for salmon wondered about the length of line they would get in such a deal.

"How much line?" was the question asked.

"Stretch your arms out wide at your side," the trading man told them. "You will get as much line as your two arms can spread."

After the first few men tried this, they discovered that some had shorter lines than others because their arms were shorter. Nobody liked that arrangement. It would make for bad feelings. Then an idea solved that problem.

Among those downriver people who had just arrived was one man with arms longer than anyone else's. Why not get him to stretch out his arms and measure for everyone? That way they would get the longest possible length and all would be the same. Long Arm agreed, and many a fishline was measured by his arms that day.[2]

September 27, 1805

"All men able to work comen[c]ed building 5 Canoes, Several taken Sick at work, our hunters returned Sick without meet. . . . The day verry hot, . . . (Capt Lewis very sick nearly all the men sick. . . .) Clark [Thwaites, Volume 3, Page 89.]

The So-yap-pos who were well enough to work began to fell the trees for their canoes in the cooler part of the day. One big tree grew along the bank of the slough, and after the So-yap-po planned where it should fall along the edge of the bank, he began chopping on it. After the canoe had been made from it, they could launch it by an easy shove into the water.

The plumy top of the pine seemed to touch the sky. Was it so tall it could not see the tiny man pecking at its base?

For a while, the tree stood motionless, as if nothing had told it that its trunk had been severed. Upheld by the arms of its comrades, it stood, while the man below watched for it to topple along the edge of the slough.

A faint breeze ruffled its topmost branches and finally broke the balance. A shudder ran down its trunk, and the tree crashed through its neighbors, tearing off branches as its top splashed into the slough, so that the water rose in two walls on either side of the tree. Like a warrior fallen in battle, the great pine lay with its top buried in mud and water.[3]

The main trunk of this tree yielded a good canoe. The So-yap-pos then cut down enough trees to make four more. They needed five canoes in all, four large and a smaller lead canoe.[4]

Many people came to watch those magic axes make chips fly faster than beavers could gnaw. Their own stone axes could not chop down great trees nor make piles of chips. They watched, wondering how fast those axes would work when it was time to hollow out the canoes. Long ago, their ancestors had learned how to hollow canoes with fire. Could those axes work faster than fire?

That question was in the minds of all who watched. They would just wait and see if the white men had a magic that worked better.

September 28, 1805

"Several men sick, all at work which is able, nothing killed to day Drewyer sick maney Indians visit us worm day" Clark [Thwaites, Volume 3, Page 89.]

More people kept coming to watch the So-yap-pos chop with their wonder-working axes: some from the Chopunnish, some from downriver, others from upriver. They crowded so close to the choppers that many could have been hit with an axe had the red-headed chief not stretched a rope between the trees to keep them from the work area.

"Stay on the other side of that rope!" he warned them.[5]

The day was sultry, too uncomfortable even for those who sat in the shade watching what others were doing. If they could not get close enough to the chopping to see how those axes worked, the downriver people saw no reason just to stand there and swelter. Nor did they want to sit in the shade of a pine tree as that old te-wel-ka guide, Toba, sat alone, paying no attention to anyone—just making flint points for his arrows.

"Let's go!" they decided. "We have seen enough. We have good, new fishhooks. Let's go try them out!"

With that, some climbed aboard the raft that had brought them, and others set out on horseback. If there was anyone who had not contrived to get some trade goods, at least nobody left without a good story to tell when the Cold Moons of winter came.

September 29, 1805

"a cool morning wind from the S. W. men Sick as usial, all the men (that are) able to (at) work, at the Canoes Drewyer killed 2 Deer Colter killed 1 Deer, the after part of this day worm" Clark [Thwaites, Volume 3, Page 90.]

A cool wind the next morning brought a pleasant change for everyone. The canoe-builders were encouraged both by the refreshing weather and by the three deer their two hunters had brought in. Although three deer would make only one meal for all the thirty-three hungry people who had to be fed, they were thankful for anything in their stomachs. Maybe next day the hunters would have even better luck. Until then, the So-yap-pos welcomed the fresh salmon, roots, and berries the Nee-mee-poo brought to them in exchange for beads and trinkets.

September 30, 1805

"a fine morning . . . cool, all at work doing some thing except 2 which are verry sick, Great numbers of small duck passing up and down the river this morning" Clark [Thwaites, Volume 3, Page 90.]

Cool weather spoke of change. Ta-yum, the heat of summer, had gone. The Moon of Pe-khum-mai-kahl, when salmon spawn in the Ki-moo-e-nim, had come. Ducklings had become grown birds ready to fly to warmer lands with their families. As if to test their wings, they flew up and down the river, growing stronger with each flight and calling to others of their kind.

"Come with us," they seemed to say. "We are leaving cold behind."

Great flocks of ducks gathered in from the ponds and streams where they had been raised. The air was filled with their quacking and the sky was darkened by their flight when flock upon flock took wing to southlands.

The cool air also told The People it was time to go back to their winter homes and prepare for the Cold Moons ahead. The river carried many canoes that sun. Some people went upriver. Others went downriver. Going and coming, they passed each other with jovial greetings all through that sun.

The So-yap-pos welcomed the cool breeze. It made them begin to feel better. More of them were able to work on the canoes, though they were still weak from sickness and lack of food.

October 1, 1805

"A cool Morning wind from the East . . . dried all our Clothes and other articles, and laid out a Small assortment of such articles as those Indians were fond of to trade with them for Some provisions (they are remarkably fond of Beeds) nothin to eate except a little dried fish which they men complain of as working of them as (as much as) a dost of Salts. . . ." Clark [Thwaites, Volume 3, Page 92.]

Twisted Hair and his brother, Te-toh-kan Ahs-kahp, stood together watching the white men's weak attempts at hollowing out their canoes.

"Too slow," they agreed. "Maybe not get finished before snow comes. Looks like we better show them how to make canoes faster."

Together, they approached the So-yap-po chiefs.

"White man makes hard work," Twisted Hair said. "We show how to make canoes easy way.

"Long ago, our ancestors learned how fire could hollow logs to make canoes. We set a row of small fires on top of log. Before fire burns too much, we cover it with mud and then scrape out charcoal to make small hollow. We set more fires in this hollow and check the burn with mud. Scrape charcoal again. We do this again and again until all pitchwood in center is burned out. Only hollow shell is left for canoe."

The white chiefs listened as they watched the exhausted workers dig at the pitifully small cavities in the logs. Their faces brightened with relief.

"Burning out the hollers makes more sense," Captain Lewis said. "We could finish five canoes in no time and be on our way."

Captain Clark added, "When the canoes are finished we will need good men to guide us downriver. Will you both go as our guides?"

Twisted Hair and Te-toh-kan Ahs-kahp spoke quietly to one another before they answered. Then Twisted Hair said, "We go just to Celilo Falls. We do not know the river below that."

"Good!" laughed the red-headed chief. "The sun has dropped behind the hill now. When next sun rises, show us how to burn out our canoes."

October 2, 1805

"... Burning out the holler of our canoes, men something better nothing except a small Prarie wolf killed to day, Our Provisions all out except what fiew fish we purchase of the Indians with us; we kill a horse for the men at work to eate &c.&c." Clark [Thwaites, Volume 3, Page 92.]

When the new sun came, Twisted Hair's young men showed the So-yap-pos how to set the fires in the cavities of their logs, how to stop the burning by putting mud on the fire, and how to scrape out the charred wood. The white men were surprised and pleased to see how fast they could hollow out the wood with this method.

Although their success with their canoes helped to make them feel better, the men were miserable with hunger, for they had nothing to put in their stomachs. It seemed like they were hungry all the time.

Their small root supply was almost exhausted. There was not enough food to nourish the canoe builders. The red-headed chief sent his men, Frazier and Goodrich, with six horses to Oyaip for roots and dried fish. To make sure they kept on the right trail and met the people most willing to trade, Joyous Heart went along.

The group had far to go and a steep mountain to climb before they reached the Prairie. Even with Joyous Heart leading the most direct way, it took them all that sun to climb out of the Koos-koos-kee River canyon to the prairie above.

The men had much bargaining to do before they could load six horses with all the roots and dried fish they could carry. Then they had to wind their way down the steep trail to the river and ford it before their mission was accomplished.

Since the root supply would not arrive from Oyaip in time for their next meal, the So-yap-pos ate a soup made from a small coyote the red-headed chief killed. It was not enough to satisfy anyone's hunger.

In exchange for a few fish, the white chiefs then gave out a small piece of tobacco, three broaches, two rings, a piece of ribbon, and a kerchief divided five ways. Even this additional food was not enough to sustain all the men who had been working. In desperation, the chiefs ordered a horse killed for their evening meal. The workers finally went to sleep with full stomachs.

October 4, 1805

"a cool wind from off the Eastern mountains, I displeased an Indian by refuseing him a pice of Tobacco which he tooke the liberty to take out of our Sack. Three Indians visit us from the Great River South of us. The two men Frasure and Guterich return late from the Village with fish roots &c. which they purchased as our horse is eaten we have nothing to eate except dried fish & roots which disagree with us verry much. (Capt. Lewis Still Sick but able to walk about a little.)" Clark [Thwaites, Volume 3, Page 94.]

Though many curious on-lookers had returned to their villages to prepare for winter, more visitors kept arriving to watch the progress on the canoe building. Three had come from as far as the Ta-ma-nam-mah [Salmon River].[6] All stood watching the men work as they had the sun before, burning, mudding, scraping.

Twisted Hair and Te-toh-kan Ahs-kahp watched as the canoe building came to an end. They realized that the So-yap-pos would leave soon. They remembered their promise to guide the white men down the river, but they had not said where they would start guiding.

The two men talked about that matter.

"Might as well ride horses downriver with our cousins this sun," Twisted Hair said.

"A-a-a-a! Wait on the big fishing island for canoes to come. Then go with So-yap-pos," Te-toh-kan Ahs-kahp agreed.

So it happened that, when a group of downriver people rode back to their own area, Twisted Hair and his brother rode with them. They knew how they would keep their promise, but they did not think to tell the So-yap-po chiefs of their intentions.

While other people watched the canoe building, Weasel Tail, one of the visiting spectators, fixed his eyes upon the sacks of trade goods piled inside a pen of pine boughs. One open sack held the So-yap-pos' tobacco. Weasel Tail wanted a piece to chew, and when he thought no one was looking, he slipped his hand through the pine branches and helped himself.

But someone had seen! The Red-Head's sharp eyes saw and he made it clear that the tobacco had to go back into the sack.

Thwarted, Weasel Tail's face turned dark with anger, but he returned the tobacco and went away, humiliated that he had been caught.

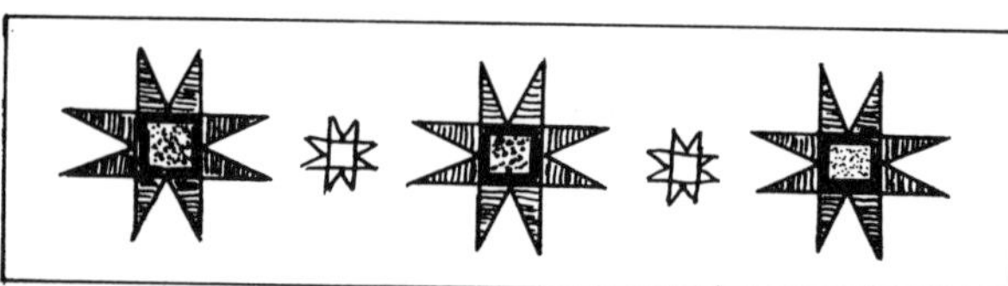

Past sundown Joyous Heart and the two So-yap-pos returned from Oyaip with loads of dried fish and roots on their horses. Food again! Even though it made many of the white men miserable, they ate it. It was food, and they were starving.

October 5, 1805

"a cool morning wind from the East, collected all our horses, & Branded them 38 in No. and delivered them to the men who were to take charge of them . . . Lanc[h]ed 2 canoes to day one proved a little leakey the other a verry good one" Clark [Thwaites, Volume 3, Page 94.]

Next morning when the red-headed chief came upon Ya'amas Wakus and Joyous Heart, he inquired, "Where is Twisted Hair? Where is Te-toh-kan Ahs-kahp?"

The two answered with shrugs and the sign, "I know not."

The So-yap-po glanced around as if to catch sight of the missing men, but they were nowhere to be seen.

Out of necessity Clark then spoke to the sons of Twisted Hair.

"Friends, your people have promised to care for our horses over winter. When we come back in the spring, you bring us all our horses and saddles. We give you two guns and powder.

"This sun we round up all our horses, mark them, and turn them over to your care. We give gifts to your men who help us."

At these words, the men from Twisted Hair's camp jumped on their own horses and helped run the So-yap-pos' herd into the narrow strip of land between the slough and the river. There they sat on their mounts and watched the So-yap-pos work.

As some of the white men caught the horses, others cut off the foretop and touched the left shoulder of each horse with a hot iron. Blue smoke carried the bad smell of burned flesh and hair. The white chief explained that this burn would mark the horse for life. No more hair would grow there. It would always be as smooth as a man's forehead—always easy to see. They branded thirty-eight horses that way.

Before he turned them over to the care of the Twisted Hair men, the So-yap-po chief gave Ya'amas Wakus and Joyous Heart each a knife and other small gifts.

Then Ya'amas Wakus, Joyous Heart, and their friends rode around the milling horses, shouting "Hi-ya! Hi-ya!" as they drove them to the river bank. Urged on by the frightful noises behind them, the horses plunged into the water and swam to the opposite shore. There, on the slopes of Tap-toop-pa (The-Mountain-That-Looks-Like-Tepee-Poles-Set-in-Place)[7] the horses could graze on ripened grass through the Cold Moons.

IMPRESSION OF THE LEWIS & CLARK BRANDING IRON

After the horses had gone, the So-yap-pos tested their first two canoes in the water of the slough. All anxious minds held the question: "Will those canoes be water-tight?"

By prying and pushing, the men worked the canoes over skid poles to the water's edge. Then they eased the first canoe into the still water of the slough.

"Whoopee!" they yelled as the canoe slipped into the backwater and rode straight up. But their spirits fell as they saw water begin to seep inside. It LEAKED!

Crestfallen, yet breathless with suspense, the So-yap-pos eased the second canoe into the water. Only after they saw it riding sound and water-tight did they give a loud cheer.

Their red-headed chief ordered the leaky canoe to be pulled out of the water and repaired.

The stay of the So-yap-pos was nearing its end.

October 6, 1805

". . . had all our Saddles Collected a whole dug and in the night buried them, also a Canister of powder and a bag of Balls at the place the Canoe which Shields made was cut from the body of the tree. The Saddles were buried on the Side of a bend about 1/2 mile below. all the Canoes finished this evening ready to be put into the water. . . ." Clark [Thwaites, Volume 3, Page 96.]

After darkness fell and all men should have been ready for sleep, the So-yap-pos moved quietly about their camp. They talked in low voices.

The Nee-mee-poo wondered what those men were doing in the dark that they had not wanted to do in the daylight. Whatever it was would wait until after the So-yap-pos left next sun. Daylight would show what the darkness had hidden.

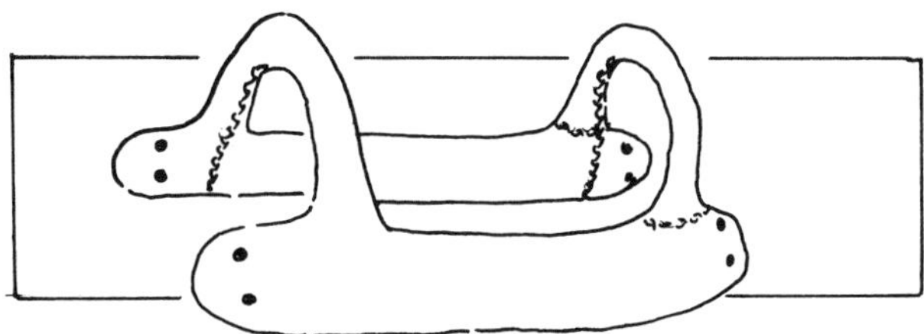

October 7, 1805

"I continue verry unwell but obliged to attend every thing all the Canoes put into the water and loaded, . . . as we were about to Set out we missd. both of the Chiefs who promised to accompany us, I also missed my Pipe Tomahawk which could not be found." Clark [Thwaites, Volume 3, Page 98.]

The canoes were finished, water-tight, and ready to go.

The So-yap-pos had spent the night before quietly packing their gear and caching powder and saddles for their return trip in the spring. To his dismay, the red-headed chief discovered that Sergeant Floyd's pipe-tomahawk was missing. Clark had guarded it carefully ever since Sergeant Floyd had died before the party reached Fort Mandan. He had intended to present it to Sergeant Floyd's family as soon as the expedition returned to the United States.

Because his Brother-Chief Lewis was still sick, Clark was everywhere directing. He told where each person was to ride and what baggage should go in each canoe. Finally, he took one long look at the camp they were leaving and another long look at the people waiting in the canoes.

Again Clark asked of the crowd assembled to watch their departure: "Where is the chief, Twisted Hair? Where is Te-toh-kan Ahs-kahp? They promised to guide us down the river to the Falls. We are ready to go. Where are they?"

And all answered with shrugs and the sign, "I know not."

He then questioned them, with mistrust in his face, "My pipe tomahawk is gone. Do you know who has it?"

Again, the answer was a shrug and the sign, "I know not."

He asked no more, but turned, entered the lead canoe, and shouted, "Shove off!"

One after the other, the canoes carried the So-yap-pos around the bend and out of sight.

Free to wander over the abandoned campsite, the Twisted Hair people searched for any precious scrap that might have been left. When their curiosity was satisfied, they faced the matter of getting themselves and their horses across the river to their winter home at the foot of Tap-toop-pa.

CHAPTER 8

DOWNRIVER

OCTOBER 7, 1805

". . . proceded on passed 10 rapids which wer dangerous the Canoe in which I was Struck a rock and Sprung a leak in the 3rd. rapid, we proceeded on 20 miles and Encamped on a Stard. point opposit a run. [*Opposite Jack's Creek near Lenore.*] passed a Creek small on the Lard. Side at 9 miles, a Short distance from the river at 2 feet 4 Inches N. of a dead toped pine Tree had buried 2 Lead Canisters of Powder." Clark [Thwaites, Volume 3, Page 98.]

Twisted Hair and Te-toh-kan Ahs-kahp had stopped on their way downriver to tell their friend, Big Heart, about white men who would soon come down in canoes.

Big Heart was thinking about this as he rode out on the hills above the river to inspect his horse herd. Strange men with hair on faces, one black man, a huge dog, two te-wel-ka men, a te-wel-ka woman and her baby! That is what Twisted Hair and Te-toh-kan Ahs-kahp had said.

Suddenly, much loud talk from the river below him reached his ears. Big Heart knew at once that it came from the strangers. He could not understand anything those men were saying. He could not see just what they were doing.

Curiosity forced him to work his way down the hill to a clump of thorn bushes where he could see, yet not be seen. There were those So-yap-pos, just as his friends had described them!

Five canoes had come to shore and the strange-looking men were unloading their packs on the sandy beach. They then inspected the empty shells of the canoes and ran their hands over the surface. They turned the canoes upside down and thumped and felt of the outside. They turned four canoes right side up and replaced the baggage. They left the fifth canoe upside down. A few men began to chink a weak place in its side.

"Looks like they sprung a leak coming through the rapids," Big Heart said to himself. He knew, too well, what damage a canoe could get in the rapids. It was certain that this canoe needed repair.

He watched, fascinated by the tools the strange men used, and he saw a few of the So-yap-pos walk up the bank to the dead-topped pine tree. It was not possible to see just what those men were doing, but they seemed to be digging around the foot of that tree.

Darkness fell soon afterward. The strangers did nothing more than eat and lie down to sleep, their first sleep from Canoe Camp.

Big Heart nudged his horse into a quiet walk and rode downriver to his village.

Next morning all of the people in Big Heart's village watched as the five canoes with their strange passengers splashed past. The people did not have much time to look while the canoes swept downstream, but they had much to talk about afterward.

Big Heart did not stop to talk with anyone. He mounted his horse and headed upriver, followed by his dog. When he arrived at the campsite of the So-yap-pos, he poked around their dead campfires looking for anything forgotten.

His dog sniffed in the areas where the white men had slept and where they had eaten. Then he sniffed along the path where the men had buried something near the dead-topped pine.

Big Heart's curiosity drove him to follow the dog to that spot. Right there the ground was soft and the smell of newly dug earth was strong. The dog began to dig. The dirt flew out behind until his head and shoulders were buried in the hole. Finally, no matter how hard he scratched, he was unable to go deeper. He backed out of the hole and whined.

Big Heart watched, wondering what his dog had found. When the dog gave up, Big Heart looked inside the hole. Two heavy canisters[1] had been buried there. That was what the So-yap-pos had been doing, burying something for safe-keeping. What it was he had no idea.

"If I leave these here," he said to himself, "somebody will carry them away. If I take them to my lodge, they will be safe until white men come back next spring like Twisted Hair said."

How heavy those canisters were! He loaded them on his horse and led him home. He did not know just what he had found, but he guarded the canisters as cherished possessions.

October 8, 1805

"A Cloudy morning . . . Set out at 9 oClock . . . passed Several Encampments of Indians on the Islands . . . at one of those Camps we found our two Chiefs who had promised to accompany us, we took them on board after the Serimony of Smokeing." Clark [Thwaites, Volume 3, Page 99, 100.]

Twisted Hair and Te-toh-kan Ahs-kahp, fully mindful of their promise to guide the So-yap-pos down the river, sat in complacent silence on the island at the mouth of the creek where cottonwoods grew. They had come here with their friends to inform others of the approach of the white men. Now they waited for those men to arrive.

When, in time, the So-yap-pos' canoes came into view and neared the island, Twisted Hair stood up and threw out a greeting. "The clouds rise and disappear when one meets a friend," his hands said.

But he felt uneasy when the So-yap-po chiefs came ashore. Their faces were stern and their actions were not warm and hearty with goodwill. What had offended them?

"Come aboard," both of the So-yap-po leaders signed, scowling.

"We smoke first," Twisted Hair replied, for he did not want to go on with angry men. They smoked. Words were then spoken without bad feelings, and Twisted Hair and Te-toh-kan Ahs-kahp found their places in the lead canoe.

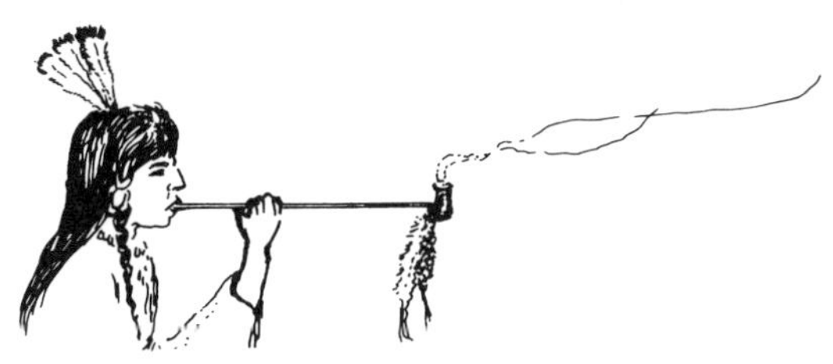

Twisted Hair and his brother knew the river well, for they had traveled back and forth on it all their lives. They knew the hazards of running through the rapids at this season when the water was low.

Here and there, the great rocks that stuck their heads above low water were easy to see and avoid. Greater danger came from the rocks that lay just beneath the surface where water deceivingly crested with gentleness. Where the stream was swift, a man did not always have time to steer clear of them.

Rocks, submerged in the river at the mouth of Ya-hotoin Creek, claimed the second canoe when the So-yap-pos came through the rapids. The canoe slammed against a rock, spun around, and struck again, nearly splitting in half.

The big man, Gass, who was steering, sailed overboard and thrashed about in the water until he reached the canoe, which had caught on a rock and was sinking with all the men on board. The men clung to the submerging canoe and yelled for help. Some baggage escaped and began to float downstream.

"Swim ashore! Swim ashore!" called the So-yap-pos who had already beached their canoes.

"Can't swim!" the luckless non-swimmers yelled back.

"Waves are too high. Too many rocks to swim," yelled the others.

One of Twisted Hair's friends who was watching from his small canoe now came to the rescue of some of the men. The So-yap-pos sent over their small canoe for the rest. By this time, they had unloaded a big canoe and used it to retrieve sunken baggage and tow the splintered canoe to shore.

Everything in the packs that had sunk was soaked and had to be spread out to dry. A few things had been lost or grabbed by hands of spectators who had come from the nearby village.

Only the few in front were lucky enough to examine

the sodden goods before a So-yap-po bellowed at them as he threw the sign, "Keep your hands off! STAY BACK! We don't want any of you taking our things."

It was too bad he had to say this just when there was a chance to examine what had never been seen before. A thing has to be felt, as well as looked at, before you can tell what it is really like. Can you tell how a moccasin or a shirt is made if you cannot turn it over in your hands? Can you tell how a tool is used if you cannot handle it? It was hard not to touch the white men's things. This brought their problem out stronger.

"We want some of those things. How can we get them?"

There was the way of simply taking something, but that was why the So-yap-pos stood there saying, "Keep back! Do not touch these things!" There was the way of yal-lept, the contest between two people giving, each vying to give the other a finer gift. There was the way of trading, but this was not a good time for that business. Perhaps next sun there would be a better opportunity to receive some So-yap-po treasure. Now darkness lay over everything like a blanket.

Again sleep came—the second sleep from the Canoe Camp.

October 9, 1805

"all day drying our roots good[s] & articles which got wet in the canoe last night. our 2 Snake Indian guides left us without our knowledge . . ." Clark [Thwaites, Volume 3, Page 100.]

The So-yap-pos went off in all directions when morning came. "Like yellowjackets when their nest has been poked with a stick," Twisted Hair thought.

Different men went to guard the wet articles which were drying slowly. Four of them pounded on the broken canoe, while others went off looking for pitch to waterproof the cracks. Another man traded for fish to take on their journey.

The Snake guide and his son kept to themselves. Nobody bothered them, but the two kept their eyes and ears open whenever the village people came near. They learned that the chief of this village had gone with a war party against their tribe. They could sense greater hostility toward them here.

"We are getting deeper into enemy country. We may come to a sad end if we continue with these So-yap-pos," the older man said. "We can slip back to Canoe Camp. Take two So-yap-po horses. Cross mountains before snow gets bad. Get home safe."

His son welcomed these words. They had no reason to stay.

When the sun dropped, father and son crossed the creek and climbed the hill as fast as if the enemy were at their heels.

By the time the red-headed chief heard about their going, the two men were out of sight; but their going troubled him. He went to Twisted Hair with the problem.

"Old Toba and his son have left on foot. They do not have their pay for guiding us over the mountains. Ask someone from this village to ride after them. Tell them to come back for their pay."

Twisted Hair shook his head.

"No!" he said. "No good to give them anything. When they go through my territory, my people will just take it away from them. Let them go."

October 9, 1805

". . . The Indians and our party were verry mery this after noon a woman faind madness. &c. &c. Singular acts of this woman in giveing in small po[r]tions all she had & if they were not received . . . She would Scarrify her self in a horid manner . . . &c." Clark [Thwaites, Volume 3, Page 100, 101.]

With the canoe repaired, their baggage dried and packed, and their stomachs full, the So-yap-pos felt in high spirits. They were ready to shove off early the next sun. Their loud, laughing voices carried far beyond their camp.

"Cruzatte! The fiddle!" they called. And one of the men, the man with only one good eye, brought out a strange hollow box with strings stretched tight on one side. He carried a stick with a horse's tail-hair stretched tight on it from one end to the other. When he rubbed this across the box, strange music came out, different from any ever heard before.

"Dance, York, dance!" the So-yap-pos shouted.

And the black man jumped up and clapped his hands. He began to make his feet move fast and his legs to swing in funny ways—different from a war dance. He rolled his eyes until the white showed all around. He laughed. Everybody laughed.

Other men sang and played on something they held up to their mouths and twanged with their fingers. They called it a Jew's harp. They clapped and yelled and danced until excitement ran through the crowd.

Ahtway, one of the women, felt the powerful force

of Iship coming over her as these strange songs and music and dances swirled around her. Ever since the power of Iship had possessed her during the Medicine Ceremony in the Cold Moons, she had been unable to control her excitement.

Now Ahtway began to sing her own song that had come to her under the spell of Iship, "Hish-a-hish-a-hish." And, as she sang, she handed out roots to those around her. It pleased her when people accepted her roots. But her spirit changed when one of the So-yap-pos refused her gift. Anger possessed her. She threw all of her root supply into the fire, snatched a flint knife from her husband, and cut her arms in several places until the blood gushed out. She wiped up the blood with her fingers and ate it. She tore off the beads and copper ornaments from her dress and thrust them upon the spectators.

Then, still singing "Hish-a-hish-a-hish," she ran about wildly and headed for the river. Her sisters grabbed her and dragged her back before she could do herself further harm. Finally, she collapsed on the sand and lay there, stiff and motionless.

When her sisters poured water over her face, she revived and was able to move about. The red-headed chief then gave her a few trinkets which pleased her. She went willingly back to her village with her family.[2]

October 10, 1805

"a fine Morning loaded and Set out at 7 oClock . . . passed a run on the Stard. Side haveing passed 2 Islands and two bad rapids at 3 miles lower passed a Creek on the Lard. with wide cotton willow bottoms [*Lapwai Creek*] . . . at 8 1/2 miles lower we arrived at the heade of verry bad riffle at which place we landed near 8 Lodges of Indians . . . on the Lard. Side to view the riffle, . . . after viewg. this riffle two Canoes were taken over verry well; the third stuck on a rock . . . Small Split in her Side which was repaired . . . we purchased fish & dogs of those people, dined and proceeded on. . . . at five miles lower and Sixty miles below the forks arived at a large southerly fork [*the Snake River*] . . ." Clark [Thwaites, Volume 3, Page 103, 104.]

Twisted Hair and Te-toh-kan Ahs-kahp enjoyed the early morning trip downriver as the canoes floated past the landmarks of their tribal myths. Beyond the cottonwood flat that marked the mouth of the creek from the Place of the Butterflies, they passed the rock formations that gave rise to some of the tales of their people:[3] the Dead Warrior Chief who lies on the rim of the canyon; the Ant and the Yellowjacket; and Coyote's Fishnet.

The brothers could well recount the legend of the Ant and the Yellowjacket.

Ant and Yellowjacket were eating dried salmon along the banks of the Koos-koos-kee.

"You have no right to eat here," Yellowjacket told Ant. "This is my territory."

"It is quite the other way. This is my territory! You have no right to eat here," Ant replied.

So they argued and bickered until they began to fight.

Coyote ordered, "Stop fighting or I will turn you to stone."

Ant and Yellowjacket paid no heed to the warning. Just as they locked jaws to tear each other to pieces, Coyote turned them to stone. There they have stood to this day.

After drifting around a bend in the river, the brothers pointed to Coyote's Fishnet. Here, Coyote had been fishing in the river when Yah-ka, the black bear, teased Coyote until he lost his temper. Coyote threw his huge fishnet over Yah-ka and tossed him to the top of the hill across the river where he turned to stone.

The canoes continued on until they came in sight of the great stone Frog. Frog squatted near the bottom of the canyon wall where he had lit after his mother-in-law pushed him from the row of dancers on the hilltop. Long before humans came to this valley, the dancers had all been turned to stone, just as we see them to this day.

Below Frog, along the bank of the river, lay a stretch of level land where a village of eight lodges overlooked the head of dangerous rapids. It was a good place for fishing people to live. Their men were skilled at managing canoes through the jutting rocks, but it was not a place for any unplanned approach.

Twisted Hair saw to it that the five canoes landed near the village. Here he pointed out the line of jagged rocks extending from one bank to the other.

During high water, most of the rocks would be covered with no great threat to canoes, but this was the season of low water. Through narrow channels between rocks, the water gushed and churned with smashing force.

Twisted Hair pointed out a likely space, saying, "That way is best." The white men agreed.

"We'll have to take the canoes through that channel, one at a time," Captain Clark said. He directed the order in which the canoes should go.

The first canoe went through safely. The second followed with no trouble. But the third slammed against a rock and split. Tossing crosswise, it wedged between rocks and was held fast by the force of the water. Oars and poles floated on downstream while the men grappled with the loaded canoe in the swift water.

Below the rapids, men, who were fishing from their canoes, watched the white men's labors with interest and understanding. When they saw the poles and oars floating past, they pushed their dugouts into the current to retrieve them for the strangers.

After a long struggle, they pulled the canoe to shore for repairs. When it was mended, the canoe followed the remaining two through the rapids with no further mishap.

By the time the split canoe was repaired and taken through the rapids, the workers were exhausted and starving. They turned to the Nee-mee-poo with such trinkets as beads, needles, and awls to exchange for salmon and dogs to eat. The women brought out plenty of salmon for the strangers' food, but few would part with their dogs. "What kind of men would eat dogs?" they wondered.

Among these people was Lee-tsu, a little girl about six summers old. Lee-tsu had been hopping about with her dog while her father and mother, brothers and sisters, uncles and aunts and cousins enjoyed themselves watching the men with fur on their faces.

Lee-tsu loved her dog. She had carried him around when he was a tiny puppy. Now he had grown too big to carry, but he went everywhere she did, ate with her, slept with her. She named him "Mox-Mox" because he was yellow.

Now Lee-tsu sat down on a big rock to watch the strange men. The dog sat beside her, his tongue out, panting. He licked her face and went on panting.

A So-yap-po with black fur on his face walked past, stopped, and looked at the dog beside the little girl. He turned to a man following him and spoke strange words. Then he licked his lips, rubbed his belly, and laughed.

He pointed to the yellow dog, and his hands said, "Who will sell this dog?"

Lee-tsu's father read the sign and thought, "Might as well. Too many dogs anyway."

Then with signs, he told the man with the black fur on his face that he would sell the dog, and he held out his hands for the trinkets that were offered in payment.

The man came over to the rock, tied a thong around Mox-Mox's neck and dragged him off. Lee-tsu could not understand what was happening. She followed her dog, and her eyes saw the terrible thing the man did with his knife.

Horrified, the little girl ran back to her parents, screaming, "My dog! That man killed my dog!"

"Plenty dogs," her mother soothed. "Lee-tsu will have another dog. See the pretty things your father got for the dog. Lee-tsu may have some pretty beads."

"Too many dogs," her father had said and stalked off—the pleasure of possessing white man's trinkets dimmed, for he loved this little daughter—and she would not be comforted.

Lee-tsu would never forget that dog, and when she grew to be a mother she would tell her children this story.[4]

After they ate, they continued on. Below the rugged rapids[5] the country opened out with wide flats on either side of the river. The close canyon walls of the Koos-koos-kee gave way to the sight of distant blue mountains and high plains, broken by canyons of other streams. The span of sky that stretched so wide to cover the earth, so high above, was an unfailing source of wonder to Twisted Hair and Te-toh-kan Ahs-kahp who had been raised in canyons.

Now, a new spectacle greeted the men. As the canoes slipped downstream, crowds of people gathered on either shore to watch. They were not just people fishing along the river, for many were on horseback. They had come—maybe one sleep, maybe two sleeps away—just to see these canoes filled with strangers.

The onlookers had plenty of time to watch the strange white men manage their heavy canoes. Many riffles still faced them, but none were as bad as those they had passed. In some places the men had to wade into the river and haul the boats over.

The brothers, Twisted Hair and Te-toh-kan Ahs-kahp, sat straight and proud, conscious of their position. To be in the lead canoe, floating past hundreds of people, was like riding at the head of a big parade—important persons in the place of honor.

By the time all five canoes were well below the rapids, the sun was on its downward path. Day was ending; but, something more than day was ending.

The river Koos-koos-kee was coming to an end. Here was Tsce-men-i-cum, the meeting of the waters. The Koos-koos-kee ended, yet it went on, constantly mingling its beautiful, clear, cold water with the blue-green of the Ki-moo-e-nim, the Snake. That river, rolling in from the south, absorbed the Koos-koos-kee's offering at the very foot of northern hills and turned abruptly toward the Land-of-the-Setting-Sun. Continuing on, it gathered the contents of every stream along the way to the great river from the north, the Columbia.[6]

A strong wind sprang up just as they came to the meeting of the waters. It was blowing upstream and the canoes had to face right into the wind as they entered the enlarged stream. The wind grew stronger until it seemed to hold the canoes in place in spite of the men's efforts to row against it.

"Halt here! Make camp for the night!" came the welcome orders. On the right-hand bank they made their camp.

Before dark, Twisted Hair and Te-toh-kan Ahs-kahp answered some questions the So-yap-po chiefs asked about The People and the country from which the Ki-moo-e-nim River came.

"Up that river—many rapids. Ten, maybe fifteen. Good fishing places. Chopunnish and some other tribes live far upstream. One chief has so many horses he can't count them. Some have large lodges with flat slab roofs."

Three days of travel by canoe had brought them thus far, and this was their fourth sleep from the Canoe Camp.

October 11, 1805

"a cloudy morning wind from the East. We set out early and proceeded on passed a rapid at two miles, at 6 miles we came too at Some Indian lodges and took brackfast, we purchased all the fish we could and Seven dogs of those people for Stores of Provisions down the river . . ." Clark [Thwaites, Volume 3, Page 100.]

At Alpowa, the village people were aware that the So-yap-pos were coming. No one was more eager to see them than the small Ta-moot-sin and his sister, We-ya-loo-hom. Ta-moot-sin had carried the coal that lit the pipe at the Oyaip council fire, and We-ya-loo-hom had played with Ba-teese, the baby of Sa-ka-ka-wea.

When the canoes did arrive, the mother of Ta-moot-sin and We-ya-loo-hom was pleased to see her brothers, Twisted Hair and Te-toh-kan Ahs-kahp, acting as guides. The feeling of friendship for these travelers grew stronger.

While the white men bought fish and dogs and ate their morning meal, the children watched. They watched when the canoes left, until the last one disappeared around the cliffs that held the river in its place.

The children had felt the goodness of these people. They would always remember this visit of the first white men to their own village.

CHAPTER 9

THE COLD MOONS

OCTOBER 24, 1805

[*At Celilo Falls*] ". . . [had] a parting Smoke with our two faithful friends the chiefs who accompanied us from the head of the river, (who had purchased a horse each with 2 rob[e]s and intended to return on horseback) . . ." Clark [Thwaites, Volume 3, Page 158.]

Twisted Hair and Te-toh-kan Ahs-kahp had felt uneasy for several suns. They had heard that the nation below the Falls was unfriendly toward the So-yap-pos. They felt they, themselves, would be killed if they continued on. Their Chopunnish nation did not extend any farther downstream, and they could not understand the language of those downriver tribes.

Together they went to the white chiefs and said, "We can be of no more help to you. We are anxious to return to our own country."

"Stay with us two more sleeps," their friends said. "Stay. We will smoke and make peace between these people and your tribe."

The brothers felt more secure. They agreed to wait that long. But, they kept their ears open for warlike words and their eyes watchful for suspicious activities of other tribes.

Mindful of the possibility of trouble, the So-yap-pos guarded a high point above the river in case they had to defend themselves. But the onlookers seemed more interested in watching the white men manage their canoes. With skill the So-yap-po rivermen guided the heavy dugouts through the boiling, churning water of the Falls. No crashing and splitting, no capsizing, no damage came to any of the five, except a little water in some.

Meanwhile, Twisted Hair and Te-toh-kan Ahs-kahp worked their way along the shoreline to the village below the Falls. Here each of them bought a horse in exchange for a robe. A horse was better than walking or trying to pole a canoe upstream all the way to the Koos-koos-kee.

The So-yap-po chiefs arrived and smoked with the chief of the village, giving him a medal. This chief seemed pleased and a friendly feeling grew between him, the So-yap-pos, and the two Nee-mee-poo.

The time came for the farewell smoke between the two brothers and the So-yap-po chiefs. Not much was said. The next sun would see the So-yap-pos turn their dugouts downstream toward the Big Water and Twisted Hair and his brother head their horses toward the Koos-koos-kee Valley.

All felt sure they would see each other again in the springtime.

HO'PLAL
[THE MOON WHEN LEAVES TURN GOLDEN]

As he rode along over the treeless plains and hills of the Walla Wallas' country, Twisted Hair's thoughts dwelt on the beauty of his homeland. It had been in the Moon of Ho'plal[1] when tamaracks in the high mountains lose their needles, that he and Te-toh-kan Ahs-kahp had left to guide the So-yap-pos down to the Falls. By this time the cottonwoods' leaves would have turned yellow and the sumacs' scarlet, and all leaves would had fallen before the two men returned to the Koos-koos-kee Valley. The sight of all the changes around them brought long thoughts to Twisted Hair, whose mind could see what his eyes could not.

"Just as the needles of the tamaracks are freed by the wind and fall to the earth in golden showers," he thought, "so there comes a time for the end of men's lives. That is Ho'plal. Now a change has come. All the trees have shed their colored leaves, and Cold is beginning."

As they continued their return trip, the brothers wondered what changes had come to their village during their absence. Their families probably had done what they always did when the Moon of Ho'plal arrived. They should all be back in their winter lodges, back from war, or from fishing, hunting, and food-gathering, with much to talk about.

Twisted Hair and Te-toh-kan Ahs-kahp stopped at all the villages along their way home to learn the news and to relate their own experiences with the So-yap-pos.

At the mouth of Ya-ho-toin Creek where the So-yap-pos had mended their sunken canoe, they visited the chief who had recently returned from war. Much change had come to him since he and his men had followed Broken Arm, Red Grizzly Bear, and Fierce-Five-Hearts to seek vengeance for the killing of the three brave warriors who had carried the pipe of peace to the Snakes.

Though they had known him well since childhood, Twisted Hair and Te-toh-kan Ahs-kahp looked at him twice before they recognized him. A deep scar now slashed through one nostril and across the end of his nose, giving his plain, dull face a fierce, threatening look.

"What happened?" his visitors asked.

The chief told them of his recent encounter with the Snakes.

"I had led my party down into Little Salmon country[2] in pursuit of te-wel-kas. We caught up with them. They were on the uphill side of a big rock—maybe high as one man, long as three or four. We were below.

"Fighting with spears, they had advantage. They could stand on top and strike down. It was hard for us to reach them from below.

"I was trying to jab my spear at one above—could reach no vital place, nothing but his feet and legs. He looked down at me, bent over, and jabbed his spear across my nose. Blood gushed out.

"In anger I cried, 'He cut my nose! I'm going over!'

"The warriors then followed me up over the rock. We killed all te-wel-kas in that party, all but this one," he pointed to a sullen young man sitting nearby. "I brought him back as my slave."

"Since then, I am 'Nusnu-ee-pah-kee-oo-keen' to upriver people, 'Neesh-ne-ee-pah-kee-oo-keen' to downriver people. My new name, 'Nose-Jabbed-with-Spear,' or 'Cut Nose,' commemorates this experience."[3]

After hearing his story, Twisted Hair and his brother had new respect for this man. Never before had they been impressed with his Power in war.

Cut Nose informed the brothers that the warriors had returned victorious. They had forty-two Snake scalps to avenge the deaths of the three who had gone on the peace mission. That meant that not a man in their war party had been killed, or they would have brought no scalps no matter how many they had killed. Scalps were just for victory.

That very night the Scalp Dance[4] was to take place.

Pika, the mother of one of the three brave warriors who had been killed while seeking peace, had wept in her endless mourning. Likewise, her son's wife had been in continuous mourning. The young woman had cut off her long hair at shoulder length and, from that time on, had not combed it. Nor had she bathed her body. The families of the other two young men had shown their grief in the same manner.

Now the deaths had been avenged. Cut Nose announced to the mourners it was time to go on with life, to start living normally.

Pika's young daughter, by marriage, bathed and then clothed herself in the beauty of white buckskin. She combed the snarls from her matted hair, but she did not braid it—just threw it back away from her face as all the other women did for the victorious Scalp Dance.

Then the chant to the evening shadows rose, calling the joys of the evening camp: "Itswa-wlts-itsqiy, itswa-wlts-itsqiy."

"Hurry, evening shadows be,
Hurry, evening shadows be,
Hurry, evening shadows be."[5]

And the people gathered. Putting aside their grief, the men of the dead man's family dressed in their finest buckskin with the porcupine quill work and the marten tippet. They joined the circle of dancers where Chief Neesh-ne-ee-pah-kee-oo-keen, himself, stood holding a fresh scalp. Up and down he waved the scalp. Standing in one place, up and down his body danced, bending at the knees. The remaining victorious warriors danced in the center, waving scalps and singing the story of their victory. Now all would know the slain warrior of their village had been avenged.

Behind the dancers stood the women, adding their voices to those of their men. No one who heard these men and women singing together ever forgot their Song of Victory. It was a sound that lifted the hearts of all from grief.

The next sun, while the village people returned to their tasks of preparing for the Cold Moons ahead, Twisted Hair and Te-toh-kan Ahs-kahp now recounted the coming of the So-yap-pos to Cut Nose.

"Strange white men came through the Oyaip soon after you left with war party. They had fur on faces and queer head-coverings. Wat-ku-ese called them 'So-yap-pos' because of their headdresses. They built five canoes and went downriver to Big Water. Our family has charge of their horses until they return in spring. They promise two sticks-that-shoot-black-sand-with-thunder when they get horses back."

A seed of envy and greed took root in the heart of the Cut Nose as he heard that story. He had missed seeing these strange men about whom his own people had told him. He had missed gaining the prestige of caring for their horses and the reward of receiving guns. He wanted these things. How was he to get them? Such thoughts began to chase each other through his mind.

When Twisted Hair and his brother departed, Cut Nose gave no voice to his feelings. But those jealous thoughts did not leave him. All through the Cold Moons, Cut Nose was to scheme how he might discredit Twisted Hair and gain favor with the strangers when they returned.

More than once, Cut Nose was to visit Twisted Hair, and, with a contemptuous swagger that spoke as loud as his words, he told Twisted Hair, "You are not taking good care of white men's horses. Not all in one place. They are scattered over the hills. No water. My men can take better care of those horses. Water them. Keep them together. We will show those So-yap-pos their horses had good care from Cut Nose people."

And it was to follow, any horse from the So-yap-po herd straying near Cut Nose territory was driven in with Cut Nose horses.

One more sun brought the Twisted Hair and Te-toh-kan Ahs-kahp to the meeting of the Chopunnish and Koos-koos-kee rivers. Here at Ah-sah-ka their band had wintered for generations. As they approached the village, cries of delight greeted them. They had been gone a long time. Now they were back, bringing small gifts of beads and shells they had obtained in trading at the Falls.

White frost glittered on twigs and dry grass when the next sun rose. Moccasins were stiff, and fingers, gathering firewood, tingled with the cold. The breath of The People and of the dogs and horses came out white. COLD was growing stronger. Everyone felt the spirit of Cold, the gusty wind, khalp-khalp,[6] that shook the tepee flaps and warned them to prepare for winter. The horses already wore their winter coats of shaggy hair. The women had stored winter food in their wecas. They had dug out the debris from their pit houses and strengthened the roof coverings with poles and branches and earth to shed the rain and snow. They had lined the walls with mats of woven rushes, and covered the floors with them. They had gathered dry willow for fuel.

The men had decided where the longhouse would be situated and whose single lodges would be put together to make it.[7] When COLD grew strong, they would be ready.

MOONS OF SEEKH-LE-WAHL AND HA-OO-KHOY [THE MOONS OF FALL DEER HUNT AND BEGINNING OF WINTER]

COLD came. It came with an icy breath that froze the grass and flowers, the ponds and creeks, the rivers and lakes. Digging roots and fishing in the streams now had to wait until warm, pleasant days came. The People would live on the food they had worked all summer to save: the dried roots and berries, bread of roots, smoked fish, and dried meat.

COLD grew stronger. Snow fell. Snow made better hunting. A man could follow tracks in the snow until he found the deer. Then, if his Deer Power was strong, he brought meat back to his family. If his Deer Power was weak, he brought back nothing, and his children were hungry, unless some successful hunter generously shared his meat.

One cold, snowy day, two men went out hunting together; both succeeded in getting a deer. When they took their game back to the lodge, one man looked at his family—not just his children, but his brothers, sisters, their children, and his mother and father—all hungry. He stripped the meat from his deer and gave each one a portion. All slept that night with full stomachs.

In gratitude, his family brought him gifts of moccasins, clothing of tanned skins, bags and baskets, until his own family was well supplied.

The other man gave his deer to his wife to prepare for the evening meal while their friends and relations looked on, hoping to be given a share.

This man and his wife looked at each other and said, "This is such a small deer! There is not enough of it to share with everyone. We might as well eat it ourselves, for there is hardly enough even for us." That family licked their lips over the meat and gorged themselves, while the hungry ones grew hungrier as they watched.

No one brought gifts to them. No new bags, no new moccasins, no fine tanned buckskin replenished their needs. In time their clothing would wear thin. Their children would have no moccasins. The clothes of all that family would grow shabby. Then the people would point their fingers at this man and his wife and say, "Ipna-ko-tahk-o-tsaya." ["You have eaten it all yourself, and your clothes are falling to pieces."][8]

As COLD continued, food supplies dwindled. In some villages, food from the summer's work was exhausted. Hunger was so great that people ate ho'pope. It had little taste, but it kept life in bodies. Ho'pope was made from the moss that grows on pine trees. When the moss was roasted, it became a black gelatinous mass that crumbled when it cooled. Ho'pope made no feast, but it was better than no food at all.[9]

Desperation forced some men to fall pine trees in

order to strip off the outer bark to expose the sweet layer beneath. This, along with the nut-like seeds they gathered, gave nourishment, but it did not stop the hunger feeling.

The Spirit of Death took people from every village that winter. Some had seen many snows, some only a few, and some had been in the beauty of youth. Wailing and keening rose as grieving families struggled against the bitter cold to bury their dead. Misery from the cold added to the burden of sorrow.

Into shallow graves, scraped out of the rock debris at the foot of cliffs, they laid the skin-wrapped bodies with their heads toward the rising sun. They dropped gifts into the graves before they covered the openings with poles and pieces of cedar, over which they placed stones and then cedar pickets upright between the stones. Finally, they sent horses of the deceased into the Spirit World to accompany the dead.[10]

When Death came for one of Cut Nose's wives, his heart was heavy with grief. He had not realized how good she had been until she was gone. Her children, her parents, brothers, and sisters felt a great loss; even his other wives missed her. After they had done everything to make her journey to the Spirit World safe and comfortable, her loved ones sent the spirits of twenty-eight horses along with her, leaving their bodies lying near her grave.[11]

After the burials, much more had to be done before living could go back to normal. Those who had handled the dead bodies had to cleanse and purify their own bodies. They made themselves vomit by thrusting osier twigs down their throats and followed that by taking sweat baths. They tore down that portion of the house where death had occurred and recovered the space. They set the possessions of the dead aside to be divided later at a feast. At this, a just man would see that greedy relatives did not take everything for themselves and leave the bereaved family destitute.[12]

WAI-LU-POOP [THE MOON OF COLDEST WEATHER]

The Moon of Wai-lu-poop was the season of coldest weather. It was a time when snow fell and the wind howled. Rains sometimes beat down day and night, or sharp cold glazed the land with ice. In the smoky gloom of the houses, it was sometimes hard to tell day from night.

While the weather lashed at the mud-calked matting of the longhouse roof, the people crowded into the comfort of the sunken room below. Family upon family squeezed in along the earthen walls, glad for any shelter from the storm.

Except for the little daylight that filtered through the smoke holes, the only light in the houses came from the row of family fires which ran down the center. Bright, clear light flared up from willow and alder wood which burned with little smoke. Pine and fir did not burn so joyously. Smoke from such fuel dimmed the light. Good light or much smoke depended upon the kind of wood the women had gathered.[13]

Around the family fires that twinkled down the center of the room, The People squatted and warmed themselves and dried their clothing. Only the need to sustain life could compel anyone to leave. Cramped quarters—jokes and squabbles—noise, vermin and smells—these things could be endured just to keep warm.

Through all the commotion ran the voices—boasting, quarreling, laughing, and joking voices. But when a storyteller's voice was heard, everybody listened.

It was when night dropped its blackness over the smoke holes that story telling was best. When the shadows from the fires grew strong and black on the walls and roof, children gave up their play and crept close to their parents. Snuggled under their sleeping robes with their feet to the fire,[14] they listened to the stories that helped pass the long winter nights.

Over and over again, through the drawn-out winters, the children listened to their elders retell the stories of the Nee-mee-poo, The People. Some stories told about how the animals lived before humans came. Some stories explained how certain landmarks came to be. Others, full of imagery, were told just for fun. No matter what kind of story it was, it was always told in just the same way. The children, hearing the stories over and over again, learned them by heart. And, in time, they would repeat them to their children and grandchildren as they had heard them.

In the Red Grizzly Bear's winter lodge, where Alle-oo-ya, Iscootim, and Koots-koots lived among brothers, sisters, and cousins of different ages, Al-la, a grandmother, told many stories.

"Al-la, what made the river?" came the questions from the children.

"Itsi-yai-yai, the Coyote," the grandmother answered.

"Al-la, where does all the water go?"

Al-la said, "I will tell you."

THE PATH FOR THE WATER[15]

Long ago, maybe a thousand, thousand years ago, water was over all the ground. It wandered everywhere around through the pine trees. It had no place to go, for there were no paths to lead it anywhere.

No people lived on earth then, just animals. The animals knew that people were coming, and they must make ready for them. They talked together.

Yah-ka, the Brown Bear, spoke first, "Water now covers the berries, the camas, and the tsa-wit. There is no food. Soon The People are coming."

Then said Titska, the Skunk, known as the Medicine Man, "Someone must dig a path for the water so it will go from the land. Then food will grow. There is yet time."

Itsi-yai-yai, the Coyote, who liked to do BIG THINGS, stood up and said, "I, myself, will dig the path for the water."

So he began to dig. He dug from the ocean, the Big Blue Water, through mountains and along on the level. Into each scratch he made along the way, streams of water flowed and raced towards the ocean. When he tired, he rested. Then he started his digging up higher. This made the falls in the rivers.

Itsi-yai-yai walked along, just looking, while his moccasins sank deep into the soft earth, leaving tracks on the edge of the canyon for The People to see.[16]

He saw that he had dug valleys so deep, they would always be warm in winter when the gray cold hung over the highlands. Grass and camas and kouse would grow early here—plenty of food for The People and horses. Then, when summer had parched the plants in the valleys, good food would still be growing in the upper country.

So were the rivers formed and things made ready for The People.

"Al-la, how did people come to live in this valley?"
"Al-la, why does rattlesnake have a flat head?"
"Al-la, why does muskrat have no hair on his tail?"
"Al-la, where did the flowers come from?"
"I used to wonder about those things when I was little," the grandmother said. "I will tell you how my grandparents answered these questions."

THE KAMIAH MONSTER AND THE COMING OF PEOPLE[17]

Before The People came to earth, a great monster lived in Kamiah Valley. Its body filled the canyon. Its head lay far upstream from Kamiah; its tail trailed off downriver.

It inhaled all the animals round about for food. Big and small, near and far, it sucked them in, until none were left. When Coyote heard about it, he was downriver, tearing out the Falls so salmon could get upstream for The Peoples' food. He quit working and started for Kamiah to see what he could do to help his friends. He traveled in a southeasterly direction towards the Seven Devils Mountains. He carried five stone knives in his pack with some pure pitch and flint for making fires. He rubbed clay on his body to blend himself with the earth. After that, he tied himself to three of the mountains with a hemp rope and fastened a bunch of grass to his forehead. Disguised in this way, he slipped through the grass to the edge of the canyon.

Right below him the head of the monster filled the valley. He had never seen anything so large.

Coyote hid himself in the grass and just looked.

Then, in his loudest voice, he shouted, "Ho! You Monster! I will either inhale you, or you will inhale me."

The Monster did not move its head, but its eyes rolled this way and that, looking for Coyote.

When it saw where Coyote was shaking the grass, it answered, "You swallow me first."

Coyote sucked in his breath with a loud "Slur-p-p-p," but the Monster only quivered and did not budge.

"You might as well try me now," Coyote said. "You have taken everyone else in. I will not be lonely."

Slo-o-o-op! The Monster drew Coyote right into its mouth. As he went, Coyote left behind him the roots of camas and kouse, beautiful flowers, and service berries for The People.

Walking along down the throat of the Monster, Coyote saw the bones of all who had died scattered around. Many of his friends were still alive, but they looked sick and hungry.

Bear came out and snarled at him. Coyote blunted his nose with a kick and went on.

Rattlesnake taunted him. Coyote stepped on his head and flattened it out.

Finally, when he came to the heart of the Monster, he looked at his hungry friends and shouted, "Why are you starving with all this around?"

He began to cut slabs of fat from the heart, saying, as he tossed them out to the hungry ones, "Smear your lips with this!"

"Bring wood!" he ordered. And when wood had been brought, he built a fire with his pitch and flint.

Clouds of smoke began to pour out of all the openings in the Monster's body—from its ears, from its eyes, from its nose, from its mouth.

Coyote kept talking and cutting at the heart of the Monster. One by one he broke all his stone knives, and still the heart hung by a piece of muscle. Coyote pulled at it with his hands.

"Get near an opening," he yelled. "When the heart is severed, the Monster will die. If you hurry, you can get out some opening before it closes. Kick the bones of the dead out as you go."

With that, Coyote yanked off the last piece of heart with his hands, and the Monster began to thrash around in convulsions. When all its openings opened up, Coyote's friends rushed out and pushed out the bones as they went.

Everyone escaped safely, except Muskrat whose tail was caught. He pulled so hard to free himself that he pulled all the hair off his tail. That is why, to this day, Muskrat has no hair on his tail.

As the Monster lay dying, the death throes made the valley wider.

Then Coyote had the bones of the dead arranged properly. And, when he sprinkled some of the Monster's blood on them, those who had died inside the Monster suddenly came to life again.

Finally the Monster lay dead, and the heat from the body rose up in steam that made fog. That is why it is always so foggy in the valley.

They carved the Monster's body, and Coyote distributed the parts, flinging some toward the sunrise to create the Crows, the Blackfeet, and the Sioux; some toward the sunset to make the Cayuses and the Yakimas; some toward the Cold to fashion the Spokanes and the Coeur d'Alenes; and from that which he tossed toward the Warm sprang the Shoshones. Not a scrap of the great Monster was left.

His friend, Fox, nudged him. "You have given everything away for people in other places. What are you going to do about The People in this valley?"

Coyote looked at his bloody hands and asked, “Why didn’t you say that sooner? I was talking so much, I was not thinking. Bring me water.”

After Coyote washed his hands in the water Fox brought, he sprinkled the bloody water over the floor of the valley. From this heart’s blood came the noble Nee-mee-poo, The People, who have lived here ever since.

Some signs of the Monster remain. When fog fills the valley, we say, “That is the breath of the Monster.” When we pass the rock mounds near the river, we say, “There is the heart of the Monster,” and over closer to the river where there lies a lower mound, “There is the Monster’s liver.”

Tota [Dad], who had fished downriver at the Falls, answered the questions, “Where did fish come from? How did they get in the river?” with his story.

THE COMING OF FISH[18]

One time winter stayed too long at Kamiah. The Nee-mee-poo had used up all their supplies of dried roots and meat. They were hungry. They did not know where to find food.

Great flocks of magpies chattered over the village, but The People paid no heed to them until they heard Itsi-yai-yai, the Coyote, call from his seat on a high point. Again and again he called.

“Follow the magpies! Follow the magpies!” he kept saying.

The People then saw that the magpies were hovering over a raft on the river. Nothing was on it, but the sound of a baby's crying came from it, "Wa-wa-wa-wa-wa!"

"Hurry! Hurry!" they said. "We must save that baby!"

They set out to follow the raft. But, though they traveled for many days, they could never once get their hands on it. Never could they see a baby on it. Always it was just ahead of them, and always they heard that crying, "Wa-wa-wa-wa!"

Finally, they came to Celilo Falls. The raft plunged over the brink, out of sight. They looked for the raft and the baby in the water below the Falls, but fish were all they could see. The water was alive with fish, jumping and wriggling, struggling to get over the Falls.

The Nee-mee-poo understood then that they had been guided to this place where the fish were. As long as they had fish, they would never be hungry again.

Grandfather's stories held the children spellbound. His voice could growl like Hah-hahts, the grizzly. His teeth could chomp and his lips could snarl like those of the fierce bear. He could make his listeners shudder with fear, or swell up with pride and courage, just by the tone of his voice, as when he told the story about finding the trail.

FINDING THE TRAIL THROUGH THE MOUNTAINS[19]

At the time when The People were coming to take the place of animals on earth, a boy was lost in the mountains. He wandered around trying to find his way back to his father and mother when he met Hah-hahts, the grizzly bear.

Now Itsi-yai-yai, the Coyote, had told the Bear that The People were coming to take possession of his territory. Bear was furious because he did not want to give up the land he loved.

When he saw the boy, the grizzly's eyes filled with hatred. He reared up on his hind legs. His teeth chomped together so that flecks of foam dribbled from his snarling lips as he lunged forward with his claws extended to shred the boy to pieces.

"So! A child of the Nee-mee-poo has come to rob me of the land I love! With one blow of my paw I will kill him, and him I will devour." Bear growled until the mountains shook and echoed his anger.

The boy just stood there before him. He answered Bear with these calm words, "I can only die. Death is only part of life. I am not afraid."

Bear stopped short in solemn wonder.

"What is that?" he rasped. "You are a different creature from the Animals. They would have cowered at my words, but you have shown the bravery of Bear, the wisdom of Coyote, and the pride of Eagles. You are of a superior race, deserving these lands. My time has come. I must show you the provisions and secrets of your new home, and I will do so gladly."

In admiration now, Bear flipped the boy onto his furry back and started into the higher mountains. Here he showed him pools and streams full of fish. He showed the boy the home of the Beavers, the Little People, who cut down trees and dammed the streams so fish could be caught more easily. He showed him the home of the moose, the elk, and the deer.

Bear climbed the backbone of the highest mountains to show the boy the way to the other side where buffalo lived on the plains toward the rising sun. Sometimes Bear would stop and stand on his hind legs to scratch a mark on the trunk of a tree so that all who came afterwards would know that he had been that way. Often the bear and the boy could hear the voice of Itsi-yai-yai, the Coyote, urging them on, for Coyote liked to use his loud voice, while Bear had not been given a loud-talk tongue.

After the boy had seen the home of the buffalo, Bear brought him back along the trail through the mountains to the camas meadows of Oyaip. He showed him the camas, the tsa-wit, and the kouse. He showed him the huckleberry, the chokecherry, and the service berry. The boy thought that all he had seen was good.

After he had done all this, Bear took the boy to the brink of the Kamiah Valley.

"Here your People are living," he said. "Go tell them what you have learned about this great land, the food that has been provided for them, and the trail that will take them across the mountains."

Bear disappeared then, and the boy returned to his People.

The rise and fall of a mother's voice, the motions of her hands, and the expressions on her face could transport the children to a land of make-believe where animals talked like humans and had problems like humans.

COYOTE[20]

There was a time when the animals could talk and act like people, but they were still animals. They predicted that human beings were coming, and they called a council to talk matters over. They talked for many days.

Finally, they decided, "You name whatever you want to be and then you be that. You act out what it is you want to be, and, if you qualify, you will be that."

They picked out judges to see who qualified.

"Well," said one chipmunk. "I'd like to be a deer."

"Well, go out there and see how you act. If you can qualify by your actions, you can be a deer," they told him.

Everytime anyone said, "I want to be this or that," the coyote would say, "I want to be that, too."

"Well," they told him. "Go out and act."

Coyote could never qualify. All the others qualified, but he was still a coyote. He was the last one and still a coyote.

"You'll just have to be a coyote," the judges told him. "That's all that's left for you to be. You've never qualified."

"Well, yes, I guess I'll have to be a coyote. But I'll exist. I'll go to every place, but I'll exist."

And that's the way it is with Coyote. He still exists.

Not to be outdone, a fun-loving uncle could charm the children with his story of the chipmunk and grizzly bear.

THE CHIPMUNK AND GRIZZLY BEAR[21]

One day, one of the animals asked, "What about day and night? How shall we have this day and night?"

Grizzly Bear spoke up with a drawl, "I want f-i-v-e y-e-a-r-s of night and f-i-v-e y-e-a-r-s of day."

Then Chipmunk, with his quick, chattering voice, said, "No! That's too long. Who wants to sleep for five years and then work for five years? We just want one day and one night. That's what we want."

So they got to arguing. They argued several days. Neither one would give the other what he wanted.

Grizzly Bear said, "No-o-o-o, I want f-i-v-e y-e-a-r-s to sleep".

Chipmunk said, "No!!"

The judges finally said, "All right! You two argue it out."

They drew a line between the two of them, and the judges said, "You, Grizzly Bear, sit on this side of the line, and you, Chipmunk, sit on the other side of the line. Now argue it out. You can have two or three days or whatever you want. Just argue it out."

So they argued for two or three days there, just as the judges told them.

Grizzly Bear kept repeating his wish, "F-i-v-e y-e-a-r-s of night, f-i-v-e y-e-a-r-s of day, f-i-v-e y-e-a-r-s of night, f-i-v-e y-e-a-r-s of day , f-i-v-e y-e-a-r-s of night . . . "

And all this time Chipmunk chattered as fast as he could, "Onedayonenightonedayonenightonedayone-nightonedayonenight!"

Grizzly Bear kept repeating, "F-i-v-e y-e-a-r-s of night, f-i-v-e- y-e-a-r-s of day . . . "

Chipmunk's tail switched up and down as he kept up his chatter, "Onedayonenightonedayonenight!"

Finally, Grizzly Bear made a mistake and said, "One day, one night."

Chipmunk had won! He had caused Grizzly Bear to make a mistake.

Chipmunk could see that Grizzly Bear was getting angry, so he started to run for home. Just as he was diving into his hole, Grizzly Bear reached out his great claws and scratched Chipmunk's back.

That is how Chipmunk got his stripes.

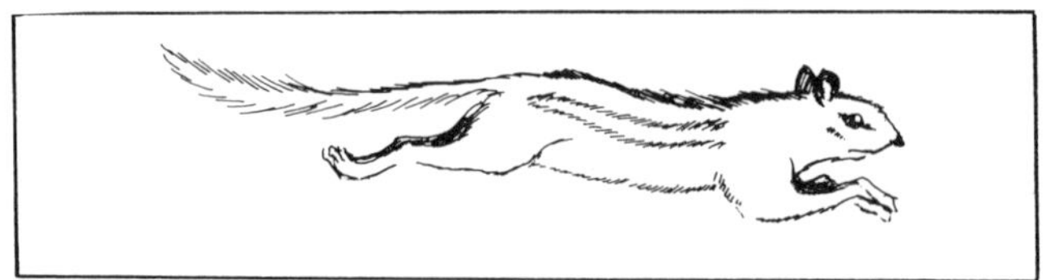

Though cramped quarters restricted their activity, the women accomplished much work that could not be done in the summer when moving about for food. Now there was plenty of time. During the day, with only the smoke-holes and firelight to illumine the interior, they worked in this smoky gloom making hemp bags for storage, hats from bear grass, and sewing clothing from smoked hides. In this half light the women twined the fibers of beargrass and hemp, working berry or root-stained material into the patterns that beautified them.[22] With their sharp bone needles and awls and thread of sinews, they stitched the tanned hides into the new moccasins, shirts, leggings, and dresses their families needed. They would fashion feather pieces and porcupine headdresses for dancing. Whatever the women had available, they used to decorate their work: elk teeth, colored porcupine quills, shells, beads—anything that seemed adaptable.

From pieces of rawhide, they fashioned their hi-sop-ti-kai, the cases for storing their ceremonial clothing, and painted designs on them.

For many women, the work this winter brought more than usual delight or despair. These women had received sharp needles, thimbles, awls, and thread from the So-yap-pos. They learned that the sharp needles pricked fingers more than bone needles, though the little caps on the end of fingers made it easier to push needles through the hides. White men's needles were hard to find, once lost. White men's thread tangled and broke. But the needles and thread were wonderful for stringing beads, the beautiful blue and white beads the So-yap-pos had brought. Women had more beads to work with than ever before. And they remembered as they worked and talked how they had obtained them from the So-yap-pos.

Then they dressed in their beautiful garments for the nightly dances in the longhouse. Their families went well dressed, too, feeling proud to be wearing clothes as good or better than others.

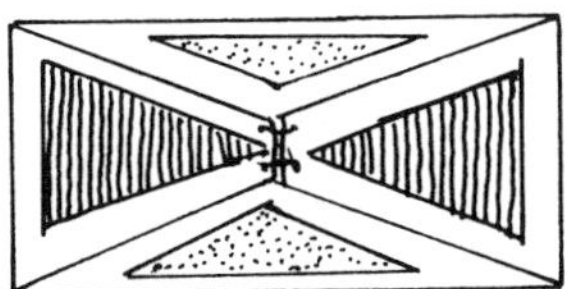
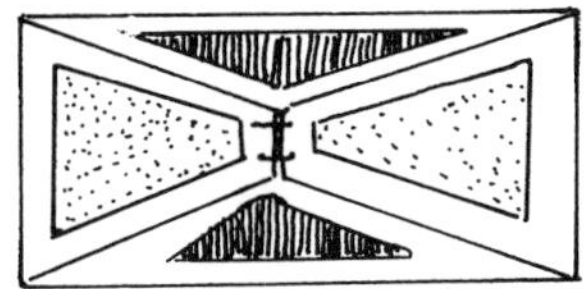

In every village that winter, while fires burned down the center of the longhouse, the Te-wats [Medicine Man] was careful to look for cracks in the packed earth floor that would let bad medicine in.[23] Bad Medicine made people forget the songs their Wyakins had given them. It weakened their Power, taking their confidence and making them afraid. Good Medicine meant strength for body and mind and spirit. It made a person able to face difficulties and dangers.

The pungent smell from the cous cous root[24] was very strong at this cold time. Many little children had sacks of these root pieces tied closely to their faces to prevent them from catching a cold. Elders were constantly chewing on the root to relieve the coughs and sore throats brought on by khalp-khalp, the gusty wind.

The menthol-like smell intermingled with the sweet smell of cedar that had been crushed into a powder.[25] Long ago The People had learned that by rubbing this powder into their sleeping furs, they were not bothered by the many fleas that were prevalent at all seasons.

Whenever the air grew foul with the reek of wet dogs, dried fish, feet perspiring in smoke-tanned moccasins, and body odors of sick or unwashed people, the doors along the wall were opened for fresh air. When the malodor of skunk or weasel was added by some tainted hunter, the doors were opened, and the air, swooping down into the lodge, thinned out the good bad-smell.[26]

When evening shadows fell, The People gathered in the longhouse for ceremonial dancing and singing. Men, women, and children came. They sat around the walls and watched. They danced and sang. They sat and watched; the children sat and watched. They watched and learned, always mindful that a man had been appointed to keep them in order.

They learned about the different kinds of special POWER that came to people. Some had DEER POWER, connected with hunting—bears, deer, wolves. Others had FLYING POWER to which all birds belonged—eagles, hawks, crows, ravens, and pelicans. Women had POWER—but the fierce animals and birds had nothing to do with it.

This was the time to see whose POWER was greatest. If a man could crawl on his hands and knees over each fire with another man on his back, his POWER would be stronger if the man on top jerked and fell off. If they got to the end together, the men changed places. If they again crossed over the fires together, they had equal POWER.[27]

Sometimes people sang the songs that had been given them by a Spirit Helper. If the words did not come, friends would try to help by singing loudly. Sometimes the singer would faint if he could not remember and would have to be dragged off the floor. Sometimes the singer would have to be revived by the smoke of cous cous blown in his face.

Children, looking on, wondered what it would be like when the time came for them to go on their lonely vigil to a mountain top. What vision would come? Who would speak? What song would come? They would learn all this when their time came.

Now was time for dancing. Strong hunters would dance the Buffalo Dance, impersonating two buffalo bulls in battle. Boys and girls followed one another in Tu-ka-wi-ut, called "Snake Dance"[28] by their friends, the Yakimas. They danced the Courtship Dance, the Match Dance, and the Moonlight Dance.

Drums throbbed and singers sang their songs while the women, standing side by side, joined in the singing and danced. Repeatedly, each woman shuffled her left foot to the left and drew her right foot to it. In this way, the circle slowly revolved around the painted, befeathered men who whooped and leaped and stomped their feet to jangle their dew-claw ankle-wraps in rhythm with the drums.

Never before had there been mirrors on headbands, necklaces, or feathered tailpieces to flash in the firelight. Never before had there been so many beads or bright ribbons and pieces of cloth displayed. Much to be desired were these mementos of the white men's coming. Some of these had been won and lost in stick games many times before they were attached to a dancer's regalia.

The parade of this new finery added enchantment to the dancing. Nobody wanted dancing to end. Every night they danced until almost morning.[29] They danced every night through the Moon of Ha-oo-khoy [December—the beginning of cold weather], through the Moon of Wai-lu-poop [January—the middle of cold weather] and through the Moon of Ah-la-tah-mahl [February—the time of swelling buds].

The days began to grow longer than the nights. The Weather Chief examined blades of grass poking through the snow. If snow was still frozen to it, bad weather was staying. Likewise, if the grass snapped in half sharply, bad weather was continuing. If the grass bent, the fish would soon arrive.[30] If the snow was not touching the grass, chinook would soon be coming.

The buds on the shrubs and trees began to swell—signs that meant the force of life would not be held back, the time when WARM would overcome COLD. These signs told the Nee-mee-poo that the season was approaching when they must leave their winter lodges and go out on the hills and prairies to dig for the first roots of the season.

When at last the grass grew green and the flowers bloomed, gladly they put the dancing behind them and welcomed the gifts of the earth.

CHAPTER 10

RETURN OF THE SO-YAP-POS

THE MOON OF LA-TE-TAHL [MARCH] PROMISED SUNshine and flowers. Buttercups nestled in the grass like droplets of sunlight. Pink birdbills, yellow bells and lamb tongues, blue bells and violets followed in their time until the Nee-mee-poo seemed to walk on bright-flowered carpets.

The first warm days called all creatures into the sunshine. Everybody came out—the ground squirrels, the rock chucks, The People. Some of The People walked around, looking for food. Some just sat in the sunshine. Others sprawled on sun-warmed boulders, looking like big bears sunning themselves.

But the Moon of La-te-tahl was a liar. Its promise of warm weather vanished in storm clouds that scudded over the prairie and covered the plants with snow.

Still, the force of life kept on working. Roots became larger the longer they waited in the ground. Whether the sun shone or not in the Moon of Ka-khee-tahl [April], kaeh-kheet roots were ready for digging, and the women began the season's harvest.

In the Moon of Ah-pah-ahl [May], after the kaeh-kheet season had passed, kouse roots were ready to harvest on the prairies above the Koos-koos-kee Valley. Then The People moved up to this higher ground to dig kouse and to make kouse bread from the freshly dug roots.

As the women of Twisted Hair's village had no good supply of kouse nearby, they grew impatient to move up to the digging grounds on Camas Prairie. As soon as they settled their minds to do this, they collected their poles, mats, bags, and digging sticks.

As always, some of the men would go along. They would help take the women across the rising river in canoes and swim the horses over. They would go with the women up the long, twisting trail to the prairie. The men would work on fishtraps[1] in the small streams near their camp as well as provide protection for the women.

But this spring the women had to wait. Chief Twisted Hair was not ready to go. He and his brother were talking over a more serious matter.

It was SPRING. The So-yap-pos had said when they returned in the spring, they would give two guns to the Twisted Hair people for wintering their horses. The men wanted those two guns more than anything else, but they did not have them yet. They knew if Cut Nose had his way, they would never get them.

All winter Cut Nose, consumed by jealousy, had bothered them with remarks about how the Twisted Hair men were neglecting the So-yap-pos' horses. He had made himself obnoxious by declaring that he could care for them much better.

Now Twisted Hair and Te-toh-kan Ahs-kahp felt threatened.

"What about Cut Nose?" Twisted Hair asked his brother. "If he gets to the So-yap-pos first, he will fill their ears with lies about our treatment of the horses. He will try to make himself important in the eyes of the So-yap-pos, and he will do what he can to get the guns for himself."

"We could go down to Alpowa and wait there for the So-yap-pos to come. We could reassure them about their horses and guide them upriver without giving Cut Nose a chance to poison their minds," Te-toh-kan Ahs-kahp said.

"Taats!" Twisted Hair sounded relieved, but he added, "I must stay and see that the women get moved up to the prairie. It is time they were digging kouse roots. You go!"

With that decided, the men moved into action. Te-toh-kan Ahs-kahp set off downriver to wait at Alpowa where he could also visit with his sister, the wife of Timuca, and their children, Ta-moot-sin and We-ya-loo-hom.

Twisted Hair and some of his men took the women and their gear across the rising Koos-koos-kee in dug-outs, while others swam the horses over. Riders and pack animals then toiled up the crooked trail to the rolling plains of kouse land above. They set up their temporary dwellings of woven mats in the shelter of a wooded knoll near the head of a small stream[2] that ran into Big Canyon. Here the men repaired an old rock dam in the creek and set in a weir of woven willow switches to catch small trout.

Where the yellow umbels of kouse blooms showed, the women dug roots. Digging was hard work. Stooping over for so long made backs ache, but the women kept on digging until they filled their bags. Then their hearts were content, and digging ceased for the day.

May 4, 1806

". . . after dinner we continued our rout up the West side of the river 3 Ms opposite to 2 lodges the one containing 3 and the other 2 families of the Chopunnish nation; here we met with Te-toh-ar-sky, the youngest of the two cheifs who accompanied us last fall [to] the great falls of the Columbia . . ." Lewis [Thwaites, Volume 4, Pages 354, 355.]

Shadows were growing long when the So-yap-pos filed into the village of Alpowa where Te-toh-kan Ahs-kahp was waiting. The Chief of Ha-so-tin, We-ah-koomt,[3] with his ever-present mountain sheep's horn dangling from his left arm, rode as the guide.

The So-yap-po leaders looked pleased when they recognized Te-toh-kan Ahs-kahp among the villagers. Here was a friend who had helped guide them on the down-river journey last fall. Now, here he was, just when they needed a guide upriver. The So-yap-po leaders took the right hand of Te-toh-kan Ahs-kahp and moved it up and down in their usual manner.

After they had settled down to talk, they asked Te-toh-kan Ahs-kahp the best way to go up the Koos-koos-kee.

Before answering, Te-toh-kan Ahs-kahp consulted with the men of Timuca's village, then said, "Cross river here at Alpowa. Trail upriver on other side is shorter and easier."

The opportunity to guide the So-yap-pos upriver had come just as Te-toh-kan Ahs-kahp had foreseen. When he said, "I, myself, will show you the way," the So-yap-pos were pleased to accept his offer.

When We-ah-koomt understood that the So-yap-pos were going to cross the river at this point, he said to them, "My people will be disappointed. They are now waiting to greet you at the meeting place of the rivers."

But the So-yap-pos did not change their plans. They gave We-ah-koomt a piece of tobacco. We-ah-koomt then turned his horse in the direction of Ha-so-tin and rode off, satisfied.

The So-yap-pos bargained for the use of three canoes to carry their baggage and men across the river. If they were to get all this done before dark, much work was in store for the whole party. The packs had to be taken off the horses and loaded into the canoes. Several times the canoes had to go back and forth across the river before all the people and baggage were on the north side. While this was being done, some of the men swam the horses across. Finally, the undertaking was finished without mishap.

But the hardships of the day were not over. The night air was freezing cold, especially for those who were wet from taking the horses across. Everybody was hungry. The food supply was exhausted. The barren hills provided no wood for fires.

The People of the village traded a little kouse bread and wood to the So-yap-pos. But they added to the white men's problems by crowding around the fires to warm themselves as well.[4]

May 5, 1806

". . . set out at 7 A.M. at 4-1/2 miles we arrived at the entrance of the Kooskooske, up the N. Eastern side of which we continued our march 12 Ms. to a large lodge of 10 families . . . arrived at 1 P.M. & with much difficulty obtained 2 dogs and a small quan[ti]ty of root bread and dryed roots. at the second lodge we passed an indian man [who] gave Capt. C. a very eligant grey mare for which he requested a phial of eyewater which was accordingly given him. while we were encamped last fall at the entrance of the Chopunnish river Capt. C. [with much seremony washed & rubd.] gave an indian man some volitile linniment to rub his k[n]ee and thye for a pain . . . the fellow soon after recovered and has never ceased to extol the virtues of our medicines and the skill of my friend Capt. C. as a phisician. . . . ." Lewis [Thwaites, Volume 4, Pages 357, 358.]

In the first light of the new sun, the So-yap-pos broke camp and started their travel up the Koos-koos-kee without eating. No food could be bought at the first village they came to. Nothing could be bought at the second village they passed, but a man of the village came out, leading a fine gray mare.

"For Medicine Man," he said. "He give eyewater—good medicine. I give horse."

The red-headed So-yap-po leader understood and rummaged in his pack for the medicine.[5] The exchange was made.

"Kah-itsi-yow-yow!" ["Thanks!"] said the one who received the eyewater as his hands signed that he gave something from his heart.

The So-yap-po sent back the same sign and led his gray mare away.

May 5, 1806

"... while at dinner an indian fellow very impertinently threw a half starved puppy nearly into the plate of Capt. Lewis by way of derision for our eating dogs and laughed very hartily at his own impertinence; Capt L.—was so provoked at the insolence that he cought the puppy and threw it with great violence at him and struck him in the breast and face, seazed his tomahawk, and shewed him by sign that if he repeeted his insolence that he would tomahawk him, . . ." Clark [Thwaites Volume 4, Page 361.]

The travelers went on upstream to a larger lodge. Here The People spared the So-yap-pos two thin dogs, some kouse bread, and dried roots for their first meal of the day.

Many people crowded around to watch the white men eat their dog and kouse stew. The famished men slurped up the food and licked their lips as if it were good.

How could anyone enjoy eating dog?

The episode gave Prankster an idea. If that So-yap-po chief liked dog, why not give him more dog? As the thought flashed through his mind, he snatched up a scrawny puppy that wobbled past him and tossed it into the man's plate. The man's stew splattered over his face, over his clothes, and over the pup. Prankster doubled up and howled in laughter at the sight. The soppy puppy sailed back into the face of Prankster, choking off his laughter and splattering his chest with stew. At the same time, the So-yap-po sprang up, waving his tomahawk and yelling words that showed his anger.

Prankster knew then that he had gone too far with his joke. He feared for his own safety, but worse than that, he saw amusement on the faces of his friends. He left.[6]

Prankster's friends had nothing to be ashamed of. They had pleased the So-yap-pos by bringing in one of the horses that had been left with the Twisted Hair people. No one said how that horse happened to be so far downriver. Maybe he had just drifted away from the So-yap-po herd. Maybe some of the Cut Nose men had ridden him down and he had come on farther.

The So-yap-pos were glad to get this horse back. They made no trouble about why he was so far from the Twisted Hair people where they had left him.

They moved on to the next village upstream, the home of Neesh-ne-ee-pah-kee-oo-keen, the Cut Nose.

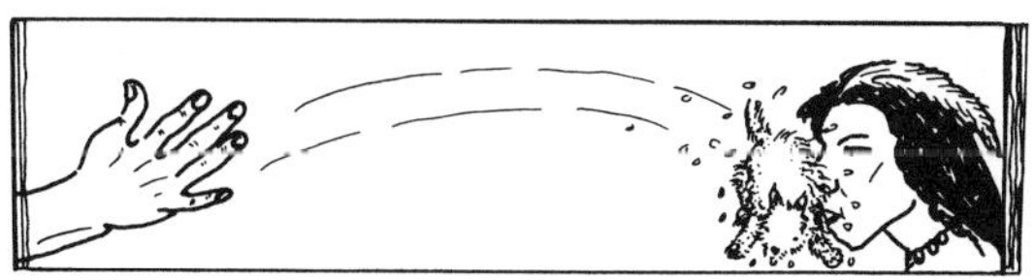

May 5, 1806

". . . after dinner we continued our rout 4 miles to the entrance of Colter's Creek about 1/2 mile above the rapid where we sunk the lst. canoe as we decended the river last fall. we encamped . . . at a little distance from two lodges . . . one of these lodges contained eight families the other was much the largest we have yet seen. it is 156 feet long and about 15 wide built of mats and straw. in the form of the roof of a house having a number of small doors on each side, is closed at the ends and without divisions in the intermediate space this lodge contained at least 30 families. their fires are kindled in a row in the center of the house and about 10 feet assunder.[7] all the lodges of these people are formed in this manner." Lewis [Thwaites, Volume 4, Pages 358, 359.]

The Cut Nose people had gone through a hard winter. COLD had come early and stayed long. Sickness struck the People and many died. With so many to feed and so much sickness, there was little food left for anyone to eat. The fish had not yet come up the river. The children were hungry all the time. The dogs were so gaunt their ribs showed.

Though the air was sharp with cold, some of the women, in desperation, had moved up to the Camas

Prairie to dig roots. By their early efforts they were hoping to send some roots back to the village to help satisfy everyone's acute hunger.

Along with the urgent need for food, there still was much sickness: sore eyes, abscesses, aching joints. Neither sweat baths nor the Te-wats with his rattles eased the pain. Word had spread that last fall a Medicine Man with the So-yap-pos had rubbed good medicine on the leg of a lame man in Twisted Hair's village, and he could walk again. That was the kind of medicine they needed.

The So-yap-pos came now, hungry and asking for food, but no one had food to spare them.

As soon as word spread through the village that the white men had arrived, people gathered around the So-yap-po leaders with their sick.

"Medicine!" they begged, showing the sore eyes and boils of the sufferers.

"No," said the So-yap-pos. "Bring dogs and horses for us to eat. Then we give medicine."

"My wife has bad sore on her back," said one man. "Doctor her. When sun comes up again, I bring you good horse to eat."

The So-yap-po Medicine Man, Captain Clark, accepted his word. He looked at the ugly abscess on the small of the woman's back to see what had to be done. With his sharp, shining knife, he lanced through the head of the abscess to let the pus run out and put in a thin roll of white cloth to keep it draining. Then he put on "good medicine"[8] and gave her some yellow powder and white powder to take every morning. Already the woman felt better.

After that, more than fifty other people came for treatment. Some brought dogs, but they were too scrawny to be good food.

The So-yap-po Medicine Man finally put his medicine and equipment away in his bag. His hands spoke to the remaining people clustered around him, "Come back when the new sun rises."

Reluctantly, the sick people dispersed. Those who felt some relief had good words for the So-yap-po Medicine Man's treatment. The rest waited in hope for the new day.

After the evening meal, Cut Nose, with his Snake slave and others from his lodges and neighboring villages, gathered around the So-yap-po camp.

At last Cut Nose was in the presence of those strangers he had been hearing about all winter. After signs of welcome, he rose to say a few words, hoping to impress the So-yap-pos with his own importance.

"I am Neesh-ne-ee-pah-kee-oo-keen, chief of this village. Great chief of Chopunnish Nation. Away with war party last fall against the Snakes at the time of your arrival."

The So-yap-pos recognized Cut Nose's position by giving him a small medal with a man's head on it. Cut Nose felt important.

Cut Nose continued, "I would have done a better job of wintering your horses than Twisted Hair. I would have guarded your saddles better. Your saddles have been taken away by some who found them. Your horses have been scattered. I am willing to help you get all back."

May 5, 1806

". . . we spoke at some length to the natives this evening with rispect to the objects which had induced us to visit their country.

this address was induced at this moment by the suggestions of an old man who observed to the natives that he thought we were bad men and had come most probably in order to kill them. . . ." Lewis [Thwaites, Volume 4, Pages 359, 360.]

The spectators understood why Cut Nose spoke as he did. But skeptics were not convinced of the white men's presence and their sincerity. Khai-yoon [Old Man] was one who rose to express his doubts and fears in quavering voice, while his hands talked.

"These men are bad," he said. "They have probably come to kill us."

The white men understood he was giving bad talk.

Sign-talk was not enough for the So-yap-pos to tell why they had come. They wanted to speak with their tongues. But how could they speak and be understood? When they learned that the slave of Cut Nose was a Snake, they found a way to give their message.

First the So-yap-po leader spoke to one of his men in one language. That man spoke to One-Who-Looked-Like-a-Badger (Charbonneau) in another tongue. He spoke to his wife, Bird Woman, who spoke to the Snake in the Shoshoni tongue. The Snake then delivered the message to the Nee-mee-poo in the language of the Chopunnish Nation.

"We come from the Land-Toward-the-Rising-Sun, far away beyond mountains, over plains, up long rivers. We bring a message from the Great Father who is chief over all. He wants all people to be friends. No more war. No more killing."

No more fighting? No more killing? That would be good if the Snakes and the Blackfeet would agree to live in peace with The People.

May 5, 1806

". . . We-art-koomt rejoined us this evening. this man has been of infinite service to us on several former occasions and through him we now offered our address to the natives." Lewis [Thwaites, Volume 4, Page 360.]

As the talk was going on about the sincerity of the white men's message, We-ah-koomt rode in from Ha-so-tin on a fine sorrel horse with ten of his men. Ever since he had left the So-yap-pos at Alpowa, their message had stayed in his mind and would not leave. He had been drawn to find the white men again and strengthen his friendship before they left the valley.

We-ah-koomt listened, then spoke, "Have you not heard the words of Wat-ku-ese, who, at the gathering on the Oyaip last fall, was glad to see these men? 'They are good men,' she said. 'Do them no harm.' "

"A-a-a-a-a-a!" they said, assenting.

By this affirmation, We-ah-koomt, with the ram's horn always dangling from his left arm, helped his people and the So-yap-pos understand each other better.

When the new sun rose, the husband of the woman with an abscess came with the horse he had promised the So-yap-pos for food. They butchered him at once, cooked the meat, and enjoyed the first good meal they had had for several days.

The So-yap-po Medicine Man, the Red-Head, was busy after that. Everyone with an ailment came to him for relief. The woman with the abscess was grateful. She had been able to sleep. A little girl who had great pain in her joints when she moved was better after the So-yap-po had bathed her in warm water and rubbed ointment on her legs and arms. Her father gave the Medicine Man a horse in gratitude for her treatment and medicine.

Most of the people came to have that good eyewater dropped into their sore eyes.

During this time, three Spokanes, who lived below the Spokane Falls, were visiting in the Cut Nose's village. They understood much of what was said through sign-talk, though they did not speak in the same tongue as the Nee-mee-poo. They told the So-yap-pos where they lived and how their river came out of a big lake in the mountains. When they saw the white men preparing to leave, one of them presented the leader with a whip he had made by fastening a lash of rawhide strips to one end of a twisted stick and a loop to go around the wrist on the other end. In return, the So-yap-po gave him a piece of narrow material as long as a man's two arms could stretch from his sides. The Spokane was pleased. This was something different that would decorate his costume.

The big sorrel horse that We-ah-koomt had ridden into camp was strong and well broke—just right for the So-yap-po chief, Lewis. When Lewis suggested trading horses, We-ah-koomt turned the sorrel over to him and took the chief's horse—a good horse, but not so big and strong.

The sun was on its downward path before the So-yap-pos were ready to move on. Te-toh-kan Ahs-kahp and We-ah-koomt, with some of their men, rode with them. There was no trouble on the way, except between the two So-yap-pos who had the job of leading a young, unbroke horse intended for food. The horse had not been led before, and it kept both men busy to keep him on the trail. Each man thought the other should take more control over the unruly horse, and they shouted bad words back and forth.

When camp was made for the night, they tied the young horse to a tree, thinking of the good feast he would provide the next day. But the horse had never been tied to a tree before, and he did not like it. He pulled back with all his strength until the rope finally broke and he was free. Giving a snort he dashed off into the darkness.

Te-toh-kan Ahs-kahp and We-ah-koomt, with his ten men, camped with the So-yap-pos that night. When they heard the clatter of hooves, they knew what had happened. "Looks like So-yap-pos' meat has run away—hahm-tits!" they chuckled together.

May 7, 1806

"This morning we collected our horses and set out early accompanyed by the brother of the twisted hair as a guide; . . . we proceeded up the river 4 miles to a lodge of 6 families just below the entrance of a small creek [*Bed Rock Creek*], here our guide recommended our passing the river. . . . a man . . . produced us two canisters of powder which he informed us he had found by means of his dog where they had been buried in a bottom near the river some miles above, they were the same which we had buryed as we decended the river last fall." Lewis [Thwaites, Volume 4, Page 367.]

After the night of sleep, We-ah-koomt and his men turned their backs to the rising sun and headed downstream toward their village at Ha-so-tin. Te-toh-kan Ahs-kahp welcomed the sun on his face as he led the So-yap-pos on their way upriver.

The men stopped on a flat bordering the river where Big Heart lived in a mat house. It was a good place to cross to the other side, and they bargained with a canoe owner to have their baggage taken over.

During the transfer of the packs, Big Heart came from his lodge with the two heavy cans he had guarded all winter.

"Dog dug and found them. Kept safe. Now I give back to you," his hands said as he presented the captains with the lead canisters they had buried last fall.

To have this ammunition restored to them surprised and pleased the white men. In return they gave Big Heart a metal fire-making tool and showed him how to strike sparks to start fire.

"Taats!" Big Heart exclaimed. "Better than gift of black sand. No gun—no need for black sand. Have to start fire all the time."

Te-toh-kan Ahs-kahp again led the way upstream[9] to the base of a solid rock cliff. On the right side, a well-worn trail led sharply up to the prairie land above.

This great expanse of level land was covered with lush grass and flowering plants. The yellow umbels of kouse plants and tsa-wit stood like signals to guide root-gatherers to the good digging grounds. Groves of tall pines dotted the land, giving shade and a source of fuel to man. As the horses followed one another on the trail, they nipped at the knee-high grass as if they could never get enough of it. Here the earth was good to man and animals.

Cut Nose had felt downcast when the So-yap-pos left his village. He wanted the distinction of being in good standing with these remarkable men. He would not lose this opportunity; he settled his mind to catch up with the So-yap-pos and cultivate their friendship.

With his te-wel-ka slave close behind, Cut Nose goaded his horse over the tracks of the men who followed Te-toh-kan Ahs-kahp. He turned from this trail long enough to visit his women's root-digging camp nearby. Here he took a small supply of roots for himself and his slave and returned to the So-yap-pos' trail.

Meanwhile, Te-toh-kan Ahs-kahp led the way over the grassy plain towards the rising sun. On the horizon, snow-covered mountains gleamed in the sunlight. Pointing to them, Te-toh-kan Ahs-kahp explained, "Man cannot cross those mountains now. Must wait until snow cover goes. Maybe one moon later. Maybe more."

Finally, they came to a canyon which seemed to slice into the level land. To get to the good ground beyond, they would have to go down to the bottom of the canyon and climb up the other side to the area where Twisted Hair's people were digging. Te-toh-kan Ahs-kahp led them down a long, steep, twisting trail to the creek at the bottom of the canyon. Here, clouds of mosquitos rose from pools left after the spring flood subsided. He led them on farther upstream to a cluster of six mat lodges, all vacant.

"People root digging," Te-toh-kan Ahs-kahp explained.

The So-yap-pos wanted to camp here for the night. In the meadow land several deer appeared. This excited the hunters, but they could not hunt in the twilight. Instead, the men ate horse meat for supper that night.

May 8, 1806

"... Neesh-ne-park-kee-ook and several other indians joined us this morning. we gave this cheif and the indians with us some venison, horsebeef, the entrels of four deer, and four fawns which were taken from two of the does that were killed, they eat none of their food raw, tho' the entrals had but little preparation and the fawns were boiled and consumed hair hide and entrals." Lewis [Thwaites, Volume 5, Page 4.]

At daybreak, when darkness had lifted up just enough to leave a bright space, but no sun, the So-yap-po hunters went out. Soon after they had left, Cut Nose, his te-wel-ka slave, and some chance companions rode into camp.

A loud noise like close thunder startled them.

"Craaack! Craaack!" The sound echoed from one side of the canyon to the other.

To the amazement of the newcomers, the So-yap-po hunters soon appeared with four deer.

Guns! More than ever Cut Nose wanted a gun. What a powerful hunter and warrior he could be if he had a gun!

Cut Nose, the te-wel-ka slave, and the other Nee-mee-poo watched the So-yap-pos cut up their venison. It looked good to them who had not eaten meat for days. They were hungry enough to eat anything. When the hunters gave them the entrails and unborn fawns along with venison, they roasted the entrails, boiled the fawns, and ate everything.

Everyone was satisfied, except the te-wel-ka slave, a young man still growing. He was still hungry, and, seeing the supply of meat, he asked with hands and voice, "More meat."

The So-yap-po chiefs refused him, knowing they had

scarcely enough to feed their party. The te-wel-ka saw only that venison was there and he was still hungry. Anger burned within him. He shut his mouth and would not speak to anyone. No messages could be passed back and forth through his voice. Finally, no one tried. No one talked to him. They acted as if he were not there.

Te-toh-kan Ahs-kahp and Cut Nose sat down and answered the ceaseless questions the So-yap-po chiefs asked about the rivers that ran toward the setting sun. Their best answer was in drawing a map that showed where the big rivers ran and where the smaller streams flowed into them. They showed where many Snake villages were located along the longest river, the Ta-ma-nam-mah, the Unknown River, [the Salmon River].[10]

When the sun passed its highest point, Te-toh-kan Ahs-kahp pointed out a steep trail[11] to the So-yap-pos. His hands told them, "You will find Twisted Hair camped on top. I now take the trail to my village in the valley."

He turned to his left then and took a trail leading down hill. As he went along he thought of what the young men of his band had to do. Now that the So-yap-pos had returned, they would want their horses.

"No horses—we get no sticks-that-shoot-black-sand-with-thunder," he mused.

Cut Nose was pleased that he now was the man who could best advise the So-yap-pos. His te-wel-ka slave, whose sullen anger wore away when the others paid no attention to him, was willing to interpret again. That opportunity came after the party finally reached the prairie and traveled a path parallel to the river canyon.

"So-yap-pos coming!" a scout called, riding into Twisted Hair's camp.

"So-yap-pos coming!"

A sense of anticipation spread as the words passed from one person to another.

Twisted Hair announced his intention of riding out to greet these men. One after another, six of his men said they would ride out with him. The thought of two guns, promised, made their faces beam with pleasure.

As they drew near the long line of approaching riders, the radiance faded from Twisted Hair's countenance. His hands sent the message, "I am glad to see you" to the So-yap-po chiefs. But he spoke no words to them. Instead, he turned to confront the Cut Nose, Neesh-ne-ee-pah-kee-oo-keen, riding along with a high and mighty look on his ugly face. The sight of him sent stabs of jealousy into Twisted Hair's heart.

Anger darkened Twisted Hair's face like the storm clouds that covered the sun. His eyes glared like flashes of lightning. His intense resentment poured forth with such fury it could almost be touched and smelled.

"Neesh-ne-ee-pah-kee-oo-keen!" he shouted. "Do you think to make yourself look good to the So-yap-pos by slandering me? Do you tell lies about our care of their horses? Do you think you will be given the guns promised to us? You are nothing! You are a detestable scoundrel—a filth-eating dog! I dare you do your worst against me!"

With that he gave a sharp grunt, closed his right fist with the thumb pushed out between the first and second fingers, and thrust it sharply toward the Cut Nose.[12]

Cut Nose was infuriated by that gesture. He glared back, bellowing, "Tsap-tsu-kelp-skin! [Twisted Hair!]

Jealous old man! Double-tongued liar! You know you have not taken good care of those horses. You know I could manage them better."

To show his desire to thrust Twisted Hair aside and take his place, Cut Nose gave a gesture of elbowing him, first with his right elbow, then with his left.

While they picked at each other in this way, the So-yap-pos looked on, wondering why they quarreled. Not understanding, they decided to move on to good water and camp for the night. The Nee-mee-poo chiefs and their followers could do as they pleased.

Twisted Hair and Cut Nose closed their lips tight. Each man led his own followers up near the So-yap-pos' campsite, but they took pains to make their camps far apart.

Before long, the So-yap-pos sent their best sign-talk man, Drewyer, to Twisted Hair's camp with a pipe. Offering the pipe, Drewyer's hands said, "Come over to our fire for a smoke."

Twisted Hair was pleased with the invitation to smoke with the So-yap-pos. Maybe the matter of the horses could be straightened out. Followed by his men, he went over at once.

Drewyer then carried the pipe to the Cut Nose with the same message.

Cut Nose merely grunted as his hands answered, "Soon."

Cut Nose did not go immediately. He was in no hurry to get near that old braggart, Twisted Hair. When he felt he had kept the group waiting long enough for his presence, Cut Nose led his men to the So-yap-pos' fire.

The pipe was passed to every man. No one refused to smoke. All seemed willing to communicate, but when the te-wel-ka was asked to interpret, he would not. Through Bird Woman, he said, "No! The quarrel is between Tsap-tsu-kelp-skin and Neesh-ne-ee-pah-kee-oo-keen."

"All we want you to do is tell us what each of them says," the So-yap-po chiefs told him. "In no way will that draw you into their quarrel."

But the te-wel-ka repeated, "It is their quarrel. Not mine. I will not get mixed up in it." He shut his mouth and spoke no more through the Bird Woman.

One of the So-yap-po chiefs then spoke with his hands, "We are sorry to find disagreement between you chiefs. What has caused this misunderstanding?"

Twisted Hair answered, "I promised to care for your horses over winter. When I returned from downriver, I had them rounded up and took charge of them. My people said the Snake guide and his son had taken two of your horses when they fled over the mountains. When Neesh-ne-ee-pah-kee-oo-keen and the big chief, Tin-nach-e-moo-toolt [Broken Arm], returned from warring with the Snakes, they were displeased that I had the honor of caring for the white men's horses. Jealous, they found fault in all I did. All winter they picked on me.

"Most of your horses are near here. Some between the forks of the rivers. Three, maybe four, at lodge of Tin-nach-e-moo-toolt at Kamiah."

Twisted Hair continued, "High water in spring took earth door from saddle cache. Some saddles maybe washed downriver. I know not. The saddles I did find I put in cache higher up. When new day comes, you stay at my lodge nearby on trail to Kamiah. I will bring your saddles. My young men will cross the Koos-koos-kee, round up horses in the forks, and bring them to you in Kamiah. There, go to lodge of Tin-nach-e-moo-toolt. I, myself, will go with you."

The So-yap-po chief, Lewis, then spoke, "Your counsel is good. We will do as you suggest. We entrusted the care of our horses to you. We expect you to gather them up and bring them to us. When you have done this, we will pay you two guns and ammunition as we promised."

Twisted Hair was satisfied. He had only to deliver all the horses and saddles, and the guns would be his. This he would do.

Cut Nose then spoke, "Tsap-tsu-kelp-skin! Bad old man! Wears two faces! Speaks with forked tongue! He promised to care for your horses, but allowed his young men to ride them hunting. Many were hurt. For that reason I, myself, and the great chief, Tin-nach-e-moo-toolt, of Kamiah, told him not to use them anymore. We saw that they were watered in the winter. We kept them together. If you proceed on to the village of Tin-nach-e-moo-toolt, I will send for your horses. I, myself, have three of them."

Cut Nose continued, "Tin-nach-e-moo-toolt has striped banner with stars you left last fall. When he heard of your return and your hunger, he sent his son and four others with provisions. They missed the way. Did not find you. At his lodge the great chief has two no-good horses for you to eat. He is expecting you."

Twisted Hair's face did not change expression while this speech was made. "Let the old fox say what he will," he thought. "He will get nowhere. The So-yap-pos have assured me of two guns."

Everyone understood the So-yap-pos' sign-talk when they replied that they would stay at the lodge of Twisted Hair next day until he brought in the saddles and horses. They would all go on to the lodge of the Broken Arm on the day after that. This put an end to the quarrel between Twisted Hair and Cut Nose.

Night had laid a blanket over the earth. Bad feelings had gone. It was time to sleep.

May 9, 1806

"We sent out several hunters . . . with instructions to meet us at the lodge of the Twisted hair. . . . one man with 2 horses accompa[n]yed the twisted hair to the canoe camp, about 4 ms. in quest of the saddles. the Twisted hair sent two young men in surch of our horses agreeably to his promis." Lewis [Thwaites, Volume 5, Page 11.]

A crow flying over to the Canoe Camp, where the So-yap-pos had built their canoes last fall, had not far to go, but men and horses had to work their way down the long, twisting trail to the river level. Twisted Hair led the way to the saddle cache on the hillside that was above reach of high water. After the men loaded the saddles and powder from the opened caches upon the pack horses, they climbed the tiresome way back to the Prairie.

A cold wind blew. Low hanging storm clouds scudded overhead. Darkness began to cover the land before they reached Twisted Hair's mat lodge. There, the So-yap-po chiefs waited to inspect the saddles and powder brought from the cache.

"Only half the saddles are here," one So-yap-po said.

"Mine is not here," another said.

"High water took saddles," Twisted Hair's hands replied.

By this time, the young men drove the So-yap-pos' horses into camp—twenty-one of the thirty-six. These were the right horses, no mistake about this. Each one showed the brand on the left shoulder, and the foretop, which had been cut off in the fall, had grown out like dancers' porcupine roaches.

The So-yap-po chiefs looked them over. Five showed hard usage. They were stiff, lame, gaunt. Three had sore backs caused by the crude saddles of the youths who had used them. The other horses were fat and sleek and full of life.

The So-yap-po men caught the horses. They tied the front feet of each horse together to keep him from wandering far away. The horses could walk with their hind legs, but their front legs had to move together in a thumping lunge whenever they moved from one clump of grass to another. Far into the night, the men could tell the horses' whereabouts by that thudding sound.

The wind grew colder. Rain fell. Hail fell. Snow began to fall—sticky, wet snow that plastered horses, packs, and the men who were out in it. Snow fell all through the night.

The So-yap-pos shivered in their open camp. Twisted Hair was glad for the protection of his mat lodge. Cut Nose saw no need to spend such a night in the open. He sought shelter with the Twisted Hair and slept there, dry and warm. Their quarrel had passed like a storm blown away.

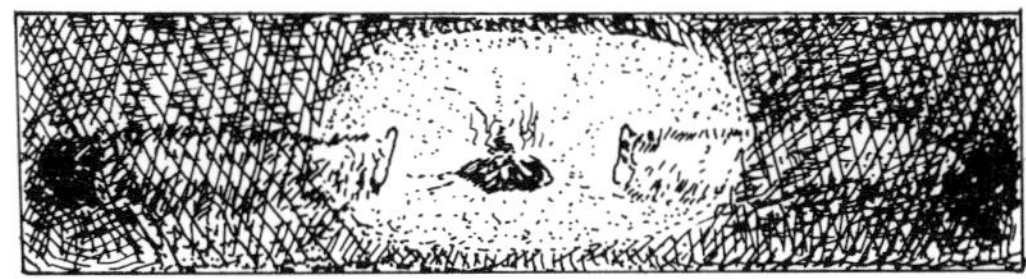

May 10, 1806

". . . we set out for the village of Tunnachemootoolt; our rout lay through an open plain course S.35.E. and distance 16 Ms. the road was slippery and the snow clogged to the horses feet, and caused them to trip frequently." Lewis [Thwaites, Volume 5, Page 14.]

By early light the snow was over a man's moccasin top, but it had stopped falling. The air was bitter cold. Men moved fast to get warm while they packed the horses for the day's journey.

"Keep moving! Keep moving!" they chattered. "You've got to keep moving or you'll freeze stiff."

With nothing more to eat than a few roots, they started toward Kamiah.

Twisted Hair rode in the lead of the single file, pointing out the best trail to take down Kamiah Creek. Behind him came the red-haired So-yap-po chief at the head of his party. Cut Nose and his men followed.

Under the horses' hooves the snow packed into hard balls which grew larger with every step. For a short distance a horse could walk awkwardly as if he were one hand higher than usual. Then he would stumble as, one after another, his snowballs dislodged and flew off to the left and to the right.

Snow turned into rain after they were well below the prairie level. The travel was no easier though. The trail became muddy and slippery. The horses had to move slowly and carefully to keep their footing.

At last they reached the flat land at the bottom of the canyon. Rain was falling there, but nothing could hold back the force of life in this beautiful valley.

CHAPTER 11

THE KAMIAH COUNCIL

MAY 10, 1806

"The Village of the broken Arm consists of one house or Lodge only which is 150 feet in length built in the usial form of sticks, Mats and dry grass." Clark [Thwaites, Volume 5, Page 18.]

Near the place called Tee-e-lap-a-lo, where many crawfish lived in the creek,[1] the house of the Broken Arm stood. If a man walked from one end of it to the other, placing the heel of one foot in front of the toes of the other all the way, he would have counted one hundred and fifty feet. Twenty-four smokes rose from the smoke-holes. Twenty-four smokes meant this was home for forty-eight families, and from that number the war chief could lead more than a hundred young men off to battle. Except for the smaller pit house, used only by women, and the sweat house, this dwelling was the winter home of all the Broken Arm people. Here, the women pounded their meal with stone pestles, cooked their mush in water-tight baskets, and sewed for their families' needs. Here, they stored their fine ceremonial garments in their hi-sop-ti-kai, the rawhide cases, and here, the families slept.

Now, a current of quiet excitement ran through this house, for young scouts had ridden down from Twisted Hair's camp on the Camas Prairie, bringing the word, "So-yap-pos coming! So-yap-pos coming! Before dark!"

They, who had been on the Oyaip last fall, remembered the wonderful things the hairy-faced men had brought. Now they would see these men again and bargain for new treasures. Their hearts warmed, and their eyes turned often toward the trail.

No one had more cause to be excited than Chief Broken Arm. He had been away at war against the Snakes when the white men had come through Oyaip. He had missed seeing them; yet he saw them well in his mind. All winter he had heard about them: men with what looked like pieces of buffalo hides stuck to their faces; one man with black skin that could not be scrubbed off; a Snake woman, Sa-ka-ka-wea, the Bird Woman, with her baby; the black dog as big as Yah-ka, the black bear, that followed at the heels of one of the So-yap-po chiefs; the horse with rabbit ears and a frightful laugh; and the chief with hair colored the same as a sorrel horse. Broken Arm saw them in his mind. Now he would see them with his eyes.

The So-yap-po chiefs had honored him last fall by leaving him a banner with red and white stripes and a blue patch in the upper corner containing fifteen smaller five-pointed white patches. They had told his people this was a "flag." Fastened to a pole stuck in the ground, the wind would make it flutter overhead, proclaiming, "Here is a great chief."

On his return from the warpath, Broken Arm had busied himself with finding a cottonwood sapling for his flag. He then secured the flag to the trimmed young tree and set this firmly into the ground.

For the So-yap-pos' welcome, Broken Arm dressed in his soft buckskin shirt and long buckskin leggings. He slipped a tippet of otterskin over his head to let it hang down the front of his shirt. It displayed trophies of battles fought, mementos of honors he had won, and the blue beads of wealth. Through the pierced septum of his nose, he adjusted a dentalium shell in the fashion of some of his people.[2] By the time he saw the white men approaching, he was ready to greet them under his flag.

Broken Arm could pick out the red-haired chief who rode at the head of the file; he recognized the big black man and the Bird Woman with her baby on her back. He, too, could not help being amused at the horse with ears like a rabbit. And, finally, he could make out the Brother-Chief bringing up the rear with the dog as big as Yah-ka at his heels.

Broken Arm flung out the sign, "I am glad to see you."

"Stop there," his hands said, pointing to a good level camping place some distance from the lodge.

The leader, Clark, directed all the men close behind him to this spot. When the last of the party arrived, that is where they made camp.

May 10, 1806

". . . I directed the men not to crowd their Lodges in serch of food the manner hunger has compelled them to do, at most lodges we have passed, and which the Twisted Hair had informed us was disagreeable to the nativs. . . ." Clark [Thwaites, Volume 5, Page 18.]

Twisted Hair, knowing how hungry these men were and wanting good feelings toward his friends, went up to the So-yap-po chiefs, forewarning, "Do not permit your men to go into this lodge and rummage for food. The people will not like it. They will treat you better if the men stay out of their lodge."

"We are hungry," the leaders said. "We want to buy food."

May 10, 1806

"... The Cheif spoke to his people and they produced us about 2 bushels of the quawmas roots dryed, four cakes of the bread of cows and a dryed salmon trout. we thanked them for this store of provision but informed them that our men not being accustomed to live on roots alone we feared it would make them sick . . . the cheif . . . told us that his young men had a great abundance of young horses and we should by [be] furnished with as many as we wanted. . . ." Lewis [Thwaites, Volume 5, Page 15.]

Broken Arm ordered roots and dried fish to be brought at once, but the So-yap-pos were not satisfied.

"We must have meat to eat along with roots or we get sick," they said. "We will trade old horses for young horses which we can eat."

"We have plenty horses," Broken Arm said with signs. "No trade. Take what you need."

He had his men bring two young horses to the So-yap-pos for food. They butchered just one for their evening meal. The other they kept for the next sun.

"After we eat, we smoke," the So-yap-pos told Broken Arm.

May 10, 1806

"... after we had taken a repast on roots & horse beef we resumed our council with the indians which together with smokeing took up the ballance of the evening. . . ." Clark [Thwaites, Volume 5, Page 17.]

While the So-yap-pos were eating, Broken Arm ordered a large buffalo-hide tepee set up nearby.

The tepee covering was a heavy, awkward bundle made of many tanned hides sewed together. Strong arms helped tug it into place and raise it on long, heavy poles. There it stood, tall and grand in the twilight, thirteen, maybe fifteen, feet across on the floor level.

Broken Arm then had an armload of wood brought for a fire to be built in the center of it. With mats around the circle and the load of dry wood in the center, the great buffalo-skin tepee was ready for the council.

Broken Arm was pleased and his hands spoke graciously to the two So-yap-pos chiefs, "Make this your home as long as you stay here."

May 10, 1806

". . . a principal Cheif by name Ho-hast-ill-pilp arrived with a party of fifty men mounted on eligant horses. he had come on a visit to us from his village which is situated about six miles distant near the river. . . ." Lewis [Thwaites, Volume 5, Page 15.]

At this time Red Grizzly Bear and fifty men rode in on their finest horses from their village upriver. Red Grizzly Bear's scouts had brought him word of the So-yap-pos' move down the canyon to the flat where Broken Arm's village stood.

Red Grizzly Bear had also been on the warpath when the white men had come through the Oyaip. He, like Broken Arm, had received a medal. As soon as he had heard of the So-yap-pos' return, he had come to meet them.

Red Grizzly Bear had heard that So-yap-pos greeted by dandling hands. That is just what those white chiefs did when they came over to greet him. They then gave him another round piece of metal, this one showing the figure of a man swinging his arms about. The So-yap-pos explained that the man was throwing out seeds which would grow into food, which in turn was good for all men. Their hands said, "Do good things to your neighbors. They will do good to you. They will not fight and kill."

Red Grizzly Bear then spoke, "When next sun comes, another chief will arrive. Very brave, he has but one eye. When he is here, all chief leaders of the Nee-mee-poo will be present. Big council will be held."

The So-yap-po chiefs then gave Broken Arm a round piece of metal. But Broken Arm's showed the head of a man, the "Great White Father," who wanted all men to live together in peace—no more fighting and killing.

Red Grizzly Bear and Broken Arm followed the two So-yap-po chiefs into the buffalo-hide lodge. Cut Nose, Twisted Hair, and as many others as could, crowded into the circle around the fire.

The black man brought roots and horse meat, and the So-yap-po chiefs ate. When they were full, they smoked and passed the pipe for all in the circle to smoke.

"We are Cap-tans," the Nee-mee-poo heard. The red-haired man, pointing to himself, said, "Cap-tan Clahk." The other man, pointing to himself, said, "Cap-tan Loose."[3]

And, by signs, they said that a "Great White Father" had sent them to tell all people to live in peace with one another.

Every man read the sign-talk, and all of them thought about the message: "Live at peace with neighbors." Did that mean no more fighting with te-wel-kas?

No one was able to give an answer. There was no more talk. That was all. Everybody just stretched out in the comfort of the fire and went to sleep.

May 11, 1806

"The last evening we were much crouded with the indians in our lodge, the whole floor of which was covered with their sleeping carcases. . . . as all those cheifs were present in our lodge we thought it a favorable time to repeat what had heen said yesterday . . . and by the assistance of the snake boy and our interpretters were enabled to make ourselves understood by them altho' it had to pass through the French, Minnetare, Shoshone and Chopunnish languages." Lewis [Thwaites, Volume 5, Pages 18 and 19.]

Just as Red Grizzly Bear had said, He-yoom-pahkah-tim [Fierce-Five-Hearts][4] arrived soon after sunrise with his following of men. They had come up from Lah-mah-ta near the Ta-ma-nam-mah River two sleeps away.

When the Captains greeted Fierce-Five-Hearts with their usual hand shake, they gave him a medal like the one they had given to Red Grizzly Bear, showing a man sowing seeds. Fierce-Five-Hearts was honored, for he knew he was equal in courage and valor to any chief of the Chopunnish nation. Had he not made ten good horse-stealing raids before he could be chief?[5] And, in the forty snows that had passed since his birth, had he not shown great Power in war? His body was still straight and strong, and he walked with his head held high, so that the left eye, blinded in battle, seemed like an emblem of bravery. Men followed him in faith that his heart was fierce as five.

The Captains invited Fierce-Five-Hearts into the big tepee where the other great war chiefs of the Chopunnish nation sat in quiet dignity, each deeply aware of his own personal achievements. A tippet of fur hung from the neck of each chief, displaying mementos of distinction and honor. To the beads, ribbons, and scalps, each had added the cherished medals given by the So-yap-pos.

Broken Arm wore the medal that showed the head of the "Great White Father"; Cut Nose also had the same kind of medal for his collection; Fierce-Five-Hearts now had a medal like that of Red Grizzly Bear, showing a man swinging his arms as he sowed seed. Red Grizzly Bear wore on his tippet that medal from the So-yap-pos along with the array of human scalps and thumbs and fingers of men he had slain in battle.[6]

These were the four great war chiefs of the Chopunnish, and to these men the So-yap-po chiefs prepared to talk. Other important men of the nation, such as Twisted Hair, crowded into the circle inside the tepee.

Young and old they came, eager to hear the words of the white men.

Black Eagle, son of a respected chief who had recently been killed by the Big Bellies, wanted to learn more of the reason for the So-yap-pos' coming. His cousin, Speaking Eagle, son of the great chief, Broken Arm, was by his side.

When all were in the tepee who could get in, the So-yap-pos called for the Snake boy, and for Sa-ka-ka-wea, the Bird Woman, and her man, Charbonneau.

May 11, 1806

". . . as all those chiefs were present in our lodge we thought it a favourable time to repeet what had been said and to enter more minutely into the views of our government . . ." Clark [Thwaites, Volume 5, Page 21.]

Mindful of the role she was to play in this council Sa-ka-ka-wea took her place with the interpreters between the Snake slave and Charbonneau. Poised and erect, she sat in the elegant white buckskin dress she had decorated during the winter moons. A wide pattern of blue and white beads ran along the length of the sleeves and across the yoke to make a garment befitting such a momentous occasion.[7] Sa-ka-ka-wea felt this council was essential to the So-yap-pos' mission; she knew the value of looking important for such a meeting. She wore this dress feeling it would increase the regard the chiefs would have for her, and they, in turn, would give more attention to the message of the So-yap-pos that passed through her lips.

One So-yap-po spoke to Charbonneau. He spoke to Bird Woman in Minnetare. She, then, spoke Shoshoni to the Snake boy, who spoke to the chiefs in their tongue.

Then Captain Lewis took a charred stick from the fire and drew a map on one of the floor mats while he explained, "Far away toward the rising sun, where the land meets Big Water, our 'Great White Father' lives.

We have come up many rivers, crossed wide prairies, passed over high mountains, paddled toward the setting sun to land's end where your river runs into Big Water."

Then Lewis made the sign for "children" and proceeded:

"Children: The Great Spirit has given a fair and bright day for us to meet together in his view that he may instruct us in all we say and do.

"I take you all by the hand as the children of your great father, the President of the United States of America, who is the great chief of all the white people toward the rising sun.

"This great chief who is benevolent, just, wise and bountiful, has sent us to all his red children to the great lake of the west where the land ends and the sun sets on the face of the great water, to know their wants and inform him of them on our return.

"We have been to the great lake of the west and are now on our return to our country. We have seen all our red children all the way to that great lake and talked with them, and taken them by the hand in the name of their great father, the great chief of all the white people.

"The object of our coming to see you is not to do you injury, but to do you good. The great chief of all the white people who has more goods at his command than could be piled up in the circle of your camp, wishing that all his red children should be happy, has sent us here to know your wants that he may supply them.

"Your great father, the chief of the white people, intends to build a house and fill it with such things as you may want and exchange with you for your skins and furs at a very low price and has directed us to inquire of you, at what place would be most convenient for us to build this house, and what articles you are in want of that he might send them.

"The people in my country are like the grass—numerous. They are also rich and bountiful, and love their red brethren.

"Your great father, the chief of all the white people, has directed us to inform his red children to be at peace with each other, and with the white people who may come into your country. Those people who may visit you under the protection of that flag are good people and will do you no harm.

"Your great father has directed us to tell you not to allow your young and thoughtless men to take the horses or property of your neighbors, but to trade with them fairly and honestly."[8]

Captain Lewis concluded, "Now we are going back to tell our 'Great White Father' what we have found. We want to tell him that you have decided to live in peace with all men, that you will welcome men who come to trade among you."

The words seemed good; but, the ideas were too new. This would have to be discussed in council among themselves before they could give the So-yap-pos an answer to take back to that "Great White Father." This message the Nee-mee-poo gave to the white chiefs by speaking first to the Snake boy who repeated it to Bird Woman, who spoke to her husband, Charbonneau, and he to the So-yap-pos.

May 11, 1806

". . . the interpretation being tedious it ocupyed nearly half the day before we had communicated to them what we wished. they appeared highly pleased. after this council was over we amused ourselves with shewing them the power of magnetism, the spye glass, compass, watch, air-gun and sundry other articles equally novel and incomprehensible to them. . . ." Lewis [Thwaites, Volume 5, Page 19.]

The sun was high in the sky when the council ended. The men filed out into the warm air to see the strange things the So-yap-pos were showing: a loop of metal that could hold fast to other metal; a long, hollow piece of metal that made a distant man seem close when you looked through it; an instrument with a needle that always pointed in the direction of the Unmoveable Star; a round instrument that had two needles, one shorter than the other, fastened together at the center and a smaller third needle that moved while something inside went "tk-tk-tk-tk-tk"; a different kind of gun that could shoot a tiny pellet without making that big noise like thunder. ("Maybe good for shooting grouse—no good for shooting bears!")

"We have heard of these things," the Broken Arm said, "but we did not believe until we saw with our own eyes. The Minnetares told three of our people who visited them after you left that you had such things. We could not believe until now."

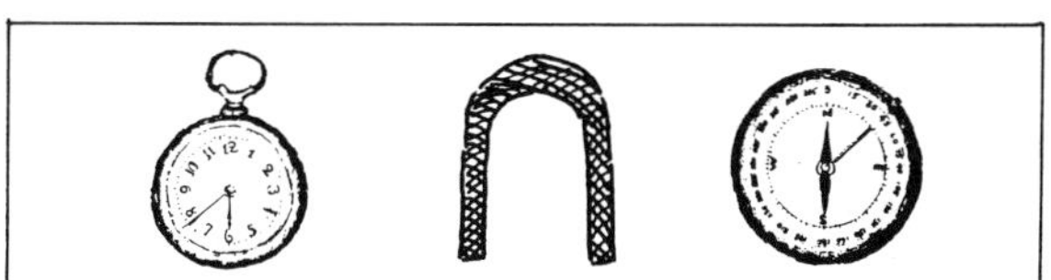

Everybody was there to see: old men and women, young men and women, and the children, all dressed in their fine clothes for this important occasion. Each one found something extraordinary.

The So-yap-po men were as interesting as the strange

tools they showed. Whenever that black man, "Yohk" (York), swaggered past them, he sent the young girls into nervous titters. He rolled his eyes at them until much white showed, and his wide grin flashed white teeth, made all the whiter against his black skin.

The men and boys looked on, some in wide-eyed wonder. They talked together and laughed at what they could not understand. Some skeptics, with eyes narrowed to mere slits, doubted what they saw.

Some of the So-yap-po men tried to learn to talk with The People. The youngest of these spoke to Black Eagle and his cousin, Speaking Eagle, who were about his own age. Pointing to himself, the young man said, "Shannon." That was easy for the other two men to say.

Then Speaking Eagle pointed to Black Eagle and said, "Tip-yah-la-nah She-mook She-mook."

Shannon tried several times before the name came easily. "Tip-yah-la-nah [Eagle] She-mook She-mook [Black]."

Black Eagle next pointed to Speaking Eagle, saying "Tip-yah-la-nah-jeh-nin," and Shannon was able to speak the name of Speaking Eagle in the Chopunnish tongue.

All three were pleased with their efforts, and a feeling of friendship grew between them.

Even though they had to talk with their hands, some of the So-yap-pos tried to tell the Nee-mee-poo strange tales of things they had seen at the Big Water.

"On shore of Big Water," one man's hands said, "we saw BIG FISH this long." And he threw a pebble as far as he could to demonstrate the size of the fish.

Disbelief met that story. Hands twirled in little circles close to heads, saying "Crazy!" "Liar!" Others signed, "forked tongues" with two fingers.

But the white men insisted they spoke truth, and someone thought to ask Bird Woman if all this was so.

"I have seen that big fish," she said. "It is true. It was as long as a man could throw a stone. The Big Water washed it up on shore in a storm. I saw it."[9]

That was enough. If Bird Woman said it was true, then it was true. But the eye of the mind found it hard to see a fish that big. Some shook their heads in disbelief, but is was remembered for telling to the little children by the light of fires in the Cold Moons.

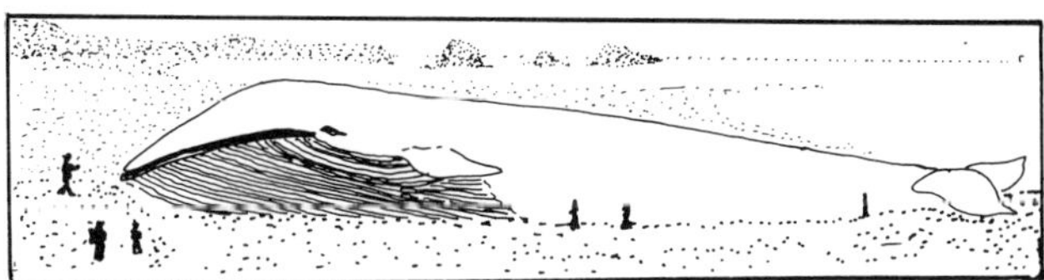

May 11, 1806

". . . A young man, son of a conspicuous cheif among these people who was killed not long since by the Minnetares of Fort de Prarie, brought and presented us a very fine mare and colt. he said he had opened his ears to our councils and would observe them strictly, and that our words had made his heart glad. . . ." Lewis [Thwaites, Volume 5, Pages 19.]

Now, through the throng came Black Eagle leading a mare and colt up to the Captains. With his hands he spoke, "Not many moons back, the Big Bellies killed my father, a great chief. I have opened my ears to your advice. From this time on, I intend to live by your counsel. Your words have made my heart happy. I give this mare and colt to show I mean to live at peace with all people."

The Captains were pleased by his words and by the gift of the mare and colt, and their good spirits grew when Twisted Hair's men brought in six more So-yap-po horses. Almost all of their horses had now been found.

May 12, 1806

"This morning a great number of indians collected about us as usual. we took an early breakfast and Capt. C. began to administer eyewater to a croud of at least 50 applicants. . . ." Lewis [Thwaites, Volume 5, Page 23.]

While the peace-making council was taking place, the sick people were finding a different kind of excitement. Word had reached their ears that the red-haired Medicine Man was among them. They had heard how he had helped others. This man used strong medicine that worked on their bodies. He was "Si-kip-te-wat" [white man's doctor][10]. They hoped he could help them, and they flocked to him for his medicine.

Eyes, stuck shut with matter; eyes, red and smarting from wood smoke; eyes, rubbed by grimy fists to clear away the sand that wouldn't go away; eyes, blurry with age; and eyes that could not see at all, brought the people of all ages to have medicine dropped in by that Si-kip-te-wat.

Some had hard, painful lumps on the sides of their necks.[11] Some had sores that did not heal. Stiff and aching joints pained others. A few could not move their limbs. And most of them had sore eyes.

The Si-kip-te-wat put drops in sore eyes. He rubbed pungent grease on stiff, aching joints. He lanced boils and applied powders. He cleansed sores and put on bandages. This man had Medicine Power different from the Te-wats, who chanted and shook rattles over their patients. He used strong medicine that worked on their bodies.

Evening shadows were beginning to fall when four men carried a man on a buffalo robe to this Si-kip-te-wat.

"Moves-No-More," they said as they laid the man down and explained his predicament as well as they could.

"He cannot move," they said. "For five snows he has not moved arms or legs. We lay him on his back, he stays. We prop him up, he stays. We put him on his side, he stays. He eats. He talks. He understands everything. He just cannot move. He is good man—big chief.[12] Will you make him walk again?"

The So-yap-po Medicine Man knelt down and felt all over the chief. He looked puzzled. He then administered some white and yellow dust for Moves-No-More to eat and advised the man's friends to give him a sweat bath.

Clark then packed his bag and went back to his men, leaving people feeling good, as much from his kindness as from his medicine.

May 12, 1806

"... The Indians held a council among themselves this morning with rispect to the subjects on which we had spoken to them yesterday. ..." Lewis [Thwaites, Volume 5, Page 23.]

While the sick received treatment, the great war-chiefs, Broken Arm, Red Grizzly Bear, Cut Nose, and Fierce-Five-Hearts, with Twisted Hair and the principal men, gathered in their own council. No interpreters encumbered the flow of thought and eloquent speech as each man, in turn, expressed what was in his heart concerning the propositions presented by the So-yap pos.

"Who is this 'Great White Father' mentioned by these men?" they wondered.

"We have never heard of such a one before. Our fathers never heard of one. Where does he come from? What Power does he have over all this land? What Power does he have to keep Snakes, Blackfeet, and Crows from attacking us if we decide to live in peace? Nothing has kept them from the warpath before this. Can any 'Great White Father' protect us?"

"Will the So-yap-pos keep their word and build trading posts where we can come and trade for their axes, blankets, kettles, moccasin-awls and beads—blue beads?"

One dissenting headman said, "We want to get our hands on more guns and the black sand and balls that make them shoot. The te-wel-ka will get more guns. We will be dead men if they have guns and we don't."

They pondered these matters at length. They thought of what it would be like, never to have more eye-drops, beads and blankets, guns or ammunition. These things they needed and wanted. They thought of the risks taken in placing trust in strangers; yet the tongues of these So-yap-pos had been straight thus far. Maybe all white men had straight tongues. That "Great White Father" must have straight tongue. Why would he send his people to them? It seemed wise to trust him. If they did not, they could cut themselves off from any good they might gain.

"A-a-a-a-a," they agreed in the end. It seemed good to trust the "Great White Father," to follow his advice and live in peace. Life looked better that way.

When the chiefs and principal men made the decision to agree to the Great White Father's proposals, it meant that every person must live by it. Everyone must agree, or it would do no good. The course they had determined must be explained to The People. The People, too, must agree.

May 12, 1806

". . . after this council was over the principal Cheif or the broken Arm, took the flour of the roots of cows and thickened the soope in the kettles and baskets of his people, . . . impressing the necessity of unanimity among them . . ." Lewis [Thwaites, Volume 5, Page 23.]

With a plan in mind, Broken Arm went straight to his lodge after the council was over. He stood for a while, just looking. The women of all the forty-eight families were busy over their cooking pots and kettles. With a deafening racket of stone pestles clacking against stone mortars, some of the women pounded dried roots into flour and meal.

No one paid attention to Chief Broken Arm until he picked up his wife's basket of kouse meal and started down the row of cooking fires, stopping to thicken the mush in each kettle or basket with the kouse meal he stirred in.

"What does this mean?" the women murmured and stopped their cooking and pounding to watch and wonder at this unaccustomed procedure.

When he had thickened the soup in every pot, Broken Arm turned and spoke in a loud voice to all the men who had drawn together.

"Open your ears to what the council has just decided," he said. "We have considered the advice of the So-yap-pos to live in peace with our neighbors and with the te-wel-kas—the Snakes, Blackfeet, and Crows. We have agreed this is good. We will no longer go to war against our neighbors. We will welcome the chance to trade with So-yap-pos who are to come to our land.

"Unless all of you agree, these words are as empty air. I invite each man who will accept the decisions of the council to come and eat of this mush. Those who do not agree will let it be known by not eating."

Without hesitation, every man stepped up and ate his portion of mush. Not one refused.

But, on hearing these words, the women burst into shrieking and wailing. They tore their hair. They wrung their hands and beat their breasts. No woman foresaw a life of peace in such an arrangement, for they knew too well what horrors befell women when te-wel-kas attacked. If their men would not fight, what was to become of them and their children?

The wailing did not sway the men from the decision made.

May 12, 1806

". . . after this cerimony was over the Cheifs and considerate men came in a body to where we were seated at a little distance from our tent, and two young men at the instance of the nation, presented us each with a fine horse. . . . The band of Tin-nach-e-moo-toolt have six guns which they acquired from the Minnetaries and appear anxious to obtain arms and amunition. . . ." Lewis [Thwaites, Volume 5, Page 23.]

To show they celebrated the decision made by all, the chiefs chose Speaking Eagle, the son of Broken Arm, and Black Eagle, the son of the chief killed by the Big Bellies, to present Captain Lewis and Captain Clark each with a fine horse as a token of whole-hearted support of their decision.

The So-yap-pos were sitting outdoors near their tepee. They rose to greet the delegation and accepted the gift of horses with acts of appreciation. They asked the chiefs to be seated and gave each one a flag, some black sand, and fifty balls for guns. Nothing held more value to Broken Arm's men. They always needed more ammunition for the six guns they had obtained from the Minnetares.[13] The white men gave red paint, ribbons, blue beads and black sand and balls to the young men who had presented the horses.

Cut Nose was pleased to receive his flag, black sand, and balls for guns, though he had no gun. He would get one, someday. To show his appreciation toward the So-yap-pos, Cut Nose had a fine horse brought up and presented it to the So-yap-pos' good hunter, Drewyer, whom he admired. This man was also a good sign-talker. Cut Nose felt Drewyer to be a man of great importance.

Broken Arm rose with dignity.

"Will So-yap-po chiefs smoke in council?" he asked, indicating the council lodge.

The men all stood up and filed into the tepee, where they sat down around the small fire.

Broken Arm spoke directly to the white men, "We have decided in council what we wish to say in answer to the words you spoke to us on the previous sun.

"Before we go on, many of our people, who are in great pain, wish to receive medicine from the Si-kip-te-wat."

The captains talked together. Captain Clark nodded and left the council fire to administer medicine to the sick who were waiting. Captain Lewis remained in the council.

May 12, 1806

". . . The father of Hohastillpilp was the orrator on this occasion. he observed that they had listened with attention to our advise and that the whole nation were resolved to follow it, that they had only one heart and one tongue on this subject. . . ." Lewis [Thwaites, Volume 5, Page 24.]

The father of Red Grizzly Bear, Old Red Bear, now a man of many snows, spoke with quivering voice and trembling hands, "My people have opened their ears wide. We have decided to follow your advice. We have but one heart and one tongue on this matter. We have long seen the benefits of living at peace. Our great desire to live at peace with our neighbors led us to send three brave men with the pipe to the Snakes last summer. They never came back. These young men were murdered. Our warriors went on warpath to avenge their death. That is why they were not on the Oyaip when you came through six moons ago. They met Snakes and killed forty-two with the loss of only those three. The blood of our friends is satisfied. We no longer want to make war against the Snakes but will accept them as friends. We value the lives of our young men too much to want them to go to war."

He continued, "Since you have not yet spoken to the Blackfeet and the Big Bellies, we do not think it is safe for our people to go over to Buffalo Country. We would gladly go if we thought those people would not kill us. It would make our hearts happy if we could live at peace with those nations, although they have shed much of our blood.

"When your forts are built, as you promised, we will come over and trade for guns and ammunition. We can live near you and feel safe. We want you to know we are friends to you. We will help you in any way we can. Though we are poor, our hearts are good.

"Some of our young men will go with you and bring back word of how our enemies receive your message. If we can make peace with our enemies on the other side of the mountains, our people will go over the latter part of the summer.

"We cannot yet decide if one of our chiefs will go with you to the land of the White Men. Before you leave, we will let you know. The snow is still too deep for you to cross the mountains. You would all die if you tried to go now. After the next full moon, the snow should be gone. Then you can find grass for your horses. That would be the time to go. Kullo. [That is all.]"

The pipe was smoked to show that all in the council accepted the proposals of the So-yap-pos.

As a sign of goodwill towards the So-yap-pos, a fat horse was given to them for their next meal. The So-yap-po who led him away patted his belly and smiled, thinking how good this horse would taste.

May 12, 1806

"... Capt. C. now joined us ... we gave a phiol of eyewater to the Broken Arm, and requested that he would wash the eyes of such as might apply for that purpose, ... he was much pleased with this present. ..." Lewis [Thwaites, Volume 5, Page 25.]

After the last council with the chiefs was finished, Captain Clark returned from treating the sick. He brought a small cup of the eye-water to Chief Broken Arm, saying, "Here is eye-water for you to wash out the sore eyes of your people. When it is gone, we will give you more."

This gave Broken Arm a good warm feeling. This medicine had great power. He had seen Si-kip-te-wat use it to make people see better. He would be able to do the same. How could he show this man his gratitude? He had nothing near at hand to give him except the shirt on his back.

Broken Arm acted as soon as the thought came to him. He stripped off his soft tanned buckskin shirt with the quill-work decorations and gave it to Captain Clark. The Captain, in turn, gave Broken Arm a white-man's shirt—light weight, compared with the buckskin, and opened down the front with slits on one side. On the other side, there were little round, flat beads with holes that were sewed through with the So-yap-pos' thread. The So-yap-pos called these "but-tons." The shirt could be closed together by pushing the buttons through the thin slits.

As if not to be outdone in the giving of gifts, one of the young men who had received the ammunition, blue beads, and red paint presented a pair of leggings to Captain Lewis. Very good work had been put into making those leggings. Surely it had taken many suns for his mother to make them.

May 12, 1806

"... we now gave the Twisted hair one gun and a hundred balls and 2 lbs. of powder in part for his attention to our horses . . ." Lewis [Thwaites, Volume 5, Page 25.]

It was time now that the So-yap-pos kept their word to Twisted Hair, whose young men had delivered almost all of their horses.

"Six horses are still missing, besides the two taken by the Snake scout and his son last fall," Captain Lewis told Twisted Hair. "When you have brought those six in, we will give you one more gun and the same amount of balls and powder."

Captain Lewis then handed over to Twisted Hair one gun, one hundred balls, and a package of black sand.

Captain Lewis next turned to address Broken Arm who had been watching the presentation to Twisted Hair. "We want to cross over the river to make our camp where we can hunt, fish, and graze our horses until the time we can get through the mountains."

"Across river is good place—good spring, good pasture. But there is no canoe to take baggage across," Broken Arm told him. "When sun comes up, we will send a man to get canoe for you."

Twisted Hair thought to himself, "Taats! So-yap-pos will be just where those six horses are grazing."

"When we get our camp established on the other side of the river," Captain Lewis said to Twisted Hair, "bring your family over and live near us as long as we stay in this country. You have good sons who know the trails through these mountains. We would like to have them be our guides."

"We will come," Twisted Hair assured him, pleased by the confidence the So-yap-pos placed in him.

The sun went down on happenings long remembered and talked about for generations to come, but The People living that day took things as they came. It was time for the stick game. Some had acquired beads and other trinkets. Some had not. It did not matter. All that could change in a stick game.

As the light waned, the players dropped their wagers onto a pile in the space between two parallel logs. Back of each log the players sat with sticks in hand, facing each other. Speaking Eagle took his place between the logs, near the wagers. He held in his hands two small bones, one marked and one unmarked. No one could see which hand held the marked bone. No one could tell, because he could shift bones from one hand to the other so fast it was impossible to tell where the marked bone was.

Speaking Eagle squatted there in the center and began to sing as he waved his arms, crossing them wildly from side to side, up and down, and back and forth. The players sang their song and beat a fast rhythm on the logs with their sticks. Now the voice of the leader rose above all, exhorting them to guess which of his hands held the marked bone.

Should a player venture a guess and the opened hand showed the wrong bone, the singing and rythmic beating began again with fresh vigor. A right guess would award the player one of the items from the pile of wagers, and the exhorting and singing and pounding resumed. It took a long, long time to play stick game.[14]

CHAPTER 12

WAITING FOR THE CANOE

MAY 13, 1806

"... administered to the sick ... collected all our horses and set out at 1 P.M. and proceeded down the Creek ... 3 miles we halted at the ... River unloaded our horses and turned them out to feed. Several Indians accompanied us to the river .. canoe did not arrive untill after sunset ..." Clark [Thwaites, Volume 5, Page 31.]

"So-yap-pos cross the river this sun," the camp Crier announced the next morning. "Anybody with sore eyes, stiff joints, or aches and pains, better go to Si-kip-te-wat before he leaves."

That was enough to set the sick people moving. Many still suffered, but nothing had given them such hope as the medicine used by the So-yap-po doctor. The line was long that morning.

The sun was almost overhead when Clark dropped eyewater into the eyes of the last one.

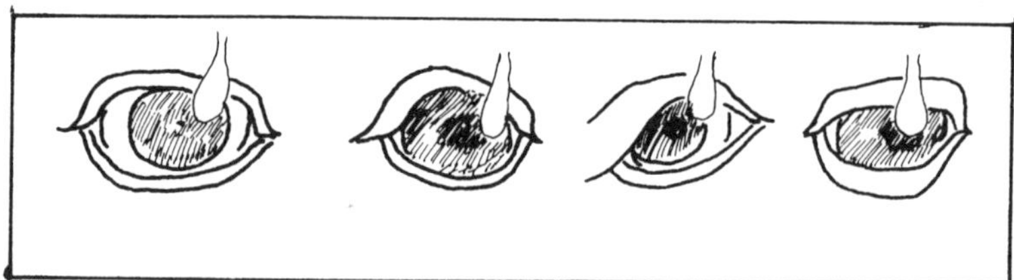

The So-yap-po camp hummed with activity. Every man argued with the horse he was trying to pack, whether the animal resisted his burden or not. Light-hearted banter passed back and forth among the thirty men, and their loud guffaws set the horse with rabbit ears to laughing with them.

The commotion drew the Broken Arm people out to watch. The boys and young men sat on their horses, ready to ride to the river with the So-yap-pos. Though the women and young girls looked on from a distance, nothing escaped their sharp eyes.

"These men do not smoke as ours do," they observed. "Our men smoke only at night around the fire and at council fires. All these men are day-time smokers. Each one has his own pipe and smokes any time during the day."

The young girls discussed the day-time smokers: the young one without hair on his face; the man with only one good eye; the red-haired man with blue eyes; the black man. They compared them all with their own brothers and cousins and friends. Each girl knew in her heart which man appealed to her most.

A driving urge to look her best beset one girl, Tom-sis [Rose]. She platted her hair smoothly into two thick braids and hung beads and wampum from her ears. What beads and shells not already fastened to her white buckskin dress were twined around her wrists, her neck, waist, and crosswise over her shoulders. Every beautiful, bright ornament, blue beads, or pieces of brass she possessed enriched her costume. In the fashion of the downriver people, she pushed a white dentalium shell through the pierced septum of her nose. She settled her mind on wearing her basket hat instead of a fur bandeau around her forehead.[1] The leaves of sweet-smelling ginger[2] perfumed her arms and hands.

When she walked along the path with her cousins, Tom-sis held her head high, fully aware of her splendid appearance, yet modestly looking neither to the right nor to the left. Except—just once, did she not look up into the sky-blue eyes of that So-yap-po who set the hot blood pounding through her body?

Though only three suns had risen since the So-yap-pos had arrived, the nearness of their camp had encouraged friendship and harmony. It was different from being camped near neighbors on the Oyaip. There, next digging season would bring friends back again. Here, these So-yap-po friends would go, never to return.

Back in the lodge of the Broken Arm, Tom-sis felt loneliness as she watched the line of horses and riders file away down the creek toward the river. Those men would be camped just across the river, but never again would all of the Broken Arm people be able to see all of the So-yap-pos in one big group. Their empty campsite left a hollow feeling to more than just Tom-sis.

Speaking Eagle and his cousins, who rode to the river with the white men, felt no such sense of loss. They saw only a chance to be near these interesting friends for a longer time. And, maybe some would gamble on races or stick game.

When they arrived at the river, the So-yap-pos found they could not get their baggage across. The canoe was not there. No one knew when it would come—maybe not for a long time.

The men took the packs off the horses so they could graze. After that, they had nothing to do but wait.

Then Speaking Eagle saw something that was to

relieve everyone's boredom. Coming across the flat were two of his cousins who had gone out early to hunt. Each man was pulling a badger by a long leather thong fastened to one hind leg. The animals could neither escape nor attack.

A group of So-yap-pos gathered around, asking what the men meant to do with these badgers. Speaking Eagle answered, "You see here two badgers, same size. We turn them loose. Each starts to dig a hole. They dig fast. Soon out of sight. Still digging. You reach in and pull badger out by tail. One of us will reach in and pull the other badger out. We bet our badger always comes out first."

Shannon, the youngest So-yap-po, called out, "Me first! Here's buttons for stakes." He laid his wager down.

Speaking Eagle turned a badger's thong over to him and said, "Let badger go. Let it dig. When out of sight, grab by tail. Pull hard." At the same time, he let go of the thong on his badger and watched.

Soon, both animals had burrowed out of sight. The men knelt in front of their holes, ready for the signal.

"Grab!" yelled Speaking Eagle, thrusting his arm into his badger's hole.

Shannon plunged his arm into his hole, getting a face-full of dirt as the badger kept clawing. He found the short tail, got a good grasp on it, and pulled. The badger seemed stuck fast. Shannon pulled harder. Still, the animal did not budge. Again he tried, putting all the strength he could into the effort until it seemed he would pull the tail off. Slowly, grudgingly, the badger yielded, but when Shannon eased up on the pulling, he received another face-full of dirt. One last strain dragged the badger out, still clawing and snarling viciously.

Too late!

Speaking Eagle sat by his badger's hole, calmly holding the leather thong of his badger.

Speaking Eagle's cousins squatted in a semi-circle, calm and complacent, with only twinkling eyes to betray their mirth. One of them took the badger's thong from Speaking Eagle, challenging another So-yap-po to try his strength and skill.

Potts laid down his wager and took the thong from Shannon's hand. Turned loose, the badgers soon burrowed out of sight again. At the given signal, each man shoved his arm into his badger's hole and began to pull.

Potts grunted and pulled, but the animal clawed dirt into his face. He strained and tugged with no result. He worked and sweated until the creature, at last, began to give up.

"He's a-comin'!" Potts yelled as he drew the badger out, snapping with rage.

But no cheers greeted his victory over the badger. His opponent squatted on the ground, calmly watching, while his badger fussed at the restraining thong. Potts, too puzzled to notice twinkles in the eyes of the innocent looking badger-handlers, passed the thong of his badger to Silas Goodrich who had bet a fishhook he could win.

But Silas did no better than his friends before him. In spite of heroic exertion on his part, his rival's badger came out first. Silas shook his head in disbelief.

"Dag-nabbit!" he growled. "What in tarnation is goin' on here? We'll all get skinned if we keep bettin' on badgers! What about a horse race? At least we'd know what we're up against."

May 13, 1806
". . . in the evening we tryed the speed of several of our horses. these horses are active strong and well formed. . . ." Lewis [Thwaites, Volume 5, Page 29.]

The So-yap-pos turned the thong of their badger over to Speaking Eagle and went off, perplexed, never to find out why they had always lost at the badger game.

Speaking Eagle took the thong and quickly slipped it from the hind leg of Old Woman Badger whose long, sharp claws had clung tenaciously to the floor of her burrow. Free at last, she slid into her hole, aching from the tail-pulling.

At the same time, the thong was released from the hind leg of Old Man Badger. His handlers had caused him such unbearable pain by pulling on the testicles under his tail, that he went limp and could be dragged out at once. He dived into the cool darkness of his hole to recover from the indignities he had suffered.[3]

Speaking Eagle and his cousins gathered up their winnings and watched with interest while the So-yap-pos raced their horses. The young men knew how the So-yap-po horses ran, for they, themselves, had ridden them throughout the winter. They looked now with critical eyes at how the So-yap-pos rode, for it took both horse and rider to win a race. The So-yap-pos rode well enough to be a challenge on another sun.

Finally the canoe arrived after sundown, not the time of day to move baggage across the river. That would have to wait until after sunrise.

It was time to sleep.

CHAPTER 13

BEARS!

MAY 14, 1806

"a fine day. we had all our horses collected by 10 a.m. . . . had all our baggage crossed over the . . . River which is rapid and about 150 yards wide. after the baggage was over to the North Side we crossed our hors[e]s without much trouble and hobbled them in the bottom after which we moved a short distance below . . . and formed a camp around a very conveniant spot for defence where the Indians had formerly a house under-ground and hollow circiler spot of about 30 feet diameter 4 feet below the serf[a]ce and a Bank of 2 feet above. . . ."[1] Clark [Thwaites, Volume 5, Page 35.]

At last, every So-yap-po and all of their horses were on the other side of the Koos-koos-kee River where the grass on the broad, flat bottom land grew belly-deep for horse feed. It was a good place for controlling the movements of the horse herd: the Koos-koos-kee River curved around the south and west edges; the tumbling Tom-me-taha Creek discouraged crossing to the east; steep hills guarded the north.

A cold spring bubbled up joyously from level ground and spilled into a tub-like hole before it gurgled off to the river. No better spot could be found for taking a cold dip after a sweat bath while, at the same time, providing convenient water for household needs.

Long before, the Nee-mee-poo, who first discovered the place, had said, "Taats!" and they had set themselves to digging a circular pit, thirty heel-to-toe feet across and as deep as a tall man's shoulders. They made it even deeper by piling the earth around the rim to drain water away from the hole. Over this they had made a roof of branches, leaves, and mats. There they dwelt for no one knows how long until, in the wisdom of the council, they moved to higher ground. Now, nothing remained but the pit, over-grown with grass, and the cold spring that laughed its way to the river.

"Just what we need!" the So-yap-pos declared as they stored their baggage in the pit and guarded it by setting up shelters of sticks and grass around the rim. "No thievin' man nor prowlin' bear'll rob us of the supplies we need for getting ourselves home."

May 14, 1806

". . . immediately after we had passed the river Tunnachemootoolt and Hohastillpilp arrived on the south side with a party of a douzen of their young men; they began to sing in token of friendship as is their custom, and we sent the canoe over for them. . . ." Lewis [Thwaites, Volume 5, Page 33.]

The canoe had just made its last trip across the river when Broken Arm, with twelve of his young men, and Red Grizzly Bear, with three old friends, arrived on the opposite bank. The group wanted the So-yap-pos to remember them as friends, and, for that reason, they sent their song across the water:

"Lawtiwa-mah-ton,
Lawtiwa-mah-ton."
[Friends together]

The So-yap-pos understood this gesture and sent the canoe back for them. Broken Arm and his son, Speaking Eagle, Red Grizzly Bear, Black Eagle, and as many other men as the canoe could hold, left their horses with caretakers and crossed over.

The So-yap-po captains invited them to smoke in friendship. There, in the soft warmth of this spring day, birds sang in the trees overhead. Bees and butterflies flitted from flowers of all colors in the field around them. They smoked and felt the beauty of the earth and the closeness of being friends together.

Red Grizzly Bear had held that feeling in his heart for many suns, and, on this occasion, had planned a gift for Captain Lewis. The right time came when one of his men rode up to the group on a horse he had just swum across the river. The splendid gray gelding glistened in the sunlight from the water that still dripped from him. The rider dismounted and handed the rein to Red Grizzly Bear.

Red Grizzly Bear then spoke at length. He assured the So-yap-pos of his friendship, of his intention to live at peace with all men, and of his desire to have more opportunities for acquiring white men's trade goods. As a token of appreciation for the honor the So-yap-pos had bestowed upon his people by their visit, he wished to present the fine horse which had just arrived. With that he handed the rein over to Captain Lewis.

To Red Grizzly Bear's delight, he received from Lewis two hundred balls and some powder for his gun, along with a square of cloth he thought would look impressive around his neck. Red Grizzly Bear thought of the hunting successes the ammunition would bring him now that he could again use his stick-that-shoots-black-sand-with-thunder.

May 14, 1806

". . . Collins killed two bear this morning and was sent with two others in quest of the meat; with which they returned in the evening; . . ." Lewis [Thwaites, Volume 5, Page 34.]

When a white hunter returned to camp to get help in bringing two dead Hah-hahts [grizzlies][2] back to camp before sundown, Red Grizzly Bear's concept of hunting bears expanded. Bears were good to eat, but they were too dangerous for one man alone to attack with arrows. Now, Red Grizzly Bear saw that one man had killed two bears with a gun! That was an act of bravery as great as killing two te-wel-kas in battle.

The thought of bear meat to eat was tantalizing! Not for a long time had anyone tasted bear, and here the So-yap-pos had a large, fat he-bear and a smaller she-bear. The So-yap-pos shared the head, neck, and shoulder of the he-bear and half the she-bear.

Speaking Eagle and his friends prepared the feast of bear meat. They built a hot fire with dry wood and heated smooth stones brought from the river. They spread the hot stones out level and laid pine boughs over them. On these they placed a layer of meat strips. On this they laid another layer of pine boughs. Another layer of meat strips went on this, and another layer of pine boughs over that. When the meat had all been layered between pine boughs, they poured a little water over it and covered the whole pile with a thick layer of earth. Long after sundown, they uncovered the tender, juicy roasted bear and everyone ate until he could eat no more.

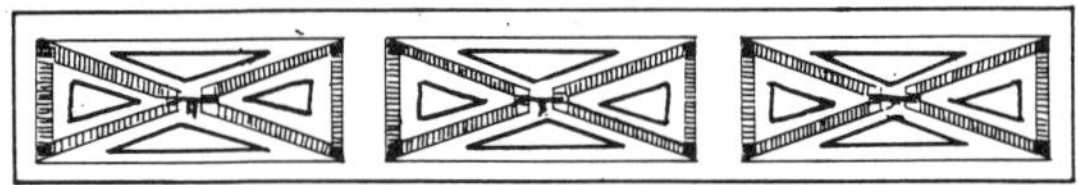

While both the So-yap-pos and Nee-mee-poo were busy preparing the bear meat, another hunter came into camp with word that he had killed a mother bear and her two large cubs. Hunting alone, he had been unable to bring the carcasses in by himself. The So-yap-pos would have to wait until next sun to bring these bears in, as darkness would soon cover the valley.

Most precious to Red Grizzly Bear were the big he-bear's claws which the So-yap-pos gave to him. They were tangible proof that a man with a gun had power over Hah-hahts, the grizzly, the animal men feared above all others.

The Nee-mee-poo knew some habits of the Hah-hahts. They knew the Hah-hahts made dens in the mountains and rid themselves of vermin in their stinking dust wallows among the exposed roots of giant cedar trees.[3] A hunter, warned by the bad smell, was wise to move at high speed away from such a place. Many a man had been killed and eaten by Hah-hahts for daring to get within an arrow shot.

The Nee-mee-poo had seen many different colors of fur in the Hah-hahts family. Some were almost pure white, while others were black, brown, grizzled, or red. All were large and fierce, but none would climb trees.[4] If a man could find a tree when he needed it, climbing a tree was his best chance to escape a charging grizzly.

Now, a tree was all that saved Ya'amas Wakus when one sun he loaded Twisted Hair's gun, as he had seen the So-yap-pos do, and went hunting.

He did not have far to go before he saw a deer. Quietly

he raised the gun to his shoulder, sighted down the barrel, and pulled the trigger.

"BOOM!" roared the gun. Down fell the deer, lifeless. Ya'amas Wakus stood there, deafened by the noise, shaken by the kick of the gun, and stunned by the thought that with one single shot he had brought down his game.

Jubilant, Ya'amas Wakus hurried back to camp and told his wives, "I shot deer up the trail. You women take care of it and pack it in."

His wives, with great pride in their man's hunting power, took their horses up the trail to bring down the meat, but in a short time they raced back to camp as fast as their ponies could run, screaming and shrieking, but making no words. Ya'amas Wakus knew something terrible had happened. He spoke to the women in a calm voice until they could get words out.

"Hah-hahts! Hah-hahts! Hah-hahts is eating the deer!" they gasped.

Ya'amas Wakus did not stop to hear more. He loaded his gun and ran up the trail to the kill. As he approached, Hah-hahts lifted his bloody muzzle and growled in a loud voice.

Ya'amas Wakus did not get too close. He just lifted his gun and fired. Hah-hahts went down, but he was not dead. He staggered to his feet and roared, louder and louder, as he lunged toward the man.

Frantically, Ya'amas Wakus loaded his gun for a second shot, but by that time the bear was too close upon him. Ya'amas Wakus dropped the loaded gun and shinnied up a tree.

Hah-hahts raged around the tree, standing on his hind legs and clawing as high as he could toward the man above him. Finally, he came upon the gun, the hated thing of the hated man!

Picking it up, he bellowed and snarled, trying to bite

it and tear it to pieces. While he had the barrel in his mouth, his claws caught in the trigger of the gun.

"BOOM," the gun roared back at him, and Hah-hahts dropped dead. He had shot himself!

Ya'amas Wakus, still shaking with the fear that had passed, went back to camp. Once more he sent his wives out. This time they brought back not only what was left of the deer meat, but also a grizzly—a prize beyond his expectations.[5]

CHAPTER 14

HORSES

WHILE BROKEN ARM, RED GRIZZLY BEAR, SPEAKING Eagle, Black Eagle and the other Nee-mee-poo were waiting for the bear meat to roast, they joined the So-yap-pos who watched a commotion in the meadow among the sixty-five horses they now owned. Two of the stallions were fighting as if to kill each other.

Lunging, plunging, screaming, they reared and slashed with their front feet. Their great teeth ripped skin and muscles. Their eyes glared wild and red. They whirled and kicked with their hind feet and struck again with their front feet, pawing and squealing. Blood gushed from their wounds, but, sustained by primordial madness, they fought on.

May 14, 1806

". . . we have found our stonehorses [stallions] so troublesome that we indeavoured to exchange them with the Chopunnish for mears or gel[d]ings but they will not excha[n]ge . . ." Lewis [Thwaites, Volume 5, Page 35.]

The So-yap-pos were worried. They needed these fine, strong animals to carry them through the mountains and plains on the way back home. But here they were, ripping themselves to pieces. What good would they be to anyone after more such fights as this?

The captains turned to the watching Nee-mee-poo.

"Trade horses?" they asked, hoping to rid themselves of the ugly problem.

No trade. After seeing how vicious those animals

were, no man wanted to be bothered with them. "See-kim kap-seese'!" ["Horse bad!"]

"Two horses for one of yours," the So-yap-pos tempted.

"See-kim kap-seese'! No trade!"[1]

May 14, 1806

". . . we came to a resolution to castrate them and began the operation this evening one of the indians present offered his services . . . he cut . . . without tying the string of the stone as is usial. he [s]craped it very clean & seperate it before he cut it. . . ." Lewis [Thwaites, Volume 5, Page 35.]

"We can't have good horses ruining each other. We'll have to geld them," the white men decided, "then they won't give us any more trouble. They'll have time to heal before we leave."

The man called Drewyer, the best hunter and sign-talker, had done the operation on other horses. He was ready to tackle the savage studs as soon as the fighting was over.

Horse-Breaker, looking on, could tell by the So-yap-pos' hands what they had determined to do. (Drewyer talked with his hands as much as with his mouth.) He had seen the results of this man's work before. How stiff those horses were afterward!

Horse-Breaker had learned a better way from his father. He wanted to show these So-yap-pos what he knew.

"Let me," his hands said to Drewyer. "Horse heals faster."

That seemed agreeable to all the So-yap-pos. Horse-Breaker waited until one of the fighters finally turned tail and ran away. Then the noose of his horsehair rope whirled through the air and over the head of the conqueror.

Before the stallion had gained his wind from fighting, he was flat on the ground with men holding ropes on his legs so he could neither stand nor kick to defend himself. Men stood around watching Horse-Breaker's method of gelding a horse. After they turned him loose, the animal no longer felt like fighting.

Horse-Breaker operated on five more stallions that evening.

Next sun the animals which he had operated on seemed to have bled more, but they were not so swollen as those Drewyer had worked on. They seemed to feel better. The So-yap-pos were impressed and Horse-Breaker felt proud that he had shown them a better way to manage horses.

Though Broken Arm and his young men decided to return to their village the next sun, Red Grizzly Bear and his companions were in no hurry to leave. They had feasted well on bear the night before and had no urge to go hunting. Besides, it was too hot to move. Here among friends, they would stay until the notion to leave came upon them.

May 15, 1806

". . . a party of 14 natives on horseback passed our camp on a hunting excurtion; they were armed with bows and arrows and had decoys for the deer these are the skins of the heads and upper portions of the necks of the deer extended in their natural shape by means of a fraim of little sticks placed within. the hunter when he sees a deer conceals himself and with his hand gives to the decoy the action of a deer at feed; and thus induces the deer within arrowshot; . . ." Lewis [Thwaites, Volume 5, Pages 38 and 39.]

Red Grizzly Bear and his old friends did not stir when fourteen Nee-mee-poo hunters rode past with their bows and arrows and deer decoys. The old men knew these young ones were headed for the Oyaip on good hunting horses. These horses were trained to respond to their riders' body movements. In open country, the horses would encircle the deer. Swiftly they would close in on it until the hunters were close enough to shoot it with arrows.

If the hunters found a deer in the woods, they would hunt on foot and use decoys to fool the deer into thinking they were just some of his family. The hunter could work his way up within arrow shot; the deer would sense no danger, until it was too late.

In their hearts, the old men hoped strong hunting Power went with the hunters, but not one of them spoke as they watched the riders disappear into the breaks of the canyon.

When the sun, which had beamed hot all day, dropped below the rim of mountains, Red Grizzly Bear and his friends decided they might as well return to their village in the cool of the evening. They left, thinking they would cross the river in the canoe, but the canoe was not in its accustomed place. Someone had taken it away.

Daylight faded.

"Might as well go back to So-yap-pos' camp for the night," they said.

It did not matter that it was far into the night before they arrived at the camp. They were among friends. They would have food, and they were safe.

Red Grizzly Bear and his friends lingered on in camp until mid-day. By then they had settled their minds to go farther upstream to find a canoe to cross the river which was rising. When they left, they took the remainder of the bear's head and the neck which the So-yap-pos had given them. Their families would have a feast!

May 17, 1806

"... no Indians visit us to day which is a singular circumstance as we have not been one day without Indians since we left the long narrows of the Columbia." Clark [Thwaites, Volume 5, Page 45.]

May 18, 1806

"... 3 Indians ... called at our camp; they informed us that they had been hunting several days and had killed nothing; we gave them a small peice of meat which they told us they would reserve for their small children who were very hungary; ..." Lewis [Thwaites, Volume 5, Page 46.]

Hunting on the camas grounds at Oyaip had brought nothing but disappointment to the hunters. Though snow still covered the ground up there, they had seen no tracks to follow, no deer to run. Discouraged, the hunting party that had set out five suns ago broke up. Some went off in one direction, some in another. Others decided to return to their village.

Three of these arrived at the So-yap-pos' camp, hungry, yet not starved, for they had taken roots and root-bread with them. Their mouths watered and their stomachs growled at the sight of some of the bear meat which the So-yap-pos brought out to share with them. Gladly they took the meat. But the memory of their little children, crying from hunger, hung heavy in their hearts. They could not eat that meat themselves.

"Our little children are hungry," they explained to the white men. "We will save this meat for them."

Sharing the customary smoke with the So-yap-pos refreshed them, and they left with good feeling in their hearts. They would not be returning to their village empty-handed. Cries of joy would greet them and smiles would drive away the tears when their children were fed.

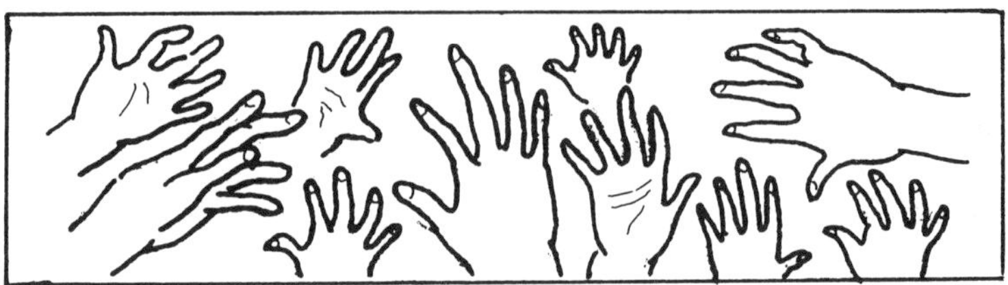

May 19, 1806

"... I sent Joseph and R. Feilds up the river in surch of the horse which I rode over the Rocky mountains last fall. he had been seen yesterday with a parsel of indian horses and has become almost wild. ..." Lewis [Thwaites, Volume 5, Page 49.]

Horse-Breaker had driven a herd of his horses upriver past the Heart of the Monster to good pasture.

"Wonder how that horse got in this bunch," he said to himself when he realized that a troublesome stallion among his horses was not his. This one had a bushy foretop and carried the So-yap-pos' brand on his left shoulder. "Bothersome horse! Maybe they'll come get him."

A feeling of relief came over him when he saw two riders approaching. So-yap-pos! Look like brothers! Maybe after that wild horse!

Their hand-talk said, "That horse belongs to our chief. We came to get him."

But the horse was no longer a gentle, manageable animal that permitted man to approach and put a rope around his neck. He whirled and turned his heels toward anyone who tried to get near. How could they separate him from the other horses? How could they catch him to lead him back?

Horse-Breaker settled the matter. The noose of his rope swished through the air to encircle the wild horse's neck. Remembering the meaning of ropes from his tamer days, the horse allowed himself to be haltered and led away, though he snorted and lunged in defiance.

The two So-yap-pos had had enough of that horse by the time they reached their camp. They were glad to turn him over to their captain.

Captain Lewis had been relying on the sure-footed strength of this horse to carry him once again across the mountains. Now, when he observed his favorite horse had turned into a snorting, plunging, wild-eyed beast, he made up his mind.

"Drewyer," Captain Lewis said, "castrate him!"

Drewyer carried out the order and tied the subdued animal to a tree. But the horse still fought restraints, and, during the night, he lunged over the rope and dislocated his hip in his struggles.

By morning, the horse was not only stiff from his operation, but in such pain from his hip that he could not walk. Warm weather increased the activity of flies around his wound. Following their nature, they laid their eggs in the open cut. Soon, the eggs hatched into maggots, and the maggots squirmed and wriggled through the flesh, bringing great suffering to the animal.

Fourteen suns were to come and go. In all that time, the horse did not eat. He could not walk. And the men who came each day to try to cleanse his hurt walked away shaking their heads in pity. The horse would not heal.

"Poor old horse! We ought to put him out of his misery."

"Shoot him!" Captain Lewis ordered at last. "And drag him off away from camp."

The order was carried out at once.

May 22, 1806

". . . being without meat at noon we directed one of the largest of our colts to be killed. we found the flesh of this animal fat tender and by no means illy flavoured. we have three others which we mean to reserve for the rocky mountains if we can subsist here without them. . . ." Lewis [Thwaites, Volume 5, Pages 54 and 55.]

When Black Eagle, the young man whose father had been killed by the Big Bellies, met the So-yap-pos on their arrival at the Broken Arm's village, he had presented the So-yap-po chiefs with a cherished mare and colt. He had chosen them from the best of his horse herd in gratitude for the message from the Great White Father.

The colt had grown since then. Every sun showed him bigger and fatter than he was the sun before, a promise that he would some day be a magnificent war-horse or buffalo chaser. But, the So-yap-pos did not look that far ahead. For two days, their only food had been roots, which disagreed with them when eaten without meat. They began to see the colt only as something to put meat into their empty stomachs, and, by noon, they determined to eat him.

They might have spared the colt if they had known that the hunters were to have success later in the day.

Across the river hunters from Broken Arm's village had ridden upon a deer and were driving it downhill at breakneck speed toward the water.

Alerted by the whoops of the hunters and the barking of Seaman, the dog, the two captains and three of their men rushed down to the river bank with their guns. Swimming away from the arrows, the deer headed straight to its death by gunfire. As its body floated downstream, some of Broken Arm's hunters jumped on a raft and retrieved it.

That one little deer did not feed many hungry mouths, but when the So-yap-po hunters brought in five more deer that evening, everyone had plenty to eat.

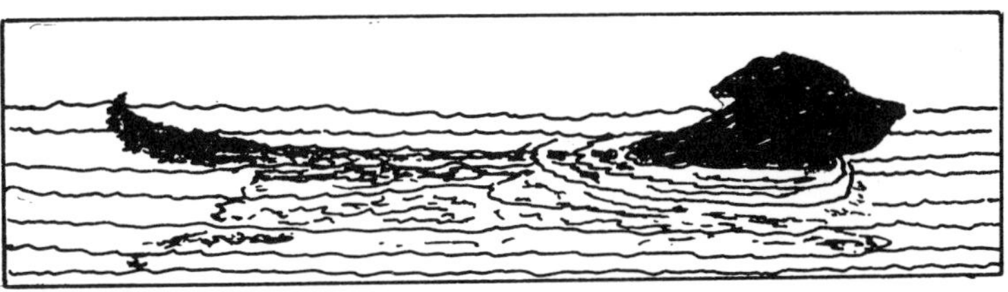

Even the two men, White Hawk and Three Feathers, who rode into camp late, received food.

White Hawk and Three Feathers had just returned from a visit to the fishery on the Ki-moo-e-nim River. It was apparent they had not spent all their time fishing. The beads and shells that dangled from their ears, the ropes of beads and shells around their necks, their paint and feathers, made a striking display of new-gained wealth. They must have had good luck in stick games while they were gone.

They recounted their exploits to their friends with laughter and words. Then their hands spoke in simple signs to the white chiefs, "Many fish in Ki-moo-e-nim. Fat fish. Later, fat fish will come to Koos-koos-kee."

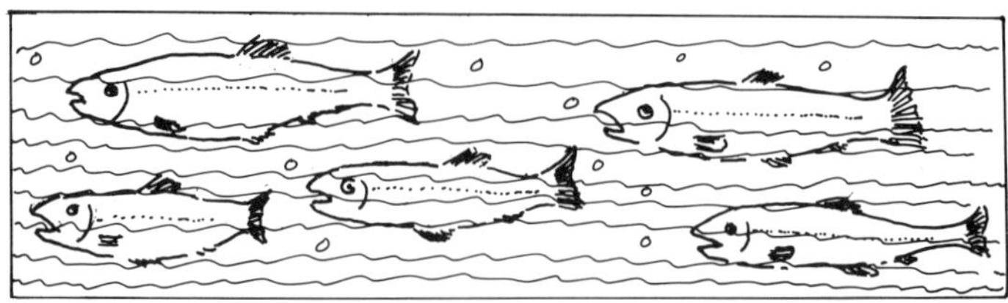

The evening meal had scarcely been eaten when many riders from the Broken Arm village gathered on the river bank across from the So-yap-po camp. They seemed to be excited about something, but they did not attempt to cross the river to disclose their news. Instead, their Crier's loud voice carried the message to the other side.

"Look out for te-wel-kas," he yelled. "They came by night to a lodge on Ta-ma-nam-mah River. Nobody killed. Nobody home. People had been warned beforehand and left. Watch for te-wel-kas!"

That news brought light sleep to every Nee-mee-poo who heard it, though nothing alarming happened during the night.

May 23, 1806

"Sergt. Pryor wounded a deer early this morning . . . my dog pursued it into the river; the two young Indian men . . . mounted their horses swam the river and drove the deer into the water again; Sergt. Pryor killed it as it reached the shore on this side, the indians returned as they had passed over." Lewis [Thwaites, Volume 5, Page 58.]

The sound of a gun shot and the deep barking of the big dog, Seaman, wakened the whole camp at sunrise.

Sleepy men roused up to see Seaman chasing a wounded deer into the river. The hunter, Pryor, was running behind, but he was too far back to get another good shot. White Hawk and Three Feathers took one look and knew what they had to do to get meat for their morning meal.

They jumped on their horses and plunged into the

river right behind the deer. Cold and swift though the current ran, the deer had strength enough to reach the opposite bank where a group from Broken Arm's village had assembled. The deer's feet had scarcely touched ground when these whooping, yelling spectators headed it back into the river. Again, the deer swam across the swift water back to the So-yap-pos' shore. As it scrambled up the bank, Pryor's bullet ended its life.

The So-yap-pos gave half the deer to the men who had followed it back and forth across the river. White Hawk and Three Feathers shared their portion with four of their friends who had come from Broken Arm's village. Before the sun reached its highest point in the sky, nothing was left of the deer.

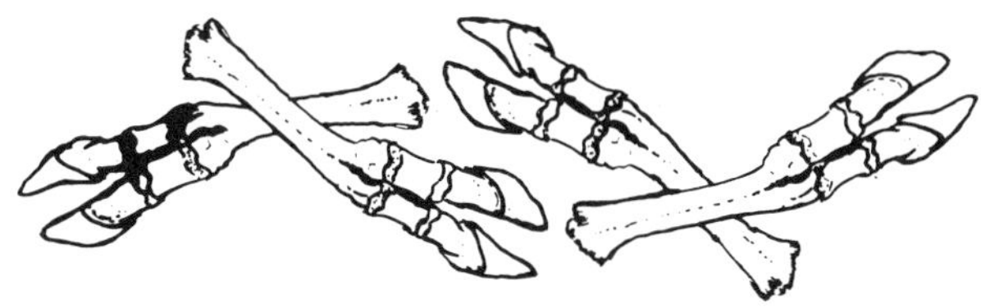

Plenty of meat made contented stomachs, but it could not banish the worry that te-wel-kas might be sneaking around to steal horses. If the Snakes found them, they could drive off a man's entire fortune in one raid.

The Chopunnish measured their wealth in horses. Some owned fifty, some sixty, and some a hundred head or more. A man with many horses could live well.[2]

What kind of life would a man have without his horses? How could his family move from one faraway root-digging camp to another without horses? Or how could the men run deer over the rugged hills? Families would not cross the mountains to hunt buffalo unless they could ride. Without their horses, few people would have much of a chance escaping the te-wel-kas. And, no man wanted to lose the fun of racing his horses. Horses meant good life for the Nee-mee-poo.

"Better go look after our horses," the men agreed when they had finished the last of the deer.

They rode off together but separated to go in different directions. Some rode up one side of the river. Some rode up stream on the opposite side. Some went up to the Camas Prairie, looking at the horse herds that ranged over the grasslands. And always, through that sun, their eyes searched for signs of the Snakes, but no te-wel-kas were seen. Their horses were still safe. The men slept well that night.

May 29, 1806

". . . Our Horses maney of them have become so wild that we cannot take them without the assistance of the indians who are extreemly dextrous in throwing a rope and takeing them with a noose about the neck; as we frequently want the use of our horses when we cannot get the use of the indians to take them, we had a strong pound formed to day in order to take them at pleasure . . ." Lewis [Thwaites, Volume 5, Page 85.]

The So-yap-pos had traded for many horses on their return journey from the Big Water. By the time they had collected their horses left with Twisted Hair's people the previous fall together with their new ones, they had acquired sixty-five horses in all. They had this herd driven closer to their camp. The men wanted to find out which horses had strong attachments with others and which horses fought. Knowing this about the animals made it easier to keep them from straying.

Every So-yap-po hunter had two or three favorite horses. Each time a hunter went out, he took a different horse from the one he had ridden the day before. This kept the horses from getting foot-sore and stiffened by constant use.

Certain So-yap-pos who were not hunters groomed these special animals—brushing, trimming feet, and doctoring cuts. Whenever a hunter needed a fresh mount, his horse had to be ready for the trail. That made a problem for the caretakers.

Catching the right horses for the different hunters gave the caretakers their hardest work. The animals had run loose so long, they were wild and skittish. The grooms could not lay hands on them. Coaxing and gentle talk did not work. The surest way of catching a particular horse was to rope him, but the So-yap-pos were not good ropers. Every time they cast a noose and missed, the horses ran and ducked and dodged until the men grew discouraged.

All the while, Nee-mee-poo horsemen watched, silently amused by the struggle between man and beast. In desperation the white men turned to the onlookers, asking them to rope certain animals for them.

Pointing, they let the ropers know which horse they needed: " . . . the brown . . . the black . . . the white . . . get the blaze-faced bay!"

Then the Nee-mee-poo rider would charge into the horse herd and, with one fling of his noose, catch the desired horse. This was sport that helped the So-yap-pos, yet left them defeated when they had to rely on their own roping.

The captains decided to solve the problem.

"Build a strong pound," they ordered their workmen. "If the horses are in a small space where they can't run, we can catch them easier."

This order set the boss-man, Gass, and his helpers to cutting trees for the fence. They laid the logs in such a way that, with the fewest logs possible, the fence was too high for a horse to jump over and too strong to knock down.

"Pound," the white men called it. It wasn't big enough to hold all sixty-five horses at once, but selected horses could be shunted into the pen and caught with less effort.

The fence was a good place to sit, watch, inspect, and make judgments. Lame, stiff, or sore-backed horses were spotted at once for treatment. The caretakers doctored and groomed daily. Sound horses were held in the pound for immediate use. The rest of the horses were turned back into the meadow to be caught on another day.

When Speaking Eagle and the youngest So-yap-po, Shannon, sat on the top pole of the fence, they both saw the same horses milling around in the pen. But each saw them in a different way. To Speaking Eagle, horses meant wealth and prestige, success in war and hunting, winning at races and games. To Shannon, they meant FOOD for sustaining life in emergency; they meant swift ESCAPE from enemies; and they meant HOPE in crossing mountains and plains towards home! And each man judged the horses according to his own values.

CHAPTER 15

GOOD MEDICINE

MEDICINE SUPPLY CARRIED BY LEWIS AND CLARK EXPEDITION

List requested by Captain Lewis

[Thwaites Edition, Volume 7, Page 236.]

15 lbs. best powder'd Bark
10 lbs. Epsom or Glauber Salts
4 oz. Calomel
12 oz. Opium
1/2 oz. Tarter emetic (sudorific or diaphorectic—causing sweat]
8 oz. Borax
4 oz. Powder'd Ipecacuana (emetic, purgative)
8 oz. Powder Jalap
8 oz. Powderd Rhubarb
6 Best lancets
2 oz. White Vitriol
4 oz. Lacteaum Saturni
4 Pewter Penis Syringes
1 Flour of Sulphur

3 Clyster pipes
4 oz. Turlingtons Balsam
2 lbs. Yellow Bascilicum (ointment: rosin, beeswax, lard)
2 Sticks of Symple Diachylon (plaster of glycerine mixed with lead salts of the fatty acids for excoriated [skinned areas] surfaces and wounds)
1 lb. Blistering Ointments
2 lb. Nitre
2 lb. Coperas

[In addition to the above, Volume 7, Page 244 lists:]

4 oz. Laudanum
1 Set Pocket Instruments small
1 Set Teeth Instruments small
1 Tourniquet
2 oz. Patent Lint
50 doz. Bilious Pills to Order of B. Rush

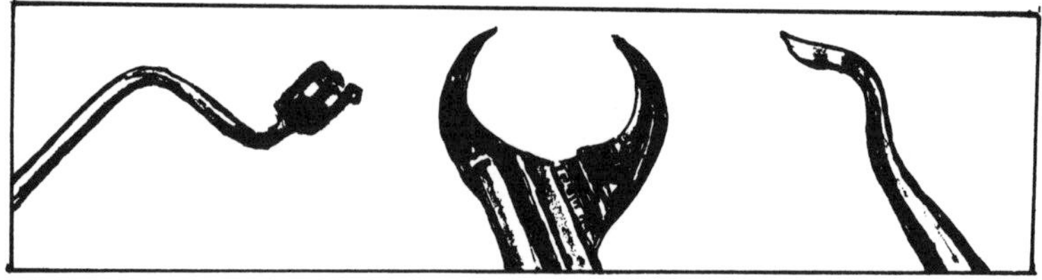

May 18, 1806

". . . at 3 P M . . . so[o]n after an old man and a woman arived the man with sore eyes, and the woman with a gripeing and rhumatic effections. I gave the woman a dose of creme of tarter and flour of Sulphur, and the man some eye water. . . ." Clark [Thwaites, Volume 5, Page 48.]

Old Man Bobcat and E-wap-na [wife] lived across the river from the Broken Arm's village, near the Heart of the Monster. They had not seen the So-yap-pos treat the sick at Broken Arm's village, but friends who had been there told them about it.

"Those So-yap-pos drop medicine in eyes. Makes them hurt, but feel better afterward. They rub arms and legs and backs with good bad-smelling medicine.[1] They give white dust and yellow dust to eat for pains in bowels.[2] You better go see those So-yap-pos. Get their good medicine."

The two thought about this news for several suns. Sometimes it was too rainy to go. Sometimes it was too hot. But one morning, when clouds covered the sun without dropping rain, Old Man Bobcat knew it was time to go.

Sometimes at night the pain in his eyes kept him from sleeping. He would lie there and think about their condition. Sometimes he thought about this in the day when E-wap-na prepared food and brought it to him. He remembered how she fetched clothing for him that he could not see to find. Even when her feet and legs and back hurt so much and she could barely move, E-wap-na took care of him.

This sun E-wap-na began to complain of pains in her bowels. She moaned and groaned with pain. Bad pain!

Old Man Bobcat settled his mind.

"E-wap-na is bad sick," he said to himself. "Bad pain may bring death. Don't want her to die. I need her. I can take anything as long as she is by my side. Better get her to So-yap-po medicine man."[3]

By the time the sun was well past its high point, Old Man Bobcat's and E-wap-na's gentle ponies had carried them safely down to the So-yap-po camp. It was just as their friends had said. These strange men, with different colored hair, talked with their hands and heard with their eyes.

It was not hard to tell the red-haired medicine man about their sickness. He dropped stinging medicine into Old Man Bobcat's eyes. It burned like fire! Good medicine! He then gave the white and yellow dust to E-wap-na to eat. The white dust was sour and the yellow dust tasted like stinking water. Good medicine! The Red-Head then rubbed some good bad-smelling water on E-wap-na's aching joints.

When Old Man Bobcat and E-wap-na left for home, they felt better than they had for many moons. Now, they would tell everyone in their village about the good medicine.

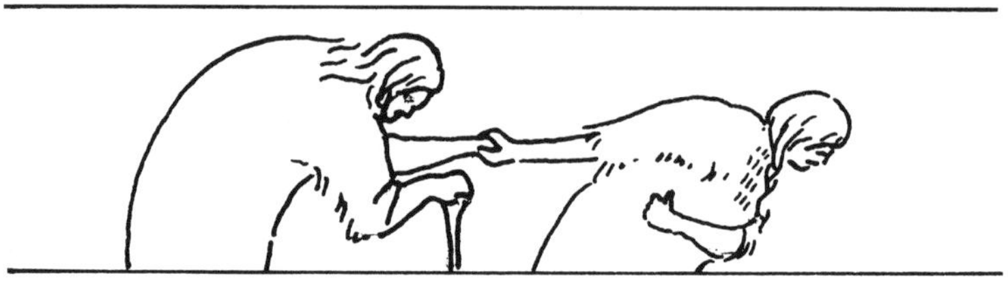

May 19, 1806

". . . about 11 oClock 4 men and 8 women came to our camp with Thompson who went to the Village very early this morning. those men applyed for Eye water and the Women had a variety of Complaints . . ." Clark [Thwaites, Volume 5, Page 50.]

Though the night-long rain had ceased, a damp chill hung over the earth. The People in Broken Arm's village found comfort of a sort around the smoky fires in their long mat lodge. But the meager warmth from the fires could not dispel the suffering of many who had sore eyes. The smoke made eyes smart, and rubbing them made their eyes feel worse. Matter formed and stuck them shut. Light was blinding.

The women suffered with more than sore eyes. Their joints ached. Their legs felt weak. They had to gather wood and bring water from the creek for cooking, even though the air was chill and damp, causing them even greater pain.

"E-nasa-pahl-we-sah," ["I'm getting tired, but I have to keep going,"] A-yat [Old Woman] groaned, as she stiffly shuffled in with a load of sticks for the fire.

"Wa-tu e-mas pahl-we'!" ["Don't force yourself!"] her neighbor answered, just sitting there doing nothing.

"What ails you?" A-yat asked her. "You look awful. Bad sick?"

That silenced her friend. She just sat still with a far-away look and began to weep.

Nobody felt good. The sick baby cried. Everybody around felt like crying.

Outside, dogs began to bark, and children ran to see who was coming.

"One So-yap-po here," they called back. The men rose in the lodge and went to meet him.

"The man, Tom-son, comes to trade for roots and bread," they reported to the women. "Crossed river in canoe."

This news lifted the spirits of everyone. Thompson had a few things to trade: awls (always needed); arm-bands, for decorations; and long, sharp knitting needles—maybe good for running through flat cakes of root-bread so they could be put on strings for drying.

More important than that, he had come in the canoe. He could take more than food back in that canoe. It had room for many sick people.

When Thompson returned across the swollen river, the canoe carried roots and root-bread, four men with sore eyes, and eight women with various ailments.

The Si-kip-te-wat began treating the sick people at once. He put eye-water into the eyes of all. He gave medicine to two women to make their bowels work. To the weepy, dejected woman he gave thirty drops of medicine that made her peaceful.[4] He showed the people how to help one another by rubbing the "good bad-smelling" water on backs, hips, thighs, and legs.[5]

The gloomy feeling that had come with the wet day left the sick people. They had received good medicine. Their spirits were high and their bodies felt much better when they crossed the rising river to their village.

May 22, 1806

". . . Charbono's Child is very ill this evening; he is cuting teeth, and for several days past has had a violent lax, which having suddonly stoped he was attacked with a high fever and his neck and throat are much swolen this evening. . . ." Lewis [Thwaites, Volume 5, Page 56.]

The sun had no clouds to hide behind this day. It warmed the air and drove away the dampness. Grass shot upward. Flowers opened their pink, blue, red, yellow, white, and purple beauty to the eyes. Robins, blackbirds, and wrens filled the world with songs of joy. Women in the villages hunted fresh roots for food. Old people dozed in the sunshine.

Across the river the So-yap-po men dried out baggage and clothing that had been soaked by rain. Their chiefs had a new, dry shelter built for themselves.

The earth seemed good for everyone.

But Sa-ka-ka-wea's little boy, Ba-teese, was sick. For several suns he had had diarrhea; but, though that had stopped, he now burned with fever. His gums, neck, and throat were swollen. He chewed on his fingers and cried, but he could not eat.

Both captains came to look at him. They felt his head and neck. How hot! They looked at his swollen gums and shook their heads.

"He is about sixteen months old now. It's obvious he's cutting more teeth," Captain Lewis said.

"That is true," Captain Clark replied. "But something more is wrong with him. See how swollen his neck is? It must be very painful. He must be getting a boil there.

It may come to a head and have to be lanced, but we'll have to wait before that can be done. Meanwhile, I'll put an onion poultice on it and give him a dose of cream of tartar and flour of sulfur. It might help."

"York, boil some wild onions until they are soft. We will use them for a poultice."

All night long, someone watched over the baby, continually keeping warm onion poultices on his neck.

By morning Ba-teese's fever was lower, but his neck, though no worse, remained swollen. In spite of all the poultices applied during the day, his neck and jaw became more swollen. More poultices, more cream of tartar did not help. He felt even worse.

Throughout the night he fussed until the captains were at their wits' end. At last Captain Lewis said, "We could try giving him a clyster (enema). It can't hurt him. It may help."

That evening they gave him an enema and a dose of cream of tartar. When morning came, the fifth day after he became ill, Ba-teese's fever was gone and the swelling was down, but a little hard lump could still be felt below his ear. More onion poultices!

From that time on, Ba-teese slowly recovered.

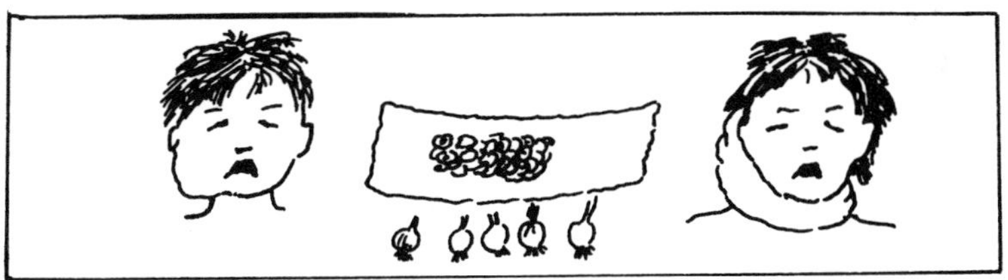

May 23, 1806

". . . at noon we were visited by 4 indians who informed us they had come from their village on Lewis's river . . . to see us and obtain a little eyewater . . ." Lewis [Thwaites, Volume 5, Page 58.]

In the village on the bank of the Ta-ma-nam-mah River, far upstream from the mouth of the Lah-mah-ta Canyon, four men sat smoking and discussing their common ailment. All of them had sore eyes.

"Eyes hurt," Speaks-with-Straight-Tongue mourned.

"A-a-a-a-a," agreed Sits-by-Fire. "Can't see to hunt."

"A-a-a-a-a," Lost-His-Horses said. "No good!"

"A-a-a-a-a! Can't see to hunt. Can't see to fish. Can't see to make arrowheads. What can we do about it?" asked Running Horse.

Speaks-with-Straight-Tongue spoke again, "I have recently heard that a party of white men with hair on faces are camped with Broken Arm. Among them is a man with red hair. He gives good medicine for sore eyes. I am going to visit him. Get some relief!"

"Kiyu'!" said the other three.

With a few provisions, the four men started on the journey, which, even on strong horses, was to take them the best part of two suns.

The small group jogged along the bank of the Ta-ma-nam-mah until they came to the mouth of the Lah-mah-ta Canyon, where they turned right and followed the creek up its narrow valley to the foot of a broad-faced mountain. The trail up this mountain was long and tedious, zig-zagging back and forth many times before reaching the top. It was "lah-mah-ta"—wearisome—and it took the horses almost from sunup to sundown to climb the trail.[6]

The four men arrived at Broken Arm's camp on the second sun, only to find that the white men had moved their camp across the Koos-koos-kee River and some distance downstream.

Undaunted, Speaks-with-Straight-Tongue, Sits-by-Fire, Lost-His-Horses, and Running Horse rode on. They swam their horses across the swollen stream and approached the So-yap-pos' camp.

Their sore eyes kept them from observing many

strange things the So-yap-pos had. But they had come only to see the red-headed doctor who had medicine for eyes. It was not hard to find that man, and it was not hard to tell him what they wanted. He seemed to know.

The red-haired Si-kip-te-wat dropped a liquid into the eyes of Speaks-with-Straight-Tongue. It burned like fire, but in a short while the burning stopped and his eyes felt better. The Red-Head likewise treated the eyes of Sits-by-Fire, Lost-His-Horses, and Running Horse. The burning was near torture. It hurt bad enough to cure anything!

Satisfied that they had received what they came for, the four men mounted their horses, swam them across the river, and began their return trip to the Lah-mah-ta Canyon.

Next sun the four worked their way down the wearisome trail. By sundown, they sat, smoking, in their village on the bank of the Ta-ma-nam-mah River, far upstream from the mouth of the Lah-mah-ta Canyon. To all who came to listen, they told about their visit to the Red-Head who had dropped strong medicine into their eyes and made them feel better.

"I speak true words. I saw that Red-Head. His medicine helped me see better," Speaks-with-Straight-Tongue assured his listeners.

"A-a-a-a-a," the other three agreed. "He had good medicine."

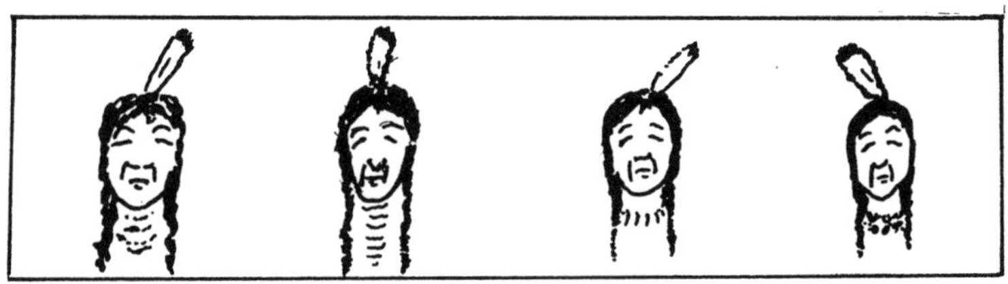

May 24, 1806

"... William Bratton still continues very unwell; ... John Sheilds observed that he had seen men in a similar situation restored by violent sweats. Bratton requested that he might be sweated . . . we consented. . . ." Lewis [Thwaites, Volume 5, Page 60.]

During the visit of the four men from the banks of the Ta-ma-nam-mah, some of the So-yap-po men were busy digging a hole. It was a round hole, three big-sized feet across and four feet deep. When they were through, they built a hot fire in the bottom and let it burn until the sides of the hole were very hot. They then scraped out all the coals and placed a chunk of wood on the bottom for a man to sit on, along with a slab of wood for his feet to rest on. After this, they made a roof frame of willow branches which curved over the top of the pit, and over this they put a covering of blankets. The sweat hole was now ready for use.

The So-yap-po, Bratton, had an ailment which the captains could not diagnose. His legs were so weak they could hardly hold him up to walk. He felt pain when he tried to sit. None of the captains' remedies had helped.

When Bratton's friend, Shields, said, "I have seen men cured by taking violent sweat baths," Bratton asked for that treatment.

Now he was ready. With all his clothes off, he was lowered into the hole. Shields tucked the blankets snugly around the edge of the roof. Bratton created steam by sprinkling water over the hot wall from a pail. He drank dipper after dipper of horsemint tea until sweat began to pour from his body.

When the men above thought he had been in the hole long enough, they pulled him out and quickly carried his steaming body over to plunge into the cold creek. Twice they dipped him into the icy water before they returned him to the hole for another sweat.

This time the men left Bratton to sweat for a longer time, and when they took him out, they wrapped him in blankets. They let him cool off slowly rather than take another cold water bath. He slept well that night.

When daylight came, Bratton was able to walk!

"I feel better than I have for a long time," he laughed. "I don't feel very much pain anywhere."[7]

May 24, 1806

". . . at 11 A.M. a canoe arrived with 3 of the natives one of them the sick man of whom I have before made mention as having lost the power of his limbs. . . ." Lewis [Thwaites, Volume 5, Page 61.]

In Broken Arm's village, the helpless Moves-No-More lay limp as he had for the past five snows.[8] Earlier when the So-yap-pos had first returned from the Big Water, their Si-kip-te-wat had told Moves-No-More's friends to give him a sweat bath and had given him white and yellow dust to eat. All this had made him feel better, he thought, but he was still too weak to move his arms, fingers, legs or toes. Moves-No-More thought all the time about how good it would be to walk again, to sit up, to feed himself, to swim, to ride a horse, to go on a hunt.

"To-ta," he said to his father. "Will you take me back to the camp of the So-yap-pos? Ask them to do something more to make me well?"

His father's heart was full of love and concern for this fine young man. He would do all in his power to restore his son's health. The father sought the help of a strong man to move the weak body of his son. He then arranged to have a canoe carry them across the river.

The So-yap-po captains greeted the family and friends of Moves-No-More kindly and looked the sick man over.

As Clark had done the first time he met Moves-No-More, now both captains shook their heads with puzzlement.

"What can be wrong with him?" they asked each other. "He hasn't had a stroke. He can't be paralyzed because his muscles haven't wasted away. He doesn't seem to have any great pain in any place, so it can't be rheumatism."

"I'll give him some laudanum to make him rest better," Captain Clark said. "And I'll give him some of our portable soup[9] to add to his diet. He may have eaten some harmful root, or he may not be getting enough good meat."

On the following sun, the captains decided that the sweat hole had done so much for Bratton, it might be what Moves-No-More needed. The two men had very similar symptons. The captains ordered the sweat hole heated again. They could think of nothing better to do for Moves-No-More.

Carefully, Moves-No-More was eased into the hole where he crumpled in a heap on the bottom, unable to sit up or to sprinkle water on the hot wall to make steam. He had to be pulled out. Everyone was disappointed at the failure.

The captains talked together about what should be done. They could see only one solution.

"This man needs some deep sweats," Captain Clark said. "Take him back to your village and give him sweats in your way. Give him doses of this yellow powder and this white powder every day. And here is some more portable soup to feed to him. All this should help him get well."

The So-yap-pos went about doing other things, supposing their directions would be carried out, but Moves-No-More did not want to be taken back. He asked his father to stay overnight and think about how he could get a sweat in the white man's way.

Father and son and the strong man who had accompanied them talked a long time. It finally came to them how Moves-No-More could manage the So-yap-pos' sweat bath.

When the next sun came, To-ta went to the captains and said, "My son asks that you try to sweat him again in your way. I, myself, will dig the hole bigger around. I will go into the hole with him and hold him up. I will sprinkle the water on the hot wall and make big steam. I will help him get out. I will do all I can to help."

"We have also been thinking," the red-haired So-yap-po said. "We will put some straps around him to suspend him in the hole. That will make it easier to keep him in place and easier to pull him out. We will see what we can do."

The father went to the sweat hole and dug it wide enough for him to get inside with the limp body of his son. The So-yap-pos fastened a strap under the sick man's arms and to this they fastened cords and ropes which they hung over a tree branch.

The father let himself down into the hole and the So-yap-pos eased the weight of the son slowly down with the ropes. They fastened the ropes to the tree when the man was in a sitting position. They covered the roof with blankets. The father began making steam.

"Drink this brew," the father said, holding the dipper of horsemint tea to his son's lips. "Make you sweat. Much sweat."

Both men had a sweat in that deep hole. When Moves-No-More was pulled out, he felt more pain than he had felt for many moons. For this the Si-kip-te-wat gave medicine. The pain left and he was able to rest.

The following day, To-ta and Moves-No-More repeated the same procedure.

When the sun rose the day after his second sweat, Moves-No-More was able to sit up! His heart was filled with joy.

"Look!" he told everyone. "I can move my arms! I can move my fingers! I feel better than I have for many moons. I am going to get well!"

The captains were pleased. All the So-yap-pos were pleased.

"You stay here with us. We will continue giving you these sweats. We think they will help you get entirely well," the white men told him.

Moves-No-More sat up almost all of that day, something he had not been able to do for a long, long time. He thought about many things—different things from what he had thought about while he lay flat on his back, snow after snow.

The next sun, Moves-No-More looked forward to another sweat, but the sky said it was going to rain. The So-yap-pos thought it was not a good time to give another sweat. But Moves-No-More was not discouraged. He washed his face all by himself. He knew he was going to get well. He could feel strength coming back into his arms and legs.

The weather permitted the So-yap-pos to build a hot fire in the sweat hole the following day. Moves-No-More was now strong enough to go into the hole by himself.

While he was inside making steam and drinking tea, they left him there for a long time. Much sweat poured from his body until he felt he could take no more.

"Enough! Enough!" he called. "Take me out!"

When he was out and properly cooled, he found that this time he could use one leg and thigh well and the other leg a little. All his toes were moving!

From that sun on, Moves-No-More made progress in using his limbs. He flexed the muscles of his arms and legs. He made fists and picked up pebbles and pine cones with his fingers to throw at any person or thing within his range. He lay on his back and waved his feet in the air. Leaning against a tree, he pulled himself up and tried to kick pine cones as far as he could. More strength came back to him with every sun that passed.

Although the So-yap-pos were busy preparing to cross the mountains to the Land-Toward-the-Rising-Sun, they kept their word to Moves-No-More. They gave him another violent sweat which left him feeling tired and drained out. He felt listless, but soon after he could move even better than before.

Two suns went by with no sweats. Moves-No-More exercised his body, trying to make every muscle work for him again. With all his efforts, his strength increased until he found that he could stand up alone! Standing alone on his feet was just the beginning of walking. Nothing could stop him now. With every tottery step he took, his strength grew, and his muscles began to function dependably.

At last he shouted in triumph, "I can walk! I can walk!"

He would now have a new name. Moves-No-More no longer fit a man who could move again. That is what he would be called—"Moves-Again!"[10]

As long as he lived, through all the other names he acquired, this man would never experience greater joy than when he became Moves-Again. Nor did he ever forget those kind So-yap-po men who had cured him with their "Good Medicine."

CHAPTER 16

MOON OF AH-PAH-AHL

IN THE VILLAGES OF THE KOOS-KOOS-KEE VALLEY, THE Nee-mee-poo read signs of nature. These signs told them what the weather would be, when it was time to dig, when the fish would come upstream, and when to start on their annual migration to the high prairies for camas digging.

When the warm suns came with rain, they said, "Now plants give plenty food in the valley."

This was the Moon of Ah-pah-ahl, the season for the digging of kouse roots and the making of ah-pah, kouse bread.

When the yellow umbels of kouse and tsa-wit appeared on the hillsides, they said, "We must go up higher for digging."

When masses of blue camas lilies shimmered in the distance like mountain lakes, the Nee-mee-poo said, "Much camas for winter."

After many nights and days of rain, there were twenty-one warm suns.[1] The deep snowdrifts in the mountains began to melt. Clear, icy water raced down the ancient scratches of Itsi-yai-yai's claws to fill and overflow the river's banks. Blackbirds sang in the swamps, and blue cranes' babies came out of their shells to show that bitter weather was gone. Swarms of gnats, flies, and mosquitos chewed on the necks of deer, thickening the deer's hide to make good moccasins.[2] The raven's cry from the top of a tall tree warned of movement below—maybe deer, maybe bear, maybe man.[3]

May 18, 1806

"... early this morning the natives erected a lodge on the opposite side of the river near a fishing stand a little above us. no doubt to be in readiness for the salmon, the arrival of which they are so ardently wishing as well as Ourselves. . . ." Lewis [Thwaites, Volume 5, Pages 46 and 47.]

Knowing that salmon would soon be coming upstream, the men in Broken Arm's village watched for the fish from a stand they had built out into the river. Made of small poles, the stand jutted ten feet into the water and three feet above the surface, allowing a man to dip his net as close to the salmon run as possible. Grandfathers of long ago had passed on their knowledge that the first salmon swam upstream in the middle of the river, not near the banks.[4]

In the evenings as they smoked, the men of Broken Arm's village gathered with their chief to talk and plan where and how they would start fishing. Everyone had a chance to give his opinion. Fish Hawk, a notable fisherman of the village, settled his mind.

"I will set up a lodge down by fishing stand," he said. "Will use it for shelter while watching for fish. Salmon will come soon."

"I will help," spoke up one who would rather fish than do anything else.

"I will also help," said another.

So the three set up a lodge across the river from the white men's camp, and Fish Hawk took his dip-net to the end of the platform to try his luck. Time after time, he plunged the net into the water, just to pull it out empty.

"The salmon are not here yet," the men reported when they returned to their village before dark. "Just have to wait."

A feeling of eagerness grew in every village, lodge, and camp in the valley. Men wanted to fish, but the big salmon run had not yet come. Women wanted to dig many bags of roots, but it was still too early to move to the prairies above. But they did not fret. The People did what they had to do. They knew how to wait.

However, the So-yap-pos did not wait with patience. They wanted to be on the way to their homeland, but the snow-roofed mountains barred their crossing. They watched for every sign of the snow's melting. Every morning and every evening they measured the rise and fall of the river.[5] Sometimes the river dropped; sometimes it rose, according to the amount of snowmelt of the day. When the river dropped into its channel and did not rise again, it would give the message, "It is now possible to cross the mountains."

The So-yap-pos' spirits fell when the water rose, and rose when the river fell, for that meant the snow was almost gone.

They asked every man who visited their camp, "Now is it safe to start over the mountains?"

And always they heard the same words, "Wait for the next full moon. Before then, horses will have no food for three suns on top of those high mountains."[6]

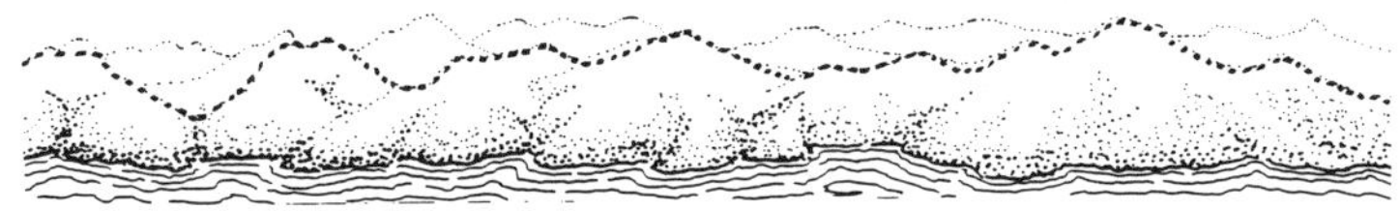

May 21, 1806

". . . we would make the men collect these roots themselves but there are several specels of hemlock which are so much like the cows that it is difficult to discriminate them from the cows and we are affraid that they might poison themselves. . . ." Lewis [Thwaites, Volume 5, Pages 52 and 53.]

Although the search for food was the first concern of all, life held more variety than it had during the snow moons. Every sun brought something new to do or see or talk about.

Every sun, like ants leaving their hill, the So-yap-pos spread out from their camp in all directions. Always ten or eleven men rode out to hunt in the hills or plains above. Even when it rained, they hunted. Others went to the villages across the river or farther upstream to trade their curiosities for roots and root-bread. Their chiefs had instructed them not to dig their own roots, for they did not know good roots from poisonous ones.

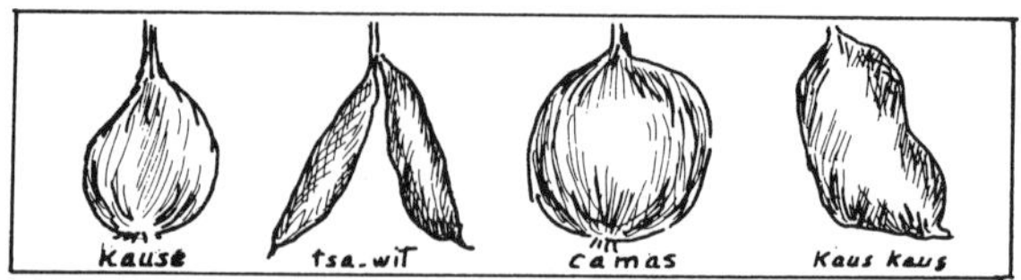

May 21, 1806

"... we set 5 men at work to build a canoe for the purpose of takeing fish and passing the river and for which we can get a good horse. . . ." Clark [Thwaites, Volume 5, Page 53.]

Whenever the So-yap-pos wanted to trade at a village, they had to borrow a small canoe, which was not always available, or swim their horses across the swollen stream. Sometimes the rise of the water forced them to stay on their own side of the river, which meant they had to travel farther to trade. Finally, an idea came to them. They talked it over with their daily visitors.

"We want to make canoe," they said. "Will carry big loads. When we leave for the Land-Toward-the-Rising-Sun, what will you give for canoe?"

"You leave canoe. Taats!" came the response. "We give one good horse."

That bargain, along with fair weather, set the men

to working in good spirits. When five suns had passed, they had finished the canoe and slid it into the river. It was a good canoe, big enough to carry twelve people, and it rode well in the water.

To the Nee-mee-poo, this canoe would be a prize.

Every day of sunshine advanced the season for digging roots. The able women were drawn to the hillsides where the plants now yielded roots of useful size. Those women who remained in the lodges made the ah-pah, kouse bread, and smoked what fish their men happened to catch. Always, moccasins had to be made. Even undecorated, everyday moccasins took a long time to sew.

May 24, 1806

". . . 4 of our party pased the river and visited the lodge of the broken Arm for the purpose of traiding some awls which they had made of the links of [a] small chain belonging to one of their steel traps, for some roots. . . ." Lewis [Thwaites, Volume 5, Pages 61 and 62.]

No one in Broken Arm's village was surprised when four So-yap-pos appeared with trade goods. Those men had come often to trade for food. This time the So-yap-pos brought sharp metal awls to make leather work easier. Women who made many moccasins gladly exchanged roots and root-bread for these labor-saving tools. When the men left at sundown, they took a big load of provisions. The bargaining had pleased everyone.

Upstream from Broken Arm's village, only eight people were present in the lodge when the So-yap-po, Goodrich, came to bargain for roots.

"People gone," they told him. "Some dig roots, some hunt, some fish in Ki-moo-e-nim River. Get fine salmon there."

They showed him the fat salmon, now drying, which had come from that fishing place. But they had little to trade him. He left with a light load.

The So-yap-po traders ranged farther and farther from their camp with their meager supply of buttons and awls, hoping to exchange them for roots and root-bread. Their visits, as well as their trade goods, seemed to add prestige to any village they visited. When Red Grizzly Bear led the two So-yap-pos, who were brothers, to a small village hidden in a canyon, their appearance caused a stir among the women, for they had not seen the So-yap-pos before. As the women lived near good digging grounds, they had an abundance of roots on hand that they generously offered in trade for the white men's trinkets.

"These things will show that So-yap-pos have visited us," the women said. "We are as important as anybody in Broken Arm's village. They can't lord it over us now."

On the next sun, more So-yap-pos visited this same village. Five men came early, obtained roots, and left. Then came the big, black man and two men who talked well with their hands. They did not rush with their trading but sat and talked. Darkness came. Still, they bargained. They slept in the village that night, but left after daybreak with four bags of roots and root-bread.

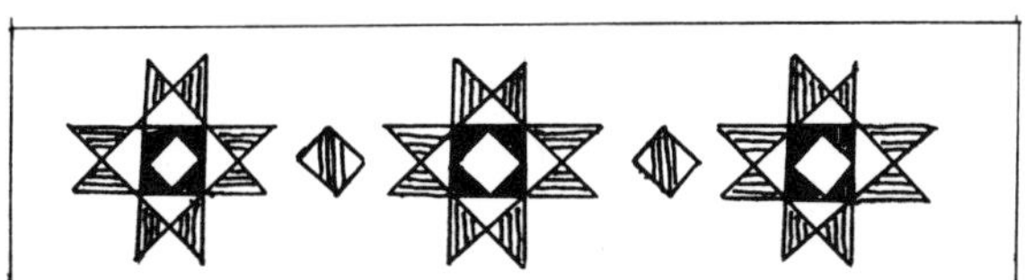

May 27, 1806

"the dove is cooing which is the signal as the indians inform us of the approach of the salmon. . . ." [Thwaites, Volume 6, Page 217.]

"Salmon coming! Salmon coming!"

This message from the dove set men to watching the river every day. Salmon still had not arrived in any great numbers, but, in time, the Koos-koos-kee would teem with salmon, and nobody would have to go to the fishery on the Ki-moo-e-nim.

The voice of the dove and the sight of those fat salmon drying in Broken Arm's village whetted the appetites of the So-yap-pos. They did not want to wait for the big salmon run. They wanted fish to eat now.

When Fish Hawk visited the So-yap-pos' camp, they asked him many questions. "How far is it to this fishing place? How long does it take to get there? In what direction is it?"

Fish Hawk said, "I, myself, will guide you to fishing place." Pointing to the southwest, he continued, "We ride up to prairie. Go that way for one-half sun to Ta-ma-nam-mah River."

Fish Hawk's friends said, "Kiyu'!"

"Good!" said the white chiefs. They gave orders to their men: "Sergeant Ordway, take Frazier and Wiser and go with Fish Hawk and his friends to Lewis's River

[Salmon River] for a supply of fish. Try to get back by tomorrow."

The men rode up Kamiah Creek to the prairie, stopping at Twisted Hair's root-digging camp to trade for a supply of roots. Determining they would be coming back the same route, Frazier asked Twisted Hair to keep the roots they had bargained for until their return trip. Twisted Hair agreed, looking forward to any visit he might have with the So-yap-pos.

When the sun was overhead, the group reached the breaks of the great river that tumbled far below. The sun had set by the time they had zig-zagged down the long, tortuous trail to the bottom of the canyon.

The Ta-ma-nam-mah River was at flood stage—rushing, churning, leaping to escape the granite walls that squeezed it into a boiling, foaming torrent. When the time was right, fishing was good here, but not now. Salmon had not yet arrived.

"Next sun we go to Ki-moo-e-nim fishery," Fish Hawk said. "Farther, but plenty of fish."

Next sun, the men worked their way down the canyon past the meeting of the Ta-ma-nam-mah and the Ki-moo-e-nim Rivers to the churning rapids that blocked the free migration of salmon upstream.[7] Here, along the narrow bank of the river, generations of fishing people had lived in a house built of split timber.

This house had been constructed a little at a time, for the timber had to come from afar. No big trees grew here. Whenever men could gather driftwood or snag a tree floating down in flood water, they used their stone axes and elk-horn wedges to split off slabs of wood for their house. Any other timbers had to be rafted or towed to this place where the flat-roofed house now stood, thirty-five feet wide and one hundred fifty feet long. Similar houses could be seen far downriver.

People often came and went here. While the men fished, the women gathered roots on the hillside and prepared the fish for drying and smoking. Whenever newcomers arrived, trading took place first, and then the new arrivals would join in the fishing and root-gathering.

When the three So-yap-pos, Ordway, Frazier, and Wiser, arrived with Fish Hawk and his friends after sundown, they wanted to trade with these people for salmon.

"Why don't they catch their own fish?" the fishermen asked. "Plenty of fish in river. Why not fish for themselves like other men do?"

Their fish meant winter food for the Nee-mee-poo, but the fishermen were curious about the goods the So-yap-pos had brought to trade for fish. They wondered what good could come with trading off the hard-caught salmon. Had the So-yap-pos brought a better way of getting food? The People thought about these things during the night.

When morning came, the white men brought out their curiosities for trading. Plainly seen in the daylight, these items became more desirable. One man had a sharp metal blade that folded out of sight between two pieces of wood. He showed how it could cut hair from his face.

"If it can do that, it will cut hides and leather. That sharp cutter will be more useful than these two shining coins I took from around the neck of the Snake I killed in our last battle," Two Crows thought to himself.

He took from his own neck two Spanish gold dollars and offered them in exchange for the white man's razor.

The So-yap-po accepted. Now Two Crows could cut many holes in his war shirt with this sharp tool. He felt fortunate to make such a bargain.[8]

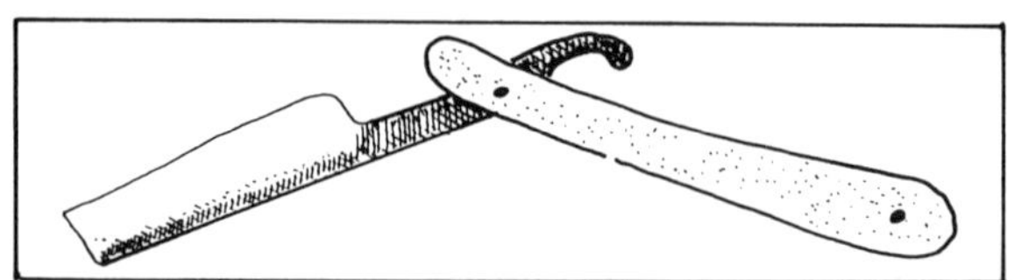

Bargain by bargain, throughout the day, the So-yap-pos at last had gathered enough fish to take back. By that time, the sun was down. They knew they would have to spend another night and start their return trip soon after daybreak.

Climbing up from the river to the rolling country high above took most of that new day. The trail, made slippery by recent rain, was steep and narrow. Men and horses alike welcomed solid footing when they reached the top.

Seven suns had come since the So-yap-pos, Ordway, Frazier, and Wiser, were led into the canyons of the Ta-ma-nam-mah and Ki-moo-e-nim. Never before had white men seen the meeting of these two WILD RIVERS, and no white man has since described the canyons with better words than they later told to the So-yap-po chiefs: “One continued rapid about one hundred and fifty yards wide, and its banks are in most places solid and perpendicular rocks which rise to a great height. Its hills are mountains high.”

As they made their way over the prairie the following sun, they were able to obtain roots from several kouse-digging groups they met. Their pack horses carried into the So-yap-po camp these roots and seventeen fat fish. Some of the fish had begun to bloat with the heat; but many were still good and so fat they were fried without extra grease for the white men’s supper.

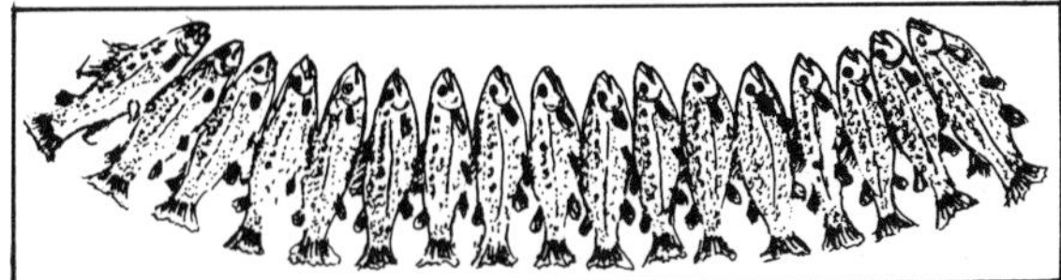

When the Broken Arm women saw the trader, Goodrich, coming into the village with his bundle of buttons and awls, they said, "Here comes that So-yap-po wanting to trade for kouse and kouse bread. Wonder if he has anything new to offer?"

Goodrich had very few articles for trading and nothing new. Although he did want roots and root-bread, that was not all he desired. He asked for goat hair to make pads for the So-yap-pos' saddles.

One after another, the women traded with him, giving him the food and goat hair he had requested. No family had a big supply of goat hair, but the several small bundles they offered filled his pack when he left that evening.

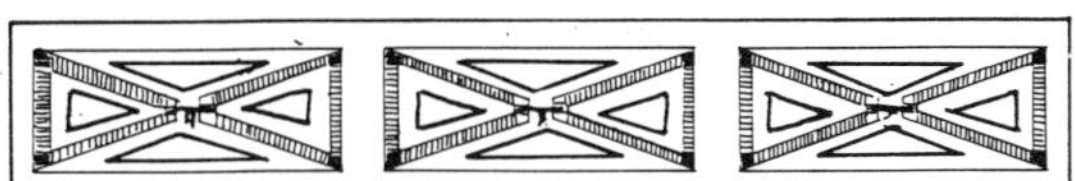

Evening shadows fell. Broken Arm and his men smoked and discussed the events of the sun just passed. While they considered what to do the next sun, one, who had just returned from visiting the So-yap-pos' camp, spoke up.

"So-yap-pos sank new big canoe," he said. "Three of them crossed river in it, swimming horses behind. On this side canoe slammed against tree standing in water, tipped over, sank. Spilled blankets, coats, trade goods into river. All floated downstream. Men and horses swam ashore. One So-yap-po had bad time, but got out.

So-yap-po chiefs sent men over in our small canoe to raise big canoe. No luck. Water too deep. Current too strong."

The men thought about this in silence while they smoked. They had hoped to make much use of this canoe when the white men left. Carrying twelve people, it would have saved many trips back and forth. Now sunk! No use thinking about it now.

"When new sun comes," Broken Arm turned to other matters, "I hunt."

"A-a-a-a," the men joined in and each added, "Kiyu'!"

May 31, 1806

"The Indians pursued a mule deer to the river opposit to our Camp this evening; the deer swam over and one of our hunters killed it. . . ." Clark [Thwaites, Volume 5, Page 93.]

Maybe twenty-five, maybe thirty men rode out with Broken Arm this day to hunt. According to the Hunting Chief's instructions, they spread out over the hills in such a way that when a deer was sighted they could converge on him. Someone's arrow was sure to get him.

They rode all morning, seeing nothing. It began to look like they would have no luck. But when the sun started to drop, Broken Arm saw a form, high up on the mountain, moving into the shadows.

Soundlessly, the Hunting Chief gave the signals that passed from one rider to another, "Blacktail above! Work your way up and around him. Drive him down and all surround if possible." The men only had to know where the deer was. They knew what to do, once they sighted him.

Before the deer was aware of their presence, men on horses were above him, in front of him, and behind him. He had no where to go but downhill. Here he found riders who chased him on the steep hillside until he ran into more men who chased him farther downhill to the valley floor, straight toward the river. No yelling men, racing on horseback, blocked his way. The deer plunged into the water and swam to the other side, leaving all those men on their panting horses to watch the end of their chase. The deer had not known that other men were on the bank in front of him—men with deadly sticks that shot black sand with thunder.

Broken Arm and his hunters saw the So-yap-pos drag their deer up the bank and proceed to skin him out. They felt no hostility toward these white men for killing their game, only gratitude. They had learned long before that the So-yap-pos were fair-minded men who shared meat when they had it.

The hunters sat on their horses near the place where the big canoe had sunk the sun before. They could see it through the clear water, wedged in among half-submerged cottonwoods. Broken Arm looked at it a long time. He looked at all those strong men with him. So many men ought to be able to lift that canoe out of the water.

"I think we can get that canoe up," he said. "If every man gets in and lifts, we could save it."

The men tried. They waded into the water around the canoe and tried to lift it by prying, pushing, and pulling. But the force of the current in the deep, icy water held it fast. The men could not budge it.

"Canoe will keep," Broken Arm said. "River will drop. Canoe will still be here. On solid ground then. We can drag it out with horses and ropes. Just leave it."

On the same side of the river as Broken Arm's village, but a long way upstream, Raven-Flying-Over was mending his fishnet. He looked up to see two So-yap-pos leading a pack-horse along the ledge of the cliff that skirted the opposite bank of the river. A rock gave way as they passed. The pack-horse lost his footing and plunged down into the swirling water, but unhurt, he swam on across the river toward Raven-Flying-Over.

The two men, after reaching a safe place to stop, waved their arms, talked with their hands, and did enough yelling to let Raven-Flying-Over understand they wanted him to drive their pack-horse back to them. He caught the horse and sent him struggling once more through the water. The river current tugged at the pack and worked the lashings loose, sweeping away a fine dressed elk skin and dissolving the vermilion paint the men had brought along for trade.

Raven-Flying-Over watched, helpless to save what the river had taken, but, with an idea, he ran up to the lodge of his people.

"So-yap-pos come," he said. "I have heard they have strange things to offer in trade for roots and root-bread. Their pack horse fell off the cliff, lost some of pack in river. I will take roots and bread over on our raft. See what they have left for trade."

He grabbed a bag of roots and some rounds of bread and ran down to the raft.

"Kiyu'!" his brother, Gray Cloud, and cousin, Sleeping Wolf, said, running after him.

The raft was awkward to handle in the swift water; but without a canoe, they had no other way of transporting cargo over the stream. The men worked with poles to shove the raft through the swift current. Sometimes it seemed they made no progress, but, bit by bit, they moved toward the bank where the So-yap-pos were resting after their misadventure.

If Raven-Flying-Over had not looked up to see how close they were to the shore, they might have succeeded. But he did look up and he missed setting his pole where it should have gone to hold the raft away from a rock. The raft, turned by the current, swung into the big rock and flipped. The men clung to the raft, but the roots and bread floated on down the river.

What more could they do but work their empty raft back upstream to their village, empty-handed?

The hapless So-yap-pos turned their horses around and started back downriver. Dispirited at losing their trade goods, they brought nothing back except the story of their mishaps.

Up to the rolling plain that lies south of the canyon of the Koos-koos-kee middlefork,[9] Black Tail's family had gone for root-digging. Where they were now living, their eyes beheld the yellow flowers of kouse and tsa-wit and the blue of camas. The air they breathed carried the fragrance of roses and syringa to the women digging roots and the men hunting in the mountains. Their world was beautiful, and they should have been happy.

They would have been happy, except that Black Tail lay dying. He had been sick a long time, ever since winter. His family had done everything they knew to help him. He had been sweated in the sweat lodge and plunged into cold water. They had brewed cous-cous for him to drink, and he had chewed on cous-cous roots. Still, every sun saw him weaker; now he had no strength left. The Te-wat came and blew smoke, shook his rattles, and chanted. He did all he could, but Black Tail grew worse. It was plain to see that he was dying.

His family faced the fact and began to determine what should accompany him on his journey to the Spirit World. His long-legged black horse would go. And he would need his weapons. Those he prized above all others were the tomahawks that had belonged to the So-yap-pos. One was both tomahawk and pipe; the other was made of stone from far away. Black Tail had given two good horses for them to Swift-Moving-Hands. Swift-Moving-Hands had stolen the pipe-tomahawk from the belongings of the red-headed chief of the So-yap-pos at their Canoe Camp last fall. He had found the other, left behind at the So-yap-pos' camp on the Oyaip. Black Tail's family decided to send them with him to the Spirit World.

While the preparations for his journey to the Spirit World were taking place, Black Tail died.

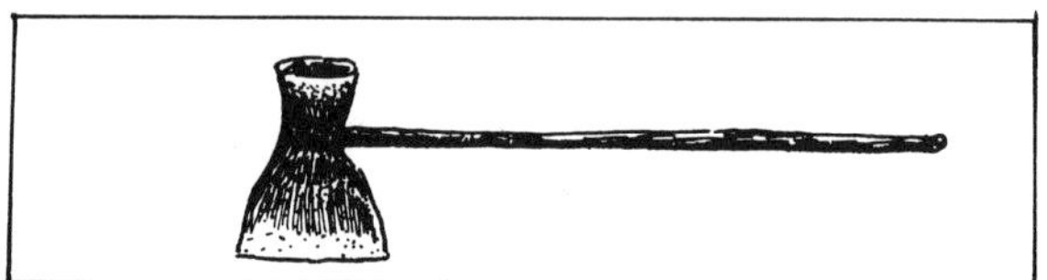

June 2, 1806

". . . his relations were unwilling to give up the tomehawk as they intended to bury it with the disceased owner, but were at length induced to do so for the consideration of a ha[n]dkerchief, two strands of beads, which Drewyer gave them and two horses given by the cheifs to be killed agreeably to their custom at the grave of the disceased. . . ." Lewis [Thwaites, Volume 5, Pages 98 and 99.]

Soon after Black Tail's family had laid out the tomahawks for burial, Cut Nose, Red Grizzly Bear, and the So-yap-pos' best sign-talker, Drewyer, arrived in the small village. The three visitors had the air of an important mission about them and made a request which upset the plans of Black Tail's family.

The So-yap-po motioned to two tomahawks that were laid out and said with his hands, "Those tomahawks belong to red-headed chief of So-yap-pos. He leaves soon. Wants tomahawks. You give me tomahawks. I give you two strands of beads and this 'kerchief."

"Tomahawks belong to Black Tail," said his son. "He paid two horses to Swift-Moving-Hands for them. When Black Tail is in Spirit World, tomahawks go with him."

Cut Nose, remembering the comfort he had received when twenty-eight horses had been slaughtered for his wife's burial, offered, "You give tomahawks to So-yap-po. I give you one horse to go on Black Tail's grave."

"Black Tail will need many horses on his way to the Spirit World. He will need horses more than tomahawks," said Red Grizzly Bear.

Red Grizzly Bear sensed a change of thought coming over the family. He added, "I, too, will give one horse to sacrifice."

A long silence fell while the family thought about this. The son finally spoke for them all, "A-a-a-a. We give tomahawks back to white man. You give two horses for Black Tail's grave. My father will have plenty horses in the Spirit World."

Black Tail's son extended his hand to receive the beads and handkerchief from Drewyer and handed the two tomahawks over. The So-yap-po was satisfied. After Black Tail's family received the two horses Cut Nose and Red Grizzly Bear had promised, they, too, would be satisfied.

June 3, 1806

"... at 3 P. M. the broken arm and three wariors visited us and remained all night. . . . To day the Indians dispatched an express over the mountains to Travellers rest or to the neighbourhood of that creek on Clark's river in order to learn from a band of Flat-Heads who inhabit that river and who have probably wintered on Clarks river near the enterance of travellers rest Creek, the occurences which have taken place on the East side of the mountains dureing the last winter. . . ." Clark [Thwaites, Volume 5, Page 104.]

Broken Arm's village had visitors. Rainbow, White Antelope, and Spotted Horse rode in from their small villages upstream. They came to discuss the Ka-oo-yit, the annual spring meeting and root feast that would soon be held on the prairie above. People from all the Nee-mee-poo villages would meet there to celebrate the end of COLD and the coming of WARM, the abundance of fresh roots to eat, and the joy of renewed friendships—the time of Lawtiwa-mah-ton.

"We have important matters to discuss in council," Broken Arm told them. "The So-yap-pos have given us new ideas to think about. They will soon be leaving across the mountains. I, myself, am going across river to their camp for a visit just now."

"Kiyu'!" said Rainbow.

"Kiyu'!" said White Antelope and Spotted Horse.

When they arrived across the river, the So-yap-po chiefs welcomed them with the invitation to sit and smoke. The pipe passed from one man to another in silence. The visitors did not talk, but their eyes missed nothing.

There was Moves-Again, moving his arms and legs and laughing with joy. There was that So-yap-po, Bratton, walking, after being too weak to move. Bird Woman's little boy, Ba-teese, was toddling about when someone was not carrying him. The So-yap-pos' strong medicine had restored health to all three. These So-yap-pos had brought good with them.

Other men of the Nee-mee-poo who were in the So-yap-po camp joined in the smoke.

"Looks like the river is beginning to drop," Yellow Dog commented. "Wonder how much snow is left on mountain tops? Wonder how our friends, the Shalees,[10] made it through the winter?"

"Maybe somebody better go find out. Two men with strong horses could travel light. Get over trail fast. Find out if all is well on other side of mountains," Two-Times-Shot said.

"A-a-a-a-a-a," all the men agreed and looked to see who would undertake this mission.

"I will go," said Looks-Ahead. "I have good, strong horses. Plenty food. I know the trail. Can travel fast. Will see if my cousins among Shalees are all right."

"Kiyu'!" said Follows-the-Trail. "I have good horses. I know the way."

"A-a-a-a! Go. Bring back news of the Shalees," said Broken Arm.

With those words, Looks-Ahead and Follows-the-Trail gathered up their provisions. The two men took only the bare necessities: root-bread for food, buffalo robes for their saddles and for warmth, and four strong, sure-footed horses to carry them over the treacherous, snow-packed trail as fast as possible. The two set out on their mission.

As the So-yap-pos watched the departure of Looks-Ahead and Follows-the-Trail, they realized these men were planning to cross the mountains.

The men had scarcely passed from sight before the So-yap-pos began asking the same questions they had asked many times before.

"Isn't it time that we could start over the mountains? If Looks-Ahead and Follows-the-Trail can go, why can't we?"

"It is not wise for you to go yet," Broken Arm said. "The messengers travel with no more than four strong horses. You have more than sixty. Many creeks to cross where horses must swim. Not enough grass growing now to feed sixty horses. Trail is steep and slippery. Wait twelve, maybe fourteen more suns. You will be able to cross then."

"A-a-a-a-a," agreed the other Nee-mee-poo who sat around.

They sat and smoked with the So-yap-po chiefs. The white men asked other questions they had asked before, "Will some of you come with us to the Missouri River? We will protect you, and we can help make peace with the tribes there."

And the answer was the same as it had been before, "No one will go at this time. Later in the summer some of us plan to go over and spend the winter in Buffalo Country."

Then Captain Lewis spoke, "Send two or three of your young men with me as far as the Great Falls. They can wait for me there until I return from exploring up Marias River. I will try to bring about good understanding between them and any Big Bellies I meet. The young men will return to you with word of the intentions of the Big Bellies, whether peaceful or warlike. You will then know what to expect. You will know if you will have to keep on guard against them until the white men can come and build forts to protect you."

Broken Arm answered, "We will select young men when we have big council. My people are preparing to move up to plain above for Spring Festival, the Ka-oo-yit. My people will soon be gone." He continued, "We will discuss the matter there. If the red-headed chief will visit my village, I have good gifts for him."

"On the sun after the next sun, I shall cross the river for a last visit with you," Captain Clark promised.

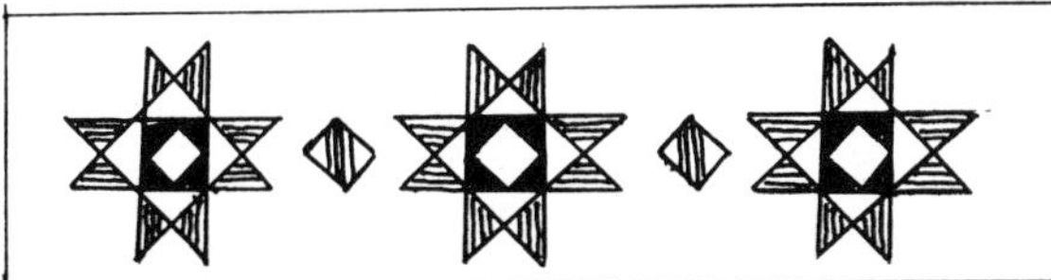

Ever since he had promised at the Kamiah Council to move his camp across the river near the camp of the So-yap-pos, Twisted Hair had had cause to reconsider that idea. Mostly, he had heard strong objections from the women.

"We don't want to move across the river to that place," they told him. "There is not enough good root-digging there. Down in the valley the season will soon be gone. We are already here where digging is good. We want to have big supply of roots when snow flies. We don't want to go."

Twisted Hair had seen the good judgment behind their arguments. He would not disrupt the pattern of his women's work. If he was to have food to eat when winter came, the women would have to gather roots now, whenever, wherever they could.

As soon as the So-yap-pos recovered their six horses at their present campsite, Twisted Hair had received his two guns. He had what he wanted. What could be gained now by turning away from the traditional root-gathering patterns? He settled his mind to let the women dig where they wanted. He would not move his people close to the So-yap-pos' camp as the white men had requested.

June 5, 1806

"... Frazier who had permission to visit the Twisted Hairs Lodge at the distance of ten or twelve miles did not return this evening. . . ." Clark [Thwaites, Volume 5, Page 110.]

Twisted Hair was glad enough to see the So-yap-po, Frazier, return for the packet of roots and bread he had left ten suns before when on his way to the fishery. From him, Twisted Hair learned that the So-yap-pos were getting ready to leave the valley and start over the mountains to Buffalo Country and beyond.

"Night lays a blanket of darkness for sleep," Twisted Hair said. "Next sun, I will go with you to So-yap-po camp."

True to his word, Twisted Hair was ready to set out for the river soon after daybreak. Two of his sons, Joyous Heart and Ya'amas Wakus, and the So-yap-po, Frazier, went along with him.

They reached the river bank opposite the So-yap-pos' camp just as Captain Clark, Drewyer, and three other men were tying up their canoe.

Hands sent the greeting, "I am glad to see you."

"Cross the river to our camp," Captain Clark said, indicating the canoe that had brought his party over. "Captain Lewis will be there to greet you. He will be happy to see you. I am now going to visit Broken Arm as I promised him."

Twisted Hair looked at the river, high over its banks, racing and boiling and carrying driftwood. Crossing in the canoe at this stage would be dangerous, but better than swimming over on horseback. The men tied their horses to cottonwood trees and pushed off in the canoe. Skillfully, they dodged the floating debris and reached the opposite bank without mishap.

June 6, 1806

"I visited the Broken Arm to day agreeable to my promis of the 4th. inst and took with me Drewyer & three other men I was receved in a friendly manner. . . ." Clark [Thwaites, Volume 5, Page 112.]

Several chiefs of small bands who had ridden into Broken Arm's village that day inquired about the So-yap-pos.

"We have heard they want all tribes to live in peace," they said. "That sounds good, but how will it work? We want to hear that message from the white men, themselves."

"You can hear for yourselves," Broken Arm told them. "The Red-Head will visit here this sun."

When Captain Clark rode into the village with his men, the Broken Arm greeted him warmly. Their hands said, "I am glad to see you."

The visiting Nee-mee-poo chiefs then asked him for the message about living at peace with their neighbors. Every word the red-haired chief spoke about not fighting and killing they kept in their hearts.

While the men smoked, they talked of matters they had previously discussed regarding Nee-mee-poo guides crossing the mountains to the Missouri Falls.

"The Nee-mee-poo will not cross the mountains at this time. Later in the summer some of our people may go over into Buffalo Country, maybe spend the winter there," Broken Arm said. "We cannot send any young men to accompany you to the Great Falls just now. The council will select them—ten, maybe twelve, suns from now. All the lodges are preparing to move up to head of Kamiah Creek for Ka-oo-yit. Will hold council then and select young men. If you leave before then, the young men will follow and catch up with you."

It seemed to be the final answer to the So-yap-pos' request.

As a token of his sincerity, Broken Arm took up a hemp bag filled with roasted camas and presented it to Captain Clark, signifying his generosity with hands that said he had a big heart and did not expect a reward or something in return.

Then, pointing to the southwest, Broken Arm spoke

again, "Word has come through visiting Wai-i-let-pos [Cayuses] that a party of Snakes came to the trading place in the valley of winding waters.[11] The Snakes told the Cayuses that they had heard the So-yap-pos' message from Cameahwaite's band last fall. The Snakes said they want to follow advice of the white men. They want to make peace with Cayuses, Walla Walla, and Chopunnish."

Broken Arm continued, "There in that valley all people will be able to come together in peace. Cayuse, Umatilla, Walla Walla, and Chopunnish will meet Snakes without fighting. The flag you gave the Cayuses will fly over the trading place in that valley—a sign of lasting peace.

"When these Snakes can be found and brought to the Ki-moo-e-nim River, we will meet with them and smoke pipe of peace. Will send some chiefs from my people to go with these Snakes and take peace pipe to their nation. Will make peace that will never be broken."

Broken Arm then brought out two peace pipes—a plain one and an unusual one of stone inlaid with silver. The ornate pipe had come from the Snakes.

"One is gift to you and one will be sent to the Snakes," he said. "Take one."

Captain Clark chose the ordinary-looking pipe for himself. He took the other pipe into his hands and fastened blue ribbon and white wampum to its stem before he handed it back to Broken Arm.

"This pipe will be the emblem of peace between us," he said.

Evening shadows were growing long. The talk ended. Gifts had been presented. The last handshake had been given. The Red-Head summoned his men who had bargained for a good store of roots and bread. With a sufficient supply to add to those they already had for their journey, the So-yap-pos set off toward their camp beyond the river.

June 6, 1806

". . . The Twisted hair came with him but I was unable to converse with him for the want of an interpreter, Drewyer being absent with Capt. C. . . ." Lewis [Thwaites, Volume 5, Page 110.]

The So-yap-po chief, Lewis, gave Twisted Hair the sign, "I am glad to see you," and clasped his hands in the white man's way of greeting, but he did not seem to understand Twisted Hair's hand-talk. The two men could not communicate with signs. Neither one could understand the other and no one else in camp could interpret for them. The best sign-talker, Drewyer, had gone to Broken Arm's village with Clark.

All through the sweltering afternoon Twisted Hair and his sons rested and visited with Moves-Again, who was fast regaining his strength.

When the sun dropped behind the rim of the valley, Twisted Hair and his sons, Joyous Heart and Ya'amas Wakus, decided to return to their own home camp on the cooler prairie. Again they took the canoe back to the opposite side, where they tied it up and mounted their horses for their trip home. They did not go far when they met Clark and his men returning from Broken Arm's village. This group of So-yap-pos could communicate, and they began to ask questions.

"We will soon be starting over the mountains. Will need some guides," Captain Clark said. "Will you or your sons be able to go with us? We have found your sons to be dependable. They would be good guides."

"We will be unable to go across the mountains with you at this time," Twisted Hair answered. "It is not good time for us to leave. My brother is sick, bad sick. My heart is heavy."

Twisted Hair's brother sick? Te-toh-kan Ahs-kahp? How sick? Did he have bad cough? Did he spit blood? Did he burn with fever? The So-yap-pos would never know the answers.

The men parted and went their different ways.

CHAPTER 17

BREAKING CAMP

Although their villages were in an upheaval as The People prepared to leave for the summer, the chiefs, Broken Arm, Red Grizzly Bear, and Cut Nose, and the men from their villages slipped away from the loud voices of women, whenever they could, to spend more entertaining visits with the So-yap-pos.

June 7, 1806

"The two young Cheifs who visited [us] last evening returned to their village on Commeap C. with some others of the natives. Sergt. Gass, McNeal, Whitehouse and Goodrich accompanyed them with a view to procure some pack or lash ropes in exchange for parts of an old sain [seine], fish giggs, peices of old iron, . . . they were also directed to procure some bags for the purpose of containing our roots & bread. . . ." Lewis [Thwaites, Volume 5, Page 114.]

Speaking Eagle and Black Eagle had stayed all night at the So-yap-pos' camp. They had watched the So-yap-pos trying to pack up their possessions without having enough bags or strings and ropes to lash the baggage on their horses' backs. The problem was enough to make a man scratch his head in bewilderment, but the white men had determination born of necessity.

Each man searched for scraps of unneeded articles which could be exchanged for the bags and strings they needed. Bits of old fish net, some fish gigs, and pieces of old iron, old iron files, and a few bullets were all they could collect. The So-yap-pos, Gass, McNeal, Whitehouse, and Goodrich, took the odd collection along for trade when they crossed the river with Speaking Eagle and Black Eagle who were returning to Broken Arm's village.

It was not a good time to trade for packing materials. The women would not part with their bags, strings, and ropes. They needed them for their own packing; besides, the So-yap-pos offered nothing of any use at this time. Sergeant Gass and McNeal realized they were getting nowhere and decided to return to their camp where they could be of more use. Whitehouse and Goodrich stayed all night and managed to obtain a few strings, but no woman wanted to part with a precious bag made of beargrass twined with hemp.

While the small group of So-yap-pos was bargaining, Red Grizzly Bear had crossed the river to the So-yap-pos' camp. Leading a fine horse, he rode slowly around until his eye lighted on Frazier.

"I am glad to see you," his hands said.

He dismounted and ceremoniously presented the horse to Frazier, saying, "Red Grizzly Bear is grateful for moccasin boots you made him. Let this horse go with you."

To signify that he wanted nothing in return, Red Grizzly Bear held his right hand, with the back down, in front of his right breast and moved his hand in a sharp cutting motion to the left several times. Then he raised his right hand with the back to the right, his extended fingers touching. Pointing upward, he moved his hand outwards and downwards to signify "gift."[1]

Frazier was not expecting this fine gift. He was pleased.

June 8, 1806

". . . The Cutnose visited us today with ten or twelve warriors; two of the latter were Y-e-let-pos [Willetpos] a band of the Chopunnish nation residing on the South side of Lewis's river whom we have not previously seen." Lewis [Thwaites, Volume 5, Page 117.]

Cut Nose, who had camped nearby ever since he had come into the Kamiah Valley with the So-yap-pos, also decided to join Red Grizzly Bear and see the So-yap-pos for a final visit. With him came a group of his men and two visitors from the Cayuse band. They had brought good horses with them.

The sight of such fine animals aroused the So-yap-pos' interest. They milled around among the horses, feeling of feet, legs, backs, and found them sound. Then they brought up some of their own horses with sore backs.

"Trade?" their hands asked. "This tomahawk goes with this horse."

"Taats!" said one Cayuse, and he exchanged his good horse for the one with a sore back. "Sore back will heal."

The So-yap-pos continued dickering until they had traded off, straight across, two more sore-backed horses for two good horses with sound backs. The trade was satisfactory to every man involved.

June 8, 1806

". . . in the evening several foot races were run by the men of our party and the Indians; after which our party devided and played at prisoners base untill night. after dark the fiddle was played and the party amused themselves in danceing. . . ." Clark [Thwaites, Volume 5, Page 118.]

When evening shadows began to fall, the exuberant white men challenged each other and their visitors to foot races. Their hunters, Drewyer and Reuben Fields, who spent most of their waking time tramping up hill and down after game, were the swiftest runners among the So-yap-pos. The other men whose main duties were in camp had less speed and stamina; but all were urged to race for the exercise.

Sun-Going-Down had never seen the white men run, had never raced against them. Now, with his friends and cousins, he stood among them. Altogether, a group of more than forty men stood about, intent on proving who was swiftest.

For a while Sun-Going-Down watched small groups of men race. In his heart he felt he could do better than any of them. Was he not the fastest runner in all the summer races on the Oyaip? Could he not outrun a swift horse for a short distance?

When the speedier runners were set to run against each other, Sun-Going-Down slipped into the line without saying a word. At the signal, he was flying ahead, hair floating on the breeze, showing the heels of his moccasins to those who followed.

The last race found Sun-Going-Down lined up with long-legged Drewyer and wiry Reuben Fields. By now he knew he would have to run faster than he had ever run before if he were to beat them.

So fast were these three men that they left the others far behind, and so equal were their strength and speed that not one was more than the width of a hand ahead or behind the others at the finish.

After the runners had regained their breath, Captain Lewis said, "You men need more exercise. Now for Prisoner's Base." Pointing to one of the Field brothers, he said, "Joe, you choose men for one side."

To Joe's brother, Reuben, he said, "Choose for the other side."

"Yes, sir!"

"Yes, sir!"

Joe Fields scratched a long line in the dirt, and about sixty feet from that, Reuben Fields scratched another long line. First one, then the other, chose a man to stand behind his line, until half the men stood behind one line and half behind the other. Potts ran out into the center, daring someone from the other side to catch him. When he saw Shannon coming, he turned and ran as fast as he could toward his base. He did not get there. Shannon touched him, and Potts then had to go to Shannon's side where he stood in a little pen scratched out in the dirt. Goodrich darted after Shannon, but Shannon escaped to his line. Frazier dashed after Goodrich and caught him, sending him to the pen with Potts.[2]

In this way the game went, back and forth, back and forth, until every man on one side had been captured and put in the "prisoners' pen."

By the time the game ended, the visiting spectators had begun to understand the point of all the running. Maybe they would try to play that game among themselves some day.

When darkness came, the So-yap-pos continued their hilarity, even though they were tired from running.

"Play your fiddle, Cruzatte," Captain Clark said. "Let's have some music and dance."

Clouds had come in, blocking out any light from moon or stars, but a fire shed a warm glow around the circle of spectators who watched the men dancing to the fiddle music. Different from war dances of The People, these men made their legs go fast in fancy steps while their friends clapped and sang.

The black man, York, was most fun to watch. Even in the firelight, it was hard to separate him from the shadows. He seemed only a black blur in the night until the whites of his eyes flashed in the flickering firelight.

Whenever he laughed, his teeth gleamed white against his dark skin and revealed his whereabouts. When he danced, it was not like any white man's dancing and far different from the wildest war dance. His arms and legs flailed out in every direction, and his feet moved lightning-fast in a rhythm no young warrior could begin to imitate.

"Yankee Doodle, keep it up!
Yankee Doodle Dandy!
Mind the music and the step,
And with the girls be handy."

The So-yap-pos bellowed the song, laughing and clapping for the dancers.

When they could dance no more, the men went to their sleep, exhausted and happy. But the spirits of Captains Lewis and Clark had been dampened by Red Grizzly Bear's words who again warned: "You cannot cross the mountains until next full moon. You will not find horse feed on top of those mountains. Better wait."

June 9, 1806

". . . the river has been falling for several days and is now lower by near six feet than it has been; this we view as a strong evidence that the great body of snow has left the mountains, though I do not conceive that we are as yet loosing any time as the roads is in many parts extreemly steep rocky and must be dangerous if wet and slippry; a few days will dry the roads and will also improve the grass." Lewis [Thwaites, Volume 5, Page 119.]

The So-yap-po chiefs listened to the words of Red Grizzly Bear; but it was almost as if those words had fallen on deaf ears. The So-yap-pos used their own judgment.

"Round up all the horses," they ordered the next morning. "See if you can trade any more with bad backs for sound ones."

That order meant just one thing to their men. They were going to start for home.

They sang while they shagged the horses into the corral and roped six with sore backs.

"Yankee Doodle went to town
Riding on a pony,
Stuck a feather in his cap
And called it macaroni . . ."

Red Grizzly Bear and his followers looked on, understanding that the white men wanted to trade for better horses, but there was nothing to interest them in the So-yap-pos' horses. Only one man decided to trade. He had plenty of horses. He knew there was nothing wrong with the white man's horse but a sore back. Just keep ill-fitting saddles and heavy packs off horses' backs—they would heal.

Red Grizzly Bear realized these friends were preparing to leave, regardless of what he had warned them about the conditions in the mountains. He also realized that his entire village was ready to move up to the headwaters of Kamiah Creek for the annual Ka-oo-yit, The Peoples' Spring Root Festival. He must go with his people.

Red Grizzly Bear could not tell these white men in words what they had meant to him. His simple signs could not express all his feelings of regret that the So-yap-pos were leaving. He stood silent as the two white chiefs offered their hands for one last handshake. Then, Red Grizzly Bear, pointing to his breast with his right thumb and giving his right hand a forward thrust upward, signed, "I go."[3] With that he set his face toward his village and the life of his people. Not once did he glance back at the friends he was leaving.

After Red Grizzly Bear and his men had gone, Broken Arm crossed the river for a final talk with the white men before leading his people to their place at the Ka-oo-yit.

These So-yap-pos had been good friends, had brought guns and tools, had healed many people. Now they were leaving, maybe never to return, but the message of living at peace with neighbors would remain. Broken Arm thought of these things as he received the captains' handshakes.

Cut Nose lingered in the So-yap-pos' camp. He had something important to do. Now was the time to rob that eagle's nest he had seen downriver. Before this, it had been too soon. If he put it off any longer, it would be too late. The nest would be empty.

It was a trip that would take a good horse if he was to return quickly with young eagles. Remembering a good horse that had gone to the white men in trade, he asked to ride him on this errand.

The eagle's children were just as he thought they would be: old enough to live without their mother's warmth at night, too young to fly. Their fluffy gray feathers would soon grow long enough to use in war dance costumes.

When the sun was at it highest point, Cut Nose returned. He had two half-grown eagles, subdued by leather hoods fastened over their eyes. He intended to keep them captive by tying thongs to their legs and pegging the thongs to the ground. He would feed the young eagles and when their tail feathers had grown out, he would pluck them. That was the easiest way of getting the Power their feathers would bring him.

Black Eagle, the young chief who had presented Lewis and Clark with the fine mare and colt at the Kamiah Council, rode into the So-yap-po camp with ten of his friends that evening. They all rode on good horses. Again, the sight of such fine animals fired the white men with the urge to trade. They, themselves, wanted to keep their best horses and trade off only the nondescript animals, but again they met with little success. When one of the So-yap-pos offered Black Eagle's friend a well-worn leather shirt and a low-spirited horse for a strong horse, the trade was made.

Black Eagle's friend took the shirt as a memento of the So-yap-pos' visit, and he took the spiritless ewe-necked horse in exchange for the strong-limbed, sure-footed animal he had ridden into camp. His new horse was not much good, but good enough.

Like the evening before, the So-yap-pos were in high spirits. They ran races and challenged the visiting Nee-mee-poo. They played Prisoner's Base. They sang and danced, but they went to bed earlier. When morning came, they were going to start HOMEWARD.

June 10, 1806

"This morning we arrose early and had our horses collected except one of Cruzatt's and one of Whitehouse's, which were not to be found; after a surch of some hours Cruzatt's horse was obtained and the indians promised to find the other and bring it to us at the quawmash flatts where we purpose encamping a few days. at 11 A. M. we set out with the party each man being well mounted and a light load on a second horse, beside which we have several supenemary horses in case of accedent or the want of provision, we therefore feel ourselves perfectly equiped for the mountain." Lewis [Thwaites, Volume 5, Page 120.]

Black Eagle and his party watched the train of sixty-six horses carry their white friends away on the dusty trail. At the foot of the steep hill that rose from the valley floor to the Oyaip Prairie above, they disappeared into a grove of pine, tamarack, and fir.

For a long time, Black Eagle sat on his horse, thinking and feeling all that these men had meant to him. He breathed deep breaths of dusty, warm air, heavy with the perfume of roses and honeysuckle. For the rest of his life, those smells would bring to him the memory of this day—when the So-yap-pos left the valley of the Koos-koos-kee.

When No Horns, one of Broken Arm's hunters, had ridden into the hills north of the river that morning, his mind was on getting meat for his family. They had eaten nothing but roots for many suns. He had thought he could kill some kind of game to satisfy the craving for meat, but he had found nothing. He was coming home empty-handed.

To his surprise, as he went around a bend in the trail, he met the whole party of So-yap-pos coming up the hill toward him. Single file they came, all those men and more than sixty horses.

As they drew near, No Horns threw out the sign, "I am glad to see you."

The red-haired chief threw back the same sign. Then his hands pointed to Whitehouse and said, "Whitehouse lost one horse. Have you seen him?"

No Horns looked at Whitehouse and the horse he was riding. He knew at once which horse was missing. He had roped that horse many times for Whitehouse.

He replied, "I have not seen horse. I will find him. Bring him to Oyaip."

The white men continued up the hill toward the prairie and No Horns went his way.

No Horns did not arrive at his village, for he met seven of his friends, bent on following the So-yap-pos to Oyaip.

"We camp with So-yap-pos," they told him. "Maybe have luck hunting. Maybe not. So-yap-pos—good hunters—always share meat. We will eat well."

No Horns listened to his stomach and joined his friends in their plans to get a good meal from the white men. They pressed their horses so hard up the steep hill that they overtook the party of So-yap-pos before they had reached the level prairie land.

That night they camped with the So-yap-pos. Though a So-yap-po hunter brought a deer into camp for the evening meal, the white men, for the first time, did not share their food. They wanted to save everything they could for provisions to get them over the mountains and home.

The So-yap-pos were hungry that night, too, for some of them ate ground squirrels for dinner.

June 11, 1806

"... five of the Indians also turned out and hunted untill noon, when they returned without having killed anything; ..." Lewis [Thwaites, Volume 5, Page 123.]

Soon after dawn, the So-yap-po hunters set out. Only two brought back game: one Yah-kah, black bear, and two bucks. Even then, they kept all that meat for themselves. No Horns and his friends were not that lucky. They had killed no game and came back to camp with nothing. Hungry, they looked expectantly at the So-yap-pos' meat, but it became clear that the meat was not to be shared. No Horns and his friends subdued their hunger with the root-bread they always carried with them. All that time they wondered why the white men did not keep the custom of sharing food with men who had none.

"Looks like So-yap-pos want to keep all that meat for going over the mountains," No Horns said. "We better go home. No luck here."

Just then one of the white men came over, leading a small sluggish horse. Pointing to No Horns' big black horse, his hands asked, "Trade?"

Without giving much thought to the bargain, No Horns' hand said "Yes."

The men exchanged horses.

The So-yap-po was pleased with the strong animal he now owned.

No Horns, disappointed that he had no meat to take home, released his pent-up feelings on his new mount. With a keen lash of his quirt, he moved the horse into an unaccustomed burst of speed and dashed after his friends.

June 12, 1806

"... an indian visited us this evening and Spent the night at our camp." Lewis [Thwaites, Volume 5, Page 131.]

Joyous Heart had not been able to visit with the So-yap-pos much after they returned from their winter camp. He had first met them on the trail to Oyaip last fall and guided the red-headed chief down to Twisted Hair's fishing camp. Now Joyous Heart heard that these men were headed back toward Oyaip, getting ready to cross the mountains to Buffalo Country.

Joyous Heart settled his mind to visit these men one more time while he could. Alone, he rode up from the river to the So-yap-pos' camp. He found them near the camas roasting pits where they had camped in the fall.

The pits were still there, waiting to be used later in the summer; but now they were hidden by camas blooming everywhere. All over the Oyaip, blue camas spread until the Prairie seemed like a vast lake. Joyous Heart rode through this expanse of blue until he reached the So-yap-pos' camp at the eastern edge.

It was now past sundown. Mosquitos swarmed in clouds over every living creature. The white men, in little clusters, squatted around small smudge fires, trying to drive off the tormenters.

As Joyous Heart rode up, the Red-Head greeted him. Between swats at mosquitos, his hands said, "I am glad to see you."

Joyous Heart felt the goodwill of these white men. He slipped off his horse and bent down beside friends in the smoke of a smudge fire.

June 12, 1806

"... The indian who visited us yesterday exchanged his horse for one of ours . . . and received a small ax and a knife to boot, . . . and set out immediately to his village, . . ." Lewis [Thwaites, Volume 5, Page 133.]

Captain Lewis led out one of his horses to show to Joyous Heart. The horse had not entirely healed from castration. He was stiff and could not travel well. Lewis needed a horse that could go up and down steep mountains and climb over logs.

He pointed to Joyous Heart's good horse and asked if he would trade. He held up a small axe and a knife. With his hands he said, "I will give axe and knife along with this horse in trade for your horse."

Axe?! Ever since last fall when he had first seen the So-yap-pos cut trees faster than beavers at Canoe Camp, Joyous Heart had wanted an axe. Without hesitation, he turned his strong horse over to the So-yap-po and received the axe, knife, and trade horse. That horse's condition did not matter. He would get better, maybe. The real treasures were the axe and the knife.

Joyous Heart was elated. Then suddenly he grew alarmed. His people sometimes demanded the return of a gift. Maybe the So-yap-po would want him to give the axe and knife back to him.

Joyous Heart jumped on his horse and rode toward the river as fast as the beast could move his stiff legs. If the white man wanted his treasures back, he would have to catch him first and take them.

Joyous Heart now owned an axe. It was the one thing of the So-yap-pos that he had wanted most, even greater than his desire for a gun, now that his father, Twisted Hair, owned two. He chopped all the time with his axe. Before anyone else was awake in the morning, he was up chopping. As long as he could see, he chopped. Wherever he went, he took the axe with him and chopped as he went along.

One day when his friends called to him to come along with them, Joyous Heart jumped on his horse with his axe in his hand. He kicked the horse with his heels to speed him on and gave him a hard whack with the axe at the same time.

When he caught up with his friends, they asked, "Why is your horse bleeding?!"

Joyous Heart looked back. Blood was pouring from a deep gash in the horse's hip. He knew then what he had done.

"I wondered why he was limping," he said. "I have been chopping so much lately, I wasn't even thinking when I chopped him."

Joyous Heart turned that horse loose so he could heal. He rode another horse and took care not to chop him.[4]

June 13, 1806

"Ordered Rubin Fields and Willard to proceed on to a small prarie in the Mountains about 8 miles and hunt untill we arrive the[y] set out at 10 A.M. Soon after they set out all of our hunters returned each with a deer except Shields who brought in two in all 8 deer. Labeech and P. Crusatt went out this morning killd a deer & reported that the buzzds. had eate up the deer in their absence after haveing butchered and hung it up. . . ." Clark [Thwaites, Volume 5, Page 133.]

When daylight came, the So-yap-po hunters started out in different directions. Before the sun was at its highest, seven came back with eight deer. Two men came back saying they had killed a deer and hung it up, but when they went back to get it, they found nothing but skin and bones. Buzzards had picked it clean.

June 14, 1806

". . . We have now been detained near five weeks in consequence of the snows; a serious loss of time at this delightfull season for traveling. I am still apprehensive that the snow and want of food for our horses will prove a serious imbarrassment to us as at least four days journey of our rout in these mountains lies over hights and along a ledge of mountains never intirely destitute of snow. every body seems anxious to be in motion, calculation is to reach the United States this season; this I am determined to accomplish if within the compass of human power." Lewis [Thwaites, Volume 5, Page 134.]

Every warm day on Oyaip Prairie increased restlessness among the Lewis and Clark Party.

"We have waited five weeks for the snow to go from the mountains. We can't wait much longer if we want to get home to the United States before next winter. Why can't we start now?" the men asked.

The two captains spent much time considering when they should start.

"I want to get home this season if we possibly can," Captain Lewis said. "I fear we may run out of horse feed when we cross the high snow-covered ridges, but we will try it."

"Good!" said Captain Clark, and he turned to give orders to his men.

"Get all your gear packed for an early start in the morning. Round up the horses and hobble them so we won't have to hunt for them."

June 14, 1806

". . . we had our articles packed up ready for a start in the morning, our horses collected and hobble[d] that they may not detain us in the morning. we expect to set out early, . . ." Clark [Thwaites, Volume 5, Page 134.]

HERE, IMPATIENCE OVERCAME DISCRETION!

CHAPTER 18

THE FIRST ATTEMPT

JUNE 15, 1806

"Collected our horses early with the intention of makeing an early Start. Some hard Showers of rain detained us untill AM at which time we took our departu[r]e from the quawmash fields and proceeded with much dificuelty owing to the Situation of the road which was very sliprey, and it was with great diffculty that the loaded horses Could assend the hills and Mountains the[y] frequently sliped down both assending and decending those steep hills. . . . we arrived at the Camp of R. Fields & Willard on Collin's Creek [*Lolo*] . . . here we let our horses graze in a small glade and took dinner. . . . we proceeded on . . . passing over some ruged hills . . . to a Small glade of about 10 acres thickly covered with grass and quawmash, near a large Creek [*Eldorado*] and encamped. we passed through bad fallen timber and a high Mountain this evening. from the top of this Mountain I had an extensive view of the rocky Mountains . . . Several high pts. to N & N.E. covered with Snow. a remarkable high rugd mountain[*Seven Devils*] in the forks of Lewis's river nearly south and covered with snow. . . ." Clark [Thwaites, Volume 5, Page 136 and 137.]

Hard rain showers prevented the men from getting an early start the next morning. Neither man nor horse felt like moving fast in the rain. Loading the packs on the horses took longer than usual, but finally the long line of horses and riders left the Oyaip.

Travel was slow. Rain had made the trail muddy. The horses slipped when climbing the hills. They slipped when they went down hill. They had to cross swift streams and jump over trees that had fallen across the trail. Step by step, stumbling and slipping, they moved on over a high mountain and down to a grassy flat by a creek. Here they camped for the night with food and rest for all.

June 16, 1806

"Collected our horses early and Set out at 7 AM proceeded on up the Creek [*Eldorado*] . . . crossed the creek to the East and proceeded on through most intolerable bad fallen timber over a high Mountain on which great quantity of Snow is yet lying premisquissly through the thick wood, and in maney places the banks of snow is 4 feet deep. . . . we deturmine to proceed . . . . . . continued our rout through a thick wood much obstructed with fallen timber, and interupted by maney Steep reveins and hills which wer very high. the Snow has increased in quantity so much that the great part of our rout this evening was over the Snow which has become sufficiently firm to bear our horses, otherwise it would have heen impossible for us to proceed as it lay in emince masses in some places 8 or ten feet deep. . . . we arived early in the evening at the place [*on Hungery Creek*] I had killed and left the flesh of a horse for the party in my rear last Sept. . . " Clark [Thwaites, Volume 5, Page 139.]

When they set out early next morning, they found traveling even more difficult. Much fallen timber lay across the trail leading up a high mountain. Snow lay in deep piles in the dense woods. Their path took them down deep ravines and over high hills. The farther they went, the more snow they found, until at last they traveled on top of hard packed snow, eight or ten feet deep. Night camp was at another grassy glade near a creek bottom.

June 17, 1806

"We collected our horses and set out early; we proceeded down hungry creek ahout seven miles passing it twice; . . . beyond this creek the road ascends the mountain to the hight of the main leading ridges which divides the Waters of the Chopunnish and Kooskooske rivers. this . . . mountain we ascended about 3 miles when we found ourselves invelloped in snow from 12 to 15 feet deep even on the south sides of the hills with the fairest exposure to the sun; here was winter with all it's rigors; . . . if we proceeded and should get bewildered in these mountains [*Willow Ridge*] the certainty was that we should loose all our horses and consequently our baggage inst[r]uments perhaps our papers and thus eminently wrisk the loss of the discoveries which we had already made if we should be so fortunate to escape with life. . . .

under these circumstance we conceived it madnes[s] in this stage of the expedition to proceed without a guide who could certainly conduct us to . . . (Travellers (Creek) Rest) . . . we therefore came to the resolution to return with our horses while they were yet strong

. . . and again to proceed as soon as we could procure such a guide . . . having come to this resolution, we ordered the party to make a deposit for all the baggage which we had not immediate use for, and also all the roots and bread of cows which they had except an allowance for a few days . . . we left our instruments papers &c. . . . our baggage being laid out on scaffoalds and well covered we began our retrograde march at 1 P.M. having remained about 3 hours on this snowey mountain. we returned . . . to hungry creek, which we ascended about 2 miles and encamped. . . .

this is the first time . . . that we have ever been compelled to retreat or make a retrograde march. . . ." Lewis [Thwaites, Volume 5, Pages 140, 141, 142.]

Their trail this day led them up to the main ridge which divides the waters of the Chopunnish from the Koos-koos-kee. As they climbed higher up this ridge, they found themselves in snow, twelve to fifteen feet deep. All around them was snow. They could find no trace of trail, no trail signs. They could not tell which ridge to follow.

"We'd be fools to try to go any farther without guides," the captains decided. "We had better make a cache and store all the baggage we don't need. Then we must go back to Oyaip and wait until we can get a guide. We can never make it without one."

Even the most impatient men could see the wisdom of this decision. They set to work, cutting branches from exposed trees to make a platform which they lashed securely to standing trees. On this they piled their baggage and securely wrapped it.

No one was happy to have to return to Oyaip, but all were relieved that they would not face the snowy mountains without a guide.

June 18, 1806

"This morning we had considerable dificuelty in collecting our horses they having Strageled off . . . in serch of food on the Sides of the mountains among the thick timber, at 9 oClock we collected them all except 2 one of Shields & one of Drewyers. we Set out leaving Shields and LePage to collect the two lost horses and follow us. We dispatched Drewyer and Shannon to the Chopunnish Indians in the plains beyond the Kooskooske in order to hasten the arrival of the Indians who promised to accompany us, or to precure a guide at all events and rejoin us as soon as possible. We sent by them a riffle which we offered as a reward to any of them who would engage to conduct us to Clarks river [*Bitterroot River*] at the entrance of Travellers rest Creek [*Lolo Creek*]; we also directed them if they found diffcuelty in induceing any of them to accompany us to offer the reward of two other guns to be given them immediately and ten horses at the falls of the Missouri . . . we had not proceeded far this morning before J. Potts cut his leg very badly with one of the large knives; he cut one of the large veins on the iner side of the leg; Colters horse fell with him in passing hungary creek and himself and horse were driven down the Creek a considerable distance roleing over each other among the rocks. he fortunately escaped with[out] much injurey or the loss of his gun. he lost his blanket. . . . after dinner we proceeded on to the near fork of Collins Creek and encamped in a pleasant situation at the upper part of the Meadows [*Eldorado Meadows*] . . . Musquetors Troublesome." Clark [Thwaites, Volume 5, Pages 145 and 146.]

During the night the horses wandered into the thick woods on the hillsides trying to find grass. The next morning two were missing.

"Shields and LePage, you stay here and hunt for those horses. Follow us when you find them," Captain Lewis ordered.

"Drewyer and Shannon, since you are both good at communicating with the Indians, we need you to go to the big Chopunnish encampment on the plains. See if you can hurry up those fellows who promised to be our guides. Give this rifle to anyone who will lead us over the mountains. If that won't do the trick, offer them another gun at once. Tell them we'll give them ten horses at the falls of the Missouri."

Drewyer and Shannon took the guns and set off immediately towards the southwest. The rest of the party, unmindful of the hazards before them, turned more to the northwest. Their way out of the canyon was up a steep hill through heavy brush and over fallen timber. Some men cleared the trail by whacking down the underbrush with any practical tool they possessed. One miscalculated blow with his large knife caused Potts to slice through a vein in his leg. Letting the others struggle on, the captains halted to check the bleeding and dress Pott's wound.

Rampaging Hungery Creek threatened disaster to any life that tried to cross. Both men and horses realized this. The men knew they had to choose a likely crossing to get to the other side.

The horses set their feet down deliberately on the slippery rocks of the the creek bed, firmly resisting the crashing force of the water.

All seemed to go well with this crossing. One by one

the horses carried their riders or packs safely over the torrent, until Collins attempted to cross. His horse accidently slipped in midstream and lost his footing. The swift current tumbled horse and rider over and over as it swept them downstream. When they finally climbed out of the creek, Collins still had his gun, but his blanket had floated away.

The day ended better than it had begun, except for mosquitos.

June 19, 1806

". . . At 2 P.M. J & R Feilds arived with two deer; John Sheilds and LaPage came with them, they had not succeeded in finding their horses. late in the evening Frazier reported that my riding horse that of Capt. Clark and his mule had gone on towards the Quawmash flatts and that he had pursued their tracks on the road about 2-1/2 miles . . . the musquetoes have been excessively troublesome to us since our arrival at this place particularly in the evening. . . ." Lewis [Thwaites, Volume 5, Page 147.]

The men rested and let the horses graze.

Shields and LePage came into camp late without their lost horses. Soon after their arrival their friend, Frazier, reported to the captains.

"Captain Lewis, Sir," he said, "your riding horse along with Captain Clark's horse and mule have gone on ahead toward the camas grounds. I followed them for two and a half miles, but couldn't catch up with them."

That problem would take care of itself next day. Night was falling by this time and the men had another problem to face. Clouds of mosquitos swarmed about them in such magnitude, they were in torment.

June 20, 1806

"... as we shall necessarily be compelled to remain more than two days for the return of Drewyer and Shannon we determined to return in the morning as far as the quawmash flatts and indeavour to lay in another stock of meat for the mountains, our former stock being now nearly exhausted as well as what we have killed on our return. . . ." Lewis [Thwaites, Volume 5, Page 149.]

While the So-yap-pos were busy making their preparations to start across the mountains toward home, the Nee-mee-poo were getting ready to start on their annual root-gathering and fishing travels.

Before they could move from their lodges in the valleys, the women gathered all the bags they could find to hold their root harvest. They would pack their fine clothes, along with their spare clothes, in their hi-sop-ti-kai. Finally, they rolled up the reed matting needed to cover their summer shelters and were ready to leave.

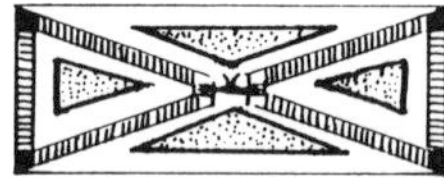 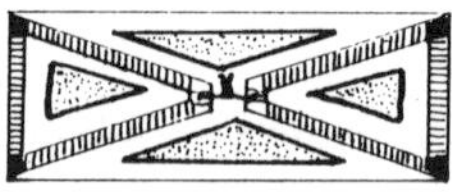 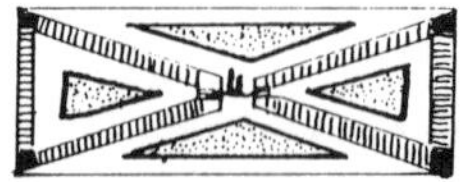

Red Grizzly Bear's village, near the river in the Kamiah Valley, teemed with activity. Mothers, busy pounding roots, needed help and called out to the children, "Watch the little ones! Keep them away from the creek!"

"Go to the spring and bring water."

"Help blind grandmother find a place in the sun."

And the children helped. Sometimes they helped, thinking about the good times ahead. Sometimes they helped for fear of the Whipping Man. The children of the Nee-mee-poo were not punished by their parents; but, disobedience, quarreling, and teasing did not go unheeded. Each family had its own designated Whipping Man—the head of another family—who appeared with switches hidden under his robe to mete out punishment when due.

No boy or girl ever wanted to face the Whipping Man. Some ran and hid when they saw him coming. Others gritted their teeth and took their punishment bravely.

With terrible solemnity the Whipping Man would look into the faces of the unruly children, spread his robe down on the ground and say, "Kum-noo-kun!" ["Come here!"] Then each child had to lie down or stand on the robe and receive stinging lashes from his switch.

After the switching, the Whipping Man lined the penitent ones up and lectured them.

"You must do what your mother says!"

"You must be good and show respect for your grandmother!"

"Your grandmother's water basket is empty! That should never be! Show your kindness by going to the spring for water."

"Never laugh at a man with one eye nor at anyone with a crippled foot!"

The children remembered these things long after the Whipping Man had gone his way.

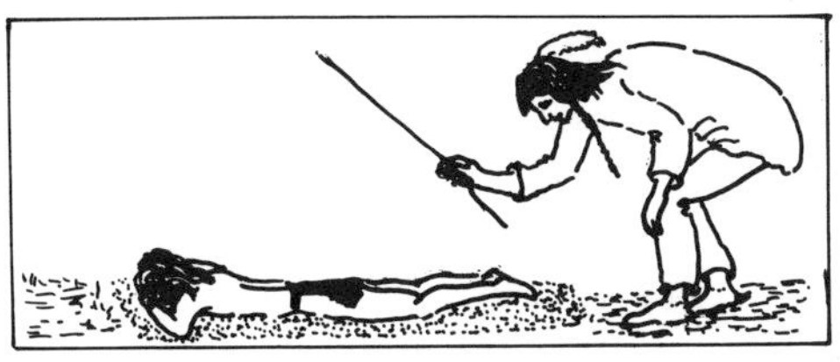

Among the small boys in Red Grizzly Bear's village were Alle-oo-ya, Iscootim, Koots-koots, and Hahahts-tah-mal-we-yaht [Grizzly Bear Commander]. One afternoon, these boys were challenged by Peem, an uncle of Koots-koots, to play ip-paht-tah-khahts, a game that tested their bravery and endurance.[1]

Peem, pointing to some boulders, said to the boys, "Sit on these rocks, back side sticking over. I will whack each of you on the seat with my hand. If I knock you off and make you cry, I win. If you don't cry and come back for more, you win and you can do what you want to me."

This game was hard on all. One by one, Peem knocked the boys off the rocks; but they came back for more and shed no tears. Peem whacked and swatted, until his hands were too sore to strike another blow.

The boys had won, and they took him at his word. They could do anything they wanted. They pulled Peem's hair, rubbed dirt on his face, kicked him, and pulled off his breechclout to mark his defeat.

This victory strengthened their confidence in themselves to the point that, when a boy their own age swaggered up with a challenge, they felt they could face anything.

"I can outrun any of you," he bragged. "I am the fastest runner in this village."

Alle-oo-ya, Iscootim, Koots-koots, and Grizzly Bear Commander wondered what this one had in mind, for he was a whiner, a tattle-tale, a trouble-maker! He tormented them constantly. If they retaliated, he told his mother and she called the Whipping Man to punish them. Although he was as large as any of them, the boys called him Me-yap-khah-wet [Baby].

"I'll race you," said Alle-oo-ya boldly.

"Me, too!" said all the rest.

They raced. Me-yap-khah-wet ran fast, but not the fastest. Just when it looked like Grizzly Bear Commander was going to take the lead, Me-yap-khah-wet tripped him and made him fall. The race ended with a burning desire for vengeance in Grizzly Bear Commander's heart.

Pee-kah [mother] should have been busy, but instead, she sat staring at a heap of mats and bags filled with dried meat. The family of her new son-in-law had brought those mats and bags of meat as a gift when they had paid their ceremonial visit two suns back. Their gift had closed the wedding ritual between her daughter, Black Cricket, and White Antelope.

Now Pee-kah sat, looking back at what had taken place in her family. It had been in Ah-pah-ahl, the Moon of Kouse Bread, when her daughter, Black Cricket, had gone to live with White Antelope's people. Then Black Cricket returned to her home. Her family took horse-loads of tanned deerskins, new moccasins, robes, and decorated hi-sop-ti-kais to White Antelope's family who were pleased with Black Cricket and the beautiful gifts.

Thinking of all the hard work that had gone into making those gifts, then looking at the heap of ordinary-looking mats of rushes and the bags of dried meat, Pee-kah spoke to the grandmother.

"Doesn't look like much," she said. "Not enough!"

"Maybe had poor luck hunting," the grandmother answered.

"Maybe," Pee-kah said, "but it seems like they could have brought more."

All thoughts about this inequality vanished then, for her son of nine summers came up bleeding and bawling. One look at the blood streaming from his forehead, down over his face, was enough for his mother to guess the cause of his plight.

"Ha-ha-tswal kap-sees!" ["Those dirty, stinkin' boys!]" she raged. "They are always making you miserable. What did they do this time? The Whipping Man will give them a good beating for this."

Pee-kah took her bleeding son to the Whipping Man and demanded that those boys be punished. The Whipping Man took one look at the wound and decided the boys deserved a beating more than ever. Wearily, he gathered up the switches he used on trouble-makers. It seemed no sun ever sank to rest without his having to use switches on those boys.

When the boys came before him, the Whipping Man asked of Grizzly Bear Commander, "Did you do this thing?"

"Yes," Grizzly Bear Commander answered. "Me-yap-khah-wet is always doing something to us, then telling his mother and making us get whipped for doing nothing. This time I threw a rock and hit him on the head. Might as well do something to get whipped for."

The Whipping Man understood and let them go.

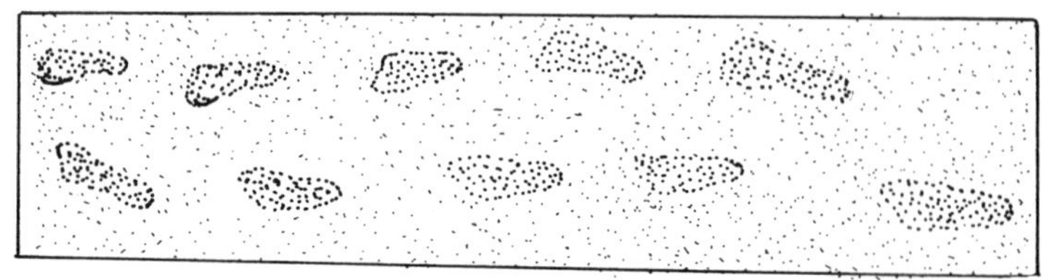

At last the time came when Red Grizzly Bear said, "Next sun we move up to Te-pah-le-wam[2] for root-gathering festivities."

That meant everyone in the village would be leaving, from the oldest grandparents to the youngest babies. It meant many horses had to be caught. These horses would bear the burdens of mats, bags, and tepee covers on their backs, since the travois of the Plains did not work well in the mountains.

Some horses would carry The People with small children riding behind their mothers or grandmothers. Some gentle horses would carry two or three older children at once, while others would carry the proud children who had learned to manage a horse alone.

From every village in the valley, the Nee-mee-poo climbed up to the broad, rolling plain to Te-pah-le-wam where their ancestors had gathered for generations. Here was space for everyone. Here was an unlimited supply of camas for the women to dig. And here was a track for racing horses. Everything needed for a good time was at this place.

It was the time of Ka-oo-yit, a time to celebrate the end of all the long, dark days in the communal houses and the beginning of the new season of living in the open air. It meant more than just the work of root-gathering. It meant the celebration of the joy of being alive.

After their shelters were set up, the women began to dig roots. The first event of the season was the big Root Feast, which everyone anticipated with pleasure.

When at last a large supply of roots had been dug, the women worked together to prepare the feast of steamed roots for all to share. With two women working at each cooking basket, they heated water by plunging smooth hot rocks into the water-filled basket. Using forked sticks, the women had to work fast to take the rocks out and replace them with other hot rocks, time after time, until the water boiled. Then they put the roots into the basket and kept the water boiling until the roots were cooked. At last, they piled the roots on mats and the feast was ready.

The children could hardly wait. Koots-koots, who had closely watched the progress of the cooking, stared transfixed at the size of a certain root lying on the mat right before his eyes. Koots-koots had never before seen a root so large. It had to be the biggest root in the world! He could wait no longer. His hand reached out and picked it up from the pile of roots, his mouth watering as he held it. It would taste so good!

Just as he opened his mouth to taste that tempting root, he heard a voice behind him say, "YOU BETTER NOT EAT THAT ROOT! YOU MIGHT GROW UP, HAVE FAT WIFE!"

Koots-koots shuddered at the thought. FAT WIFE? He had never even thought about having a wife. He did not want one. Especially, he did not want a FAT one.

Reluctantly, Koots-koots put the big root back on the mat and took a smaller one. Just then a man's huge hand reached down and took that big root. Koots-koots looked up to see who had done this thing.

Uncle! Koolkooltom, his uncle was eating that big root.

Always, Koots-koots was to remember that biggest root in the world and to wonder how it tasted; but, he would never know.[3]

Among the people who enjoyed this Root Feast were guests from the Skitsuish [Spokanes] tribe who lived near Lake Waytom [Lake Coeur d'Alene] and the big falls in the Spokane River. These people had brought disturbing news to the Nee-mee-poo.

"Last winter," they said, "Big Bellies killed many people on other side of mountains. Many Snakes. Many Shalees."[4]

Shalee Woman, one of Red Grizzly Bear's wives, was deeply distressed. She thought of her brothers and sisters on the other side of the mountains. She longed to hear what had become of them. But there was no way to find out, unless someone crossed those snowy mountains. She could do nothing but grieve and quietly weep.

Her son, Koolkooltom,[5] was also distressed. He had aunts and uncles and cousins and friends among the Shalees. He would never be at peace in his heart until he knew whether they had survived the winter attack by the Big Bellies. Unlike his mother, he could do something.

Koolkooltom, this eldest son of Chief Red Grizzly Bear and Shalee Woman, would not be dissuaded. He was a grown man. He knew the way; he had been over the mountains many times. He would cross those mountains now and learn how his relatives had fared.

"I will go over to Shalee country. See what happened," he announced to his friends.

"Kiyu'," Ya'amas Wakus, son of Twisted Hair, volunteered.

No one else offered to leave the good times of Ka-oo-yit to make the hazardous trip over the mountains.

The two[6] set out as soon as necessary preparations had been made. Well-mounted and with four extra horses, they headed for the Oyaip, unburdened by self-doubts.

June 21, 1806

"We collected our horses early set out on our return to the flatts . . at the pass of Collin's Creek we met two indians who were on their way over the mountains; they had brought with them the three horses and the mule that had left us and returned to the quawmash grounds. these indians returned with us about 1/2 a mile down the creek where we halted to dine and graize our horses . . . as well as we could understand the indians they informed us that they had seen Drewyer and Shannon and that they would not return untill the expiration of two days; the cause why Drewyer and Shannon had not returned with these men we are at a loss to account for. we pressed these indians to remain with us and to conduct us over the mountain on the return of Drewyer and Shannon. they consented to remain two nights for us and accordingly deposited their store of roots and bread in the bushes . . . and . . . returned with us, as far as the little prarie about 2 miles distant from the creek, here they halted with their horses and informed us they would remain untill we overtook them or at least two nights. they had four supenumery horses with them . . . at seven in the evening we found ourselves once more at our old encampment where we shall anxiously await the return of Drewyer and Shannon." Lewis [Thwaites, Volume 5, Pages 153 and 154.]

"Wonder if we'll meet up with So-yap-pos," Ya'amas Wakus asked.

"Maybe, maybe not," Koolkooltom answered.

The sight of Drewyer and Shannon riding downhill toward them answered that question and raised more.

"We turned back from the mountains," Drewyer explained. "Too much snow. Not sure of trail. We go now for guides."

"We cross mountains to visit Shalees," Koolkooltom told the two white men. "You will find my people near the head of Kamiah Creek. Maybe get guides there."

"Our party may be on the Oyaip where horse feed and hunting is good. If you see them, tell them you saw us," Drewyer said. He and Shannon continued on their way.

But on the Oyaip, only silent messages spoke to Koolkooltom and Ya'amas Wakus. Dead campfires, hoof prints, and trampled grass told them that the So-yap-pos had been there six suns back and left.

Still . . . Captain Lewis's saddle horse, Captain Clark's two horses, and that rabbit-eared horse were up to their bellies in grass, eating ravenously. Their owners had not gone on without them. Koolkooltom and Ya'amas Wakus knew at once that the animals had returned to this good pasture after they had found themselves in a deep canyon without enough to eat.

"Looks like the So-yap-pos are not far ahead of us," the two men determined. "Probably looking for these horses. We better take them along, back where they came from."

Next sun, when ready to start into the mountains, the two men herded the So-yap-pos' horses along the trail with their own four extra horses. With their stomachs full, the horses, by habit, fell into single file and followed their leader. Up steep pitches and down into canyons, over logs across the trail, the little caravan made its way to the ford of a deep, swift creek, which they crossed.[7] Here, they met the large group of So-yap-pos and horses toiling up toward them.

The captains were glad to get their strayed horses and asked that Koolkooltom and Ya'amas Wakus return with them to better grazing ground downstream.

While they ate, the men talked. "Did you see our two men, Drewyer and Shannon, on your way?" was the first question.

"A-a-a-a-a! Two sleeps more they come," was the answer.

"Will you stay with us and lead us over the mountains when they come back?" was the next question.

"We stay two sleeps," came the answer.

With that, Koolkooltom and Ya'amas Wakus cached their roots and bread in the bushes and went with the So-yap-pos to a small prairie upstream. Here was a good place to camp.

"We wait here two sleeps," they said. "Good horse feed here."

The grass was sufficient for six horses, but not for the sixty-odd that carried the So-yap-pos and their baggage. Only their return to Oyaip would guarantee the white men food for themselves and their animals.

That morning Captain Lewis and Captain Clark talked together, deciding what was best to do.

The strenuous return trip, in and out of deep canyons, through thick brush and over logs, had already disabled two good horses. One horse choked and coughed as if he had distemper. The other, Cruzatte's horse, had jumped over a fallen log and snagged himself badly in the groin.

"We'll have to leave Cruzatte's horse here until we return from the camas flats," Captain Lewis said. "He'll never amount to anything now. Too bad. He was a fine horse."

Captain Clark then spoke to Sergeant Gass, "Sergeant, stay here with Reuben and Joe Fields. We want them to hunt until we get back. Keep an eye on Koolkooltom and Ya'amas Wakus, too. Try to persuade them to wait for our return."

The Red-Head then mounted his horse to lead the rest of the party up the trail back to Oyaip country.

Koolkooltom and Ya'amas Wakus had given their word that they would wait two sleeps. They stayed in camp with the boss-man, Gass, who watched the horses and doctored the injured one. The two Fields brothers went hunting.

One sleep passed.

Another sun rose. Koolkooltom and Ya'amas Wakus again stayed with the boss-man. The hunters brought in nothing but a pheasant that evening, just a taste of meat for each of the five men.

The second sleep passed. Now Koolkooltom and Ya'amas Wakus could go. Before the new sun was at its highest, they took the roots from their cache in the bushes, gathered their spare horses, and went on their way. By evening they reached meadows where their horses could graze. Here they made camp and went fishing.

Pleased with two salmon-trout they had caught, they returned to camp. As they were preparing the fish for their supper, their horses pricked up their ears and looked toward the trail. A whinny told the men that horses were approaching.

Life-long training made them wary, ready to defend themselves, but one glimpse of the riders set them at ease. It was the boss-man, Gass, the brothers, Reuben and Joe Fields, and one more So-yap-po, Wiser. Friends and hunters!

One of the men set out at once to hunt. He brought back a duck, and all shared food together.

"Next sun," Gass said, "all our party will be coming. Will you wait until they come?"

Koolkooltom and Ya'amas Wakus thought about that request. Their food supply might give out before they crossed the mountains if they delayed too long. They made no promise.

When morning came, the boss-man urged, "Stay one more night. We will give each of you a pair of moccasins."[8]

Moccasins were almost as necessary as food; they always needed more. How could a man get good moccasins any easier than by waiting? They settled their minds at once.

"A-a-a-a, we stay," Ya'amas Wakus said.

All day mosquitos and no-see-ums swarmed in clouds around the men and horses. They chewed around the eyes, in the ears, and between the legs of the horses, until the animals could neither eat nor rest in comfort. Their only relief came from standing in the smoke from little smudge fires which the men set. One man was assigned to stay in camp and keep the smoke rolling up throughout the day.

CHAPTER 19

KA-00-YIT

AFTER THE BIG ROOT FEAST, THE ROUTINE OF DAILY LIVING ran along under the excitement of the encampment, like water flowing under a blanket of ice: courting, marriage, birth, death, and vision quests. Hunting, fishing, and root gathering never ceased, for no matter what else happened, the scrounging for food went on and on. This was Ka-oo-yit[1], the beginning of a new season.

In the family of Koots-koots, Yah-tsah, the elder brother, who was no more than twelve summers, lay asleep. That morning he had just returned from his vision quest with Kah-lah-tsah, the grandfather, after being gone five sleeps searching for his Wyakin on the high mountain top.

Now, gaunt, famished, fevered, depressed, and exhausted, Yah-tsah rested and would not speak to anyone. He had already told the grandfather everything he could remember about the quest. After he had eaten, slept, and the fever had gone, he might tell others how he had gone to the top of a high mountain where grandfather had left him, saying he would return after five sleeps.

That first night alone, Yah-tsah had been close to the stars, and he had heard coyotes. His stomach had gnawed with hunger, but there was nothing to fill it. Finally, he had slept restlessly, and when the sky began to grow light, he had turned his face toward the rising sun and had sung a prayer of thanks for its warmth.

He had kept his face turned to the sun as it moved on its way to sunset. He was thirsty, but his stomach had forgotten to hurt from hunger. As the sun went down, a great storm swept over the mountain tops, drenching him with rain and filling little hollow places in the rocks with water. Though Yah-tsah felt bitterly cold, he drank and sang a song of praise for the drink.

When daylight came, he turned his face toward the sun again, but his head felt light and his body burned. He was grateful for the sips he could still draw from the water pockets in the rocks.

Yah-tsah did not see clearly now. Everything looked blurred. Even sounds seemed hard to make out. As he sat in the shade of a rock, he tried to focus his eyes on the place where a woodpecker was making a "rat-a-tat" noise somewhere nearby. At last he caught the flash of red in a tree. It seemed too big and blurry to be real; but there it was—a red-headed woodpecker, swaying on a branch of a tree below him. Yah-tsah listened until he heard clearly the song the bird made. He tried to make that sound. Again and again he tried. For the next three suns until his grandfather appeared, that was all Yah-tsah tried to do. He was sure he had it.

Grandfather appeared on the fifth sun as he had promised. The first thing Yah-tsah did was to sing the woodpecker's song to him, hoping for his approval.

Grandfather listened intently, and asked him to sing it again. Then gently, but firmly, he said, "You almost have it, grandson, but not quite. A song must be just right, or it will have no Power for you. Some other time we try again."

They returned to the encampment, where his understanding family gave the young boy food and allowed him to rest. They reassured him that another time would come when Yah-tsah would receive his Wyakin. Perhaps it would have more Power than that of the woodpecker.

While Yah-tsah, the elder brother, had been gone on his vision quest, a baby had been born. Nearby, hanging from the sturdy branch of a big pine, this tiny newborn baby swung in his te-cas. That morning his mother had brought him up out of the birthing place of the alwi'tas, the women's lodge, for all to see.

"Ninna-nin-nin," ["Dear little thing,"] the girls and women crooned as they passed the baby, asleep in his te-cas, from one admirer to another.

"What will his name be?" they asked.

And the baby's mother answered, "For now, he will be named after the first thing I saw as I came from the alwi'tas: 'As-ah-ek-sach-t-nim-e-wai-oo-ko-i-in-samne-pah-hak-e-nee.' ['Crows-Flying-Out-of-Rock-Creek-Canyon-With-Mouths-Wide-Open.']"[2]

That baby would have many names before he was an old man; but, that name would be the longest of all.

Evening shadows fell. Except for the pale moonlight and the glow of campfires, darkness lay like a blanket over the great encampment. It was a time of good feelings and friendship, a time for visiting and stick games, a magical time for dancing and serenading.

"See! The moon is shining. We can have the Moonlight Dance," laughed Morning Star to the four girls and five boys who gathered around her. "Just enough light to have good dance."

"A-a-a-a!"

They had scarcely voiced this agreement before they formed a circle with boy, girl, boy, girl, boy, girl holding hands. Three times around the circling dancers went, then they turned and went three times around. Next, the girls all stood in the center, facing the boys. Three times around, the boys circled the girls in one direction, while the girls went around the opposite way. Three times they reversed directions before the boys took the center and the circling in opposite directions was repeated. At last, they all joined hands as in the beginning, boy, girl, boy, girl, and they swung their hands back and forth, back and forth.

All the time they danced, they sang a song without words. There was no story to tell, no great deed to remember. They sang and danced just for fun.[3]

Like all the animals and creatures of the earth, now was the time when young men felt a force within them that yearned for the favor of women. How was a man to know what girl, if any, liked him, or if more than one girl liked him, or if some girl from a distant village might like him? And, like their fathers and brothers before them, the young men settled their minds to find out.

To make themselves most attractive to the girls, the young men primped. They shined their long black hair with bear oil, adorned themselves with feathers and paint, and those who had the prized dentalium shells, thrust them through the septums of their noses.

"We will have serenade," announced Kah-hah-toh, called the Short One by his friends. Kah-hah-toh was the keeper of the large piece of stiff rawhide on which the serenaders drummed. He brought it out and invited all who could find a handhold to join in the serenade.

As many of his friends who could, grasped the edge of the large piece of stiff rawhide with one hand and beat a rhythm with a stick in the other hand.

Ten or twelve men could crowd around Kah-hah-toh's rawhide. With Kah-hah-toh leading the singing, they danced their way to the first tepee where they sang to the young woman within, "Come on over!"

Lah-kahts-koots-koots, Little Mouse, well knew when she heard this call that, if she appeared at the door of her tepee, she was expected to go out to the serenaders and stand behind the man she liked best and sing with him. Before she dashed out without thinking, she stayed in the shadows of the lodge and looked at the men outside. She did not want to stand behind the tiny Kah-hah-toh, whose head came just to her shoulders. She did not want to sing with Crane's Legs, her cousin. Her eyes were drawn to the dashing Ka-hap, Wildcat, from Lah-mah-ta, and would not leave. She made her choice. With no more hesitation, she stepped out of her doorway and took her place behind Ka-hap.

Singing, "Come on over," the serenaders approached a second tepee where Ko-yas-ko-yas, Bluejay, waited expectantly. She knew before they came which man she would choose. Straight to the leader of the serenaders she went, and took her place behind Kah-hah-toh.

In this way they went from one tepee to the next, singing out the invitation for young girls to join them. One after another they came, and no man was left without a girl behind him.

Sometimes several girls chose the same man. Kah-hah-toh felt flattered that Akh-akh, Magpie, had chosen to stand behind him. That he, the Short One, should have more than one woman behind him made him feel good. In serenading he was equal to any man, regardless of size. He sang more lustily than ever.

But not every girl was pleased when another joined her in following the same man.

Bluejay was furious that Magpie would pick the man she had already chosen.

"I am singing with Kah-hah-toh," Bluejay yelled at Magpie. "Go choose somebody else."

"I am singing with Kah-hah-toh. I will not go elsewhere!" Magpie retorted.

With this, Bluejay gave her rival a push that sent her staggering. Magpie came clawing back to yank the thick black hair of her opponent.

Kah-hah-toh spoke forcefully, "Enough! There is room for both."

The two women stopped their squabbling and sullenly followed on behind Kah-hah-toh. As the serenading progressed on into the night, their wrath weakened.

They all sang. The singing did not stop until every tepee, known to house a young maiden, was serenaded. By then, the first rays of light were peering under the cover of darkness. The ill humor of the competing women had vanished.

Kah-hah-toh felt good about that serenade. Two women had fought over him.[4]

It was while the serenaders were midway around the great encampment that two So-yap-pos broke the usual order of activities. A number of the Nee-mee-poo had not seen such men before, although they had heard of them. To some people, the men were objects of curiosity. To others, they were intruders; but to the people from the Kamiah Valley, they were welcomed friends.

Drewyer, the good sign-talker, and young Shannon, who could understand some of the speech of the Nee-mee-poo, sought out the lodge of their friend Tin-nach-e-moo-toolt, Chief Broken Arm.

If Broken Arm was surprised at the sight of them, he did not show it. It was as if he had been expecting them. But knowing they came with a purpose, he motioned them to sit and smoke.

At length, Drewyer spoke. "We have come to ask again for guides over the mountains. We tried, but had to turn back. We cannot cross over without them."

"This is a matter to come before the whole council," Broken Arm told them. "We have not met in council. Next sun we meet. Decide who will go as guides as we promised your leaders."

Just as Broken Arm promised, when the next sun rode high in the sky, he sent the Crier to call the chiefs and headmen to council: Twisted Hair from Ahsahka; Timuca from Alpowa; Cut Nose from Ya-ho-toin; Five-Fierce-Hearts from Lah-mah-ta; Red Grizzly Bear from Kamiah Valley; Broken Arm from Tee-e-lap-a-lo in Kamiah Valley. The chiefs and their important men pondered and smoked.

Drewyer and Shannon, with signs and the few words they had learned of the Chopunnish tongue, spoke their message.

"We have come for guides," they said. "We cannot find our way over the mountains without guides. We tried. Snow was too deep. Could find no trail. We returned to Oyaip. Here is one gun for a man who will come to guide." And Shannon lifted the gun up high for all to see.

This was a serious matter to think about. No one spoke, but all were thinking as they smoked. They wanted more guns, but they had to consider other things as well. Looks-Ahead and Follows-the-Trail had started to cross the mountains in the Moon of Ah-pah-ahl. They had found too much snow in the mountains—too much soft snow. They had come back.

Should they send ANY man over the mountains at this time to guide the So-yap-pos? Should they send more than one? Who would go? Who would get the gun?

Seeing their reluctance to commit themselves, the white men again spoke, "We give one more gun right now to men who will go as guides. We give ten good horses when we reach the falls of the Missouri."

The chiefs' eyes narrowed to slits as they peered through the cloud of kinnikinnick smoke rising from the pipe. This offer gave them more to think about. They needed all the guns they could get, but they had to weigh the matter fairly. Crossing the mountains was dangerous and tricky. It was an undertaking that called for courage and skill, for understanding the course of the trail, and for knowledge of survival in the harsh conditions on those high snow-covered mountains. To undertake this mission called for the brightest and bravest of the young men, and there was no assurance that they who went out would come back.

Many smokes and many speeches later, Broken Arm announced to Drewyer and Shannon, "It is decided. Three young men will go: my son, Speaking Eagle, Black Eagle, whose father was killed by Big Bellies, and Ahs-kahp, the brother of Cut Nose. All skilled in knowledge of finding the trail through the mountains."

Drewyer and Shannon felt a burden lift from their spirits.

The spirits of the three young men also soared, for they were anxious to cross the mountains with their friends, the So-yap-pos.

Speaking Eagle and Black Eagle began at once to prepare for the taxing journey ahead. They fully realized the dangers they might have to face: sudden, violent mountain storms; snow slides; lack of horse feed; the odd chance of missing the trail. For that, each knew he could rely on the judgment of the other two. For their survival, a supply of roots, spare moccasins, warmer clothing, warm robe, and three or four extra horses were essential.

The brother of Cut Nose, Ahs-kahp, took the preparations more lightly. It was hot on the Prairie. All he needed here were his moccasins, breechclout, and a small tanned robe. He could not be persuaded that bitter Cold still gripped the mountain ridges in its Power. He felt equal to the trip, clothed as he was.

Sustained by the knowledge that they had been over the trail enough times to find the way again, the men felt confident they would accomplish this mission and return. With their survival supplies packed on their horses, they put worries behind them and looked forward to continued friendship with the So-yap-pos, to receiving the rewards of guns, and to renewing relationships with their cousins on the other side of the mountains.

Without looking back, the three rode off with Drewyer and Shannon in the early dawn of a new day.

CHAPTER 20

CROSSING THE MOUNTAINS

JUNE 22, 1806

"This morning by light all hands who could hunt were Sent out, the result of the days performance was greater than we had even hopes for. we killed eight Deer and three Bear. we despatched whitehouse to the Kooskoo[s]ke near our old encampment above Collins Creek in order to precure some salmon which we understand the nativs are now takeing in considerable quantities near that place. we gave Whitehouse a fiew beeds which I unexpectedly found in one of my waistcoat pockets to purchase the fish. . . . neither Shannon Drewyer nor Whitehouse returned this evening. . . . Clark [Thwaites, Volume 5, Page 156.]

This morning the So-yap-pos awoke on the Oyaip Prairie. Disappointment at having to return diminished when the hunters brought in eight deer and three bears they had killed. At least they had plenty of meat for a few days, but the thought of getting good salmon tantalized them.

Captain Clark, toying with the contents of his coat pockets, found a few beads he could use in trade.

"Whitehouse!" he called. "Go down to the fishery on the river and buy some good salmon for us with these beads."

Whitehouse rode off with a light heart. He would welcome a change of diet as much as any man.

June 23, 1806

"Apprehensive from Drewyer's delay that he had met with some difficulty in procuring a guide, and also that the two indians who had promised to wait two nights for us would set out today, we thought it most advisable to dispatch Frazier and Wiser to them this morning with a vew if possible to detain them a day or two longer; and directed that in the event of their not being able to detain the indians, that Sergt. Gass, R & J. Fields and Wiser should accompany the indians by whatever rout they might take to travellers rest and blaize the trees well as they proceeded and wait at that place untill our arrival with the party. . . . at 3 P.M. Drewyer Shannon and Whitehouse returned. Drewyer brought with him three indians who had consented to accompany us . . . for the compensation of two guns. one of those men is the brother of the cutnose and the other two are the same who presented Capt. Clark and myself each with a horse . . . at the Lodge of the broken arm. these are all young men of good character and much respected by their nation. . . ." Lewis [Thwaites, Volume 5, Pages 156-157.]

Koolkooltom and Ya'amas Wakus had stayed in camp as long as they had promised the So-yap-pos.

"We better move on if we are to get across the mountains before our food is all gone," they decided. They started out.

Only a short time after they left, Gass, Reuben and Joseph Fields, and Wiser appeared to find their camp deserted except for Frazier.

"They just left," Frazier told them.

"Then we've got to catch up with them. If Drewyer and Shannon can't find guides, we are going to need these fellows," Gass said.

The four men hastened on.

Loud cheers sounded in the Oyaip camp as six riders approached.

"Here comes Whitehouse back from the fishery!"

"Looks like Drewyer and Shannon have brought our guides!"

Into the throng the returning So-yap-pos rode with three Nee-mee-poo: their friends, Speaking Eagle and Black Eagle, and a third, known as Ahs-kahp. He was a brother of Cut Nose.

Speaking Eagle and Black Eagle were carrying the guns they had been given for guiding the So-yap-pos homeward. Ahs-kahp would receive his when they got across the mountains.[1]

"Hurray! Now we can cross the mountains!"

And the So-yap-pos began at once to prepare for an early start in the morning.

June 24, 1806

"We collected our horses early this morning and set out acompanyed by our three guides . . . we nooned it as usual at Collins's Creek where we found Frazier solus; the other four men having gone in pursuit of the two indian men who had set [out] from Collins's Creek two hours before Frazier and Wizer arrived. after dinner we continued our rout to Fish Creek [*Eldorado Creek*] a branch of Collins's Creek . . . here we found Sergt. Gass Wiser and the two indians whom they had prevailed on to remain at that place untill our arrival; R. & J. Fields had only killed one small deer . . . at Collins's Creek and of this they had been liberal to the indians insomuch that they had no provision; they had gone on to the branch of hungary Creek at which we shall noon it tomorrow in order to hunt. we had fine grass for our horses this evening." Lewis [Thwaites, Volume 5, Page 158.]

Next morning the So-yap-pos traveled without hesitation or guesswork to the camp on Collin's Creek where Frazier waited for them alone.

"Koolkooltom and Ya'amas Wakus didn't wait any longer than they said they would," Frazier explained. "Gass, the Fields brothers, and Wiser went ahead to catch up with them and ask them to wait for all of us."

The party continued until they found Gass and Wiser with Koolkooltom and Ya'amas Wakus waiting for them at Fish Creek. The Fields brothers had gone ahead to hunt. Here everyone camped where grass was good.

June 25, 1806

"last evening the indians entertained us with seting the fir trees on fire. they have a great number of dry lims near their bodies which when set on fire creates a very suddon and immence blaze from bottom to top of those tall trees. they are a beatifull object in this situation at night. . . . the natives told us that their object in seting those trees on fire was to bring fair weather for our journey. . . ." Lewis [Thwaites, Volume 5, Page 159.]

Koolkooltom and Ya'amas Wakus had been reluctant to wait for all the So-yap-pos to accompany them. Hunting had not been good. The food supply they had cached in the bushes was not sufficient to satisfy their immediate hunger and to sustain them while crossing the mountains. They could not wait much longer lest they run short of food.

The sight of Speaking Eagle, followed by Black Eagle and Ahs-kahp, at the head of the long file of So-yap-pos descending into camp, relieved Koolkooltom and Ya'amas Wakus. Those three guides meant no more waiting for So-yap-pos. Everyone would be moving along the trail when the new sun rose. They would now move with assurance they were on the right ridges. No better guides could be found among the Nee-mee-poo than Speaking Eagle, Black Eagle, and Ahs-kahp. Koolkooltom and Ya'amas Wakus were glad they would be traveling with these three friends.

The group of young guides and their friends laughed and jested together that night around their campfire, partly out of comradeship, partly because they faced unknown hardships and adventures in the mountains.

Squatting around their campfire, they looked at the great fir trees nearby whose lower branches were dead and dry. Ya'amas Wakus remembered how his grandfather had taught him to use such trees to bring good luck.

"Set fire to those dead branches," he said. "Will then have good weather for traveling."

"A-a-a-a," his friends agreed. "We will help. Make big fire for good weather."

Ya'amas Wakus grabbed a burning stick from the campfire and touched it to the dead limbs of the tall fir behind him.

WHOOSH! Flames roared up the trunk of the tree in an explosive flash, sending sparks high into the black night sky. The friends raced from one tree to the next with torches until the whole meadow shimmered in the glare from blazing evergreens.

"Why do you do this?" the So-yap-pos asked as they watched the spectacle in amazement.

"To bring good weather. Better travel. Better hunting," said Ya'amas Wakus, who loved the excitement.

After the fire subsided, sleep came to all.

June 25 , 1806

"We collected our horses readily and set out at an early hour this morning. one of our guides complained of being unwell, a symptom which I did not much like as such complaints with an indian is generally the prelude to his abandoning any enterprize with which he is not well pleased. we left them at our encampment and they promised to pursue us in a few hours. at 11. A.M. we arrived at the branch of hungary creek where we found R. & J. Feilds. they had not killed anything. here we halted and dined and our guides overtook us. . . ." Lewis [Thwaites, Volume 5, Page 159.]

When dawn came, it did not look like the fire the guides had lit had brought fair weather. It was raining, and the rain did not make Ahs-kahp, brother of

Cut Nose, feel well. He shivered as if in the middle of winter. Eager to go with Speaking Eagle and Black Eagle, he had not thought to wear more than what he wore in the warm valley. Except for his breechclout and moccasins, he had only a light elkskin robe dressed without the hair—not enough to keep warm in the cold mountain air.

Ahs-kahp went to the So-yap-pos with his teeth chattering.

"Sick," he said with shaking hands. "Bad sick. Stay here."

Speaking Eagle spoke then to the So-yap-po leaders, "Go on ahead. We catch up with you."

The So-yap-po chiefs looked at each other, then at the pitiful Ahs-kahp.

"We'll have to go on and trust them to come," Lewis said. "We can't do anything else." And the captains gave orders for their party to move on up the trail.

Speaking Eagle turned to Ahs-kahp, "You take sweat. Get warm. Feel no cold."

Working fast among the steaming embers from last night's fire, Ahs-kahp's friends formed a little hut of branches and covered it with their robes. They built a fire and heated rocks red hot. Ahs-kahp crawled inside and dropped water from his horn cup on the hot rocks until the hut was full of steam and sweat poured from his body.

"I'm coming out," he yelled. As his friends pulled the robes from the entrance, Ahs-kahp backed out and plunged into the icy creek. Again he crawled into the sweathouse for another sweat. He cooled off more slowly this time. His body felt a glowing warmth that cold air did not seem to penetrate. Now he was again ready to travel.

They set out at once and caught up with the big party who were camped on a small meadow to rest and eat.

Captain Lewis looked hard at Ahs-kahp, not shivering now, but still cold. Rain had soaked through his thin robe to his skin. The captain pulled a small buffalo robe from his pack and handed it to Ahs-kahp.

"Wrap up in this," he said. "Keep warm and dry. The air will get colder."

Ahs-kahp pulled the robe around his shoulders. With the warm hair next to his body, no cold could touch him. The buffalo robe blocked out the dampness and chill that surrounded him. His heart felt warm toward this So-yap-po.

June 26, 1806

"we passed by the same rout we had travelled . . . to our deposit on top of the snowey mountain to the N. E. of hungary Creek. . . ." Lewis [Thwaites, Volume 5, Page 161.]

Fog veiled the mountains as the long line of horses and riders set forth in the morning. Sometimes the fog hid the guides at the head of the line from the view of those at the end. Sometimes the leaders disappeared around a bend in the trail; but, no one felt lost, for always the horse ahead could be seen.

All morning the zig-zag path led them up a long, steep hill through mist and fog to the snow line. Now the horses could travel on hard-packed snow as if on a smooth road. Deeper than a man's height, snow covered the rocks and fallen trees and made travel safer and faster.

By midday, the party reached the top of the mountain where the So-yap-pos had cached their baggage on their first attempt.[2] Nothing had tampered with the hide-covered packs stored on poles they had fastened between trees. In spite of the cold, the men worked fast and cheerfully to transfer their unmolested goods to the backs of their horses.

They then broke into squads of about three each and built small fires and cooked food for themselves. The horses stood, resting in the snow, with nothing to eat. Heads hanging, shifting weight from one foot to another, they waited.

June 26, 1806

". . . the indians haistened to be off, and informed us that it was considerable distance to the place which they wished to reach this evening where there was grass for our horses. . . ." Lewis [Thwaites, Volume 5, Page 161 and 162.]

Speaking Eagle, Black Eagle, and Ahs-kahp ate quickly, then rose and walked among the So-yap-pos, urging them with hand-signs and voices to make haste.

"Hah-mtits! Horse feed lies far ahead. Hah-mtits! Must find horse feed before dark. Hah-mtits!"

No more talk! The men mounted their horses and began the climb up a higher mountain that loomed ahead. One by one the So-yap-pos followed the guides. Their sixty-six horses with those of the guides and their extras formed a procession of almost eighty horses. Against the backdrop of the awesome white mountains, they were mere specks, like ants toiling single file along the ridgepole of a house. And in a sense, they traveled a ridgepole. No matter whether Speaking Eagle, Black Eagle, or Ahs-kahp led them up hill or down, on side hill or crest, they followed a dividing ridge. On the right hand, the waters ran into the Lochsa. On the left, they drained into the Chopunnish. The watershed was the way through these mountains.

With confidence the guides pressed on, never hesitating, never in doubt. The mountains had not changed since they had last crossed them. They remembered the way. Even where the deep snow covered all markers on the trees, they could tell which dividing ridge connected with another.

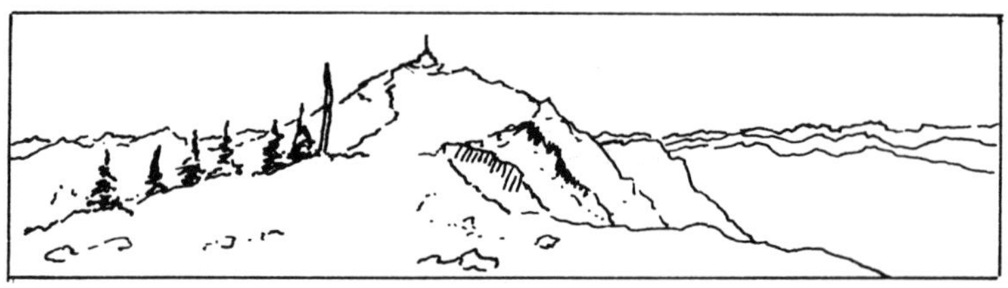

The way was long and darkness was beginning to fall when, at last, they reached their goal [*Bald Mountain*]. Here, on a treeless mountainside exposed to the sun, the snow was gone. Grass was green and a spring gurgled out of its bed in the mountain. To find all this at the end of the grueling day was reward enough.

Tired though they were, the men cheerfully relieved the horses of their packs before they prepared their own dinner and beds for the night. The horses, revelling in the freedom from the burdens, rolled and shook themselves, drank the spring water, and ate their fill of the sweet green grass.

As all these preparations for the evening were going on, a lone rider straggled into camp with two horses. From the appearance of his horses, he had not spared the animals in his effort to catch up with the party.

Ya'amas Wakus took one look and said softly, as if to himself, "White Wolf, my cousin. Before we left, his thoughts were going back and forth like a tree in the wind. He must have settled his mind to join us."

The So-yap-po captains wondered what had brought this young man on a journey by himself. They went to the group where Speaking Eagle, Black Eagle, Ahs-kahp, Koolkooltom and Ya'amas Wakus were talking to White Wolf.

"What brings you over this trail, alone?" they asked White Wolf.

And White Wolf answered simply, "To go to the Great Falls with you."

The captains looked at Koolkooltom and Ya'amas Wakus. "And you?" they asked. "Are you also planning to go to Great Falls?"

"No. Just far enough to visit camp of our friends and cousins, the Shalees," was the answer.

The captains asked no more questions and went on.

June 27, 1806

"We collected our horses early and set out. the road still continued on the heights of the same dividing ridge on which we traveled yesterday . . . on an elivated point we halted by request of the Indians and smoked the pipe. . . ." Lewis [Thwaites, Volume 5, Page 164.]

Deep canyons still held the darkness of night when Speaking Eagle guided the column of riders and horses along the high ridge in the direction of the Land-Toward-the-Rising-Sun. Though clouds obscured the brightness of the sun, the mountain tops glowed with the light of day. Every step seemed to lead up into more brilliance as the mountains rose higher.

With utmost confidence, Speaking Eagle, Black Eagle, Ahs-kahp and their friends rode on. Here and there, they could point out to the white men the trail markers on the trees where the snow had melted sufficiently. In a few places where the ground was bare, they showed the old road. But the snow lay deep where the sun did not reach. Signs of the trail were so scarce and far apart that the sight of one brought reassurance, even to the guides.

Higher and higher they climbed, until there was nothing more to climb. Even the eagle that soared above them seemed to have only the clouds for his roost.

Long ago the ancient ones had stood in awe at this place where they had left a cone of rocks built around a tall pole. Its silent message reminded travelers to pause and ponder on the meaning of their world.

Through the voice of Itsi-yai-yai, the Coyote, a brooding spirit spoke to all who would listen:

"Frail Human, standing tall with head near the stars above,
Proud-standing, with feet on the birthing-place of rivers,
Safely have you come thus far through these mountains.
How could you tell which way to go?
Looking up, what do you see? Nothing but sky.
Looking down, deep canyons.
Behind—mountains. To right and to left—mountains.
Looking ahead—mountains. Mountains as far as eyes can see.
You, who are but a mere Human! How can you find your way?
Something Greater than you has been your Guide."

Awe and wonder filled the hearts of Speaking Eagle, Black Eagle, Ahs-kahp, Koolkooltom, Ya'amas Wakus, and White Wolf as they drew near the cairn. Never did they pass this place without stopping to smoke and meditate, nor would they now.

They stopped and called back, "Smoke here."

The long line halted. While their leaders smoked the pipe with the guides, the riders waited and absorbed the scene spread out before them. The horses rested.

The point on which the cairn was built jutted out into a canyon where strong winds had repeatedly blown the snow from the rocky promontory. Here, the men squatted and smoked, spellbound by the magnificent view. With their backs to the sun, they faced steep snow-covered slopes of winter; turning around, they saw grass and flowers of summer.

After the smoke, the guides swung onto their horses and led the way down a steep mountain, crossing the heads of two streams that ran into the Chopunnish. They then climbed up to the main ridge. Finally, they arrived at a mountainside, bare of snow, where grass was starting and flowers were blooming.

"Red Mountain," they said. "Sleep here. Let horses graze."

Speaking Eagle pointed out the trail to the fishery in the canyon of the Lochsa.

"When we go over with our families to Buffalo Country," he said, "some men go that way to fish. Then go up river and meet families in meadow at head of Koos-koos-kee."

For the first time since starting over the mountains, men saw big game—three black-tail deer. But no one could get a shot. The deer disappeared. Supper consisted of roots boiled with bear's oil.

Speaking Eagle, Black Eagle, and Ahs-kahp counted four sleeps since they had begun to guide.

June 28, 1806

"... at 12 oClock we arived at an untimberd. side of a mountain with a southern aspect just above the fishery [*Powell Junction*] here we found an abundance of grass as the guid[e]s had informed us. . . ." Clark [Thwaites, Volume 5, Page 168.]

In order to follow the dividing ridge this day, the guides led the procession over high knobs and down through deep hollows. Every step the horses took was on massive drifts of hard-packed snow that covered rocks and fallen trees. They could travel faster on snow, but sometimes they slipped, and sometimes a horse would punch through a soft spot up to his belly. Then he struggled and floundered around in the snow before he could get his four feet firmly under him again. With a heavy pack on his back, the effort was exhausting.

The sun was at its highest when they reached a mountainside with plenty of grass for the tired and hungry horses. With their packs still on, the horses fed greedily while the men held a conference.

"From here, no grass at sundown," Black Eagle told the So-yap-pos.

"We will camp here then. Let the horses feed and rest," the captains agreed. "There's no water here. We'll have to melt snow." There was plenty of snow!

The guides counted the fifth sleep from the time they started over the mountains.

June 29, 1806

"... we pursued the hights of the ridge on which we have been passing for several days; it terminated at the distance of 5 ms from our encampment and we decended to, and passed the main branch of the Kooskooske . . . when we decended from this ridge we bid adieu to the snow. . . ." Lewis [Thwaites, Volume 5, Page 169.]

Next morning, Speaking Eagle, Black Eagle, and Ahs-kahp talked with the So-yap-po chiefs.

"This sun we come to hot springs. Plenty grass. Maybe find deer at licks there." These reassuring words put new spirit into every man who understood them.

"We will send Drewyer and Reuben Fields on ahead to the warm springs to hunt," the captains said. "They will have no trouble finding the trail from here on."

As Speaking Eagle, Black Eagle, and Ahs-kahp often talked to Drewyer with hands and words, so now they pointed out to him and Fields the most direct way to go.

Long before the slow-moving troop could get started, the two men had gone on.

Along the dividing ridge, the snow-packed trail continued until it broke over into the valley of the Koos-koos-kee. As the trail descended, the snow covering became thinner, finally disappearing entirely before the party reached the river.

The snow was gone! The great mountains lay behind!

The sight of a slain deer, hanging from a tree near the river, added to the good spirits of the So-yap-pos. Reuben Fields and Drewyer had been successful. The next meal would be more than plain boiled roots. A pack horse soon received the extra burden.

The long file of horses began to cross the main branch of the Koos-koos-kee.

Before the last horse had struggled over the smooth stones on the bed of the swift water, Speaking Eagle, Black Eagle, and Ahs-kahp had climbed far up the steep mountain trail on the opposite side. By the time the last horse and rider had reached the summit, the guides had arrived at a broad meadow where the grass was thick and tall [*Packer Meadow*].

The sun was overhead. While their horses fed in deep grass, the humans prepared their own dinner and rested.

A check on the horses, before they took to the trail again, showed that two horses had been left behind.

"Joe Fields and Colter, back track and find those animals," Captain Lewis said. "One is my extra saddle horse and the other has a pack we can't afford to lose. And keep on the look-out for game. We'll camp at the warm springs tonight."

Before sundown the guides had led the expedition to their evening campsite in the meadow near the hot springs. This had been their goal for the day. As on the entire journey over the mountains, no accident or incident had prevented these guides from reaching their desired camping place.

Here were the hot springs! This marvel of hot water bubbling out from the base and spaces between tall gray cliffs delighted everyone who stopped there. From three different sources the water ran: very warm in one, much too hot for comfort in the other two. Long ago, visitors had dammed the warm spring with stones and gravel to make a pool that seemed to say to every traveler, "Come in! Enjoy my warm water. You will feel better when you leave."

The guides wondered who had been here last. Before anyone else could clutter up the signs with his own footprints, the guides looked sharply around as they went toward the pool area. Tracks would leave them messages.

"Look!" Black Eagle called. "Footprints! Made many sleeps ago."

"Two men! Barefoot!" Ahs-kahp said, inspecting the depressions in the wet ground. "This far from pool men wear moccasins."

"Maybe had no moccasins. Maybe escaped from Big Bellies with just their lives. Must be true that Big Bellies raided Shalees as Spokanes said!" Speaking Eagle spoke in alarm. Worry and sorrow for their friends weighed on their hearts. They showed the barefoot prints to their So-yap-po friends.

The message was a warning to all. "Big Bellies may be near. Murderous, treacherous te-wel-kas."

For the time, though, worry over friends sank under the pleasure of swimming in warm water. Each man stayed as long as he could in the pool. Then he dashed out and ran to the nearby Aha-tes Creek[3] where he plunged into its icy water. After that he raced back into the warm pool. Again, he rushed for a dip into the ice water, and, again, he dived into the warm water. As long as they could stand it, the men bathed this way: from warm to cold, from cold to hot, from hot to cold, from cold to hot. When they had had enough, they quit after a hot plunge.

The So-yap-pos went about their bathing differently. Shouts and laughter echoed from the gray cliffs as they cast off their clothes with glee and jumped into the warm water.

"Bet I can stay in longer than you," Shannon challenged Potts, who was recovering from the bad cut on his leg.

"How long did you stay, Captain Lewis?"

"Nineteen minutes was all I could take," Captain Lewis answered.

"I could only stand it ten minutes, it was so hot," Captain Clark said. "I'm still sweating."

Languid or relaxed as the warm bath had affected them, the men went to sleep that night with full stomachs and a feeling of great relief and accomplishment at having crossed those mountains.

Speaking Eagle, Black Eagle, and Ahs-kahp counted the sixth sleep since they had left the Oyaip.

June 30, 1806

". . . a little before Sunset we arrived at our old encampment on the S. side of the Creek a litle above its enterance into Clarks river [*Traveler's Rest, or Lolo Creek, Montana*]. here we Encamped with a view to remain 2 days in order to rest ourselves and horses . . . we found no signs of the Oatlashshots haveing been here lately. the Indians express much concern for them and apprehend that the Minetarries of Fort d[e]Prarie have destroyed them in the course of the last Winter . . . " Clark [Thwaites, Volume 5, Page 174 and 175.]

The new sun came up with promise of fair weather. Signs of deer in the country raised the hopes of the hunters. Drewyer and Joseph Fields went on ahead to hunt. Before the rest of the party was on the trail, a small deer came to lick at the warm springs and was felled by a So-yap-po's gun. At least some meat with their meal was assured.

Speaking Eagle, Black Eagle, and Ahs-kahp led the party down the valley. Sometimes the trail ran on the bottom land, sometimes on the sides and tops of steep ridges. Nothing seemed so difficult as compared to the trail through the mountains they had just completed, yet an accident did occur.

As they followed along the steep side of a high hill, the hind feet of Captain Lewis's horse slipped over the edge and he dropped off the trail. His rider toppled over with him and slid forty feet before he could stop himself. The horse thrashed about trying to regain his footing. But for all the frantic struggles, neither horse nor man was hurt.

When they stopped for their midday meal, Shields killed a deer. Soon after they were on the trail again, he killed another.

As evening drew near, the So-yap-pos came upon three deer left by the hunters, Drewyer and Joseph Fields, who had gone ahead in the morning.

Six deer in one day! No plain boiled roots for supper that night!

All that day they had followed along the course of a creek. As light began to fade, they arrived at a good campsite on the south side of the creek, a little above where it emptied into the river [*Bitterroot River, or Clark's River*].

This was where Black Eagle, Speaking Eagle, Ahskahp, Koolkooltom, Ya'amas Wakus, and White Wolf had hoped to find their friends, the Shalees. They scurried around, looking for fresh signs, but none could be found. No one had been in this vicinity for a long time.

"Those barefoot tracks back at the hot springs spoke of someone in great distress. Something terrible has happened to them!" they mourned.

With heavy hearts, they counted seven sleeps from Oyaip.

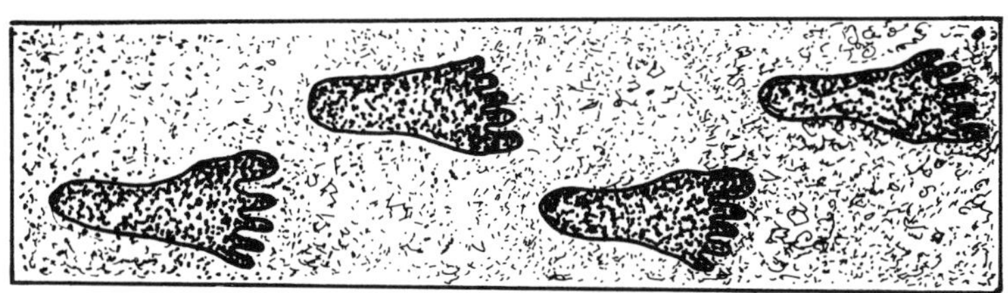

July 1, 1806

"We Sent out all the hunters very early this morning by 12 oClock they all returned haveing killd. 12 Deer six of them large fat Bucks, . . . as Capt. Lewis and Myself part at this place we make a division of our party and such baggage and provisions as is

Souteable. . . . one of the Indians who accompanied us swam Clarks river and examined the country around, on his return he informed us that he had discovered where a Band of the Tushepaws (Shalees) had encamped this Spring . . . & that they had passed Down Clarks river . . ." Clark [Thwaites, Volume 5, Page 179.]

When the new sun rose, the six Nee-mee-poo men held their own discussion while the So-yap-pos prepared to divide food.

"Things don't look good for anybody going into Buffalo Country just now. Pah-kees attack," Ahs-kahp said.

"A-a-a-a," the rest agreed.

"We better not go any farther," said Speaking Eagle. "We better go home."

But Koolkooltom was not satisfied. "I came to visit friends and cousins among Shalees," he said. "I want to find out what happened to them. I am going to swim across. Look for signs."

When no one offered to go with him, Koolkooltom swam the river alone and began his search for traces of his friends. Like a dog sniffing scents on a trail, he scurried through underbrush and over open ground with eyes that read every track and sign.

Not only his friends, but the So-yap-pos, as well, awaited his return. What he reported was reassuring to all.

"Shalees made their encampment over there, maybe one, maybe two moons past. Sixty-four lodges. They moved downriver, maybe to good camas grounds on a branch of this river."

July 2, 1806

". . . in the course of the day we had much conversation with the indians by signs, our only mode of communicating our ideas. . . . I prevailed on them to go with me as far as the East branch of Clark's River and put me on the road to the Missouri. I gave the Cheif a medal of the small size; he insisted on exchanging names with me . . ." Lewis [Thwaites, Volume 5, Page 180.]

Now that the concern for their friends, the Shalees, was lessened by evidence of their being alive, Speaking Eagle spoke to the So-yap-po captains.

"Friends," he said, "my brothers and I have counseled together about continuing this journey with you. We have brought you safely over the mountains as we said we would. Now we do not want to go farther. We want to return home."

"Friends," Captain Clark answered, "you have been good guides. We could not have crossed those mountains without your help. But one more thing we ask of you. Captain Lewis and I are taking separate routes from this point. Go with Captain Lewis for two more sleeps. Show him the right road to take through the mountains to the Great Falls of the Missouri."

"A-a-a-a-a! We will go," the six men agreed.

Turning to Ahs-kahp, brother of Cut Nose, Captain Clark said, "We promised three guns for guides. Speaking Eagle and Black Eagle received their guns before we started over the mountains. Now we give the third gun to you." In addition, Clark gave the three guides some powder and balls for ammunition.

Ahs-kahp beamed with satisfaction. He now owned a gun.

Lewis then honored Black Eagle with a small round medal remembering the many kindnesses Black Eagle had shown him. He then delighted Black Eagle's friends by tying blue ribbons around the hair of each one.

When Black Eagle received the medal from Captain Lewis, he thought in his heart, "This man is good friend! Can be trusted. To show my admiration and respect for him I wish to honor him by exchanging names." To Captain Lewis he spoke with his hands, making it clear that exchanging names with his friend was a great honor. When the So-yap-po chief understood, he consented.

"Friend," Black Eagle said, "my father was one to be trusted, as you are. He was killed by Big Bellies. To honor you I would bestow upon you his name, Heume-ya-kah-likt, meaning 'White Grizzly Bearskin Folded.' "

The So-yap-po repeated the name as he had heard it, "Yo-me-kol-lick," trying to remember the sounds. "I am honored to receive that name."

Then White Wolf came forward to honor Captain Lewis with the gift of a horse.

"I have opened my ears to what you have told my people in council. It is my hope that you see the Big Bellies and make good peace with them. Tell them it is our desire to be friends with them. Show them this horse, given as a token of our sincerity," spoke White Wolf.

Hearts were lighter that night. Plenty of good, fat deer meat filled their stomachs that evening, for the hunters had brought in twelve deer that day. They lay down for the eighth sleep since leaving Oyaip.

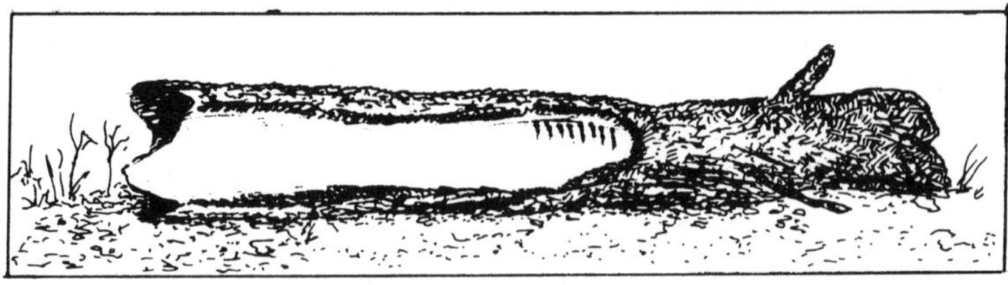

There was not much to do when the new sun came up. The hunters went out as usual, but came in with only two deer. Captain Clark had most of the meat dried for future use.

The man, Shields, worked at repairing guns. The muzzles of two guns had burst. He sawed them off and made short guns out of them. They looked good.

Captain Clark saw Speaking Eagle looking at those short guns and spoke with his hands, "Do you want to trade the long gun we gave you for guiding us for this short gun?"

"A-a-a-a-a," Speaking Eagle said, thinking that a short gun would handle better. He handed over his long rifle for the sawed-off gun.

"Wonder how it shoots," he said, and straight way fired it at a ground squirrel sitting on his mound some distance away. The shot was good. Speaking Eagle was pleased with his trade and shot several more rounds.

Much talking with hands went on with the So-yap-pos that day. Understanding one another was growing easier.

By observing the men drying meat, dividing food supplies, reorganizing packs, putting guns and ammunition in shape, and portioning out the horses, it was clear the parting would take place on the next sun.

Captain Lewis meant to go downriver, taking Drewyer, Gass, the Fields brothers, Frazier, Werner, Thompson, Goodrich, and McNeal, his dog, Seaman, and seventeen horses. All the Nee-mee-poo guides and friends would go with him for two sleeps.

Captain Clark would go in the opposite direction, upstream, taking Charbonneau, Sa-ka-ka-wea and her little boy, Ba-teese, the black man, York, the other So-yap-po hunters and workmen, and the remaining horses.

July 2, 1806
". . . the Musquetors has been So troublesom day and night since our arival in this Vally that we are tormented very much by them and cant' write except under our Bears [i. e., biers]. . . ." Clark [Thwaites, Journal 5, Page 181.]

When they had finished giving directions to their men, each So-yap-po chief crawled under his light tent to get away from the hordes of mosquitos. As they were often seen to do, they pushed little sticks up and down and across thin, white "leaves," making black marks that meant nothing to the curious Ya'amas Wakus and his friends.

The day wore on, marked by the diligence of the So-yap-pos in preparing for their separation. Every man was checking his gun and gear to make sure he would be ready for the new adventures ahead.

The evening shadows brought a cool breeze to drive off the mosquitos. To Speaking Eagle and his friends, who had not been active during the day, it was now a pleasure to move about. An urge for activity welled up in them, and they raced their horses for the sheer joy of feeling their hair floating on the breeze. Some of the So-yap-pos joined in the racing. Then they all tested their own swiftness by challenging each other to foot races. As had happened in the past, no one person came out ahead all the time.

The ninth sleep from Oyaip came.

CHAPTER 21

THE PARTING

JULY 3, 1806

"Took leave of Capt. C. and party to-day. gave one of my shirts and a handkercheif to the two Indians whom we met on Collin's Creek and detained some days. . . . All arrangements being now compleated for carrying into effect the several scheemes we had planed for execution on our return, we saddled our horses and set out . . ." Lewis [Thwaites, Volume 5, Page 183.]

The sun had risen well above the mountain tops before each party of So-yap-pos was ready to go its way. The men gave each other vigorous handshakes, hearty slaps on the back, and loud calls of "Good-bye!" "We'll meet you on the Missouri!" "Take care of yerselves!" And then they mounted their horses.

Captain Clark turned toward the south and took the trail following the Bitterroot River upstream. To his right loomed the sharp outlines of the precipitous Bitterroot Mountains which dropped abruptly to the western edge of the Bitterroot Valley. Behind him followed his man, York, the interpreter, Charbonneau, the Bird Woman and her little boy, twenty men, and some twenty-six pack horses.

As Clark turned to the south, Captain Lewis turned toward the north, following the Bitterroot River downstream. To his left the Bitterroots reared their ragged heads sharply along the the western edge of the valley.

Speaking Eagle and his five tribesmen led the way down a well-worn path along the west bank of the river. Captain Lewis and Seaman, his big black dog, followed with Drewyer, Gass, Reuben and Joe Fields, Frazier, Werner, Thompson, Goodrich, McNeal. The extra horses brought up the rear.

The sun was almost at its highest when they saw, on the opposite bank, a muddy stream emptying itself through two channels into the river.[1] Below this point, the guides stopped to confer with the So-yap-pos.

"Here is best place to cross and get on road to Buffalo Country," Speaking Eagle said. His friends agreed.

The river was wide and swift. How could the So-yap-pos cross without getting their food supplies, extra clothing, blankets, and other items in their baggage wet? There were no trees here big enough to make a canoe.

Gass, the carpenter, said, "We could build rafts by using a few small trees and branches and what driftwood we can scrounge up. These would take us over."

That was a workable idea. But wood was scarce.

Without stopping to eat, the men scurried around, gathering dry drift logs and dry limbs until they had enough to piece three small rafts together. Only then did they take time to eat.

The sun was already halfway down toward the horizon. They had to work fast and hard to get everything across the Missoula River before sundown.

The guides made their own crossing simple. They just swam their horses over, towing their belongings behind in little round boats they fashioned from deerskin. All the extra horses followed and swam safely to the other side.

It remained, now, for the So-yap-pos to get themselves across. Three rafts loaded with baggage and manned by one or two men crossed over. The baggage was unloaded and a man on each raft returned for more cargo. Back and forth they went, and every time a raft crossed, the current carried it farther down stream.

Captain Lewis and two men who did not swim well were the last over. When they set out, the current swept the raft into swift water that raced between small islands and willow-covered sandbars. Just as they neared shore, the raft sank below the surface. Willow bushes raked Captain Lewis off into the river, but he swam to safety. The other men clung to the raft until it bumped into the bank some distance below, allowing them to scramble safely to the shore.

At last, all were together again, the crossing accomplished. Travel resumed with the guides leading upstream to a campsite near a small creek.

As always, keen eyes examined the ground for messages left by tracks. A fresh horse track in the road just beyond the camp raised questions.

"What does this mean?" asked Captain Lewis.

"Maybe Shalee scout watching us cross over," said Speaking Eagle. "Shalee camp may be near." His voice sounded hopeful.

This night's camp was made most miserable by mosquitos. Again, the mosquitos plagued every living thing—from men and horses to Seaman, the dog. The horses grew frantic until the men built fires that made smoke dense enough to stand in. The smoke drove the mosquitos off, where they swarmed around the edges of camp, until cold breezes from the mountains blew them away for the night.

Hunters, who had been sent out as soon as camp was made, came in with three fat deer. Captain Lewis gave a whole deer and half of another to his guides. This was more than the Nee-mee-poo men needed for their supper, but they wasted nothing. They sliced the extra meat into very thin strips, cutting parallel with muscles, instead of across the grain as the white men did. Draped over poles, high above passing animals, it would dry quickly in the sun.

"We leave this here," Black Eagle explained. "As we

come back from visiting Shalees, we will have it to eat when we cross over mountains."

Here, the guides made sure that Captain Lewis understood how to find the road to Buffalo Country and the Great Falls of the Missouri. They pointed out to him the trail that led upstream to the meeting of the rivers.

"Follow this trail along the branch that comes in just above until the Co-kah-lah-ish-kit [the Blackfoot River], the river of the Road to Buffalo, comes in from the left. The road is plain. It will lead you to the Great Falls. You cannot miss it," Speaking Eagle told him.

"When you reach dividing ridge between these rivers and Missouri, you come to forks in road. Take left hand fork. Both roads take you to falls, but left hand is better," Ahs-kahp offered.

"We cannot go any farther," Speaking Eagle continued. "It is the land of the Big Bellies. We do not want to meet te-wel-kas. We want to look for our friends, Shalees, downriver."

Captain Lewis now spoke to the three guides, "Friends, you have guided us over the mountains and we have given you the three guns we promised. We told you we would give you ten good horses if you went with us to the Great Falls of the Missouri. Now you tell us you cannot go to the Falls. No horses. You have shown us the right trail and we are grateful. No one could have done better. You are good guides."

Turning to Koolkooltom and Ya'amas Wakus, Lewis continued, "I am also grateful to you for waiting for us before we joined together at Oyaip. As yet, you have received no reward. Now, I want to give you a gift." And he gave to Koolkooltom one of his shirts and to Ya'amas Wakus a handkerchief. The men were pleased, and their hearts were warmed by these gifts.

Before the hunters went to sleep that night, the captain instructed them to go out early the next morning.

"I want to leave some extra meat for our guides who have served so well."

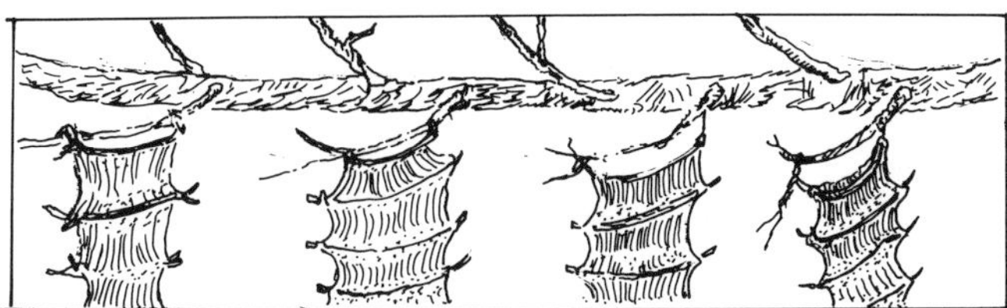

July 4, 1806

". . . at half after eleven the hunters returned from the chase unsuccessfull. I now ordered the horses saddled smoked a pipe with these friendly people and at noon bid them adieu. . . . these affectionate people our guides betrayed every emmotion of unfeigned regret at seperating from us; . . ." Lewis [Thwaites, Volume 5, Pages 187 and 188.]

Soon after the hunters went out at daybreak, the watchful eyes of Ya'amas Wakus caught sight of a man on horseback swimming across the river toward them.

"Looks-Ahead, my cousin!" Ya'amas Wakus said. "Finally made it across the mountains."

Looks-Ahead rode his dripping horse up to Captain Lewis and his hands said, "When Koos-koos-kee began to drop, I started over the mountains with Follows-the-Trail. Snow too deep, too soft. Had to turn back. I, alone, tried again. Followed your trail. Four suns behind. Now I find you."

Captain Lewis gave out a small amount of black sand and balls to the guides and their comrades. This pleased them, but it added to the somber looks on their faces. It meant that every act of their So-yap-po friend was bringing the moment of separation closer.

That moment came soon after the hunters returned. They had not had any luck. They had no extra meat to give to their Nee-mee-poo friends. The guides would have to depend on the meat they were drying from the day before.

Lewis now settled his mind. He and his party must move on. But before he gave the order to start, he shared one last smoke with these friends he must leave behind.

Finally he rose and shouted, "Saddle up!" "Let's get going."

"Friends," Black Eagle said sorrowfully. "We will not see you again. We know if you meet the te-wel-kas, the Big Bellies, they will kill you, just as they did my father." And he gave a wail of grief.

Lewis then turned to shake the hands of Black Eagle, Speaking Eagle, Ahs-kahp, Koolkooltom, Ya'amas Wakus, White Wolf, and Looks-Ahead, saying, "Good-bye," just as he had done to the other So-yap-po captain when they parted.

But that was not the way of the Nee-mee-poo, who knew no word for "Good-bye." Tears ran down their faces as each one gave strong hugs to one So-yap-po after another.

When the last So-yap-po rider disappeared around a bend in the trail, the seven friends mounted their horses and started downriver in search of the Shalees.

Not far away, they found them at the camas grounds. There, sadness and gladness awaited them. In truth, the Blackfeet had killed some of their cousins and friends. Some had died during winter; but,many were alive and well to welcome their kinsman from across the mountains.

During the Moon of Ta-yum, the hottest time of summer, the men remained at the camp with cousins and friends, hunting and enjoying the friendship of these people. In late summer they helped move the encampment upriver to the customary location near the mouth of the creek, Aha-tes, that runs past the hot springs.

The men knew that the warm days of summer would go when the moon changed. They wanted to be across the mountains among the Nee-mee-poo before bad weather set in. They would have to start soon or run the risk of being caught in an early snow storm on the mountain tops.

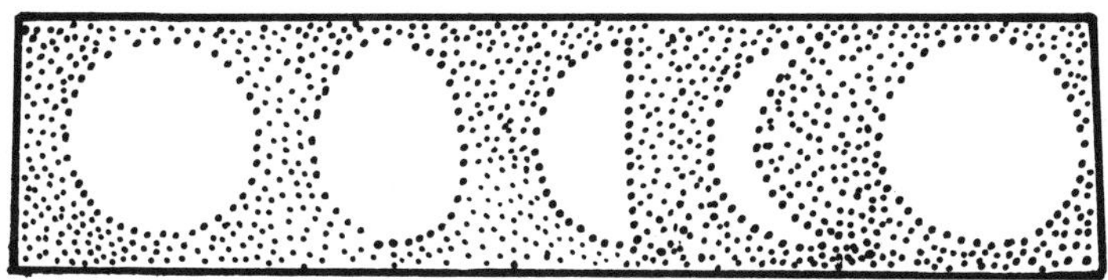

After the So-yap-pos had departed from the valley of the Koos-koos-kee, an inconsolable young woman grieved over the departure of the So-yap-pos. They had gone when the snow still lay deep in the high mountains. All of the "Daytime Smokers" had gone. Her "Daytime Smoker" had gone, never to return! Or had he? She wondered.

Tom-sis could not believe she would never again see the man she loved. Despite all her family's efforts to persuade her to go with them to the Ka-oo-yit and to take part in their summer's activities, Tom-sis refused to leave the Kamiah Valley. If her "Daytime Smoker" should return, she would be there. Her family worried over her despondency, fearing she might take her own life in the river. But when she could not be dissuaded, they were forced to go on without her.

For a time Tom-sis almost lost the will to live. She wept and cried aloud, "Enim hah-ma!" ["My man!"] "Enim hah-ma!" until she could cry no more.

Then an idea came to her. If her man had gone, never to return to the Koos-koos-kee Valley, she could follow him. She would find him, and he would know how much she loved him.

Tom-sis settled her mind and rode off as soon as she could pack an extra horse with her sleeping robes, a supply of root-bread, and baskets for berries. Her compulsion to catch up with the Daytime Smokers dispelled all fear of dangers along the way. No storms, no bears, nothing would stop her.

Many suns had gone since the So-yap-pos and their guides had started over the mountains. It was now the best season to make the crossing. The snow had melted from the trail. Enough grass for her two horses could be found on even the highest ridges. Huckleberries, ripening in the high mountains, added to her food supply. Tom-sis had only to keep her horses moving along the trail.

At length she reached the highest ridge—the place where The People left messages for others to read.[2] Even before the memory of her grandfathers, The People had, from time to time, carried rocks up to this place to use in messages. Long ago, when The People had piled rocks in a cone around a tall pole, why did they leave a hollow place inside? Was it a place for travelers to leave tokens to assure safe passage?

Visitors, unskilled in reading these rock signs, often took the wrong trail and became lost in tangled brush at the foot of the steep mountain.

Tom-sis looked at the signs. She saw where some people had taken the trail to the river to fish. She did not want to go that way. She knew the trail sign she must follow. Before she went on, she placed on a flat, river-washed rock a rose she had found blooming in the high mountains. She laid a small stone on the stem to hold the flower in place.

"Tom-sis has gone this way," the message read.

Two sleeps later Tom-sis rode out of the mountains. She passed the hot springs and finally came upon the camp of the Shalees. Here she found her cousins, Speaking Eagle and Black Eagle, along with Ahs-kahp, Koolkooltom, Ya'amas Wakus, White Wolf, and Looks-Ahead.

"Tom-sis! Why do you come?" Black Eagle asked her in surprise.

"I follow Daytime Smoker," she said. "Enim hah-ma!" ["I want to find my man!"]

"Those men are far away. We do not know where they are. They parted. Some of them went ya-wits-kin-ne-kai [north]. Some went loo-kits-kin-ne-kai [south], closer to te-wel-ka country. We do not know where your man is now."

"The moon has changed. Snow will soon be coming to the mountains. We start next sun to return to Koos-koos-kee Valley. Come back with us," her cousin, Speaking Eagle, pleaded.

Tom-sis thought about this. Her man had gone far, far away. She did not know where to go to find him. She did not want to go back to her family across the mountains. She would be safe right here among her friends, the Shalees. She settled her mind.

"I will not go back with you," Tom-sis told her cousins, "but I will not try to find Daytime Smoker. I will stay here with our friends."

All through the winter Tom-sis remained with the Shalees. When the snow had barely gone and the tiny flowers were just beginning to open their blooms, she bore a baby. The heart of Tom-sis warmed with joy at the sight of him. He did not look like the other babies in camp. His eyes were not black, but smoky blue. What hair he had was not black, but yellow like the down of a baby duck, with red lights dancing through it. This was a special baby, a gift from the man she loved, and Tom-sis called him, Al-pa-to-kate, [Father Was Daytime Smoker].[3]

"We must go," Speaking Eagle said. "Moon has changed. Snow may come soon. We must return to our homeland."

Speaking Eagle, Black Eagle, Ahs-kahp, Koolkooltom, Ya'amas Wakus, White Wolf, and Looks-Ahead turned their faces toward the setting sun.

Supplied with plenty of roots and the dried meat the So-yap-pos had given them, they rode away to retrace their journey over the high mountains. Every old campsite, the warm springs, the places where horses had slipped and stumbled, where the men had smoked, where they had been cold and hungry—every landmark along the trail brought to their minds vivid pictures of their departed friends.

When they reached the place where messages were left on the highest ridge, the seven men sat and smoked a long time in silence. They wondered about that Great White Father, away off in the directon of the rising sun, who had sent the So-yap-pos to tell everybody to live in peace.

Finally, Black Eagle spoke, "We leave a sign that points to Great White Father."

"A-a-a-a! I will help," the others said.

And they searched around, never disturbing existing signs, until they had found rocks that would tell the story. By propping a long, sharp rock against smaller rocks, they pointed it toward the rising sun. Its message was clear to them.

"This is the way to the Great White Father."

From that time on, the sign would speak to all The People who would follow.

Before they left that mountain, the men went from one rock sign to another, reading messages left recently. Some said that people had gone down certain trails to fishing places. Some told how many sleeps to good horse feed. Finally, they came to a flat, river-washed rock on which a withered rose lay.

"Tom-sis!" they spoke softly.

They turned then and continued on toward the setting sun. They were certain they would find their families on the Oyaip, for this was the season when salmon spawned in small streams and The People came again to the Prairie for the camas harvest.

Four sleeps they traveled in that direction. When the sun dropped from sight at the end of the fifth day and it was growing dark, they neared the Oyaip.

Speaking Eagle raised his voice in a loud wolf call, "OW-oo-oo-oo-oo-oo-oo! OW-oo-oo-oo-oo-oo!"—the signal for beginning the trail song to inform The People of their approach. Without words, the men's voices burst out in a resounding shout that subsided to a deep-chested rumble.

"I am a friend, and I am coming home."

Their wordless message, punctuated by occasional wolf howls, seemed endless. Over and over and over they repeated it, as they rode ever nearer to the encampments on the Oyaip.

In Red Grizzly Bear's Oyaip camp, which was in the accustomed place near that of Broken Arm, the small boys played in the twilight. An unusual sound in the distance brought them to a standstill.

"Listen! Kah-lat-tsah, I hear a wolf!" Alle-oo-ya spoke softly to his grandfather. "Way off in the mountain . . . Coming closer now."

Grandfather listened. "Do you hear anything more?" he asked.

"Now I hear men singing. Far away . . . closer, now.

Seems like they come on the trail from the mountains. What do they sing?"

"They say, 'I am a friend, and I am coming home'," Kah-lat-tsah answered. "They sing so we will know they are friends and will do them no harm."

As the voices came closer, the people in Red Grizzly Bear's camp and Broken Arm's camp waited in the dusk to see who was approaching. Speaking Eagle, Black Eagle, and Ahs-kahp, who went to guide the So-yap-pos across the mountains; Koolkooltom and Ya'amas Wakus, who went to visit Shalees; White Wolf and Looks Ahead, who had joined the party enroute! All back!

Cries of joy burst forth. People streamed from Red Grizzly Bear's camp and Broken Arm's camp to welcome the young men home. Just as the So-yap-pos had promised, they now carried three guns. One gun was shorter than the others. Most of the men wore blue ribbons tied around their hair, while one wore a white shirt, another a white kerchief around his neck, and a third a medal hanging on a thong around his neck—prized gifts from the So-yap-pos.

The People talked of many things that night: how the So-yap-pos had separated, with the Red-Head taking most of the men and horses upstream; how they had guided Captain Lewis and his men to the road that goes to Buffalo Country; how they had found their friends, the Shalees, farther downstream; how Tom-sis came to the Shalee camp; how she had refused to return with them; how they had crossed the mountains at the right time, ahead of storms, and were now home.

They talked of things to come—as far ahead as they were able to look into the future. They talked about the superiority their guns would give them over the te-wel-kas, balanced against their commitment to live at peace with their neighbors. They talked about the hope that the So-yap-pos would return and set up trading places so they could get more of the white men's goods and ammunition.

It was good that the The People could not look far into the future that night. Their hearts were at peace. They went to sleep, knowing they had helped those furry-faced white men, for they had heeded Wat-ku-ese's admonition, "They are So-yap-pos! Good men! Do them no harm! DO THEM NO HARM!"

KULLO
[THAT IS ALL!]

CHAPTER NOTES

Abbreviations

Clark. Clark, W. P. *Indian Sign Language*. L. R. Hamersley and Co., 1885, Copyright 1959, Theron Fox, reprint, San Jose 6, California, The Rosicrucian Press, Ltd. (Limited Edition Reprint.)

Criswell. Criswell, Ph.D., Elijah Harry Criswell. *Lewis and Clark: Linguistic Pioneers*. The University of Missouri Studies, Vol. XV, April 1, 1940, Number 2, published at University of Missouri, Columbia, Missouri.

Curtis. Curtis, Edward S. *The North American Indian*. 20 Vols., Vol. VIII, Cambridge, Mass., 1907-1930.

Gass. Gass, Patrick. *Journals of the Lewis and Clark Expedition* (*Journal of Patrick Gass*). Ross & Haines, Inc., Minneapolis, Minnesota, 1958.

McWhorter. McWhorter, L. V. *Hear Me My Chiefs!* Caldwell, Idaho: Caxton Printers, Ltd., 1952.

Ordway. *The Journals of Captain Meriwether Lewis and Sergeant John Ordway*, edited by Milo M. Quaife, The State Historical Society of Wisconsin, Madison, MCMLXV, Copyright 1916, Second Printing, 1965.

Phinney. Phinney, Archie. *Nez Perce Texts*. New York: Columbia University Press, 1934.

Space. Space, Ralph. *The Clearwater Story*. Forest Service, U. S. Department of Agriculture.

Thw. Thwaites, Reuben Gold, ed., *Original Journals of the Lewis and Clark Expedition, 1804-1806*, 8 vols. New York: Dodd Mead and Co., 1904-1905.

Wheeler. Wheeler, Olin D. *The Trail of Lewis and Clark 1804-1904*, Two Volumes, G. P. Putnam's Sons, New York, 1926.

Chapter 1

[1] The Oyaip Prairie was sometimes spelled 0-yaip or Weyippe in old papers. Ralph Space said on an Idaho Historical Field Trip, July 27, 1958, that the meaning of the name has been lost. Harry Wheeler agreed with Mr. Space mentioning that, until recent times, Nez Perce was not a written language. However, Mrs.

Viola Molloy, an old pioneer who lived in Orofino, said she had heard that the word meant "Field of Tents."

At the time of Lewis and Clarks' arrival to Oyaip Prairie, it was about 1,800 acres with a string of timber between two branches of the prairie. The town of Weippe is on the edge of the original prairie.

[2] Area names. Informant: Harry Wheeler.

Area names as they are known today:
Lah-mah-ta = Whitebird
Ha-so-tin = Asotin
Tsce-men-i-cum = Lewiston/Clarkston
Te-weh = Orofino
Tee-e-lap-al-lo = near Kamiah
Tis-ai-ach-pa = near Kooskia

[3] Nee-mee-poo, The People, is variously spelled: Numipu; Ni mi pu. Numipi (Nez Perce call themselves). Nun = we + pu = people. Locative suffix is commonly added to place-name in forming the name of inhabitants. Numipu—therefore = "we people." Aoki, Haruo. *Nez Perce Texts*, University of California Publications in Linguistics, Volume 90, 1979, University of California Press. Informant Harry Wheeler rendered the following variations: Ni'mi' pu; Ne'me-poo; Neu'me peu.

[4] Wat-ku-ese—Through the years the author has heard the story of Wat-ku-ese from many Nez Perces: Mary Kipp, Richard Moffett, Beatrice Miles, Harry Wheeler. The stories have been essentially the same, but with slight variations. See Chapter 4, Note 7: Thw. 3:83, footnote 1.

[5] Shalees—Undoubtedly Lewis and Clarks' spelling for the *Salish* tribe living in Bitterroot Valley—known as Flatheads today.

[6] So-yap-po—Flathead name for white man. Information from Mrs. Beaverhead, Ronan, Montana. Mrs. Beaverhead spelled the name: SOYAPPI.

[7] Potlatch Creek, Ya-ho-toin. From an 1860 map belonging to informant, Ralph Space.

Thw. 3:99—Footnote 1: "The explorers (in revision, Codex G) named this Colter Creek; it is now Potlatch Creek, the principal tributary of the lower Clearwater."

[8] Lah-mah-ta, the Wearisome Place, is known as Whitebird today.

[9] Phinney, p. 126. The preparation for a great undertaking was purification, called ipna-hoywima. This was done by a long period of fasting, sweat bathing, and hot water bathing.

[10] Phinney, p. 239. Pa'siwya—the painting of the face and body was a very important source of fighting power. A warrior, properly painted, was invincible.

[11] McWhorter, pp. 19-21. Red Bear was later called "Many Wounds" for his eighty battle scars, and in 1842, age 90, was called the "Bloody Chief."

[12] Komsit—kause porridge. Informant: Edith Types, 1967.

[13] Spoons. Informant: Harry Wheeler, 1957. "They nearly always carried their own spoons. When being served, they always said, 'Give me two.' They would take two spoonfuls, all they wanted."

[14] "Eat! Make you strong." Informant: Walter Sewell.

Chapter 2

[1] Phinney, p. 22. Known as hila'wtakitsa, this refers to the apportioning of a big haul of food owned in common, particularly in case of salmon fishing by net. One man officiates in the distribution and the position requires someone who is just, a good talker, and a diplomat generally.

[2] September 4, 1986, Mylie Lawyer, Lapwai, daughter of Corbett Lawyer, gave this information: "My father always said the names of the three little boys were Alle-oo-ya, Barnabas, and Is-coo-tim. Alle-oo-ya (Alieu) became Chief Lawyer of the 1855 Treaty."

The name "Ish-coh-tim" appears on the 1855 Treaty; but the Indian name of Barnabas has been lost. Since Barnabas was a missionary-given name, the name of "Koots-Koots" (meaning Little One) has been substituted in this account.

[3] Arrow chief. Informant: Harry Wheeler, 1957.

[4] Beards. Thw. 5:29. ". . . in common with other savage nations of America they extract their beards. . . . I am convinced if they had shaved their beard instead of extracting it would have been as well supplyed in this particular as any of my countrymen." Lewis

[5] We-ya-oo-yit. Informant: Harry Wheeler. We-ya-oo-yit: the word used to designate the coming of the first men—Lewis and Clark. It means "the coming"—the first party passing through (Lewis and Clark Party).

Chapter 3

[1] Kate C. McBeth, *The Nez Perces Since Lewis and Clark*, Fleming H. Evell Co., New York, 1908, p. 26. Dandle: Nez Perces had never seen a handshake before.

[2] Thw. 3:82. Celilo Falls, the ancient fishing grounds. Water backing up from The Dalles Lock and Dam, a vital link in the development of the Columbia River and the Pacific Northwest, inundated the Celilo Falls.

[3] Lewis and Clark obtained horses from Shoshones near Lemhi Pass, Salmon, Idaho, from Sa-ka-ka-wea's brother Cameahwaite. Saddles and bridles would have to be Indian made.

[4] *Nez Perce Country—Official National Park Handbook*, p. 46, ". . . . in the spring of 1805, even as the Lewis and Clark expedition was heading west on the Missouri River, a group of Nez Perces managed to reach the home villages of the Hidatsa, or Gros Ventre, Indians near present-day Bismarck, North Dakota, and buy six guns from them. The Nez Perces got safely back to their band in the Kamiah Valley in Idaho with the guns, and when Lewis and Clark were at Kamiah, they gave the Indians powder and balls for the weapons."

[5] Butchered horse. Thw. 3:74. A hunting party found a stray horse that Clark directed be killed and hung in a tree for the larger party of men coming with Lewis.

[6] A-hot-mo-tim-nim (He-Has-a-Joyous-Heart), who, like a cheerleader, had a "Joyous Heart," was probably one of Twisted Hair's sons. Harry Wheeler was uncertain whether Ya'amas Wakus (Looks Like Mule Deer Doe) and Joyous Heart were two different men or whether A-hot-mo-tim-nim was a nickname for Ya'amas Wakus.

Chapter 4

[1] Thw. 3:82. Clark found Twisted Hair to be a "Chearfull man with apparant siencerity . . ."

[2] Thw. 4:355, 356. Te-toh-kan Ahs-kahp, "People-Coming-Look-Like-Brothers," is Tetoharsky, Nez Perce Chief, in the Lewis and Clark Journals. "Tetoharsky" is a name that has mystified historians. The Author.

Harry Wheeler explained the concept of the name in this way: The two words,

"Tetokan" = People and "Ahskahp" = Brothers, expressed the thought, "People are coming. They look like brothers."

[3] The Red-Head. Criswell, p. xxiii. ". . . Although Captain Clark had acquired many of the qualities of the gentleman of his day, all his life he remained a bluff, hearty, good-natured character who appealed strongly to backwoodsmen and to Indians, who, in his later years as Indian agent, affectionately referred to him as 'the Red-head' . . ."

[4] Chief Timuca, chief from Alpowa, was Timootsin's father. Timootsin later became Chief Timothy. (See Chapter Notes, Chapter 5, Note 3.)

[5] Baby left hanging in tree. Informant: Jack Harlan, *Lewiston Morning Tribune.*

[6] A black Newfoundland dog named Seaman, who belonged to Capt. Lewis, accompanied Lewis and Clark on their expedition. For further reference see *We Proceeded On;* Publication No. 2, July 1977, "Our Dog Scannon—Partner in Discovery" by Ernest Staples Osgood and *We Proceeded On;* Publication No. 2A, March 1986, "Call Him a Good Old Dog, But Don't Call Him Scannon" by Donald Jackson.

[7] Wat-ku-ese. Thw. 3:83, footnote 1. "There is a tradition among the Nez Perce Indians that when Lewis and Clark first visited the Chopunnish, the latter were inclined to kill the white men,—a catastrophe which was averted by the influence of a woman in that tribe. She had been captured by hostile Indians, and carried into Manitoba, where some white people enabled her to escape; and finally she returned to her own tribe, although nearly dead from fatigue and privations. Hearing her people talk of killing the explorers, she urged them to do no harm to the white men, but to treat them with kindness and hospitality—counsel which they followed.—O. D. Wheeler" See Chapter 1 Notes, Number 4.

Chapter 5

[1] Thw. 6:115. The Lewis and Clark Journals contain a table titled "Names of Indian Nations and their places of General Residence." This table provides estimates of number of houses, or lodges, and estimated number of residents at the time of the Lewis and Clark Expedition.

[2] Thw. 7:238. Burning glass—a convex lens for producing an intense heat by converging the sun's rays; very similar to a magnifying glass.

[3] Ta-moot-sin, son of Timuca, became the Christian, Chief Timothy, a life-long friend to missionaries and white settlers.

[4] Carrying coal for pipe. Information from manuscript of Pauline Evans, Sacajawea Museum, Spalding, Idaho, as told by Chief Many Wounds.

[5] *Wild Flowers of the Pacific Coast,* by Leslie H. Haskin. Metropolitan Press, Publishers, Portland, Oregon, 1934, p. 263. "Kinnikinnick is an Eastern Indian word signifying, a mixture, and was applied to any smoking preparation, containing such various ingredients as native tobacco, hemlock gum, sumac bark, spicebush bark, red dogwood bark, dried leaves of the poke plant, and those of the present species. The name kinnikinnick was finally applied to certain plants used, rather than to the prepared mixture. The *engages* of the Fur Companies brought the name to the Pacific Coast, where it became the common appellation of this plant." Botanical name: Arctostaphylos uva-ursi (L)

[6] Thw. 7:238, 239. List of articles purchased for Expedition.

[7] Camas is found in low swampy lands. Stuart, Hon. Granville. *Montana as It Is,* C. S. Westcott and Co., N. Y., 1865, p. 10. "It is a bulbous root about the size of a plum. It has a sweet, gummy taste, and is very nutritious. It forms an important item of food among the Indians from Montana to the Pacific Ocean. They dig

it, cook it in kettles, and dry it. It becomes very hard and will keep for years if kept dry. It is also very good, boiled when freshly dug. White men, Indians, and hogs are very fond of it."

[8] Phinney, p. 77. Ipna'naksa—The literal translation is "She thinks herself." This device of addressing one in the third person is commonly used in derisive statements.

[9] Whipping Man: The Nez Perce parents did not whip their children. Instead, a designated man performed the punishment. Informant: Harry Wheeler.

[10] Beargrass hat incident. Information from manuscript of Pauline Evans, Sacajawea Museum, Spalding, Idaho, as told by Chief Many Wounds.

[11] Scrubbing York. Informants: Charlie Adams and Walter Sewell.

Chapter 6

[1] Bushels of pestles have been unearthed on Oyaip Prairie by plows of farmers.

[2] See Chapter 9 "The Cold Moons" for the complete legend of the Coyote making the path of the Clearwater River and the Kamiah Valley.

[3] This island is known today as China Island. The remnants of it are located by the railroad tunnel just upstream from Orofino. The island feature was destroyed when the tunnel was made.

[4] In recent times this area was occupied by Riverside Mill which has since been removed.

[5] Orofino Creek (Rock Dam Creek of Lewis and Clark). Boulders, choking the mouth of this creek, formed a veritable dam to spring run-offs. With the Clearwater River at flood stage, the creek could not discharge its waters and caused serious flooding to the City of Orofino for years, until the United States Army Corps of Engineers dredged it in 1963.

[6] The ford crossed between the present site of the Camas Prairie Railroad depot (Orofino) and the lower end of the Orofino Riverside Cemetery.

[7] Walter Sewell claimed the stump of the tree was in evidence in the early 1900s. The porch of a house was built over it, but the stump has disintegrated. The location was near the Orofino railroad depot as it stands today.

[8] This flat is known as Chase's Flat, named after L. G. Chase who homesteaded it.

[9] Housing development has nearly filled in Chase's Slough.

Chapter 7

[1] Fishhook story told by Camille Williams, Nez Perce, 1941.

[2] Long Arm story told by Camille Williams, Nez Perce, 1941.

[3] L. G. Chase, a homesteader, dragged remains of the tree out of the slough with his team of horses. The top of the tree Chase dragged out had an axe-pointed butt end where it had been cut off. A portion of the stump was cut off at ground level and taken to the World's Fair in Portland, Oregon, in 1905 and the rest of the stump was blasted out when the first highway was built. Walter Sewell, the informant, took a piece of it.

[4] Four large and one small canoe: Gass, p. 174.

[5] Rope story. Informants: Charlie Adams and Walter Sewell.

[6] Ta-ma-nam-mah—Salmon River. Informant: Harry Wheeler.

[7] Tap-toop-pa—Winter home of Twisted Hair. Flat across North Fork, north side of Clearwater. Informant: Harry Wheeler.

Chapter 8

[1] Wheeler, p. 6. ". . . In order to preserve their powder and to economize space, etc., the former had been packed and sealed in small canisters of lead, each containing powder enough for the canister when melted into bullets, they, of course, having to mold their own balls. This arrangement was a wise and ingenious one. Not once in the entire exploration did they experience danger from a powder explosion, and these lead canisters also enabled them to cache the powder with perfect freedom."

[2] Iship. Curtis. " 'Iship' comes in a dream . . . The person to whom it comes sings a song in a strange language, dances violently and continuously, and gives away possessions. Cuts self. If person does not recover by fall, he will surely die."

[3] These rock formations can be seen along the Clearwater River and some of them are pointed out by road-signs on Idaho State Highway 12.

[4] Lee-tsu and her dog, Mox-Mox. From Pauline Evans' manuscript: Peo-peo-tah-likt's mother's dog.

[5] These rugged rapids were submerged by the Washington Water Power Dam at Lewiston and now by the back waters of Lower Granite Dam.

[6] Columbia River. (Information obtained in Astoria, Oregon; source is anonymous.) In 1792, American Merchant Captain Robert Gray was the first to cross the hazardous bar of the Columbia. He named the river after his ship.

Chapter 9

[1] Ho'plal. Spelling as used by the Museum of Nez Perce National Historical Park, Spalding, Idaho. The explanation of the meaning has sometimes been enriched by comments of informants; this applies to the words Sekh-le-wahl, Ha-oo- khoy, Wai-lu-poop as found in Chapter 9. J. J. Miles provided the information for this interpretation of Ho'plal.

[2] Little Salmon country. This point was a huge rock in the Little Salmon Valley just south of Riggins, Idaho.

[3] Cut Nose's story. Informant: Harry Wheeler.

[4] Scalp Dance. Informant: J. J. Miles, March 2, 1956. "If my son should get killed, I would mourn for him maybe a month. The chief would say, 'We are going to have a scalp dance.' That would start in the evening. There would be no more mourning for me. I would dress up. I would dance in scalp dance, holding up the scalp of the enemy. Standing in one spot I would dance up and down, just my knees and body moving.

"All the women would throw their hair back away from their faces instead of braiding it. It would be a victory dance. (No scalps would have been taken if any of our warriors had been killed in this battle that avenged my son's death.) All the women would stand back of the men. The men and women would sing together as they danced.

"It sounded real pretty, singing together."

[5] Itswa-wIts-itsqiy. Phinney, p. 264. "The derivation and literal meaning of the word are unknown. It was used to address and beckon the evening shadows which bring all the joys of evening camp."

[6] Khalp-khalp. Phinney, p. 327, xa'lpxalpnim—gusty wind. Page 306, xa'lpxalp (pronounced "khalp-khalp")—"Gusty Wind is the spirit of cold. The name is taken

from the noise made by the north wind when it viciously lashes and flaps the pliable door-piece of a lodge."

[7] Indian lodges. Curtis, p. 69.

[8] Ipna-ko-tahk-o-tsaya. An obsolete word explained by this story. Informant: Harry Wheeler.

[9] Ho'pope. Informants: Harry and Ida Wheeler.

Phinney, p. 351: "ho'pop. Baked pine tree moss made into a black porridge was a very sweet and tasty food."

Thw. 5:8. ". . . we are informed that they were compelled to collect the moss of the pine boil & eate it in the latter part of the last winter."

[10] Graves. Curtis, p. 51.

[11] Twenty-eight horses. Thw. 5:99. ". . . a wife of Neeshnee-parkkeeook died some short time since, himself and hir relations sac[r]eficed 28 horses to her."

[12] Customs at death. Curtis, pp. 51-52.

[13] Firewood fuel. Informant: J. J. Miles.

[14] Sleeping position. Chuinard, M.D., Eldon G. *Only One Man Died*, Ye Galleon Press, Fairfield, Washington, 1979, p. 54: "That the white man learned the value of the Indian practice of sleeping with the feet to the fire is shown by James Tilton's description: 'The best hospital I ever contrived was upon the plan of an Indian hut. The fire was built in the midst of the ward . . . the patients laid with their heads to the wall round about, and their feet were all turned to the fire."

[15] "The Path for the Water." Informants: Charlie Adams and Walter Sewell.

[16] Coyote's moccasin tracks. Informant, Pauline Evans showed the author the "tracks." They are large rocky, shallow depressions shaped somewhat like the impression of a moccasin with a heel and toe outline ascending the side of the hill. Many of these rock outcroppings can be seen on the north side of the Clearwater River, opposite Spalding Park.

[17] Kamiah Monster, based on Archie Phinney's rendition and stories from informants: Harry Wheeler, J. J. Miles, and Alec Pinkham.

[18] "The Coming of Fish." Informants: Charlie Adams and Walter Sewell.

[19] "Finding the Trail through the Mountains." Adapted. John P. Harlan, *The Lewiston Morning Tribune.*

[20] "Coyote." Alec Pinkham.

[21] "The Chipmunk and Grizzly Bear." Alec Pinkham.

[22] Beargrass and hemp articles. The Nez Perce women were skilled in the art of intertwining native hemp with leaves of beargrass (Xerophyllum tenax) to make bags, hats, pouches, cups. Beargrass, dyed with native plants, was used to work designs into each article. The process was slow, taking many days to finish a bag as small as 12 inches by 12 inches. Bags as large as 18 inches by 24 inches or larger used for carrying roots and root bread were highly prized.

[23] Medicine Man looking for cracks in floor. Curtis, p. 69.

[24] Cous cous. From teachings of Harry Wheeler: The root "kouse" is not a pungent, disagreeable one. It is used for food. The root "kouse-kouse" (cous-cous) is very strong, pungent, and disagreeable. It is entirely different from the food root, "kouse." It is used for medicine, especially colds. It grows high up in the mountains.

Cous cous has been identified as Canby's Lovage (Ligusticum canbyi).

[25] Crushed cedar. Informant: Walter Sewell.

[26] Good-bad smell. Phinney. Idiom meaning strong smell.

[27] Power test. Curtis, pp. 69, 71, 72.

[28] Snake Dance (Tu-ka-wi-ut). Alec Pinkham.

[29] Dance all night. Curtis, pp. 69-72.

[30] Weather Chief. Informants: Charlie Adams and Walter Sewell.

Chapter 10

[1] Thw. 5:8. Description of fishtrap: ". . . on the creek near our camp I observed a kind of trap which was made with great panes to catch the small fish which pass down with the stream. This was a dam formed of stone so as to collect the water in a narrow part not exceeding 3 feet wide from which place the water shot with great force and scattered through some small willows closely connected and fastened with bark, this mat of willow switches was about 4 feet wide and 6 long lying in a horozontal position, fastened at the extremety. the small fish which fell on those willows was washed on the Willows where they [lie] untill taken off &c. I cought or took off those willows 9 small trout from 3 to 7 Inches in length. . . ." Clark

[2] Known as Wheeler Canyon today.

[3] Thw. 4:351-357. Contains information regarding We-ah-koomt, chief near Asotin, Washington.

[4] The party was on the north shore of the Snake River, near Wilma, Washington.

[5] Thw. 4:357, 340. The eyewater was a concoction of acetate of lead and sulfate of zinc.

[6] Prankster incident occurred four miles below the mouth of Potlatch Creek.

[7] Thw. 4:358, 359. Neesh-ne-ee-pah-kee-oo-keen's (Cut Noses') lodge.

[8] Thw. 4:359. The "good medicine" was basilicon ointment. Wood, Remington, & Sadtler. *United States Dispensatory—Nineteenth Edition.* J. B. Lippincott Co., 1907, p. 315. Basilicon ointment is used for treatments of burns, chilblains, and blisters. It is made of rosin, yellow wax, and lard.

The yellow powder was sulfur and the white powder cream of tartar.

[9] The party went up Jack's Creek from Lenore, Idaho.

[10] Information from Thw. Atlas Volume, Map #44.

[11] Location is Wheeler Canyon.

[12] Hand gesture. Clark, p. 149. An insulting gesture signifying abhorrence and defiance.

Chapter 11

[1] "Tee-e-lap-a-lo" means "place of crawfish." The location is along Lawyers Creek, south of Kamiah. Informant: Harry Wheeler.

[2] Thw. 5:30. ". . . the ornament of the nose is a single shell of the wampum. . . ." Information recorded in Footnote 1: "The wampum was made of a shell (Dentalium, or a related genus). . .—Ed."

[3] Literary license! If the Nez Perces tried to pronounce the English names of the explorers, the sounds would have been much as given. Nez Perce language has no "r". The Author.

[4] Thw. 5:18. Lewis wrote "Yoom-park-kar-tim." What he heard was more like "Heyoom-pahkah-tim" = Fierce-Five-Hearts.

[5] Horse stealing raids. McWhorter, p. 11.

[6] Thw. 5:30-31. Description of tippets, and in particular, Red Grizzly Bear's tippet: ". . . but the article of dress on which they appear to b[e]stow most pains and ornaments is a kind of collar or brestplate; this is most commonly a strip of otterskin of about six inches wide taken out of the center of the skin it's whole length including the head. this is dressed with the hair on; a hole is cut lengthwise through the skin near the head of the animal sufficiently large to admit the head of the person

to pass. thus it is placed about the neck and hangs in front of the body the tail frequently reaching below their knees; on this skin in front is attatched peices of pirl, beads, wampum peices of red cloth and in short whatever they conceive most valuable or ornamental. I observed a tippit woarn by Hohastillpilp, which was formed of human scalps and ornamented with the thumbs and fingers of several men which he had slain in battle."

[7] Mrs. Pauline Evans of the Sacajawea Museum in Spalding, about 1945, had such a dress, purported to have been worn by Sa-ka-ka-wea at the Kamiah Council.

[8] Thw. 5:299-301. This speech was adapted from a speech prepared for the Yellowstone Indians. Footnote 1 reads: "This fragment, found in the Clark-Voorhis collection was evidently prepared by Clark for the Indians whom he hoped to meet upon the Yellowstone, but did not see. It furnished a good example of his methods in Indian diplomacy.—Ed."

[9] Information regarding the "big fish story." Thw. 3:293. ". . . we are told by the Indians that a whale has foundered on the Coast to the N.W. . . ." Thw. 3:314. "Capt. Clark set out after an early breakfast with the party in two canoes as had been concerted the last evening; Charbono and his Indian woman were also of the party; the Indian woman was very impo[r]tunate to be permited to go, and was therefore indulged; she observed that she had traveled a long way with us to see the great waters, and that now that monstrous fish was also to be seen, she thought it very hard she could not be permitted to see either (she had never yet been to the Ocean." Lewis, January 6, 1806. Thw. 3:324. ". . . this Skeleton (of the Whale Capt. Clark) measured 105 feet. . . ." Clark, January 8, 1806.

Nez Perce reaction to the whale from Mary Kipp and Walter Sewell.

[10] Si-kip-te-wat. Informant: Beatrice Miles.

[11] Thw. 5:20. ". . . many of the natives apply to us for medical aid which we gave them cheerfully so far as our skill and store of medicine would enable us. schrofela*, ulsers, rheumatism, soar eyes, and the lost of the uce of their limbs are the most common cases among them. the latter case is not very common but we have seen th[r]ee instances of it among the Chopunnish. . . ." *Scrofula—a tuberculous degeneration of lymph glands, especially in the neck.

[12] Thw. 5:20. ". . . a Cheif of considerable note at this place has been afflicted with [loss of uce of limbs] for three years, he is incapable of moving a single limb but lies like a corps in whatever position he is placed, yet he eats heartily, digests his food perfectly, injoys his understanding, his pulse are good, and has retained his flesh almost perfectly, in short were it not that he appears a little pale from having lain so long in the shade he might well be taken for a man in good health. I suspect that their confinement to a diet of roots may give rise to all those disorders except the rheumatism & soar eyes, and to the latter of these, the state of debility incident to a vegetable diet may measureably contribute. . . ." Lewis, May 11, 1806. Thw. 5:22. Clark records: ". . . a Chief of considerable note who has been in the situation . . . for 5 years."

[13] Guns from Minnetares. See Chapter 3 Notes, Number 4.

[14] Thw. 5:26. Stick game information from the *Journals*, various Nez Perce informants, and from Author's personal observation.

Chapter 12

[1] Thw. 5:30, 31. Description of Chopunnish woman's dress.

[2] Puchth = wild ginger, sweet-smelling plant used as a perfume. Informant: Angus Wilson.

August 28, 1966, Mrs. Pete Beaverhead, Flathead Tribe, Ronan, Montana, said long ago her people called the Nez Perces the "Clean Indians" or "Tsah-ah." They were proud of their appearance: clean shawls, robes, perfume from a plant.

Thw. 5:20 ". . . The Chopunnish notwithstanding they live in the crouded manner before mentioned are much more clenly in their persons and habitations than any nation we have seen since we left the Ottoes on the River Platte. . . ." Lewis, May 11, 1806.

[3] Badger game. Informant: Harry Wheeler.

Chapter 13

[1] In modern times this site was occupied by the Twin Feathers Lumber Mill, opposite the town of Kamiah, Idaho. Mary Kipp, a Nez Perce, lived in a small house on the same flat near a fine cold spring that bubbled out of the ground. Her sweat house sat a few feet from this.

Ordway, p. 357. "With the exception of Fort Mandan and Fort Clatsop the explorers occupied this camp a longer time than they remained in any other one place during the entire course of the expedition. Although not named by Lewis and Clark the camp has been named by students of the expedition, in honor of the neighboring Indians, Camp Chopunnish. It was occupied from May 13 until June 10, 1806, exactly four weeks. The site of Camp Chopunnish is less than two miles below Kamiah, Idaho, on the opposite side of the Kooskooskee (Clearwater)."

Today, the area is referred to as Long Camp.

[2] Criswell, pp. cxxiv, cxl, xcli. ". . . The Indians had told them (Lewis and Clark) of the grizzly bear long before they ever encountered it, describing it as yellow or white and calling it the *white bear* or the *yellow bear*. Lo and behold, when they saw it, it was neither, but was predominantly brown, with grayish or "grizzly" tips to its long hair. And yet, it should be said, in justice to the Indian, that he was the one who finally set the Captains right in their attempt to separate this species from the varieties of common black bear in that territory. And it is to be noted that they finally came around to a term denoting the whitish characteristics of the hair of this animal. But they scorned to use the outlandish Indian terms *hoh-host* (for the grizzly) and *yack-kah* (for the black). Their aversion to Indian terms, though not outwardly expressed, does not lack much of being as marked as that of the Indian for American words."

". . . *grizzly bear*, a name finally attached to one of the most remarkable of their (Lewis and Clark) discoveries. Their attention to this bear was not only due to the fact that it furnished endless excitement, sport, and danger to them; they seemed to sense the fact that the animal would play a big part in the annals of western settlement, as it did. . . . they wrote long descriptions of *Ursus horribilis*, assigning . . . many different names to him.

[3] Dust wallows. Informant: Harry Wheeler.

[4] Thw. 5:38. Grizzlies don't climb trees.

[5] "The Bear That Shot Himself." Informant: Harry Wheeler.

Chapter 14

[1] Trading horses between the Indians and the Lewis and Clark expedition. Ordway, p. 363. "Tuesday 3rd June 1806. ". . . my horse that I wrode over to the

kinooenim river nearly failed and his back verry sore and poor & in low Spririts and as luck would have it an Indian brought me a large good strong horse and Swaped with me as he knew my horse to be good when in order to run the buffaloe which is their main object to it horses that will run and Swap their best horses for Servis, for them that will run if they are not half as good as otherways."

[2] Many horses. Gass, p. 255. " (May 9, 1806.) Between the great falls of the Columbia and this place (Nez Perce Prairie), we saw more horses, than I ever before saw in the same space of country. They are not the largest size horses, but very good and active."

Chapter 15

[1] Good bad-smelling medicine. An idiom meaning a very strong smelling liniment.

[2] White dust = cream of tartar; yellow dust = flour of sulfur.

[3] Older people. Thw. 5:69. "Chopunnish appear to be very attentive to their aged people and treat their women with more rispect than the nations of the Missouri."

[4] Thirty drops of laudanum. Thw. 5:50.

[5] Good bad-smelling water. Thw. 5:50. "Volitile leniment."

[6] Known today as Whitebird Hill.

[7] Thw. 5:60. "William Bratton still continues very unwell; he eats heartily digests his food well, and has recovered his flesh almost perfectly yet is so weak in the loins that he is scarcely able to walk, nor can he set upwright but with the greatest of pain."

Wheeler, Chapter 15. Mr. Wheeler states that Bratton was suffering from lumbago and the sweat bath was a "kill-or-cure" process.

[8] Moves-No-More: See Chapter Notes, Chapter 11, Note #12. Thw. 5:63. Regarding treatment of "Moves-No-More": ". . . I am confident that this would be an excellent subject for electricity and much regret that I have it not in my power to supply it." [Lewis]

Author's Note: Even though all research into Moves-No-More's affliction would be supposition, there are two modern diseases that have symptoms similar to his: Guillian-Barre Syndrome which is a virus of the nerves; myasthenia gravis, a chronic debilitating disease characterized by rapid fatigue of certain muscles, with prolonged time of recovery of function. The muscles do not waste away. It is thought that the patient lacks some chemical concerned with nerve transmission.

A letter from the author was directed to Dr. Chuinard, author of *Only One Man Died: The Medical Aspects of the Lewis and Clark Expedition.* In Dr. Chuinard's response of September 9, 1987, he raises the possibility of "Move-No-More's" affliction as a gene inheritance. Dr. Chuinard also raises the questions: is the condition something different and indigenous to the Nez Perce; could the chief have been malingering or have hysteria?

[9] Portable soup was the 1804-1806 version of instant soup, probably consisting of dried and powdered vegetables, etc. Captain Lewis requested 150 pounds of "Portable Soup" for "Provisions and Means of Subsistence." Thw. 7:234.

[10] Moves-No-More and Moves-Again are fictitious names. Wheeler, p. 44. "The names of these Indians vary in the course of their life."

Chapter 16

[1] Twenty-one warm suns. Thw. 6:215—218. Meteorologic Tables show 21 days of sunshine May, 1806.
[2] Thick deer hide. Informant: Walter Sewell.
[3] Raven's warning. Informant: Walter Sewell.
[4] Salmon run. Thw. 6:216. ". . . they say that these fish are now passing by us in great numbers but that they cannot be caught as yet because those which first ascend the river do not keep near shore; they further inform us that in the course of a few days the fish run near the shore and then they take them with their skimming netts in great numbers. . ."
[5] Daily check of river swell. Thw. 6:216, 217.
[6] Crossing mountains. Thw. 5:117, 118. ". . . one of the indians informed us that we could not pass the mountains untill the full of the next moon or about the first of July, that if we attempted it sooner our horses would be at least three days travel without food on the top of the mountain; . . ." Lewis
[7] Churning rapids. Thw. 5:103. Location: Wild Goose Rapids.
[8] Razor for gold coins. Gass, p. 267. ". . . One of these men got two Spanish dollars from an Indian for an old razor. They said they got the dollars from about a Snake Indian's neck they had killed some time ago. . . ."
[9] The plateau on which the town of Clearwater, Idaho, is located.
[10] Shalees. Thw. 5:164. A band of Flat-Heads.
[11] The Grande Ronde Valley.

Chapter 17

[1] Clark, p. 187. "Gift." ("By itself"—p. 91; "Give"—p. 187.)
[2] Game of Prisoner's Base. E. 0. Harbin, *The Fun Encyclopedia*, Abingdon-Cokesbury Press, New York, Nashville, p. 174.
[3] Clark. ("I"—P. 222; "go"—P. 188.)
[4] Chops horse. Informants: Charlie Adams and Walter Sewell.

Chapter 18

[1] Ip-paht-tah-khahts. Informant: Harry Wheeler.
[2] Prairie near Grangeville.
[3] The Root Feast. Informant: Harry Wheeler. Mr. Wheeler said this actually happened to him as a youth.
[4] Big Bellies killing Snakes and Shalees. Thw. 5:158. ". . . they also inform us that they have heard by means of the Skeetsomis[h] Nation & Clarks river that the Big bellies of Fort de Prarie killed great numbers of the Shoshons and Ottelashoots which we met with last fall on the East fork of Lewis's river and high up the West fork of Clarks river &c."
[5] Koolkooltom. McWhorter, p. 21. ". . . The eldest son of Red Bear was Koolkooltom, Sr., Selish for 'Red Arrow Point.' "
[6] Although the Lewis and Clark Journals do not identify these two Indians in any way, they could have been the two mentioned in *The Clearwater Story* by

Ralph Space, p. 18: "Some Indians say one of the guides was the son of Twisted Hair and another the son of Red Grizzly" (Hah-hahts il- pilp).

[7] Space, p. 18. Collins Creek of the Lewis and Clark Journals is Lolo Creek of today.

[8] Moccasins. Gass, p. 277. (June 24) ". . . We gave each of the Indians a pair of mockasons, and they agreed to stay to day and wait for the party. . . ."

Chapter 19

[1] Ka-oo-yit is a general term for the celebration of the end of a period and the celebration of a beginning of a new period.

This chapter is a montage of Nez Perce customs, games, and incidents which have actually happened to Nez Perce individuals. Although they may not have occurred during the Lewis and Clark sojourn, they serve to create a mental backdrop against which Drewyer and Shannon appeared, asking for guides.

[2] Crows-Flying-out-of-Rock-Creek-Canyon-with-Mouths-Wide-Open: This was indeed a man's real name. His English name was Edward Raboin, and he lived in Toppenish, Washington.

[3] The Moon Dance. Informant: Alec Pinkham, May, 1965.

[4] The Serenade Dance. Informant: Alec Pinkham, May, 1965.

Chapter 20

[1] Author's note: The Journal entries are somewhat ambiguous as to the distribution of guns to the guides.

[2] Cache location. Space, p. 17. The cache was on Willow Ridge below Sherman Saddle.

[3] Aha-tes Creek: Indian name for Lolo Creek, Montana. Lewis and Clark called this creek: Traveler's Rest. Informant: Harry Wheeler.

Chapter 21

[1] Thw. 5:184. The Hell Gate River joins the Bitterroot to form the Missoula, or Clark's Fork. The name "Hell Gate" was changed by civilization to "Missoula" —unaware that the Indian word meant the same. Informant: Ralph Space.

[2] Location known as "Post Office." Informant: Walter Sewell.

[3] Told to Wilma Ogston by Albert Moore: "Al-pa-to-kate means 'Father Was Daytime Smoker.' This was given to Indian son of William Clark—William Clark was day time smoker." Albert Moore's version of the name was "Al-pa-to-kate"; Josiah Red Wolf's version was "Ha-la-too-kit."

APPENDIX

NEZ PERCE CHIEFS NAMED BY LEWIS AND CLARK

TWISTED HAIR

Nez Perce Name: TSAP-TSU-KELP-SKIN or TSAP-TSU-KALPS-KIN

Source of information: Harry Wheeler, Corbett Lawyer, J. J. Miles, Joseph Blackeagle

Concept: Hair twisted on side of head

Territory: Area around the confluence of the Clearwater and North Fork Rivers (Ahsahka and Orofino).

TE-TOH-KAN AHS-KAHP—TETOHARSKY

Nez Perce Name: TE-TOH-KAN AHS-KAHP

Source of information: Harry Wheeler

Concept: Te-toh-kan = People; Ahs-kahp = Brothers

You would look out and see people coming. You would say, "Tetohkan Ahskahp," meaning "people coming, looks like brothers."

Territory: Te-toh-kan Ahs-kahp belonged to Twisted Hair's band. He was one of the Nez Perces who went downriver with Lewis and Clark.

NOTE: The Nez Perces did not recognize Lewis and Clarks' "Tetoharsky" as a corruption of the name *Te-toh-kan Ahs-kahp*. "We have no 'r' in our language," they said. Lewis and Clark, coming from Virginia, must have pronounced "r" sounds as "ah" and "ah" sounds as "r." They must have said "squaw," yet they wrote "squar." They must have heard "Te *toh* kan *Ahs* (ars) kahp (ky), yet they wrote "Te-toh *hars* ky."

YA'AMAS WAKUS: Not specifically named by Lewis and Clark, but mentioned by Clark, October 5, 1805:

"Collected all our horses . . . and delivered them to the men who were to take charge of them." This man may also have been known as Ahot-mo-tim-nim which means "Joyous Heart" in the same sense as a cheerleader. Due to the lack of authentic Nez Perce names of this period, the Author has used literary license in naming one man "Ya'amas Wakus" and another "Ahot-mo-tim-nim" (Joyous Heart).

Source of Information: Harry Wheeler

Concept: Ya'amus means "Blacktail Doe." Wa-kus means "like or same." Thus, Ya'amus Wakus means "looks like Blacktail Doe."

Territory: Same as Twisted Hair's. He was either the brother or son of Twisted Hair. (Harry Wheeler believed he was a son.)

NEESH-NE-EE-PAH-KEE-OO-KEEN—CUT NOSE

Nez Perce Name:

Neeshneparkkeook—Lewis and Clark Journals, Volume 5, Page 6;

Nooshnu-apa'h-ken-kin—Olin D. Wheeler, Volume I, Page 267;

Nusnu-epah'-kee-oo-keen— Harry Wheeler

Concept: "Neeshne" is the "down river" Nez Perces' word for nose. "Nusnu" is used by the "up river" people. The word means "Nose Jabbed With a Spear." He had received the wound in a battle with the Snakes on the Salmon River. (Harry Wheeler—informant.)

Territory: Area around the junction of Potlatch Creek and the Clearwater—Arrow Junction.

TIMUCA

No translation was given for this name in the *Lewiston Tribune* article of July 14, 1940. He was the father of Ta-moot-sin, (Timothy, first convert of the Spaldings).

Territory: Below the confluence of the Clearwater and the Snake—Alpowa.

DEFINITION OF CHOPUNNISH

From *American Indian*, Vol. VIII, by Edward Curtis:

Former custom of wearing a dentalium shell transversely in the septum of the nose. Were called "Apupe'" by Apsaroke. (Ape' meaning "nose"; apano'pe—meaning "nose hole" or "nostril.") Apadhuhopi—Called Apa-hopi' by Hidatsa.

Native tradition says that Nez Perces, hearing themselves called "Apupe'" by the Apsaroke, occasionally referred to themselves by their translation of that term "Tsup-nit-pelu," and this probably is the origin of the Chopunnish of Lewis and Clark.

CHOPUNNISH

After descending the last of the Bitterroot Mountains, Captain Clark came out on Weippe Prairie where he found Indians encamped.

On September 21, 1805, he wrote, "The two villages consist of about thirty double tents, and the inhabitants call themselves Chopunnish or Pierced-nose."[1]

"Chopunnish or Pierced-nose" . . . since that time the meaning of the word has become a matter of speculation. One theory is that the word is a corruption of Tsutpeli, a Nez Perce word of self-designation[2]; another is that it may be a Sioux word, Tsunit pelun, corrupted from a Nez Perce form.

Haruo Aoki, a linguist from the University of California who has analyzed the Nez Perce language, states that he has learned of a self-designation: "cu' .p?nit." He writes, "The word "cu' .p?nit" 'pierce with a pointed object' also exists and appears close in form to Chopunnish. Clark *could* have changed the final "t" to "sh" on the analogy of many national names in English that end in 'sh' such as British, Irish, Scottish, Turkish, Spanish, and so on. If this proposed etymology is correct, and I suspect it is because many instances of Chopunnish are immediately followed by the phrase 'or pierced noses,' then the oldest name for Nez Perce meant "nez perce'."[3] Though Aoki's phonetic system represents the sounds of the word as accurately as possible, the lay person can understand it only after hearing the word pronounced. When a Nez Perce expresses, "to pierce with a sharp object," one hears, "Tshahp.n," which sounds very much like "Chop.n."

What, then, is 'nish'? 'Nish-ne', or "neesh-ne," was the word the downriver Nez Perces used for nose, according to the Nez Perce historian, Harry Wheeler. The upriver Nez Perces said, 'nus-nu.' "Neeshnepahkeeook" is written in the Journals as the name for Cut Nose. 'Nish-ne' or 'neeshne,' as the explorers spelled it, meant 'nose' and may have been more generally used at that time. Just as the practice of piercing the nose was borrowed from the downriver Indians, the word 'nishe-ne' may have come from the downriver Nez Perces.

The word "Chopunnish" is descriptive of the hand-sign used to designate the Nez Perces. To make this sign, one holds the right hand with the back to the right in front of the right cheek and close to it. The index finger is extended and pointed to the left with its tip a little to the right of and a little lower than the nose, and other fingers and thumb closed. Move the hand to the left with the back of the index finger passing under and close to the nose.[4] "Tshahp.n!" or "Chop.n!": a sharp object pokes through.

1. Thw. 3:78.
2. Spinden, Herbert J. *The Nez Perce Indians*. American Anthropological Association, 1980. Page 172, note 1.
3. Aoki, Haruo. *Nez Perce Grammar*. University of California Publication, Linguistics 62, 1970, page 3.
4. Clark.

Through what? "nish-re"—the nose. "Pierce with a sharp object the nose" = Chopunnish or Pierced Nose.

NAMES FOR NEZ PERCES

1805—Chopunnish—Pierced Noses—Lewis and Clark
1807—Choconish—Gass' Journal
1830—Chopunish—Kelly, Oregon, (68)
1845—Nezpercies—Hastings, Guide to Oregon, (59)
1859—Nezperces—Kane, Wanderings in North America, (290)
1901—Nimipu—Lyman—Oregon Historical Society Quarterly, II (288)
1901—Numipu—Mowry—Marcus Whitman (259)
Sa-ap-tin—Gatschet, Okinagan (MS BAE) Okinagan name
1853—Sa-aptins—Schoolcraft—Indian Tribes III, Map (200)
1841—Sha-aptan—Scouler in Journal, Royal Geo. Soc., London, XI (225)
1841—Shahaptemish—Gairdner in Jour. Royal Geog. Soc., London, XI (256)
Tchu't pelit (own name)-Gatschet—M.S. BAE
Tsut-peli (own name)

Smithsonian Institution
Bureau of American Ethnology, Bulletin 30
Handbook of American Indians North of Mexico, Edited by Frederick Webb Hodge, Part II, 1910

SA-KA-KA-WEA—"BIRD WOMAN"

FROM: *The Trail of Lewis & Clark*, Vol. I, Olin D. Wheeler.

"The orthography of Bird-woman's name, as given by the captains, is wrong. The word is Hidatsa, not a Shoshone word, and is formed from two Indian words. In a letter to me, Dr. Washington Matthews of Washington, D. C., an army surgeon and author of a Hidatsa dictionary, says:

'In my dictionary I give the Hidatsa word for bird as "Tsa-kaka." "Ts" is often changed to S, and K to G in this and other Indian languages so "Sacaga" would not be a bad spelling and thus Charbonneau may have pronounced his wife's name, but never "Sacaja." (The Hidatsa language contains no "j".) I fancy all this confusion may have arisen from an editorial mistake and that Captain Lewis (or Clark) did not form his "G" well. "Wea" (or wia or mia) means woman.'

There are four simple forms in which the word may be correctly used: Tsakakawea, Sakakawea, Sakagawea, Sacagawea. The last more nearly approaches the form used by Lewis and Clark and is, perhaps, the preferable one to use."

TWISTED HAIR

Both Harry Wheeler and Corbett Lawyer claimed to be descended from Twisted Hair's band, but they differed widely in the location of Twisted Hair's ancestral home. Harry Wheeler maintained that Twisted Hair's district was that area through which Lewis and Clark, in 1805, traveled from the Weippe Prairie through the valley of the Clearwater to the junction of that river with the North Fork. On the flat, near the present town of Ahsahka, was Twisted Hair's winter home. This seems in keeping with the fact that Lewis and Clark left their thirty-eight horses here for Twisted Hair to care for during the winter. It was in this area that descendants of the Twisted Hair band received allotments.

Corbett Lawyer said on February 11, 1959, that Twisted Hair's ancestral home was at Kooskia and that he was buried at Selway Falls. He said Al-we-yas was Twisted Hair's brother. He, himself, was descended from Tsap-tsu-kalps-kin, whose son, Aleiya, was the first Lawyer (the Lawyer of the 1855 Treaty). According to Wheeler, the Lawyers came from around Rock Creek, on the breaks of the Salmon River. Their allotments were not in the Ahsahka-Orofino area.

BIBLIOGRAPHY

ANDRIST, RALPH K. *To the Pacific With Lewis and Clark*. New York: The American Heritage Publishing Co., 1967.

AOKI, HARUO. *Nez Perce Texts*. Berkeley: University of California Press, Linguistics Vol. 90, 1979.

BAKELESS, JOHN. *The Journals of Lewis and Clark*. New American Library: Mentor, 1964.

BUTLER, ROBERT B. *A Guide to Understanding Idaho Archeology*. Pocatello, Idaho: Idaho State University Museum, Special Publication, 1966.

CATLIN, GEORGE. *Letters and Notes of the North American Indians*. 2 vols.: Dover, 1973.

CLARK, ELLA. *Legends of the Pacific Northwest*. Berkeley: University of California Press, 1953.

CLARK, W. P. *Indian Sign Language*. Philadelphia: L.R. Hamersley and Co., 1885, copyright 1959, Theron Fox, reprint, San Jose 6, California, The Rosicrucian Press, Ltd. (Limited Edition Reprint).

COUES, ELLIOT, ed. *History of the Expedition Under the Command of Lewis and Clark*, 3 vols. New York: F.B. Harper, 1895. Reprint, New York: Dover Publishing Co., 1965.

CRAWFORD, HELEN. *Sakakawea*. North Dakota Historical Quarterly, Vol. 1, No. 3, April, 1927.

CURTIS, EDWARD S. *The North American Indian*. 20 vols., Vol. VIII, Cambridge, Massachusetts, 1907-1930.

DEVOTO, BERNARD. *The Journals of Lewis and Clark*. Boston: Houghton Mifflin Co., 1953.

DOUGHERTY, JAMES. *Of Courage Undaunted: Across the Continent With Lewis and Clark*. New York: Viking Press, 1951.

EVANS, PAULINE. *Manuscripts of Indians' Stories* (unpublished). Spalding, Idaho: Sacajawea Museum, circa 1950.

GASS, PATRICK. *Journals of the Lewis and Clark Expedition (Journal of Patrick Gass)* Ross & Haines, Inc., Minneapolis, Minnesota, 1958.

HAINES, FRANCIS. *The Nez Perces, Tribesmen of the Columbian Plateau*. Norman, Oklahoma, University of Oklahoma Press, 1955.

HODGE, F. W. *Handbook of American Indians North Mexico*. Vol. 2, Washington, D.C.: Bureau of American Ethnology, 1907.

HOSMER, CHARLES K., ed. *History of the Expedition of Lewis and Clark*. 2 vols. Chicago: A.C. McClurg and Co., 1904.

JOSEPHY, ALVIN M., JR. *The Nez Perce Indians and the Opening of the Northwest*. New Haven and London: Yale University Press, 1965.

MCBETH, KATE. *The Nez Perces Since Lewis and Clark*. New York: Fleming H. Revell Co., 1908.

MCWHORTER, L. V. *Hear Me My Chiefs!* Caldwell, Idaho: Caxton Printers, Ltd., 1952.

———. *Yellow Wolf*. Caldwell, Idaho: Caxton Printers, Ltd., 1940-1968.

NEZ PERCE TRIBE. Allen Slickpoo, Sr., Director; Leroy Seth, Illustrator; Deward Walker, Jr. Technical Advisor; *Nu Mee Poom Tit Wah Tit, Nez Perce Legends*. 1972.

QUAIFE, MILO M., ed. *The Journals of Captain Meriwether Lewis and Sergeant John Ordway*. The State Historical Society of Wisconsin, Madison, MCMLXV, Copyright 1916, Second Print, 1965.

PHINNEY, ARCHIE. *Nez Perce Texts*. New York: Columbia University Press, 1934.

SALISBURY, ALBERT AND JANE. *Two Captains West: An Historical Tour of the Lewis and Clark Trail*. Seattle: Superior Publishing Co., 1950.

SPACE, RALPH. *Lewis and Clark Through Idaho*. Lewiston: Tribune Publishing Co., 1963.

———. *The Clearwater Story*. Forest Service, U. S. Department of Agriculture (no date).

SPINDEN, HERBERT J. *The Nez Perce Indians*. American Anthropological Association, 1908.

THWAITES, REUBEN GOLD, ed. *Original Journals of the Lewis and Clark Expedition, 1804-1806*. 8 vols. New York: Dodd, Mead and Co., 1904-1905.

WALKER, DEWARD E. *American Indians of Idaho*. Vol. I. Aboriginal Cultures, Idaho Research Foundation, 1973.

WHEELER, OLIN D. *The Trail of Lewis and Clark 1804-1904*. 2 vols., New York: G.P. Putnam's Sons, 1904.

SECONDARY SOURCES—BOOKS

ANDRIST, RALPH K. *By the Editors of American Heritage, The Magazine of History*. New York: American Heritage Publishing Co., Inc., 1967.

BAITY, ELIZABETH CHESLEY. *Americans Before Columbus*. New York, The Viking Press, 1951.

———. *America Before Man*. New York: The Viking Press, 1953.

BEAL, MERRILL D. *I Will Fight No More Forever*. New York: Ballantine Books, 1971.

BILLARD, JULES B., ed. *The World of the American Indian*. Washington, D.C.: National Geographical Society, 1974.

BRANT, CHARLES S., ed. *Jim Whitewolf, The Life of a Kiowa Apache Indian*. New York: Dover Publication, Inc., 1969.

BRISBIN, GEN. JAMES S., ed. *Belden, the White Chief*. New York: C. F. Vent, 1870.

BROWN, DEE. *Bury My Heart at Wounded Knee*. New York: Holt, Rinehart and Winston, 1970.

BRYAN, ALAN LYLE. *Paleo-American Prehistory*. Pocatello, Idaho: Occasional Papers of the Idaho State University Museum, No. 16, 1965.

BUNNELL, CLARENCE ORVEL. *Legends of the Klickitats*. Portland, Oregon: Binfords and Mort, Publishers, 1935.

BUTLER, B. ROBERT. *A Guide to Understanding Idaho Archaeology*. Pocatello, Idaho: The Idaho State University Museum, 1966.

CARTER, DENNY. *Henry Farny*. New York: Watson-Guptill Publications, 1978.

CHESHIRE, GIFF. *Thunder on the Mountains*. New York: Modern Literary Editions Publishing Co., 1960.

CHUINARD, M.D., ELDON G. *Only One Man Died*. Ye Galleon Press, Fairfield, Washington, 1979.

CLARK, ELLA E. AND MARGOT EDMONDS. *Sacagawea of the Lewis and Clark Expedition*. California: University of California Press, 1979.

CLUMPNER, MICK. *Nez Perce Legend*. Wayne, Pennsylvania: Banbury Books, Inc., 1983.

CRISWELL, PH.D., ELIJAH HARRY. *Lewis and Clark: Linguistic Pioneers*. The University of Missouri Studies, Vol. XV, April 1, 1940, Number 2. University of Missouri, Columbia, Missouri.

CURTIS, EDWARD S. *In the Land of the Head-Hunters*. 1915. Reprint. New York: Tamarack Press, 1975.

———. *Portraits from North American Indian Life*. United States: A & W Visual Library, Outerbridge and Lazard, Inc., 1972.

DEMPSEY, HUGH A. *History in Their Blood*. New York: Hudson Hills Press, 1982.

DRANNAN, CAPT. WILLIAM F. *Thirty-One Years on the Plains and in the Mountains*. Chicago: Rhodes and McClure Publishing Co., 1909.

DYE, EVA EMERY. *The Conquest*. Chicago: A. C. McClurg and Co., 1902.

ERDOES, RICHARD AND ALFONSO ORTIZ, ed. *American Indian Myths and Legends*. New York: Pantheon Fairy Tale and Folklore Library, 1984.

FISHER, VARDIS. *Tale of Valor*. New York: Pocket Books, Inc., 1960.

FORDE, C. D. *Habitat, Economy and Society*. London: Dulton Advanced Geographics.

HANNA, A. AND WILLIAM H. GOETZMANN, ed. *The Lewis and Clark Expedition*, by Meriwether Lewis. 3 vols. Reprint, New York: J. B. Lippincott Co., 1961.

HANNUM, ALBERTA. *Paint the Wind*. New York: The Viking Press, 1958.

HINES, DONALD M. *Tales of the Nez Perce*. Fairfield, Washington: Ye Galleon Press, 1984.

HOWARD, HELEN ADDISON. *Saga of Chief Joseph*. Caldwell, Idaho: The Caxton Printers, Ltd., 1965.

JOHNSON, DOROTHY M. *Indian Country*. New York: Ballantine Books, 1948.

JONES, NARD. *The Great Command*. Boston: Little, Brown and Co., 1959.

JOSEPHY, JR. ALVIN M., ed. *The American Heritage Book of Indians*. New York: American Heritage Publishing Co., Inc., 1961.

———. *The Patriot Chiefs*. New York: The Viking Press, 1951.

LAFARGE, OLIVER. *Laughing Boy*. New York. Signet, 1971.

LAVENDER, DAVID. *The American Heritage History of the Great West*. New York: American Heritage Publishing Co., Inc., 1965.

LONGFELLOW, HENRY WADSWORTH. *The Song of Hiawatha*. New York: Maynard, Merrill, and Company, 1899.

MCCRACKEN, HAROLD. *George Catlin and the Old Frontier*. New York: Bonanza Books, 1959.

MCCURDY, JAMES G. *Indian Days at Neah Bay*. Seattle, Washington: Superior Publishing Co., 1961.

MCLUHAN, T. C. *Touch the Earth*. New York: Pocket Books, 1972.

MARTIN, FRAN. *Raven-Who-Sets-Things-Right*. New York: Harper and Row, Publishers, 1975.

MARRIOTT, ALICE. *The Ten Grandmothers*. Norman: University of Oklahoma Press, 1945.

MATHEWS, JOHN JOSEPH. *Wah'Kon-Tah*. Norman: University of Oklahoma Press, 1932.

MAXWELL, JAMES, ed. *America's Fascinating Indian Heritage*. Pleasantville, New York: The Reader's Digest Association, Inc., 1978.

NESBITT, PAUL EDWARD. *Stylistic Locales and Ethnographic Groups: Petroglyphs of the Lower Snake River*. Pocatello, Idaho: Occasional Papers of the Idaho State University Museum, No. 23, 1968. (Paper)

PELTIER, JEROME. *A Brief History of the Coeur D'Alene Indians, 1806-1909*. Fairfield, Washington: Ye Galleon Press, 1981.

POLLOCK, DEAN. *Joseph, Chief of the Nez' Perce*. Portland, Oregon: Binfords and Mort, Publishers, 1950.

RADIN, PAUL. *The Autobiography of a Winnebago Indian*. New York: Dover Publications, Inc., 1963.

SALISBURY, ALBERT AND JANE. *Two Captains West*. Seattle, Washington: Superior Publishing Co., 1950.

SLICKPOO, SR., ALLEN P. *Nu Mee Poom Tit Wah Tit (Nez Perce Legends)*. Idaho: Nez Perce Tribe of Idaho, 1972.

SANDERSON, WILLIAM E. *Nez Perce Buffalo Horse*. Caldwell, Idaho: The Caxton Printers, Ltd., 1972.

SANDOZ, MARI. *Crazy Horse*. Lincoln, Nebraska: The University of Nebraska Press, 1961.

SPALDING, REV. H. H. *The Gospel According to Matthew* (Translated into the Nez Perce's Language). New York, American Bible Society, 1871.

THORP, RAYMOND W. AND ROBERT BUNKER. *Crow Killer*. New York: Signet Book, 1959.

TOMKINS, WILLIAM. *Indian Sign Language*. New York: Dover Publications, Inc., 1969.
TWOHY, PATRICK J. *Finding a Way Home*. Spokane, Washington: The University Press, 1983.
UNDERHILL, RUTH, PHD. *Indians of the Pacific Northwest*. Washington, D. C.: U. S. Department of Interior, Bureau of Indian Affairs, 1960.
WALDO, ANNA LEE. *Sacajawea*. New York: Avon, 1978.
WARREN, ROBERT PENN. *Chief Joseph of the Nez Perce*. New York: Random House, 1983.
WATERS, FRANK. *Book of the Hopi*. New York: The Viking Press, 1963.
WILLIAMS, J. GARY AND RONALD W. STARK, ed. *The Pierce Chronicle*. Moscow, Idaho: Idaho Research Foundation, Inc.
WOOD, ERSKINE. *Days with Chief Joseph*. Portland, Oregon: Binfords and Mort, no date.
ZIM, PH.D., HERBERT S. *The Rocky Mountains*. New York, Golden Press, 1964.

SECONDARY SOURCE—ARTICLES

The American Indian, Spring, 1950, Vol. V, No. 3, New York: Association on American Indian Affairs, Inc.
AOKI, HARUO. *Nez Perce and Proto-Sahaptian Kinship Terms*. University of California, Berkeley. Reprinted from International Journal of American Linguistics, Vol. 32, No. 4, Oct. 1966.
———. *Nez Perce and Northern Sahaptin: A Binary Comparison*. University of California, Berkeley. Reprinted from International Journal of American Linguistics, Vol. 28, No. 3, July, 1962.
CAVANAUGH, ROBERT M. *An Illustrated Guide to the Pacific Northwest Indian Center*. Kalispell, Montana, 1974.
CRAWFORD, HELEN. *Sakakawea*. Reprint from North Dakota Historical Quarterly, Vol. E, No. 3, April, 1927.
Chief Joseph's Own Story. Fairfield, Washington: Ye Galleon Press, 1984.
Chief Joseph's Own Story. Cambridge: Press of the Black Flag Raised, #7, 1970.
EVANS, JOSEPH AND CATHERIN. *A Brief Sketch of Idaho and American History*. Spalding, Idaho. (Unpublished).
EWERS, JOHN C. *George Catlin: Painter of Indians of the West*. Reprinted from the Annual Report of the Smithsonian Institution for 1955.
FLETCHER, ROBERT H. *American Adventure*. New York: American Pioneer Trails Association, 1945.
Following Lewis and Clark across the Clearwater National Forest. Missoula, Montana: Department of Agriculture, June, 1971.
From Where the Sun Now Stands, Vol. 1, No. 10. Lapwai, Idaho.
FUHRMAN, LEIGH (Hahots-yaya). *A Legend of Nee Mee Poo*. Richland, Washington: Valley Herald News, 1965.
GREENE, BERNICE. *Appendix C—Wild Plants and Their Uses by Indians of Interior Salish Speaking Groups of the Chelan County Region, Washington*. October, 1985.
HALSEY, CHERYEL AND ROBERT BEALE. *Lewis and Clark and the Shahaptian Speaking Americans*. Fairfield, Washington: Ye Galleon Press, 1983.
"Indian Wars." *Real West Magazine*, Americana Book No. 9, Fall, 1966.
KNUDSON, RUTHANN. "The Columbia Plateau: Foods and Trade." *The Journal of Forestry*, pp. 31-33, reprint. September, 1980.
———. "Fish, Roots, Game, and Trade in the Columbia Plateau." *The Journal of Forestry*, pp. 542-546, reprint. September, 1980.
LILJEBLAD, DR. SVEN. *The Indians of Idaho*. Idaho Historical Series, No. 3. Boise, Idaho: The Idaho Historical Society, Dec., 1960.
Montana, Vol. 5, No. 4, Autumn, 1955.
MURPHEY, EDITH VAN ALLEN. *Indian Uses of Native Plants*. Palm Desert, California: Desert Printers, Inc., 1959.
PRICE, GLADYS BIBEE. *Nun-Mip-Ni-Sheek "We Remember."* Pendleton, Oregon, 1959.

———. *Te-Yok-Keen "Hear Ye."* La Grande, Oregon: 1962.
RAPHAEL, RALPH B. *The Book of American Indians.* Connecticut: Fawcett Publications, Inc., 1953.
ROBERTSON, MELVIN L. *The Nez Perce Indians of Idaho—A Brief History.* Lapwai, Idaho, 1954.
STRANAHAN, C. T. *Pioneer Stories.* Lewiston, Idaho: The Lewiston Tribune, 1947.
TORGESON, GLENDA. "Plants of Southwestern Idaho." *Idaho Archaeologist,* Vol. VI, No. 1 & 2, Fall & Winter, 1982, p. 20.

INDEX

Abbreviations used:
C. - Chapter
JE - Entries from Lewis & Clark Journals
LCJ - Lewis & Clark Journals
LCE - Lewis & Clark Expedition

Aha-tes Creek (Lolo Creek, Mo.; Traveler's Rest in LCJ), 296, 311, 331 C.20/n.3
A-hot-mo-tim-nim. *See* Joyous Heart
Ah-pah. *See* kouse bread
Ah-sah-ka, 100
Alle-oo-ya, meeting Clark on Oyaip, 14; history of, 321 C. 2/n.2
Al-pa-to-kate (Father Was Daytime Smoker) 311-314; 331 C.21/n.3
Alpowa, 37, 93, 122, 123, 124
Alwi'tas (women's lodge), 275
Apparel: Broken Arm for receiving LCE, 147; buffalo robe, 288; dancers 119-120; dress of Sa-ka-ka-wea's, 7. *See* Tippets
Appearance of Nez Perce: 43, 98; young men 276-277
Arrow Chief, 14
Ask-kah-poo, 2

Bald Mountain, 290
Barnabus (Koots-koots), meeting Clark on Oyaip, 14-16, 321 C.2/n.2; mentioned, passim
Ba-teese, (Jean Baptiste Charbonneau, son of Charbonneau and Sa-ka-ka-wea) 49; treatment of illness (JE) 200, 201
Bathing in Lolo Hot Springs, 296-297
Beads, use of, 117
Beard pulling incident, 19
Beards, Indian's habit of plucking out, 19; 321 C.2/n.4
Beargrass articles, 325 n.22
Bear meat, eating of, 177
Bed Rock Creek, 133
Big Bellies, as enemies of Nee-mee-poo, 5, 30; killing of Black Eagle's father, a notable chief, 152, 157; mentioned, passim
Big Canyon, 123
Big Heart, finding lead canisters, 78-80; returning lead canisters, JE 133, 134
Bird Woman. *See* Sa-ka-ka-wea
Birthing place, 275
Bitterroot Mountains, 305
Bitterroot River (Clarks River) JE 257, 299, 305
Black Eagle (Tip-yah-la-nah She-mook She-mook), fictitious name applied to son of notable chief who had been killed by Big Bellies, 152; JE 157, 162
Blackfeet, enemies of Nee-mee-poo, 4, 5, 26, 45; mentioned, passim
Blackfoot River (Co-kah-lah-ish-kit), 308
Branding Iron of LCE - Impression of, 74
Bratton, (William Bratton), sweat bath, JE 203, 203-205, 329 n.7
Breath of the Monster, 110
Broken Arm (Tin-nach-e-moo-toolt): as chief and preparing for war with Snakes, 7, 8, 140, 145; flag left by LCE, 146; appearance for meeting LCE, 147; mentioned, passim
Brother-Chief, 36, 76
Buffalo Dance, 119
"Buffalo robes on faces," description of LCE members by Nez Perce, 15, 17, 18. *See* Beard pulling incident
Burial, 103, 226. *See* Horses, sacrificed
Burning glass, lighting council fire, 44

Calendar, Nez Perce, xxvii
Camas, 22; harvesting, preparing and roasting, 1, 7, 47, 48; patty-cakes, 47-48; about, 322 C.5/n.7
Camas lilies, 211
Camas Prairie, 122, 127, 192
Cameahwaite, 234, 321 C.3/n.3
Camp Chopunnish (Long Camp) referenced, 166, 174 (see JE), 328 C.13/n.1
Canisters, lead: buried, JE 78, 79; found by Big Heart, 50; returned to LCE JE 133, 134; 324 C.8/n.1. *See* Big Heart Story
Canoe Camp, 62-72
Canoe, building of at Camp Chopunnish 214; sinking of, 221; Broken Arm and men attempt to retrieve, 223
Canoes for trip to Pacific Ocean: finding wood, 53, 57-59; building at Canoe Camp, 62-72, passim; hollowing out with fire, 66, 69-70
Castrating of horses, 182-183, JE 187
Cayuse tribe (Wai-i-let-pos; also, Willet-pos), friends of Nee-mee-poo, 109, 234, 239

Cedar crushed, use of, 118
Celilo Falls (The Falls), 20, 25, 37, 69, 94, 110, 111, 321 C.3/n.2
Charbonneau, (Toussaint Charbonneau, husband of Sa-ka-ka-wea), 130, 152, 154
China Island, 323, C.6/n.3
Chopunnish, definition of, 333, 334
Chopunnish nation: 94; chiefs and principal men of, 151, 279; people of, 18; villages and locations of, 1
Chopunnish River (North Fork River), 37, 58, 62, 97, JE 256, 290, 293; meeting at Koos-koos-kee River (Clearwater River), 100
Chopunnish villages, meaning of names, 1
Clark (Capt. William Clark): Clark administering medical aid to Nez Perce 125, 128-132, 158-168, 197-210; 327 n. 11; Clark's mishap with horse, 35; personality of, 322 C.4/n.3
Clark's Fork, 306
Clark's River (Bitterroot River), 299, JE 300
Clearwater, Idaho, 330 C.16/n.9
Clearwater River. *See* Koos-koos-kee
Clothing. *See* Apparel
Coeur d'Alene tribe, 109
Co-kah-lah-ish-kit. *See* Blackfoot River
Collins Creek (also called Traveler's Rest). *See* Lolo Creek
Colter's Creek (also called Ya-ho-toin). *See* Potlatch Creek
Columbia (Great river from the north; also Great river from cold country), 24, 37, 92
Communicating with Nez Perce, 130, JE 150, 152, 154, 156; Drewyer and Shannon's ability, 258, 279; inability to, JE 235; with signs, JE 300
Council: with Nez Perce on Oyaip, 43-47, at Kamiah, 149-154, during Ka-oo-yit to determine guides, 279-280; of Nez Perce chiefs accepting L&C proposal 163-165
Courtship Dance, 119
Cous cous root, use of, 117, 119; 225; 325 n.24
Coyote, The, (Itsi-yai-yai), 54, 106, 107, 110, 112; and the Guiding Spirit, 292
Coyote's moccasin tracks as seen at Spalding, Idaho, 106, 325 n.16
Criers (camp), announcing by, 9, 12, 20-21, 43, 168, 190, 279
Crows tribe, (as enemies of Nee-mee-poo), 160-161
Customs. *See* Nez Perce Customs
Cut Nose, 9; Nose-Jabbed-with-Spear, 97; description of, 96; encounter with Snakes 96-97; conflict with Twisted Hair over care of LCE horses, 138-143; mentioned, passim

Dances: Buffalo Dance, 119; Courtship Dance, 119; Match Dance, 119; Moonlight Dance 119, 275-276; Serenade Dance 277-278; Tu-ka-wi-ut, "Snake Dance," 119
Dandling hands. *See* Handshakes
Daytime Smoker. *See* Al-pa-to-kate
Deer hunting, method, 183, JE 184
Distribution of food, 12
Dogs, eating of, 89, JE 93; procuring of, JE 125, 125; throwing pup into Lewis's face, JE 126, 126-127. *See* Story of Lee-tsu, 89-90.
Drewyer (George Drouillard), best sign talker, 139, 182; along with Shannon seeking guides over Bitterrroots, JE 275, 258
Dwellings of Indians: alwi'tas (women's lodge), 275; Broken Arm's lodge, JE 145, 145; Cut Nose's lodge, JE 127; flat-roofed house, 218-219, ish-nash, 2, 22; longhouse, 101, 104; pit, 101, 145, 175; tepee, 2, 148

Eldorado Creek, (Fish Creek in LCJ) JE 254, JE 255, JE 284
Eldorado Meadows, JE 258
Enemies (te-wel-kas) of Chopunnish: Sioux, 5; Blackfeet, Big Bellies, Snakes, 38; Crows, 160; mentioned, passim
Eyewater (eye medicine), popularity of: 132, JE 158, 158, JE 165, 168, JE 196, 196-199; JE 201; efforts made to obtain, 202-203; description of, 326 C.10/n.5

Falls, The. *See* Celilo Falls
Fierce-Five-Hearts (He-yoom-pahkahtim), 9; description of, 151; mentioned, passim
Fish Creek. *See* Eldorado Creek
Fishery on the Ki-moo-e-nim, 217, 218
Fishing methods. *See* Nez Perce Methods of
Fishing stand, 212
Fishing weirs, 123
Fishtraps, 122; description of, 326 C.10/n.1

Flag of U.S., presented to Twisted Hair, 45; presented to Broken Arm, 46, 146
Flatheads. (*See* Shalees)
Floyd, Sergeant Charles, pipe-tomahawk, 76
Food, and preparation of: bear meat, 177; deer meat, JE 136, 136; meat, drying 307; salmon, smoking, 28; pine inner bark, 103. *See also* Camas; Ho'pope
Fort Clatsop, 328 C.13/n.1
Fort Mandan, 76; 328 C.13/n.1
Forts, building of, 230

Gelding of horses. *See* Horses, castration of
Gifts, giving and receiving of; mentioned, passim. *See* Medals
Great Falls (of the Missouri), 230, 233, 291, 301, 308
Great White Father (also Great Father; Great White Chief), President Thomas Jefferson: 30, 150, 152-154, 159-160; message left at Indian Post Office, 315
Great river from the north. *See* Columbia
Grizzly bear (Hah-hahts): information about, 178, 328 c. 13/n.2; killing of, JE 176, 176-178; unable to climb trees, 178
Guides: asking for, 167, 235; LCE in urgent need of, JE 256; chosen to show LCE over Bitterrroots, JE 280, 283
Guiding Spirit, told through the voice of Itsi-yai-yai, the Coyote, 292
Guns (sticks-that-shoot-black-sand-with-thunder; also, strange or queer sticks): about, 22, 56; Clark showing how to operate, 34; exchanging sawed off rifle for one given guide, 303; given to guides who showed the way over Bitterroots, JE 257, 280, 284, 301, 331 n.1; Nez Perce's desire and importance of owning, 160, 318; promised to Twisted Hair for care of horses, 59; six guns purchased by Nez Perce from Minnitares, 160, 161, 163, 321 C.3/n.4

Hahahts-il-pilp. *See* Red Grizzly Bear
Hah-hahts. *See* Grizzly bear
Handshakes, 14, 20, 321 C.3/n.1
Headman, duties of, 12
Heart of the Monster, 110, 186, 196
Hemp, articles, 325 n.22; bags, 53, 238
He-yoom-pahkah-tim. *See* Fierce-Five-Hearts
Ho'pope, 102, 325 C.9/n.9
Horses, in relation to LCE: branding and cutting foretops for identification, 73; castrating of, 182-183, 187; causing alarm by butchering a Nee-mee-poo horse, 24, 321 C.3/n.5; Clark's mishap with horse, 35; intended for food, 71, 131-135, 141, 165, JE 188, JE 255; LCE obtained for westward journey, 321 C.3/n.3; leaving with Twisted Hair's people, 59; number owned by LCE for homeward trip, 180, 192; Twisted Hair returning of, 142, 157, 166, 231; ten offered to guide Lewis to Missouri Falls JE 257, 280
Horses, in relation to Nee-mee-poo: ability with, 187, JE 192; castrating of, 182-183; sacrificed to send to Spirit World with deceased, 103, 227; racing at Oyaip, 26; regard for, 191, 194
Hot Springs, 294, 296
Hungary Creek (variously spelled: Hungery; Hungrey; Hungry) JE 256, 258, JE 284, JE 286, 288
Hunting chief, duties of, 12, 222

Illnesses. *See* Clark administering medical aid to Nez Perce; Moves-No-More; Bratton
Indian Post Office. *See* Post Office
Ip-paht-tah-khahts, game of endurance and bravery, 261-262
Iscootim, meeting Clark on Oyaip, 14; 321 C.2/n.2, mentioned, passim
Iship, spell of, 86, 324 C.8/n.2
Ish-nash. *See* Dwellings
Itsi-yai-yai. *See* Coyote

Jack's Creek, JE 78, 78
Jefferson, President Thomas. *See* Great White Father
Joyous Heart (A-hot-mo-tim-nim), 26, 28-29, 56-58, 321 C.3/n.6; mentioned, passim

Kaeh-kheet season, 121
Kamiah, 7; Broken Arm's village, 140
Kamiah Creek, 218, 233, 243, 268
Kamiah Monster. *See* Nez Perce Indian Lore
Ka-oo-yit, 228, 230, 233, 243, 273; meaning of, 265, 331 C.19/n.1
Kause porridge (komsit), 10
Ki-moo-e-nim (Snake River), 8, 24, 92; mentioned, passim
Kinnikinnick, 46, 322, C.5/n.5
Komsit. *See* kause porridge
Koos-koos-kee middlefork, 225

Koos-koos-kee River (Clearwater River), 7; Clark's desire to go to, 24; Twisted Hair's fishing camp on, 27; how the river flowed, 37; meeting at Chopunnish River (North Fork River), 100; moving LCE down to Canoe Camp on, 53; mentioned, passim

Koots-koots. *See* Barnabas

Kouse bread, 121, 211

Kouse root digging season, 121, 123

Lah-mah-ta (Whitebird), 9, 151

Lah-mah-ta Canyon, 202

Lake Coeur d'Alene (Lake Waytom), 267

Lake Waytom (Lake Coeur d'Alene), 267

Lapwai Creek, JE 87

Leisure activities of LCE described, JE 239, 239-242

Lenore, JE 78

Lewis (Captain Meriwether Lewis), 25, 45; arrival on Weippe Prairie, 36; address to chiefs and principal men of Chopunnish Nation, 153-154; presenting a guide with a buffalo robe, 288

Lewis and Clark Expedition, list of members, xxv-xxvi; language as hear by Nez Perce, 150; purpose of mission described, 30; camping on China Island, 55; only retrograde march of, *See* Retrograde march; across the Bitterroots homeward, second and final attempt, 288-295; separating into two groups, 303-306

Lewis's River (Salmon River). *See* Ta-ma-nam-mah River

Lighting council fire. *See* Burning glass

Little Salmon, 96, 324, C.9/n.2

Liver of the Monster, 110

Locations, today's names, 320 n.2

Lochsa River, 290

Lodge, description of Broken Arm's; description of Cut Nose's. *See* Dwellings

Lolo Creek, Montana. (Collins Creek and Traveler's Rest, variously spelled: Travellers Rest.) JE 254, JE 256, JE 257, JE 268, JE 283, JE 284, 298, 331 C.18/n.7

Looks-Like-Mule-Deer-Doe. *See* Ya'amus Wakus

Long Camp. *See* Camp Chopunnish

Longhouse, making of, 101; description, 104

Many Wounds. *See* Red Grizzly Bear

Marias River, 230

Match Dance, 119

Meanings of names of villages, 1

Measuring river for snow melt, 213, 242

Medal, description of peace and friendship (Jefferson), 30

Medals, gift of: of peace and friendship given to Twisted Hair, 30, to two principal men at Oyaip Council, 45, to Cut Nose, 129, to Broken Arm, 149; of man sowing seeds given to Red-Grizzly-Bear, 149, to Fierce-Five-Hearts, 151; given to chiefs present at Kamiah Council, 151; given to one of guides (Black Eagle), JE 300, 301

Medicine Ceremony, 86

Medicine supplies, list of, carried by LCE, 195-196

Medicine used, 326 C.10/n.8, 329 C.15/nns.1,2,4,5. *See also* Eyewater

Methods used by Nee-mee-poo: catching salmon, 212; fishing, 33, 34; gelding horses, JE 182, 183; hunting deer, JE 183, 183; preparing food, 215; routine of women, 215. *See also* Nez Perce customs; Food and preparation of

Minnetares, (variously spelled: Minetarries), 49, 152, 155, JE 298

Missoula, *See* Clark's Fork

Missouri Falls. *See* Great Falls

Missouri River, 230

Moonlight Dance, 119; 275-276

Moon of: Ah-pah-ahl, 121; Ah-la-tah-mahl, 120; Ha-oo-khoy, 101, 120; Hi-lal, 14; Ka-khee-tahl, 121; La-te-tahl, 121; Pe-khum-mai-kahl, 68; Seekh-le-wahl, 101; Ta-yum, 1, 6, 311; Wai-lu-poop, 104, 120

Moons of. *See* Nee-mee-poo Calendar, xxvii

Moves-Again, 228, 235. *See* Moves-No-More

Moves-No-More, 158, 159, 205-210; about affliction, 327 n.12; 329 n.8

Myths of Nez Perce, Rock Formations: Ant and the Yellowjacket, 87; Coyote's Fishnet, 87, 88; Dead Warrior Chief, 87; Frog, 88; 324 C.8/n.3

Names, changes during lifetime, 10, 210, 275, 329 n.10

Names, different names applied to word *Nez Perce*, 335

Nee-mee-poo. *See Nez Perce entries*

Nee-mee-poo, (*Nez Perce; The People*), names of characters; authentic names and their meanings, xxiii; fictitious names and their meanings, xxiv-xxv
Nee-mee-poo, The People, 1, 5; meaning, 320 n.3
Nee-mee-poo calendar, xxvii
Nee-mee-poo glossary, xxvii-xxix
Neesh-ne-ee-pah-kee-oo-keen. *See* Cut Nose
Nez Perce. *See Nee-mee-poo entries*
Nez Perce, different names applied, 335
Nez Perce. *See Myths of*
Nez Perce character depicted: cleanliness and appearance, 327 C.12/n.2; concern for hungry children, JE 185, 185-186; concern for older people and wives, 197, 329 C.15/n.3; good character of guides, JE 283; regret shown at departure, JE 309, 310
Nez Perce Chiefs referred to by LCJ, 332-333
Nez Perce Customs: burials, 103, 226; daily activities at summer camp, 273; exchanging gifts between bridal parties, 263; food, apportioning of, 320 n.1; game of Ip-paht-tah-khahts, 261-262; gift giving (yal-lept), 83; killing horses for deceased, 103, 226, 227; Lawtiwa-mah-ton, Song of Friendship, 1, 175, 228; mourning, 98; obtaining eaglets for feathers, 244; preparing to move, 53, 122, 123, 260, 264; preparing for a trip, 229, 281, 312; preparing for war, 9, 10, 320 nn.9,10; preparing for winter, 100, 101; Stick Game, 167; wedding ritual, 263; women's activities during winter confinement, 116, 145. *See also* Whipping Man; Crier
Nez Perce Indian Lore: Baby left hanging in te-cas, 39; Badger, the game of, 171-173; Ba-teese and the beargrass hat, 50; The Bear Who Shot Himself, 178-180; Big Fish Story, 156, 157, 327 n.9; Chant, Itswa-wlts-itsqiy, 98; The Chipmunk and Grizzly Bear, 115; The Coming of Fish, 110; Cooing of dove to announce arrival of salmon, JE 217; Coyote, 114; Finding the Trail Through the Mountains, 112; Fishhook Story, 63-64; Fishline Story, 64; Generous Deerhunter and Selfish Deerhunter, (Ipna-ko-tahk-o-tsaya), 101-102; Joyous Heart and his prized axe, 250-251; The Kamiah Monster and The Coming of People, 107; Koots-koots and the Root Feast, 266; Lee-tsu and her dog, 89-90; Lighting Fir Trees on Fire, JE 285, 285-286; Making of good deer hide, 211; Nee-mee-poo, The People, creation of, 110; The Path for Water, 105; Raven's cry, 211; Rope barrier story, 66; Scrubbing York with Sand, 50, 51; Tom-sis and her daytime smoker, 169, 311-314; Wat-ku-ese, 4-6; 40-42. *See also* Nez Perce customs; Nez Perce traditions; Rituals of Nee-mee-poo
Nez Perce maiden, appearance of, 169
Nez Perce methods of. *See* Methods
Nez Perce traditions: location of root digging camps, 1-11, 231; annual root-gathering and fishing travels, 260; root-gathering and Root Feast, 264, 265; lighting fire to fir trees to bring fair weather and good luck, JE 285, 285-286. *See also* Nez Perce Customs; Nez Perce Indian Lore; Rituals of Nee-mee-poo
North Fork River. *See* Chopunnish River
Nusnu-ee-pah-kee-oo-keen. *See* Cut Nose

Orofino Creek, 323 C.6/n.5
Oyaip Prairie (Weippe Prairie; The Prairie); 1, 13; Clark arriving at, 16; LCE return to on retrograde march, 270; variously spelled and meaning 321 n.1.; mentioned, passim

Packer Meadow, 295
Peace pipe, 8, 234
People, The. *See* Nee-mee-poo
People, The (The Nee-mee-poo), creation of, 110. *See* Nez Perce Indian Lore
People-Coming-Looks-Like-Brothers. *See* Te-toh-kan Ahs-kahp (also known as Tetorharsky)
Pestles of stone, 53
Pierced-Nose people, sign for: 18, 147, 169
Pine trees, 57-60; yellow pine, 59
Pipe tomahawk belonging to Sergeant Floyd, missing, 76; found, 226
Pit house. *See* Dwellings
Post Office, Indian, 312, 315, 331 n.2
Potlatch Creek (also Ya-ho-toin; Colter's Creek): 9, 82, 96, JE 127, 320 n.7.
Powell Junction, 294

Power: in war, 9-11; hunting, 3; deer, 101, 118; flying, 118; of women, 118
Power test, 119
Prairie, The. *See* Oyaip Prairie
Prisoner's Base game, JE 239, 240-241
Purpose of LCE as explained to Indians, 45, 130, 150, 153-154

Red Bear (father of Red Grizzly Bear), 2, 3, 7, 163, 320, n.11
Red Grizzly Bear (Hahahts-il-pilp): preparing for and going to war, 7-10, 13; meeting LCE, 149; mentioned, passim
Red-Head, name Indians used for Clark, 34
Red Mountain, 293
Retrograde march of LCE, JE 256, 256-259; 268-269
Rituals of Nee-mee-poo: Broken Arm thickening people's soup to show unanimity, JE 161, 161; Power Test, 119; preparation for war, 9; name exchanging 301, 302; *See also* Nez Perce Customs; Nez Perce Indian Lore; Nez Perce Traditions; Vision Quest
Rock cairn 292, 293
Rock Formations. *See* Myths of Nez Perce
Root bread, 199, 248
Root Feast, 265
Roots, preparing. *See* Food and preparation of

Saddles, 21; antler-pronged, 54; illustration of Indian saddle, 75
Sa-ka-ka-wea, 49; about, 335; appearance for Kamiah Council, 152, 154; speaking Shoshoni, 130, 152
Salish. *See* Shalees
Salmon: arriving on Koos-koos-kee, JE 212; fall run, 7; run at Collins Creek, JE 282; spear, description of, 33, 34
Salmon River. *See* Ta-ma-nam-mah
Scalp Dance, 98, 99, 324, C.9/n.4
Scalps, Snake, collecting of, 97
Scannon, Lewis's dog, description of, 40, 322 C.4/n.6
Seaman. *See* Scannon
Serenade Dance, 277-278
Seven Devils Mountain, 107, JE 254
Shaking hands, 149
Shalees (also called Salish; Flatheads): friends of Nee-mee-poo, 4, JE 228, 229, 320 n.5; mentioned, passim
Shelters. *See* Dwellings
Shoshoni language, spoken by Sa-ka-kawea, 130, 152
Sign language, for: derogatory gesture, 138; "I go," 243; "gift," 238; Pierced Nose, 18
Si-kip-te-wat, White Man's Doctor. *See* Clark
Sioux, as enemies of Nee-mee-poo, 5
Skitsuish. *See* Spokane tribe
Slave. *See* Snake slave
Smoking, 185, 233; peace pipe, 234; at council, 44, 150, 165; in friendship, 176; LCE as observed by Nee-mee-poo, 169; ceremony of, JE 81, 81, 139, 228, 279, JE 291, 291-293, 309, JE 310, 315
Snake Dance (Tu-ka-wi-ut), 119
Snake guide. *See Toba*
Snake River. *See* Ki-moo-e-nim, 8, JE 87, 92
Snakes, enemies, war with Nee-mee-poo, 8-11, 96, 140, 146; mentioned, passim
Snake scout. *See* Toba
Snake slave, owned by Cut Nose, 129, 130, 135-140, 152, 154
Song of Victory. *See* Scalp Dance
So-yap-pos, 5, 29, 41
Spalding, Idaho, Coyote's moccasin tracks, 106, 325 n.16
Speaking Eagle (Tip-yah-la-nah-jeh-nin), fictitious name applied to son of Broken Arm, 152, 156, 162
Spell. *See* Iship
Spirit Helper, 5, 9, 119. *See* Wyakin
Spirit World, 6; preparing for, 226, 227
Spokane River, 267
Spokane tribe (Skitsuish), friends of Nee-mee-poo, 109, 267, 296
Stick game, 26; described, 167; 189
Sticks, queer, or strange sticks. *See* Guns
Stick-that-shoots-black-sand-with-thunder. *See* Guns
Story telling. *See Nez Perce Indian Lore*
Sweat baths, 128, JE 204-209; illustration of, 207; 287
Sweat house (also Sweat lodge), 145, 225

Ta-ma-nam-mah river (Salmon River; also, Lewis's River), 8, 137, JE 254; mentioned, passim
Ta-moot-sin, (variously spelled Timootsin). *See* Timootsin
Tap-toop-pa, 74, 77, 323 C.7/n.7
Tee-e-lap-a-lo, 2, 7, 145, 326 C.11/n.1
Te-pah-le-wam, 264, 265
Tepee. *See* Dwellings

Tetoharsky. *See* Te-toh-kan Ahs-kahp
Te-toh-kan Ahs-kahp (Tetoharsky; also, People-Coming-Looks-Like-Brothers), 33, 56, 57; guiding LCE down river to Celilo Falls, 81-93; guiding LCE up the Clearwater River, 123, passim; name explained, 321 C.4/n.2, 332; mentioned, passim
Te-wap-poo, 2, 57
Te-wats (Medicine Man), 117, 128, 158, 226
Te-wel-kas. *See* Enemies
Timootsin (variously spelled Ta-moot-sin): 44, 49, 93; Chief Timothy, 322 C.4/n.4, C.5/n.3
Timothy, Chief. *See* Timootsin
Timuca, 37, 44, 322 C.4/n.4, C.5/n.3, 333
Tin-nach-e-moo-toolt. *See* Broken Arm
Tippet, description of Broken Arm's, 147; description of, 151; 326 C.11/n.6
Tip-yah-la-nah-jeh-nin. *See* Speaking Eagle
Tip-yah-la-nah She-mook She-mook. *See* Black Eagle
Toba, Snake guide/scout, 67, 84, 85; with son, takes two LCE horses, 140; 166
Tomahawk, 226
Tomahawk, pipe, 76
Tom-me-taha Creek, 174
Tom-sis, 169, 311-314
Tradegoods, giving and receiving of; mentioned, passim
Trading posts, 160, 318
Trail song, 316, 317
Travelers Rest. *See* Lolo Creek
Tsap-tsu-kelp-skin, Nee-mee-poo name for Twisted Hair. *See* Twisted Hair
Tsce-men-i-cum, 92
Tu-ka-wi-ut. *See* Snake Dance
TwistedHair(Tsap-tsu-kelp-skin): 7, 29, 30, 36, 44; character depicted, JE 36, 321 C.4/n.1; drawing map for L&C, 37; appearance, 43; speaking at council, 45; agreeing to care for LCE horses, 59-60; as guide, 55-93, passim; conflict with Cut Nose over care of LCE horses, 138-143; 150, 151, 159; receives one gun and ammunition for care of horses, 166, 167; receives second gun, 231; history of, 336; territory, 20, 23; mentioned, passim

Umatilla, 234

Victory Dance, 8
Vision quest described, 273-274

Wai-i-let-pos (also Willetpos). *See* Cayuses
Walla Walla, 95, 234
War dance, 9, 10
War party, 8
War path, 8; preparation for, 9
Wat-ku-ese: story of 4-6, 7; reference in LCJ, JE 28, 28; going to Oyaip (Weippe) to protect LCE, 30, 31; admonishing not to do LCE harm, 40, 318; 322 C.4/n.7
We-ah-koomt, Chief of Ha-so-tin, 124; praise of, JE 130, 130-133
Weather Chief, 12, 120
Weippe Prairie. *See* Oyaip
Weirs. *See* Fishing weirs
We-ya-oo-yit, meaning of, 19, 321 C.2/n.5
Whale. *See* Nez Perce Indian Lore, Big Fish Story
Whipping Man, 50, 260-264
Whitebird. *See* Lah-mah-ta
Wild Goose Rapids, 330 C.16/n.7
Willow Ridge, JE 256
Wyakin (Spirit Helper): 5, 8, 9, 10, 117, 119. *See* Vision quest

Ya'amus Wakus (Looks-Like-Mule-Deer-Doe): 33, 56, 332; mentioned, passim
Ya-ho-toin. *See* Potlatch Creek
Yakima tribe, 109
Yal-lept (gift giving), 83
York: alarm he caused, 38-41; scrubbed with sand, 50, 51; mentioned, passim

The Author

Zoa Lourana Shaw Swayne, author and illustrator, was born in Torrington, Wyoming, in 1905. She passed away Dec. 22, 2000.

She was raised in the Pacific Northwest. She majored in art at the University of Idaho, in Moscow, graduating in 1931 with a BS degree in education. After seven years of teaching, Zoa married Samuel F. Swayne, an attorney. They made their home in Orofino, Idaho, which lies within the boundaries of the Nez Perce Indian Reservation.

Living in Nez Perce country, which the Corps of Discovery passed through in 1805-1806, Zoa became intensely interested in Lewis and Clark stories told by one generation of Nez Perce to the next. By 1935 most of these stories lingered only in the memories of very old members of the tribe. Realizing the stories were in danger of being lost, Zoa began writing them down. As a member of the Nez Perce Development Advisory Committee in 1962-1963, she gained deeper insight into Nez Perce history, culture and present-day problems.

In *DO THEM NO HARM!* the author combines Nez Perce stories about Lewis and Clark with excerpts from the journals of the explorers to interpret the daily happenings during that historic period.

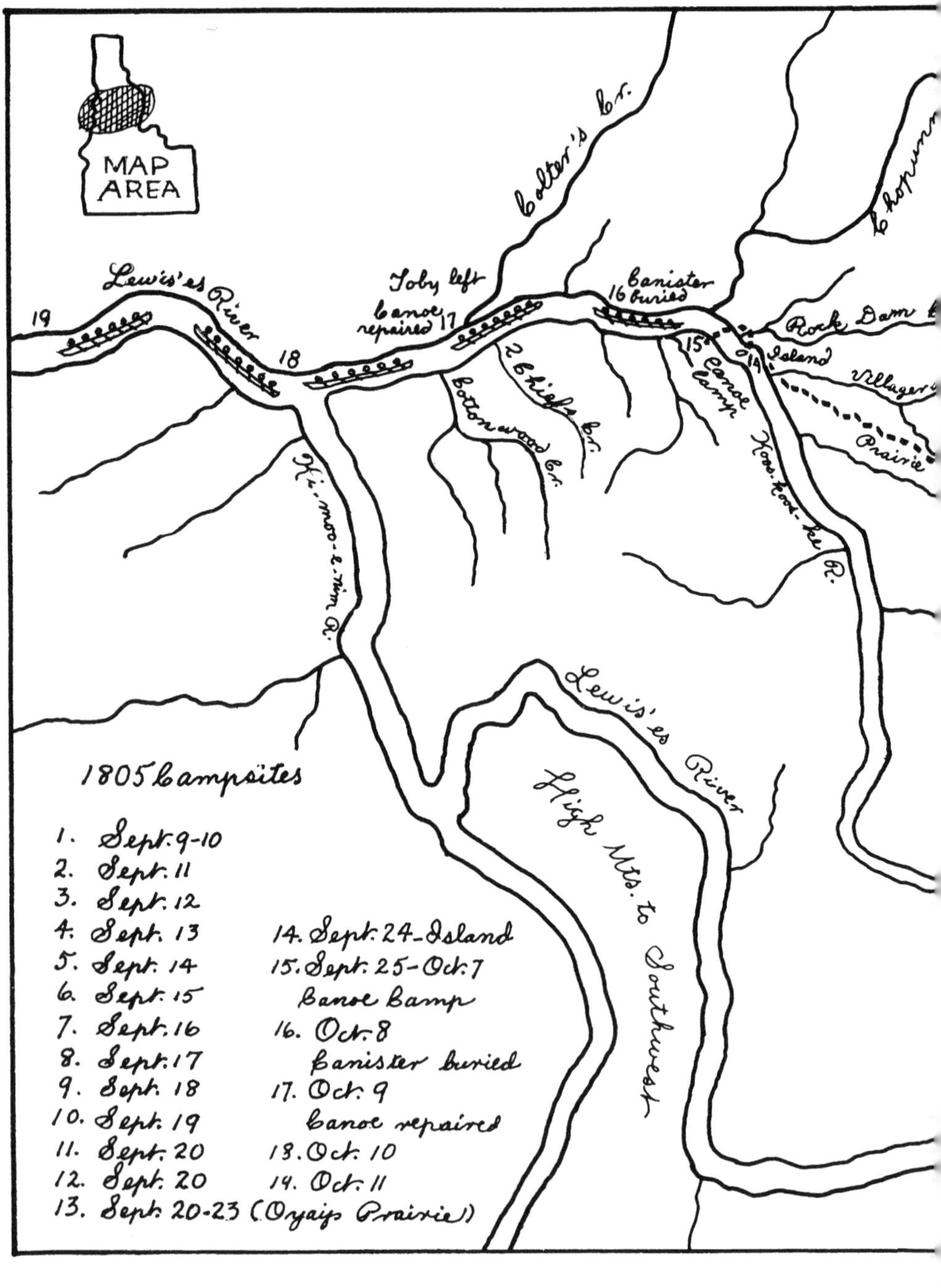

MAP AREA

Lewis'es River
Colter's Cr.
Chopunn
Toby left
Canoe repaired 17
16 Canister buried
Rock Dam
15 Canoe Camp
14 Island
Villages
Prairie
19
18
2 Chiefs Cr.
Cottonwood Cr.
Koos-koos-kee R.
Ki-moo-e-nim R.
Lewis'es River
High Mts. to Southwest

1805 Campsites

1. Sept. 9-10
2. Sept. 11
3. Sept. 12
4. Sept. 13
5. Sept. 14
6. Sept. 15
7. Sept. 16
8. Sept. 17
9. Sept. 18
10. Sept. 19
11. Sept. 20
12. Sept. 20
13. Sept. 20-23 (Oyaip Prairie)
14. Sept. 24-Island
15. Sept. 25-Oct. 7 Canoe Camp
16. Oct. 8 Canister buried
17. Oct. 9 Canoe repaired
18. Oct. 10
14. Oct. 11

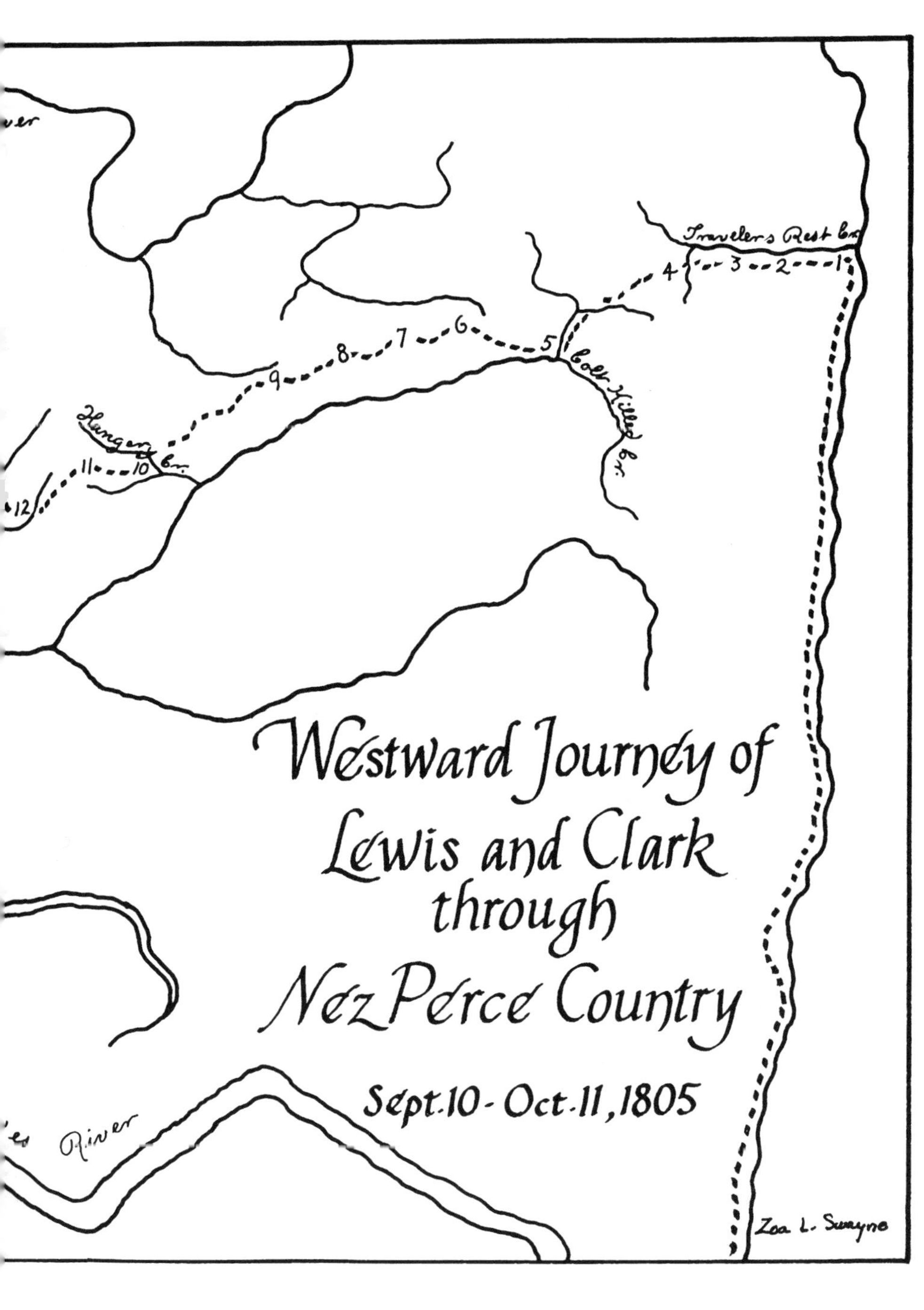
Travelers Rest Cr.
1
2
3
4
5
6
7
8
9
10
11
12
Colt Killed Cr.
Hungery Cr.
River
Westward Journey of
Lewis and Clark
through
Nez Perce Country
Sept.10 - Oct.11, 1805
Zoa L. Swayne

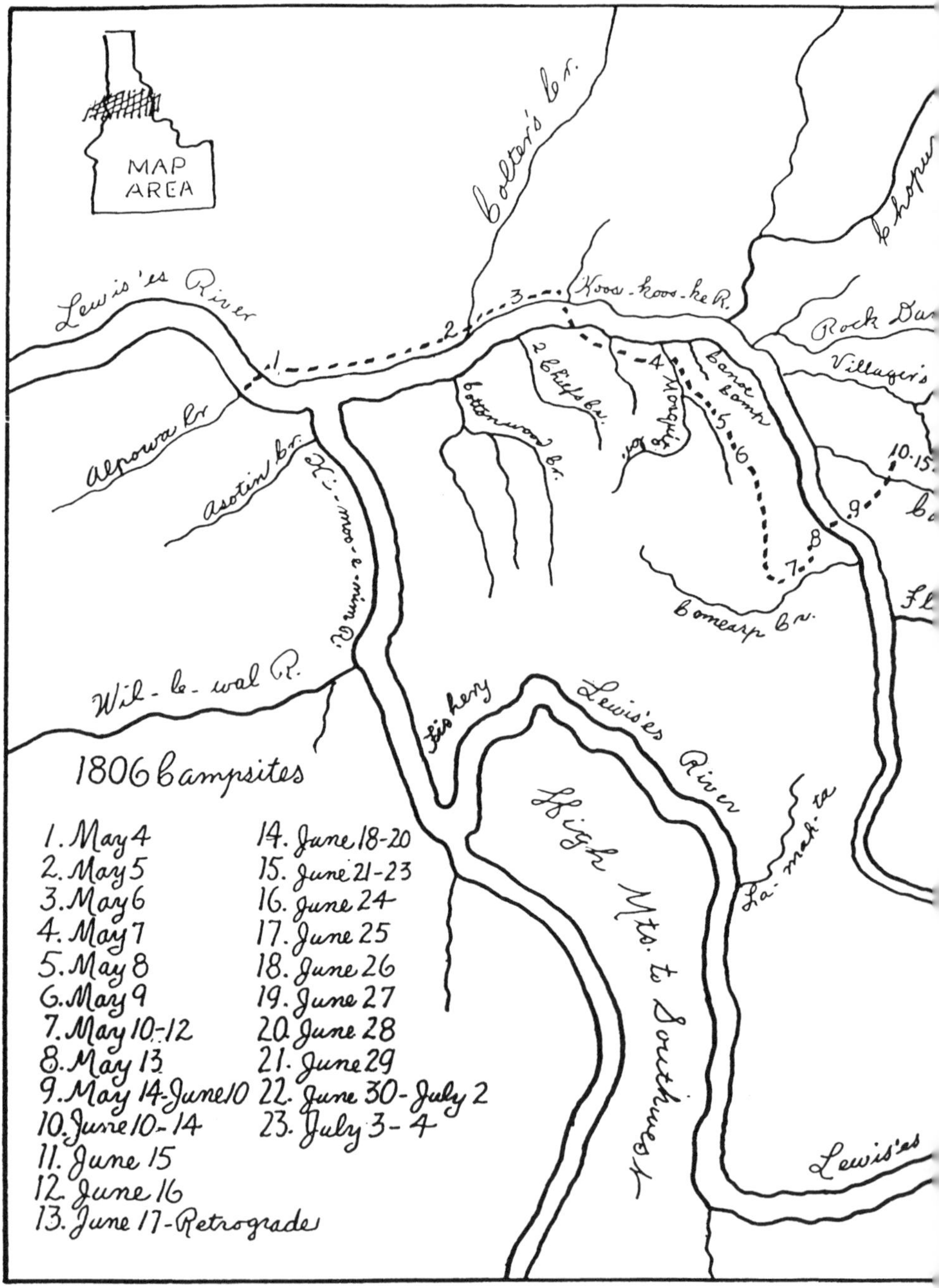

MAP AREA

Colter's Cr.

Lewis'es River

Koos-koos-ke R.

2 Chiefs Cr.

Cottonwood Cr.

Musquito Cr.

Canoe Camp

Alpowa Cr

Asotin Cr.

Ki-moo-e-nim R.

Commearp Cr.

Wil-le-wal R.

Fishery

Lewis'es River

High Mts. to Southwest

La-mah-ta

Lewis'es

1806 Campsites

1. May 4
2. May 5
3. May 6
4. May 7
5. May 8
6. May 9
7. May 10-12
8. May 13
9. May 14-June 10
10. June 10-14
11. June 15
12. June 16
13. June 17-Retrograde
14. June 18-20
15. June 21-23
16. June 24
17. June 25
18. June 26
19. June 27
20. June 28
21. June 29
22. June 30-July 2
23. July 3-4

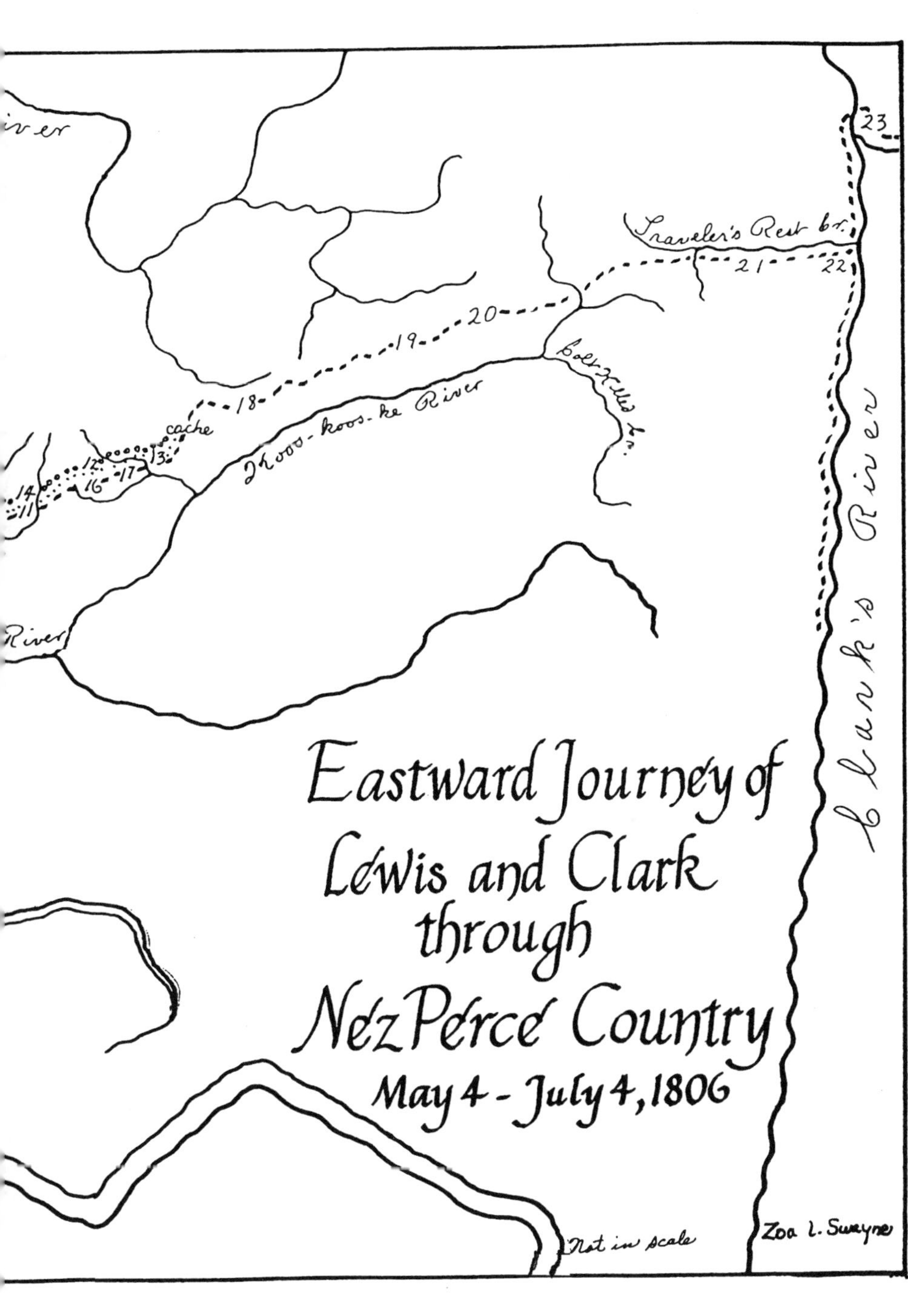

iver
23
Traveler's Rest br.
21
22
20
19
18
Bolt Killed Cr.
Clark's River
Kooskooske River
cache
12
13
14
11
16
17
River
Eastward Journey of
Lewis and Clark
through
Nez Perce Country
May 4 - July 4, 1806
Not in scale
Zoa L. Swayne

Other Books From Caxton Press

Dreamers: On the Trail of the Nez Perce

ISBN 0-87004-393-5 (cloth) $24.95
6x9, 450 pages, photographs, maps, index

Yellow Wolf: His Own Story

ISBN 0-87004-315-3 (paper) $16.95
6x9, 328 pages, illustrations, maps, index

Chief Joseph Country
Land of the Nez Perce

ISBN 0-87004-275-0 (cloth, boxed) $39.95
9x12, 316 pages, maps, illustrations

Hear Me, My Chiefs!
Nez Perce Legend and History

ISBN 0-87004-310-2 (paper) $19.95
9x12, 640 pages, 5 maps, 48 illustrations

On Sidesaddles to Heaven
The Women of the Rocky Mountain Mission

ISBN 0-87004-384-6 (paper) $19.95
6x9, 268 pages, illustrations, index